Praise for Gone Without Trace

'Well-researched, shocking, moving and exciting, *Gone Without Trace* shows that a British writer can take on the most vigorous of Americans'   *TLS*

'A terrific page-turner. Heart-stopping action and a heroine with guile as well as guts'   Harlan Coben

'A fast-paced thriller ... Carver's best book to date, and as the first four were terrific, it makes this a "must read"'
Mystery Women

'I loved it. Hard, fast and real – a solid gold A-grade thriller with a tremendous story and a great lead character ... Captain Jay McCauley is going to be one of the best'   Lee Child

'If you like the kind of hard-hitting, action-packed stories that I do, then I strongly suggest you try C. J. Carver. You won't be disappointed'   Simon Kernick

'Jay McCauley is gutsy, resourceful, and a little short of bionic – something like a female James Bond, but none the less likeable for that ... she is a splendid addition to the gallery of robust Action Women'   Laura Wilson

'An exciting adventure ... Jay is something of a superwoman – multilingual, multiskilled, indefatigable'   *Literary Review*

C. J. Carver was born in the UK and has driven London to Saigon and London to Cape Town. Adventure runs in the genes with a mother who set the land speed record in Australia and a father who was a jet fighter pilot. C. J. lives in London. Visit C. J.'s website at www.cjcarver.com.

By C.J. Carver

GONE WITHOUT TRACE

C. J. Carver

I. S. Macpherson

28·12·09

An Orion paperback

First published in Great Britain in 2007
by Orion
This paperback edition published in 2008
by Orion Books Ltd,
Orion House, 5 Upper Saint Martin's Lane,
London WC2H 9EA

An Hachette UK Company

A CIP catalogue record for this book
is available from the British Library.

Typeset by Deltatype Ltd, Birkenhead, Merseyside

Printed and bound in the UK by
CPI Mackays, Chatham ME5 8TD

The Orion Publishing Group's policy is to use papers that
are natural, renewable and recyclable products and made
from wood grown in sustainable forests. The logging and
manufacturing processes are expected to conform to the
environmental regulations of the country of origin.

www.orionbooks.co.uk

This book is for all those dedicated to the fight against human trafficking. You are making the difference.

Acknowledgements

I am deeply indebted to Lieutenant Colonel Arthur L. Shemwell III for sharing his extensive knowledge with me, as well as his rakija. Thanks also to Emine for her generous hospitality. I had a ball. Also grateful thanks to Rromir Imami for showing me his home country and advising me on all things Macedonian. Many thanks to Robert Bruce, Head of Trafficking in Human Beings Investigation Section, UNMIK Police HQ in Kosovo. Also to Monica Portillo, OSCE, Anti-Trafficking, and Zoran Bogatinov at NATO HQ, Skopje.

Thanks also to my UK advisors: Flight Lieutenant Rav Sandhu, Sergeant Will Thorpe, Detective Superintendent Lin Handley, Detective Superintendent John Briggs, and Sergeant Clive Blake; and to Sophie Woodforde and the team at the National Missing Persons Helpline.

To Broo Doherty, my agent and my trusty supporter, and lastly, to Jane Wood, my indefatigable editor, for giving so generously of her time and creativity.

As is customary in these cases, I must profess that all mistakes are mine.

One

Jay was chatting to Lily when she saw him. It was just a glimpse out of the corner of her eye, but she knew she wasn't mistaken from the way her body reacted. Electricity brushing the surface of her skin. Her gut tightening. She had learned from her army days never to ignore her physical instincts. She had the scars to prove it.

Wondering if she was imagining things, she squinted against the bitter wind to study the man's squat, brick-like shape. For a moment she went numb with the shock of recognition, but then her brain kick-started. Holy crap, she thought, her eyes widening. It really is him.

Milot Dumani. She could barely believe it. Five years had passed and he'd put on weight. The hard jaw-line was now soft and loose, his saddlebags pronounced, but the set of his mouth hadn't changed. It looked as small and hard and mean as ever.

Jay took shelter behind Lily's generous form as she showed her another photograph of a different girl. Lily ponderously shook her head. '*Jo*,' she said – No. Lily's real name was Ljliana, and when they'd first met she'd been surly and rude until Jay had spoken to her in her native language – Albanian. Being a linguist had its uses, and never more so in breaking the ice with immigrants, legal or illegal.

Today, Lily was wearing a lime-green Spandex body suit with silver platform shoes and a man's yellow jacket that came down to her knees. How the woman hadn't frozen where she stood was a miracle. Jay had only been on the street for an hour and her face was already beginning to chap from the raw February weather howling straight from the Atlantic and across the Bristol Channel into the city centre. It was a miserable day, with a sky the colour of metal filings and the air clogged with traffic exhaust. Cars had their headlights on, and people walked with their shoulders hunched, faces pinched.

'Do you know that guy?' Jay pointed out Milot. He'd stopped half-way down the street and was talking to one of the girls.

Lily shook her head. 'Why? Do you?'

'Not personally, but I saw him a few times, in the Balkans.'

Lily studied Milot. 'I wouldn't take him on no matter how much he paid me. He's got that look about him, like he'd enjoy hurting you.'

Jay was impressed at Lily's perspicacity. The last time Jay had seen Milot was in Tetovo in 2002 – post-conflict Macedonia – where he'd been laughing with his cronies, hanging out in a coffee bar. He was a pimp-cum-trafficker who had shot one of his girls in front of the others to keep them in line. He then hacked off the girl's head and roped it on the front of his car like a trophy. The girl had asked if she could telephone her mother. She hadn't even turned sixteen.

All Jay could remember was her scalding white-hot fury at seeing him driving around town with the girl's head on his fender. She was filled with savage rage, for Milot Dumani was untouchable. No policeman, no army officer, no NATO bigwig had the power to arrest him. The Mafia had ruled Tetovo back then. She could picture the girl's severed head as if it were yesterday, her skin soft as molten candle wax, the blood seeping from the scraps of torn flesh at her neck, her milky dead eyes staring dully ahead. The anger Jay had felt still made her breathless, as though she'd been hit with a tyre-iron against her heart.

'Cigarette?'

Jay jumped when Lily offered a pack of Rothmans. She shook her head.

'You've given up?' Lily looked surprised.

'Trying to.'

'Good for you.'

Jay swallowed. No way would she start smoking again just because the past had reared its ugly head. That would be too stupid. She tried to ignore Lily lighting her cigarette but she couldn't miss the delicious whiff of smoke before it was whipped away by the wind.

'You sure?' Lily was watching her.

Jay firmed her resolve. 'I'm sure.'

'You want a toffee instead? I've got some treacle dabs.'

Despite her tension, or perhaps because of it, Jay's sweet tooth perked up. Stuff her promise not to snack.

'Lily, I *love* treacle dabs.'

She had just popped one in her mouth when Lily said, 'How's your gorgeous detective inspector, then?'

'Er, I'm not sure.'

'You're not staying with him this weekend?'

'No. Not this time.'

She usually timed her trips from London to Bristol to coincide with the weekends so she could spend more time with Tom, but after their difficult dinner last weekend she had no idea where their relationship stood. She hadn't dared ring him. She hadn't had the guts.

'Anything wrong?' Lily was surveying her with a frown.

'Everything's fine,' Jay said, trying to lie and, as usual, failing.

'You've broken up? What happened? Did he have an affair with one of his pretty little constables? Or was it an ex-girlfriend? They're the worst. They know all the right buttons to press.'

To Jay's relief a Vauxhall Cavalier pulled up next to them, distracting Lily from fantasising any further.

'It's Harry,' Lily said, brightening. 'I know Harry, he's a regular. I'll see you when you're next down, shall I?' She squeezed Jay's arm affectionately. '*Lamtumirë*, sweetie. Farewell.'

Lily was the only person who ever called Jay sweetie. She'd been called many things – including stubborn, impulsive and insane – and the diminutive made her smile.

3

'*Lamtumirë*, hon.'

With half an eye on Milot, Jay watched eleven stone of underdressed prostitute heave herself into the passenger seat. Lily's customer looked half her age, a white-collar worker with a spare shirt on a hanger in the back, not the type of guy Jay imagined going for a lank-haired and badly dressed tart with pudgy feet crammed into high heels two sizes too small, but since Lily's theory was that clients deliberately went for women who were total opposites from their partners at home, it made sense. Lily had to be the perfect antidote to any BMW driver's image of a brittle, too-thin and gym-obsessed wife.

While Lily was driven away, Jay saw Milot turn from the girl and start walking down the street. Jay stared after him. A sense of foreboding tightened in her chest. Could she let him go? Allow him to vanish as though she'd never seen him? What if she heard of a girl's body found floating in the Bristol Channel with her head sawn off?

Switching her mobile phone to vibrate, Jay set off after Milot. She would see where the scumbag was going and then make a report to the local police, alerting them to the fact they had a thug, a brutal Mafia lapdog in their midst. That's if the cops didn't already know him, of course.

Milot was walking purposefully, looking straight ahead but occasionally glancing at his wristwatch. A man with an appointment. A man without a map of the city and – more worryingly – who looked as though he knew his way around. It wasn't his first visit. She could tell he felt comfortable here by the relaxed set of his shoulders, the lack of paranoia in his actions. No darting glances over his shoulder or sudden turns to throw off anyone behind him.

Sucking on her treacle dab, Jay put herself in trigger position, staying close to the target, senses alert, blood humming, and although Milot didn't know her, she knew she'd be lucky to follow him a hundred yards without getting pinged. Sadly, she'd never been able to 'go grey', which her intelligence course instructor regretted when he trained her. At five feet eleven inches she was too tall to go unnoticed, too long-legged, and

4

with the distinctive saddle of freckles across her nose and her curly mane of conker-coloured hair she blended into any crowd about as well as a horse standing on a railway platform. Men always came back for a second look. Even when she'd had a buzz-cut and was wearing muddy fatigues and boots big enough to stamp the life out of an elephant, men still looked.

She was so intent on Milot she almost missed the patrol car cruising past, but at the last minute she shrank back, checking to see who was inside. Please God not Tom. If he spotted her she didn't know what he'd do. Leap out and manhandle her into the back of his car, probably, for an in-depth interrogation.

She didn't recognise anyone in the squad car and brought her attention back to her quarry. The wind gusted sleet into her face, razor-sharp cold. It was so bitter, she felt as though she could be on an assignment in Moscow. Near the Market Gate footbridge she spotted a small-scale drug dealer. Another black guy, hoodie raised, was hanging around, possibly thinking of buying. Skin and drugs, you could be in the middle of an ice age and there would always be punters.

She saw Milot's right foot turn out a fraction, indicating he was going to change direction, but she didn't dive into a shop or try to hide. It was too late. He'd already stopped and glanced over his shoulder.

He was looking straight at her.

Two

Jay didn't break her stride. She kept walking, her body language loose and relaxed. Her thumb was hooked nonchalantly over the strap of her handbag, her gaze fixed in the distance. She could see the traffic banking at the traffic lights ahead, hear the engines roaring beneath the underpass, but she didn't take it in. Every sense was concentrated on Milot.

She felt his eyes slide over her without pausing.

One second, two seconds, three.

She could feel his stare running from the ground up, checking out the length of her legs, her ass and her waist, her breasts.

Jay stalked past him. She was so close she could almost see his nose hairs. She wondered if she imagined the smell of cigars wafting from him, that stench of nicotine and cheap cologne that followed the Albanian Mafia wherever they went, and then she was past him.

A quick glance showed he was still watching her. She was surprised; usually his sort preferred girls in their teens or early twenties, and she was pushing thirty. A horn blared nearby and he was instantly distracted, his head jerking around, his hand automatically brushing the front of his jacket. She wondered whether he was armed, or if it had been a purely reflexive gesture. She had no intention of finding out if she could help it.

Milot turned and followed in Jay's footsteps. She increased her pace a little. Following a target from ahead was tricky but not impossible, unless your target wanted to screw you. However, there was another way she could look at the situation. She was so obviously not part of a surveillance team, he couldn't dream she'd be following him.

Soon they were in the back streets of St Pauls, a myriad dirty alleyways and neglected streets with potholes and cracked pavements. It was the roughest end of the city, full of drug dealers and petty criminals. There were bars and clubs with no hoardings outside, no advertisements – places where you knocked on the front door and someone checked you out from behind the curtain before letting you in. Jay recognised a couple of private clubs as she passed, where girls she knew worked. Girls from Moldova, Poland and Lithuania. Beautiful girls, young girls. Girls who had a university education but couldn't find work anywhere else.

Her boots echoed on the pavement, the mist of her breath drifted past her face in the freezing air. To her surprise, he didn't react when she dropped back and allowed him to overtake her. She gave a narrow little smile. He had got complacent while putting on all that weight. He was losing his touch.

She made a couple of surveillance checks to see if anyone else was keeping tabs on Milot; looking for multiple sightings of the same person. She saw an elderly man a few times, and a young woman with a pushchair who could have been his backup, but it was too easy to get things wrong in this situation and when Milot turned into George Street a few minutes later, she wasn't surprised when they were nowhere to be seen.

Everything was text-book perfect until Milot ducked into an alley. Traffic roared in the distance as Jay peered after him. His stumpy, overweight figure scrunched rubbish and grit underfoot. Pausing next to an industrial-sized wheelie bin, he raised his fist and banged it three times against a blue metal door. The door opened and he slipped inside without looking back or checking over his shoulder. The door clanged shut behind him.

Jay waited a couple of minutes before moving after him. She didn't expect the metal door to sport a company logo, but she wasn't going to leave without a closer inspection.

As she'd suspected, the door held few clues. No bell, no number, not even a handle; just an average-sized keyhole. Steam wafted from a kitchen vent alongside, smelling of curry. Jay glanced inside the wheelie bin to see bulging black plastic sacks nestling alongside a couple of broken garden chairs. There were flattened cardboard boxes of potato chips, pre-cooked broccoli and carrots. A Frisbee that looked as though a dog had chewed it. A melted kitchen spatula.

She would, she decided, phone Trinity Road cop shop. She wouldn't speak to Tom, but his trusty PA, Anne. However, if Anne knew Jay was just around the corner, she would be hurt that she hadn't popped in. Jay checked her watch – twelve o'clock – and wondered if Tom would be at lunch yet. Then again, he might not even be there. He might be investigating a murder on the other side of town, but she didn't want to risk bumping into him. Not until she'd straightened out her head.

Somewhere, a footstep echoed off the damp brick walls. A single step, no more, as though someone had been standing, waiting for a long time, and had finally given in against the interminable boredom and shifted their position.

Instantly she forgot about Tom.

Shit, she thought. Her skin started to tingle.

She looked both ways, up and down the alley, but couldn't see anyone. She took several deep breaths and told herself she wasn't on the front line any more, that there were no gunmen waiting to shoot her, nobody about to chuck a grenade at her. Shaking her head, she replaced the wheelie bin lid. Jay hadn't been in a war zone for five years, not since her tour in Iraq, but she still reacted to things that other people didn't register. Like dodging plastic bags in the road in case they contained a roadside bomb, or obsessively checking the car behind her in case it was driven by a suicide bomber.

One day she hoped to walk down the street without flinching. Or sit anywhere in a pub instead of insisting on the chair with its back against the wall and beside the nearest exit. Survival habits died hard.

8

Jay thought she'd calmed herself until her mobile vibrated in her pocket.

'Jesus,' she muttered, fumbling to answer it. She was almost overwhelmed with longing for a cigarette. It was a rude reminder of how infrequently she had an adrenalin rush these days.

'Hello?'

'It's me.'

It was Nick, her boss for the past two years, calling from London and expecting her to recognise his voice as usual.

She said, 'Hi, me.'

'Any luck with the photos?'

'No, but the girls will keep their eyes peeled.'

'Damn. I was sure we'd find them there. All the evidence pointed to Bristol . . . ' There was a sound of rustling paper, then Nick said, 'Where are you?'

'In St Pauls checking out a restaurant wheelie bin.'

Brief silence.

'Why?'

'I saw Milot Dumani slip in a back door beside it.'

'You what?'

She was about to fill Nick in when she became aware of a man standing at the entrance to the alley, silhouetted against the pale grey daylight. She glanced left to see another man at the other end. They both started walking towards her.

Dark-skinned and unshaven, they wore jeans and sneakers and thickly padded windcheaters. Big, confident guys who looked like truck drivers except for the fact that one of them appeared to be holding some sort of weapon close to his body. From the way he was carrying himself, she took it to be a baseball bat.

She felt a momentary rush of shame. Pure humiliation.

Milot hadn't lost his touch after all. He had been aware of her following him all that time, and had called for backup.

'Nick, two men are approaching me. They don't look friendly.' She spoke rapidly, telling him where she was. 'Call the cops, would you?'

'On it,' Nick said.

She hung up, put her phone in her pocket and swung right. No point in dialling nine-nine-nine with Nick on her case, she didn't want the distraction. There was little doubt her opponents would win if it came to a fight. She might be tall and relatively strong, but these guys had at least eighty pounds on her.

She had to see if she could bluff her way through.

Walk with confidence, as though you belong, she told herself. *Head up, shoulders back, and don't show your fear.*

She walked straight for the guy who didn't appear to have a weapon. She didn't look behind her, but strode out, making for the alley's entrance as though the man didn't exist. He stopped, filling up the alley entrance like a haystack.

'Excuse me,' she said, sounding irritable, 'but could you let me pass? I'm already late.'

She could hear the other man, behind her, closing in. He was breathing with a faint rasp, as though his lungs were congested.

Her body was on high alert, listening to the man behind, her vision trained on the one in front, watching his hands, his eyes. She was seconds away from colliding with him.

Raising her hands, she made shoo-ing motions. 'Look, I really don't have time for this . . . '

'Stop there,' he said. Aggressive, hard.

She felt a moment's confusion. His accent was American. Not Macedonian, not Albanian, not from anywhere in the Balkans.

He brought up his hand as though to grab her. Memories she'd locked away burst into the light. For a moment she froze, her breathing strangled in her throat, and then her training took over. The second she felt him touch her bicep, she twisted, pretending to fall into his arms and throwing him off balance. Using her elbow she stabbed him hard in the sternum. It was a short, cruel blow, and he hadn't expected it, hadn't braced himself, because she heard the soft 'oof' as the air left his lungs. Then she hit him again. Drove home her advantage with the same jab, but harder.

When his knees buckled she spun round to the second man, who was scrabbling inside his jacket. She tried to kick him in the groin but she was out of practice and too slow. He twisted aside and her blow went wide. Off-balance, her shoulder smacked against the wall. She was bringing up her hand, wanting to chop it against the man's throat, doubtful if she'd make it but still going for the blow, when she felt something hard and cold rammed behind her ear.

'Make another move, I blow your head off.'

Three

Jay twisted to look into the face of a third man. The man with the gun. A pair of steady brown eyes gazed back.

'Turn around,' he said.

She did as she was told.

'Place both hands on the wall.'

Jay complied. Her heart was pounding like a road drill, but she did her best to keep her fear from showing. She turned her head and watched the man she'd winded scrape himself off the ground. He was groaning and looked as though he might be sick. The other guy gave him a helping hand. Both were sweating hard.

The man with the gun said, 'Legs apart.'

She was surprised he'd asked. Usually they just kicked them aside. She felt his hands pat her down. Shoulders, arms, flanks, waist, outer thighs, then inner. No pausing or lingering at any point. Briskly professional. Not your usual bloke, she thought. Nine times out of ten they couldn't resist a quick feel of your boobs or a grab of your backside.

He said, 'Don't move unless I say so.'

Her linguist's ear picked up the melting pot of accents in his voice. Most people would think he was British but she heard the faintest of lilts from Holland and France, maybe even Algeria, but she couldn't work out if he came from one of those countries or if he was just a Brit who'd lived overseas for a while. He definitely wasn't an Albanian thug, yet despite the fact that she should have been cheered by this, her stomach thought otherwise and was squeezed tight with apprehension.

'Who are you?' she asked.

He didn't reply. He pocketed her mobile phone before taking a fiver from her jeans pocket that she'd forgotten about. After he replaced it he walked a couple of paces away and picked up her handbag. He opened it and extracted her wallet. Taking out her driver's licence and Visa card, then a bunch of keys, he gave them each a quick once-over before putting them back. He then reached a hand into the pocket of his bomber jacket and took out a mobile phone, flipped it open. He punched in some numbers, then took a couple of steps back and dropped his voice. She couldn't hear what he said, but she knew she was the topic of conversation when he retrieved her driver's licence and flicked his gaze between her and the photo-card as he spoke, obviously reciting the number. He was on the phone for less than thirty seconds before he hung up and came to stand close again. The pistol was held comfortably in his right hand, pointing at her chest. She could see the words *Pietro Beretta* stamped on its muzzle.

Still looking at her, bomber jacket spoke to the man Jay had winded. 'Get the car.'

The man nodded and began walking.

'You' – he spoke to the other man – 'walk ahead of us to the street. We'll follow you.' He cut his eyes to Jay. 'Won't we, Miss McCaulay?'

'What if I refuse?' She made her voice mocking to cover her growing anxiety. 'Will you shoot me?'

By way of reply he brushed her hair aside and planted his other hand on her neck. She felt his forefingers against her carotid artery. Christ, no! All he had to do was dig them in and he'd cut off the supply of blood to her head. The pain would be excruciating, but worse, she'd lose consciousness in seconds.

'Just walk,' he said quietly.

She'd be an idiot if she even thought of tangling with him. He had the build of a swimmer, tall and muscular with broad shoulders – and she wouldn't stand a chance. He looked as fit as a leopard and just as ruthless. With his hand fisting her collar and the pistol pressing in the small of her spine, Jay moved ahead of him and along the alley. When they came to the street, he let go of her collar and slid his arm beneath her coat and around her waist. The embrace was intimate and anyone glancing at them would assume they were lovers. They wouldn't see the Beretta which had slid to rest against her belly.

Outwardly, she tried to keep calm. Inwardly, she was panicking, trying to think how to break free without getting shot. Impossible.

'Keep walking,' he told her.

Aside from his pal sloping ahead of them, there was nobody about. Not even a dog. If she screamed, she doubted the cavalry would charge to her rescue. Maybe a couple of curtains would twitch, but that was all. People around here wouldn't want to get involved. Not unless there was a bag of narcotics or a suitcase full of money ripe to be nicked.

'You had some good moves back there,' he said. His tone was conversational. 'But you're out of condition.'

Jay turned her head to stare at him, speechless.

'You should train more.'

Before she could respond, a grey sedan came into view, and slowed to a stop beside them, engine running. The driver was a woman. The man Jay had winded was in the passenger seat. His pal went to the rear door and opened it. He stood back like a chauffeur waiting for her to step inside.

'Hop in,' bomber jacket told her.

His arm slid from her as he stood back, waiting for her to comply. Everything appeared civilised and polite, but her skin was springing with sweat despite the cold. Outnumbered four to one, without a weapon, there was no point in fighting, much as she'd love to give it a go to try and buy some time. She'd be unconscious, locked in the boot and half way to Cornwall by the time the cops arrived. Nick would only just have alerted them, and despite the fact that Trinity Road Station was only three streets away, it was already too late.

For the first time this week, she longed to see DI Tom Sutton.

'Inside,' bomber jacket prompted once more. His voice was low and calm, and Jay opted to do as she was told for the time being and folded herself on to the back seat. The car reeked of stale cigarettes, coffee and takeaways; the odour of boredom. From the litter in the footwells, which included a couple of soft-drink cans and a burger carton, she guessed it had been used as a stakeout vehicle for some time. Did this mean they were from one of the UK's security forces? Had they been watching Milot?

The men were professionals. They had obviously done this before, and their reticence could be part of a ploy. By deliberately not telling her who they were, or where they were going, they could be trying to keep her worried and vulnerable so that when they eventually got to their destination, she'd be easy to crack. Cops couldn't use that approach, but other security services had few qualms about kidnapping people without any introductions.

It was a 'snatch'.

She felt the woman watching her from the rear-view mirror. Somehow Jay wasn't surprised to see it was the same woman who'd been trailing behind her and Milot, but now without the pushchair. She was faintly pleased she'd pinged the woman and wondered if she'd been right about the elderly man too.

The man she'd winded had upended her handbag's contents on his lap and was picking through her wallet. Squinting at her driver's licence, he said, 'Who the hell are you?'

'Doesn't it say?'

'Hardly.' He gave a snort. 'Your licence shows a name but that's about it. No cutesy key ring, no pictures of your children or your cat, no tampons, no tissues, no sunglasses, nail files, lipsticks—'

'No guns or flick-knives, either.'

'True. But you can't say it's the sort of handbag a normal woman carries.'

'I'll take that as a compliment,' she told him, and then bomber jacket climbed inside, effectively sandwiching her in the middle of the back seat. No chance of flinging herself out en route, then. Her mouth was dry, the surface of her skin tight, but she forced herself to try and relax. Save her energy. Tucking a lock of hair behind her ear, she rotated her neck and gave her shoulders a roll. She could already feel a bruise forming where she'd hit the wall.

'Keep your hands where I can see them,' bomber jacket said.

Jay spread her palms on her thighs and leaned her head against the headrest, concentrating on appearing as imperturbable as her captor. This attempt to seem calm was a complete lie, but that was one of the good things about the army. It trained you to keep a cool head even when the shit hit the fan.

'Where are you taking me?'

Bomber jacket gave her a perfectly blank look and remained silent. She could have been talking to the white cliffs of Dover for all the expression on his face. When the woman driver glanced at him in the rear-view mirror, he gave her a nod. She started the car and pulled out.

Jay wanted to ask if anyone had a cigarette but kept quiet. Even if they had a carton of duty-free in the glove box they probably wouldn't have given her one, just used her nicotine habit against her.

Nobody said a word during the ride out of Bristol and on to the M4, seventy-three miles in the fast lane to the outskirts of Heathrow.

They pulled up at the rear of a bland, two-storey office building that could have housed anything from an insurance company to a heroin processing laboratory. The car park contained a dozen cars of average make, none of which you would look at twice. There were grey and blue Ford hatchbacks, Toyotas and Mazdas. No bright colours. It was as though every vehicle had been bought to blend in without being noticed.

Jay was escorted through a pair of double doors and up a short flight of stairs. She noted the synthetic grey carpet and white walls, fluorescent lighting and cheap plastic door handles. There were no pot plants and no pictures on the walls, giving the place a utilitarian and soulless atmosphere. In the background she could hear the hum of the A4 – lorries and buses and cars roaring along the old London road – but otherwise it was quiet.

At the top of the stairs was another corridor lined with doors, all closed. She was led to the second door on the left, where bomber jacket knocked twice before pushing it open. He gestured Jay inside. The two guys from the alley stayed in the corridor with the woman driver, who was holding Jay's handbag. She heard the click as the door shut behind them.

The room had more of the same grey carpet, white plastic fittings and fluorescent strips. A row of windows overlooked a handful of warehouses and a high fence topped with razor wire defending one of the runways. An odour of some kind of cleaning fluid hung in the air.

Three people sat at a table in the middle of the room, two men, one woman. One man was in his fifties, the other in his mid-thirties. The woman looked a little younger than Jay, but not much, and was maybe in her late twenties. Pale skinned, she had pink cheeks and short-bobbed hair as black and shiny as a jackdaw's wing. Her eyes were dark and intelligent, her chin small and sharp. She held Jay's gaze unflinchingly and without expression. Having met dozens of women like her, Jay immediately recognised the type. She could almost smell the woman's ambition from across the room.

The older man had iron-grey hair and wore a pair of half-moon spectacles. He looked her up and down and said, 'Take a seat.' His tone was offhand, expecting her to do as he said, like a Colonel expecting a foot-soldier to jump at his command, but he wasn't a superior officer and she wasn't in the army any more.

Jay didn't move.

'We haven't got all day,' he added caustically.

She didn't like being pushed around, let alone kidnapped, and it was an effort not to let her apprehension flare into anger. Instinct told her it wouldn't be a good idea to black this guy's eye, much as she was tempted to.

'I'll sit, but only after I've made a call.' She was amazed how calm her voice was. She sounded as though she was putting in a request for a train ticket. Emboldened, she kept going. 'Actually, let's amend that to several calls. First to the police, the next to my lawyer. Then maybe Amnesty International, they might be interested to hear about the abuse of my human rights.'

'Your rights were cancelled the second you attacked one of my men,' he said coldly.

'The Bristol police have been alerted—'

'I called them off, so I suggest you sit down and shut up.'

Jay struggled to hide her alarm. If he had the power to call off the local cops, he had the power to keep her here indefinitely. And she'd been right about the lack of introductions. They wanted to disorientate her and keep her off-balance. Shit. This was not her idea of an afternoon's fun.

'I'd rather stand,' she said blandly. Which wasn't true, but she was buggered if she'd let the old goat bully her. She wondered what Lily would make of him. He looked that buttoned-up he had to have a spanking fantasy at least, or maybe he'd request a French maid's outfit.

She watched bomber jacket move across the room to take up position in the corner, his arms loose at his sides. He was covering the door in case she made a break for it, as well as keeping himself away from the windows and presenting himself as a target. When she caught his eye he gave her the tiniest of nods, almost imperceptible, as though to put her at ease, but she wasn't fooled. He was simply a professional doing his job.

'So,' the older man said, still looking at Jay. 'You were following Milot Dumani.'

She didn't say anything. She was watching everyone's body language. There was an air of expectation and curiosity, but also a thick underlay of caution, as though they'd released a wild animal inside the room and were unsure how it was going to behave.

The older man bit his lower lip then moistened it with his tongue as he studied her. Belatedly she took in the papers on the table and spotted what appeared to be a copy of her driver's licence. A hasty resume of her life to date, she assumed, gathered while she had been driven here. She hoped her army psych report hadn't been included.

'Ms McCaulay,' he said. 'Who are you working for?'

The question was a dead giveaway, and confirmed her suspicions. 'Am I under arrest?' Her voice was curt to cover her fear.

'Not exactly,' her questioner said, 'But—'

'I'll see myself out.' Jay made a walk towards the door but stopped when bomber jacket moved to block her. Both hands were raised, polite as a traffic cop.

'Sorry,' he said. He sounded genuinely apologetic, as though he was refusing her entry into an art gallery that was just closing.

'We just want a chat,' the older man said behind her. 'An informal conversation about our mutual friend, Milot. That's all.'

She stalked back to the table. As she surveyed the three of them, their dry-cleaned suits and gleaming shirts and soft, clean hands, she bet they never dirtied themselves in the field. They were desk jockeys, a world apart from people like her and Nick, who weren't afraid to dive into the mire if it meant getting a result.

Putting her hands on the table she leaned forward, knowing it was a mistake to adopt a confrontational pose, but she was starting to get truly pissed off.

'Okay,' she said. 'If you want a chat, why don't you introduce yourselves? My name is Jay McCaulay, but then you already know that. And you are?'

There was another long silence.

Jay put her head on one side and looked at each of them in turn. 'Oh, dear,' she said. 'It looks as though we have a stalemate, because until I know who you are and why you've brought me here, conversation is out.'

More silence.

She gave them another thirty seconds or so and then she picked up a chair and took it to the window. Sitting down, she concentrated on her breathing to try and bring her blood pressure under control. Breathe in and hold, breathe out. And repeat. As she breathed, she came to a decision. For as long as it took, she would sit here in silence and let them fester. She refused to be intimidated.

The minutes ticked past.

Gradually she felt her equanimity return. Leaning back, she adopted a careless, confident pose by lacing her fingers behind her head. She looked at the view. A Virgin Atlantic 747 was coming in to land. Five hundred feet above the ground and descending rapidly, the airplane roared past, rain steaming from its steel flanks, a magnificent feat of engineering that made her shake her head in admiration. Intellectually she knew how jet airplanes flew, but the kid in her always marvelled at how something the length of a twenty-storey office block could stay in the sky.

She could just make out the faces of people gazing through the oval windows, some of them no doubt seeing England for the first time. Her hand lifted to touch the miniature icon at her throat as she imagined Zamira to be on the plane. The girl wouldn't even notice the bad weather through her excitement.

Two more aircraft had landed before she heard the older man behind her clear his throat.

'I'm Patrick Kingsman.'

She glanced across at him.

'I'm with the Foreign Office.'

He gestured at the sandy-haired man on his left. 'This is Alistair Ingram. And this' – to the woman – 'is Laura Sharpe. Both are on attachment to the Foreign Office.'

Her spirits, which had risen on thinking about Zamira, promptly plummeted. She'd been right. For Foreign Office, she thought glumly, read MI6.

She'd been kidnapped by spooks.

Four

'MI6,' Jay said on a half sigh.

'And MI5. It's a joint operation.'

She stared pointedly at the man in the bomber jacket, who was watching her with his usual rock-like expression. 'And you are?'

'Max Blake,' he said. 'I'm working this op with SOCA. The Serious Organised Crime Agency.'

'Thank you,' she said sweetly, and was surprised to see his eyes narrow at the corners, but whether it was in irritation or amusement, she didn't know.

Kingsman pushed up his spectacles with a forefinger. 'Miss McCaulay. We'd like to know who you are working for.'

Jay turned back to the window. If she gave an inch now, they'd trample all over her.

She said, 'I want a two-way street in this conversation, okay? Oh, and I'd also like to know what *your* interest is in Milot. It might help clarify things.'

Annoyance scratched his voice. 'Just tell me which security agency you're attached to.'

'I'm not. Your files should show you that. So come on, Kingsman. What am I doing here?'

In the window she could see him stroking his throat as he studied her. Then he sighed, and leaned forward. Spread his hands on the table. 'We want to know why you were following Milot. Our own interest in him is confidential.'

'You could have got one of your men to ask the question in Bristol. You didn't have to kidnap me.'

'Until we knew who you were, we felt obliged to take every precaution. If you were an unfriendly, say, or working for Milot – or were even one of his enemies – we couldn't risk you making phone calls or signalling a colleague of yours in the vicinity. I apologise if our methods appear a trifle harsh, but we've learned over the years that taking a suspect into an unfamiliar environment helps yield better results when we talk to them.' He swallowed, suddenly looking uncomfortable. 'I'm sorry.'

Wow, an apology. That wasn't bad. It was, in fact, quite a breakthrough. It showed he'd decided to treat her reasonably straight, which meant they might just get this over with before teatime, and she could then make it to Prayers – what Nick called the weekly round-up meeting each Friday – on time. The sooner I get talking, the sooner I leave, she thought.

Getting to her feet she picked up the chair and brought it back to the table. Sat down opposite them.

'Okay,' she said. 'I work for TRACE.'

'And what does TRACE do?'

'It's an international aid agency. Tracing, Reunion and Crisis Executive.'

From the silence that followed, she wasn't sure whether they knew this already or not, and decided to keep going.

'We're like a communications network. A message board for families. We trace missing persons in post-conflict areas throughout the world, reuniting families separated by war. This can also involve identifying those killed and informing their families. During conflict we post messages between families across frontlines.'

'You wanted to deliver a message to Milot from a long-lost relative?' Laura Sharpe gave a snort.

'No. I wanted to see where he went so I could report his whereabouts to the authorities.'

The atmosphere tautened.

22

'Authorities?'

'The police. The last time I saw Milot was five years ago in Macedonia. He was expanding his THB business – trafficking in human beings – across the Balkans and into Europe. He's a nasty piece of work, and I wanted to know what he was doing over here. Where he was going.'

Laura Sharpe's expression remained sceptical. 'You're asking us to believe it was a coincidence you saw Milot in St Paul's today? And that you decided to follow him on some sort of whim?'

Before Jay could answer, there was a knock on the door and the woman driver came inside with Jay's handbag and a sheaf of papers, which she delivered to Kingsman. After he'd scanned the first page, he passed it to Laura Sharpe, and then on to Ingram. There were five pages but it didn't take them long to read them.

'It says here your offices are in London,' Kingsman said. 'What were you doing in Bristol?'

He was still looking at what appeared to be her C.V., chock-a-block with her army appointments over the past ten years. He had paused at the last page, which she assumed was the finale of her life so far. His expression hadn't changed at any point, which she hoped meant her psych report was safely tucked away elsewhere.

'I was trying to find two sisters who have disappeared.' She leaned forward, gesturing at her handbag. 'May I?'

Kingsman pushed it forward. 'Of course.'

Jay opened her handbag to see that everything seemed to be in order, including her driver's licence and credit card. Withdrawing the photographs she'd shown to Lily in Bristol, she fanned them on the table. She tried not to flinch when Max Blake materialised at her side. He had crossed the room as quietly as a cat.

Leaning past her, Blake looked at the photographs. Both girls looked around seventeen, although they were, in fact, fourteen. Both were slender as reeds with long, dark glossy hair and blue eyes, tiny waists and high, pert breasts that pushed at their skimpy t-shirts. They were tanned and looked as energetically happy and healthy as a pair of young puppies.

'They don't look English,' Blake remarked.

'They're not. They're from Moldova.'

A kink appeared between his brows. 'You think they're in Bristol?'

'We heard a rumour that some unusually pretty girls from the Balkans had just arrived there. I thought I'd check it out.'

'Trafficking?'

'Yes.'

'Did you have any luck?'

She shook her head.

Kingsman scooped up the photographs, rapped them against the table to straighten them, and then returned them to her. 'You've been to Moldova?'

'No.'

'But you've been to Macedonia.'

'And Bosnia and Kosovo.'

'You're a linguist,' Kingsman said.

'I've been known to translate from time to time.'

Laura Sharpe piped up. 'You were with TRACE in the Balkans?'

'No. I joined NATO out there with the 12 Signals Regiment. I only started with TRACE two years ago. When I left the army.' To prevent anybody asking why she'd left the Sigs, Jay barrelled on. 'Now you know who I am, can I go? I've got a meeting at four that I really don't want to miss, and—'

'How well do you know Macedonia?' Kingsman interrupted.

'Just in passing. I only went there to help someone.'

'Who?'

She frowned, but couldn't see any reason not to tell them. 'A little girl who'd been separated from her mother during the Kosovo crisis. I placed her in a refugee camp in Macedonia, where I knew she'd be as safe as possible while I tried to find her mother.'

'Did you find her?' Kingsman's eyes were bright.

'Yes,' she said, and thought: but not in Macedonia.

He went back to reading the pile of papers, not seeming to make much of it, but the memory made Jay shudder. She couldn't think what had made her promise Zamira she'd find her mother. It wasn't like her to get involved like that, let alone with a kid. She didn't even like kids. She'd obviously been shell-shocked – or suffering from some sort of parental delusion because she'd saved the girl's life – to have been so incredibly stupid, and when she'd tried to wriggle out of it the next day, Zamira wouldn't have it. Jay had dropped the girl at the refugee camp first thing, made sure she was registered, but Zamira refused to let her leave. She clung to her elbow like a burr.

'But you *swore*,' Zamira had whined for the hundredth time, reminding Jay exactly why she hadn't had children. Of all the things she disliked about them, whining was right at the top.

Jay shook her arm free of Zamira's grip. 'No, look, I have to go. The people here will find your mother for you.'

Zamira's eyes began to tear. 'But you said *you* would find her! You promised.'

'I didn't promise.' Jay tightened her jaw, refusing to feel guilty. She'd saved the girl from being obliterated by a Serbian shell, and then she'd enlisted the help of every aid agency she could find to track down Zamira's mother, Nadire. She'd spoken to the United Nations High Commission for Refugees, the Red Cross, Oxfam and CARE International – big internationals who employed tens of thousands of people – and to the smaller agencies, like TRACE, who employed just twenty-five world-wide. She'd done more than a lot of people would have.

Without looking at Zamira, Jay climbed into her jeep and pushed the key into the ignition.

'But you said . . . ' Zamira bleated.

'I've got to get back to Pristina. I've got to translate for some really important people. A Russian UN Head, two Kosovan generals . . . '

She swallowed the last of her sentence when Zamira turned and ran away, her stick-thin legs kicking out clumsily like a foal's. The little girl was sobbing, but Jay shut down her emotions. She was a soldier for Chrissakes, not a fairy godmother. Zamira would be fine. She needn't worry. The Red Cross or TRACE would reunite her with her mother. Starting the jeep, she pulled out, spinning her wheels and creating a cloud of dust that obscured the refugee camp behind her.

In Pristina, Jay had finished one meeting and was running for the next when Kiro at TRACE rang her.

'Jay? Is Zamira with you?'

'No. I dropped her off this morning, remember?'

'Bollocks,' he cursed. 'In that case, she's missing.'

Her skin went cold. 'What do you mean, missing?'

Kiro sighed, and she imagined him putting his head in his hands. 'You know what it's like here.'

Jay stared at the side of the PTT building. The refugee camp where Zamira was held over a hundred thousand refugees, and unprotected young children made tempting targets for gangsters and hoods. 'You think she's been kidnapped?'

'She's very pretty.'

'I'm on my way.'

She found Zamira curled up in a cardboard box behind the refuse dump. Crows hopped and pecked at dirty cans and the air reeked of rotting vegetables and fly-blown meat. The little girl was asleep, but her face was still red and raw from crying. Jay picked her up. Without opening her eyes, Zamira wrapped her arms around Jay's neck and said, 'I knew you'd come back.'

Jay was aware of a small, tight sensation in her chest. She couldn't think what it was. Indigestion from the handful of dry biscuits she'd scoffed on the drive down, probably.

With Zamira's small face pressed against her shoulder, Jay carried her across the camp and ducked into TRACE's makeshift office, a ten-foot by ten-foot space built out of chipboard, with a tin roof and four walls plastered with photographs and messages. There were even notes to loved ones pinned to the ceiling.

'Hey, you found her!' Kiro beamed.

'Yeah, great,' Jay replied. 'So, where's Nadire?'

'In a town called Leposavic in north-east Kosovo.' Kiro

scrabbled through a bulging folder, pausing to cast his eyes over a blue form. 'She can't leave the city. It's controlled by the Serbs.'

'Great,' she said again, and settled herself on one of the rickety deck-chairs, Zamira on her lap. The girl was watching her with wide eyes. Jay couldn't help but stare back. Sometimes she found it hard to look away, and she wasn't the only one. Zamira was the only kid in the camp who didn't have brown eyes, and people invariably did a double-take when they saw the brilliant green irises.

'Nadire's a Kosovo Muslim,' Kiro went on. 'She can't risk coming out of hiding. If she gets stopped by a Serb patrol, they'll shoot her on the spot. She told me she wants Zamira to stay here, where she's safe.'

'Safe for how long? Jesus, Kiro, I can't be popping down here all the time. My boss will go insane.'

Kiro remained silent. He dropped his gaze to the blue form and put it on his desk, then smoothed a crease from the top corner. Jay watched him, her mind exploring the possible options, desperate for a solution.

'What if I go to Leposavic?' she ventured.

Kiro immediately flung up his hands in horror. 'Sweet mother of Jesus, you're not going to smuggle Nadire out, are you?'

Jay looked away.

'You want to get yourself shot?'

'You want Zamira to get kidnapped by a bunch of gangsters?'

This time, it was Kiro's turn to look away.

Later, when she told Zamira she was going to fetch her mother, the girl regarded Jay solemnly, then slipped off the miniature icon hanging around her neck and gave it to her.

'Nana gave it to me,' she told her. 'It will keep you safe too.'

Jay didn't want to accept it, but she didn't want to cause any offence by refusing; she knew how important gift-giving was out here. She studied the miniature carving of mother and child, unsure how to react. 'Thanks,' she said, embarrassed. 'It's beautiful.'

Before she left, Jay gave Zamira her blue-enamel Saint

Christopher pendant in return. It was the least she could do, swap gift for gift.

By the time MI6 let Jay go, two hours had passed and her mouth felt sour, her eyes scratchy.

At the door, Kingsman shook her hand. 'I'll ask Alison to drive you. Where would you like to go?'

'Vauxhall, please. My car's still at the office.'

'I'm calling on you as a professional to keep this meeting confidential,' he told her. 'A single word out of place and there could be some nasty repercussions.'

It was a clear warning. Jay nodded to show him she'd heard. She was about to step through the door when he said, 'Would you return to the Balkans, given the chance?'

'Why?'

'Just curious.'

'I wouldn't mind, but at this time of year I could think of more clement places to visit.' She gave a wry smile. 'Like Barbados.'

She couldn't read his expression. She said goodbye.

He didn't say anything in return.

Five

As he strode up the rocky mountain path, Branko Morillon hoped Zamira was ready. He hadn't seen her since the autumn and he trusted she'd grown up a bit since. She had just turned fourteen then, but she'd acted like a girl half her age. Still, nearly six months had passed, and girls could grow up fast during their teens.

Take Hana, for example, Zamira's best friend. She was the same age as Zamira but she'd been ready sooner, pushing her little breasts at him, wetting her lips with her tongue and sliding her hands between her legs as she held his gaze. Hana had been panting as hard as a young bitch on heat, and as malleable as he could have wished for. She'd asked few questions and done exactly as he'd wanted.

He paused to look behind him. At the bottom of the valley he could just make out the village of Novo Selo, a clutch of ramshackle stone buildings beside a stream that was near bursting its banks and roaring from melted snow. From the distance it looked pretty and picturesque but in reality he knew its streets were stony and smeared with centuries of animal shit. The houses had no electricity or running water, and there were no brightly-lit bars to hang out in, no restaurants or coffee shops. Few outsiders visited, and those that did were greeted with cold stares. Life was hard here, brutally so in winter. He should know, he used to live in a village like that. Fingering the fine, soft cashmere of his jacket – bought on his last London trip – Branko reckoned he'd rather kill himself than return to his penniless old life in the mountains.

He continued up the track, hoping Zamira would be as compliant as Hana, but then he remembered the flare of anger behind her eyes when he'd criticised her girlish behaviour. Sighing, he admitted to himself that Zamira would probably be one of the difficult ones, which would be a shame as he really was quite fond of her. When a girl became troublesome, it made it much harder for her. He'd do his best to make sure she realised how things worked early on, and maybe she'd be all right. Better than all right, if he was honest, because she was one of the most stunning-looking girls he'd seen since he'd been in the business. He'd taken her photograph to London, and a bidding war had broken out between three of his wealthiest clients, each wanting to pay top dollar to be her first. If Zamira behaved, did the right thing, she could do really well for herself in London.

Branko wrinkled his nose against the smell of cow dung as he approached the hovel where Zamira and her mother, Nadire, lived. A simple affair with four walls, it had a red clay-tile roof supported by broad timber beams, and no windows. Like many people scratching a living in remote parts of Macedonia, the two women relied on mountain streams for their washing and log fires and candles for warmth and light during the winter.

He pictured Zamira's face, alight with amazement and joy at her first London taxi ride and he began to smile. If he played his cards right, in no time at all he'd have Zamira begging him to take her away from her shit-stinking, poverty-stricken existence.

Zamira was sulking in the shade under the ancient olive tree when she spotted Branko. She'd just had a fight with her mother, who had yelled at her to get out and not come back until she realised how lucky she was. Lucky? Nana didn't understand anything. She thought that living in the mountains was good for you when nothing could be further from the truth. It was so mind-numbingly dull, she could scream.

30

The fight had started over Hana. All Zamira had done was wonder out loud whether Hana had managed to escape boring old Novo Selo for somewhere better – Hana had been determined she'd be living in London come the spring – and her mother had gone berserk. Zamira never got to say what was on her mind; that she was hoping Hana hadn't left home. She knew it was unkind, but life without Hana would be just about unbearable.

'Hana's more stupid than I thought,' said her mother. 'She'll never get work over there. She doesn't speak a word of English.'

'Jay will help her.'

'Jay has already done quite enough helping,' her mother snapped. 'Or have you forgotten how much we owe her?'

As her mother launched into a tirade about counting their blessings, part of Zamira's mind split away, remembering when she'd first seen Jay McCaulay. She'd been five years old, crammed in the back of a truck with twenty-five others, their faces gaunt, their bodies wrapped in tattered clothes and makeshift bandages seeping blood.

She could remember crying for her mother, who she'd lost when their apartment was shelled. She recalled the two British soldiers with red berets peering into the darkness of the truck, but what she remembered most clearly was the tall female soldier with short-cropped reddy-brown hair who'd appeared in a rush. Her boot laces were undone, her shirt hanging out of her trousers. A little blue disc shone brightly alongside her dog tags.

'Hello, I'm Captain McCaulay,' the female soldier said in Albanian. 'I'm a translator with one of the British regiments, I've heard you've some wounded . . .'

Zamira felt a ripple in the air. A ripping, tearing sound she recognised with horror. She opened her mouth to shout a warning but Captain McCaulay was ahead of her and already moving, lunging forwards, diving for the truck.

Zamira felt the captain pluck her from the truck and scoop her against her chest. A protective hand went to the back of her head. Then they were crashing to the ground, rolling away from the truck and she was beneath the captain who was holding her

31

firmly. She was chanting something in English. It sounded like a prayer.

WHUMP.

The truck disappeared in a cloud of smoke and flame, completely obliterated. A hail of torn shards of jagged metal and glass fell all around them. She saw a severed leg lying on the ground. An arm. Her head and ears felt as though they'd been stuffed with cotton wool. She looked up into the captain's face, smeared with smoke, her syrup-coloured eyes blinking rapidly.

'You okay?' she gasped.

'Yes.'

If it hadn't been for Jay McCaulay, she would have been killed, and she would never have found her mother. However, since Zamira felt as though her life was already over, she couldn't be sure if she would thank Jay for saving her if she saw her right at this moment.

Now she saw her mother walking to greet Branko, the massive shape of Bear padding alongside. The sheepdog was trained to protect them and to guard their handful of sheep and their two cows from wolves. His coat was the colour of dirty snow and as dense and warm as a sheep's fleece, and he wore a thick leather collar studded with wicked spikes. He weighed over 150 pounds, and could easily kill a man, but he knew Branko and was wagging his tail.

Zamira had to force herself not to jump to her feet and run full tilt across the hillside to join them. Instead she concentrated on walking, stepping carefully, over small gullies and crevices. She didn't want to be panting like an overheated animal when Branko first caught sight of her.

She slowed even further as she neared, her heart picking up. She'd forgotten how tall Branko was, how handsome. He wore smart trousers and a beautiful jacket the colour of blueberries. He was stroking Bear's head and talking to her mother with easy familiarity.

When he looked up, she lifted her head and approached him as sedately and serenely as she knew.

'Hello, Peaches!' he called to her. 'Aren't you looking beautiful today!'

Zamira felt herself blushing and fought against ducking her head. She would show him she wasn't a child any more. Nose in the air, she walked towards him, swinging her hips like Hana had shown her.

'Very nice,' he nodded approvingly. 'You're quite the young lady, aren't you.'

Zamira felt a hot rush of delight run through her.

'Branko . . .' Her mother shot him a warning look, at which he chuckled and patted her arm.

'Don't you worry, Nadire. I love Zamira and Hana like I would my own daughters. I'd never see any harm come to them, you know that.'

'But Hana's in London.' Nadire made it sound like Hades.

'She's *what*?' Zamira forgot all about being a young lady as her jaw dropped.

Nadire continued as if she hadn't heard. 'It's not safe, letting her go there. I don't care what you say, Branko, cities are full of scum. How Hana's family could let her go, I can't imagine. How do they sleep at night? They must be so worried . . .'

'Worried about how to spend all the money Hana's sending home,' Branko snorted. 'They've more food than they can eat and Hana's father has just bought a new trailer. His daughter's earning a fortune over there and her family are as happy as a well-fed bunch of pigs.'

'What's she doing?' Zamira was jigging from foot to foot. 'Where's she living?'

'She's working as a waitress at one of the top restaurants in the West End.'

Zamira knew all about the West End from the magazines Hana had brought home from Tetovo. The West End was full of smart cars and theatres, its shop windows filled with shirts made out of silk and shoes studded with jewels. Over here, the only things you got to see in a shop window were dowdy clothes coloured grey, black and brown, sacks of vegetables and, if you were lucky, a sheep's head.

'She's earning loads of money,' Branko went on. 'She goes shopping whenever she likes, has her make-up done at the big stores, goes out for meals.' His eyes sparkled with mischief. 'She's even got a boyfriend.'

'She's not even fifteen!' Nadire protested in horror.

Branko sent her a wry look. 'Don't tell me you never had a boyfriend before then because I won't believe you. Not with your looks, Nadire, love.'

Now it was Nadire's turn to blush. 'Branko, stop it,' she scolded. 'I'm too old for your flattery.'

He laughed, straight white teeth flashing in the sunlight. His hair gleamed blue-black, and his skin was smooth and looked as though it would feel like velvet to touch. Zamira didn't think she'd ever seen anyone so beautiful.

'Peaches,' he said, still smiling. 'I came because I've a present for you.' Hurriedly he held up his hands at her mother's scowl. 'It's not make-up or perfume or anything you wouldn't approve of, Nadire, I promise.'

Reaching a slender hand inside his jacket pocket he withdrew an envelope. A letter.

Zamira gasped. 'It's from Hana?'

'Yes.'

Zamira took the letter and turned it around in her hands. The envelope was plain white, and battered at the edges from being in Branko's pocket. Her name was in bold, black letters on the front. She stared at it, feeling angry and happy and jealous all at once. Angry at Hana for leaving, happy she was living the life they'd always dreamed of, and violently jealous for the same reason.

'She's living in a beautiful apartment,' Branko went on. 'It's got a view of the park, not too far from the cinema, some nice shopping malls, and it's got a coffee shop around the corner.'

Zamira felt herself burn with envy.

'But there's a problem.'

Zamira's eyes flew to Branko's. He was watching her steadily, seriously.

'She misses you. She says she wants you to join her.'

In a flash, Nadire was standing between Branko and Zamira. 'My daughter is not going anywhere.' Her voice was low and angry. 'So you can take yourself back to Skopje and leave us alone.'

'I'm sorry, Nadire.' Instantly he was contrite. 'Of course Zamira isn't going anywhere. She'll marry a local lad and have half a dozen children and live in the mountains until she's an old woman. Won't you, Zamira?'

The look he gave her was sorrowful, and her heart ached at the understanding in his warm brown eyes,

'Leave us, Branko,' snapped Nadire. 'I don't like you filling Zamira's head with these ideas.'

'I only came to deliver the letter.'

'Just go.'

'I'm sorry if I've offended you, Nadire.' His tone had turned gentle. 'It wasn't my intention. If I can make it up to you, let me know. I'll be staying with Hana's parents for the next two days.'

Nadire crossed her arms and lifted her chin, her expression stony.

Zamira watched Branko's elegant figure stride back down the mountainside, his blueberry coat perfectly tailored between his shoulder blades, his leather boots as clean and shiny as if they were brand new. Her fingers strayed to the silver chain around her neck and the blue-enamel St Christopher. If it was the last thing she did, she'd go to London, and take Captain Jay McCaulay some home-made baklava. Jay loved sweets.

Six

The man watched Jay McCaulay unlock the outer office door and step inside. She didn't look over her shoulder or check the vehicles around her. She obviously had no clue anyone might be watching.

He switched on his car radio and settled down to wait. The street was still busy with people leaving their offices, climbing into cars, heading for the tube and home. Their heads were ducked against the wind.

TRACE's office was on the first floor of a three-storey, whitewashed building set between an upmarket Portugese deli-cum-grocery and an insurance broker. Whoever had decided on TRACE's location, had decided well. Their rent would be cheaper than if they were north of the river in Westminster, and being this close to Vauxhall they were still within walking distance of government buildings and with easy access to embassies should they need to check visas. Buzzing down his window, the watching man breathed in the smell of frying garlic and exhaust fumes and wished he was at home, in the hills.

Two lights snapped on inside the TRACE offices and McCaulay came into view. She was rubbing her eyes and yawning. He could see the outline of her breasts against her blouse. She was one hell of a good looking woman. He couldn't help wondering what she looked like naked, and whether she shouted when she came.

*

Everyone had already gone home except Nick. Dropping her handbag on the nearest desk – which she shared with her colleague Gill Fisher – Jay went and peered into Nick's office and saw he was on the phone. He was scowling, absorbed, and didn't look as though he'd appreciate being interrupted.

She went to the kitchenette and poured herself a glass of red wine, a robust Australian Shiraz that warmed her throat and belly, and started to dissolve the stress she still held inside. With a packet of caramel-coated peanuts in one hand and wine in the other, she checked the maps and wall charts to see how successful the week had been. Gill appeared to have helped reunite two families, both in Montenegro – Jay wondered if they were connected – but otherwise the week had been quiet. Nick continued to chip away at the Kosovo list. Over two and a half thousand persons were still reported missing after the war, which would keep him out of mischief for some time yet.

Returning to her desk, she checked her phone messages. All of them bar one were from her mother. She was roasting a delicious beef sirloin with Yorkshire pudding on Sunday, and Jay and Tom must come for lunch. Jay erased the messages and switched on the computer, unsure how she felt about the fact Tom hadn't rung.

Part of her was relieved, but the other part, if she was totally honest, felt a bit miffed. She knew she'd treated him badly, but if he cared for her as much as he'd intimated, he wouldn't have fallen at the first fence, would he? Her mind started replaying the scene at the restaurant, and it was only with difficulty that she hauled herself into the present. She had to stop obsessing over that damned dinner and absorb herself with something else. Like Milot Dumani.

Crunching on peanuts, she began an e-mail to Kiro in Skopje, asking if he'd heard anything about Milot recently, plus whether he had any news on the missing twins who had allegedly been trafficked through Macedonia and on to Italy. The computer hummed softly. Radiators ticked and taxi engines vibrated outside the window. Daylight eased into grey, then black.

'How many am I supposed to take?' Nick appeared in the

doorway. He was holding a bottle of High Strength Omega 3 capsules and frowning. 'My doctor told me I don't eat enough fish. I hate fish.'

Tall, and spare as a length of metal pipe, Nick had an aquiline face spoiled by a broken nose, and close-cropped hair the colour of gun metal. He worked out at the gym six days a week, but even if he never lifted another weight he'd still be three times stronger than most men his age. Jay hoped she'd be in as good condition when she reached sixty-one, but doubted it. She strapped on her running shoes most mornings but her weakness for red wine and the odd cigarette somewhat counterbalanced her training.

She kept tapping on the keyboard. 'After what went down today you want to talk about your diet?' She wasn't sure if she could look at him without raising her voice, possibly shouting at him, and she hated doing that. It showed a lack of control, and was totally unprofessional.

'My diet's important. The government recommends eating oily fish at least once a week but I can't work out how many pills that is.'

'Nick, when I was in Bristol I asked you to ring the cops, but they were called off.'

'So I heard.'

'You knew?'

She looked at him. Deployed in the Falklands and then in the first Gulf War, Nick carried copious scars, most of which weren't visible. Sure, he had a white ridge crossing his face where a bullet had shaved his cheekbone, and he was a bit deaf from traversing a mountainside rocked with exploding missiles, but it was the shadows in his eyes – dark as the bottom of any chasm – that told the real story.

Nick had left the marines after a lengthy tour in Bosnia in the Nineties. He'd gone out to try to help re-build the area and ended up paying lip service to the roadmap of reconstruction. Disillusioned and saddened at the hypocrisy, he resigned and set up TRACE in the belief he could do more himself than he could as a marine. That was the official version anyway. It omitted the

38

fact that when his wife left him, along with his daughter, he fell into a depression and the only cure appeared to be to bury himself in aid work.

'Nick ...' She respected him enormously but right now she was practically trembling from the effort of not raising her voice. 'I was in a serious situation and you let me down.'

He put the pill bottle on her desk. 'You really believe that?'

'Yes.'

'Look at it from my point of view. One minute I'm pressing the panic alarm for you, the next I've got Roger Park on the phone telling me to drop it.'

'Oh,' she said. She felt as though she'd had her chair whisked out from beneath her. Roger Park was a Cabinet minister and the chief of their board. TRACE was a private aid agency, and having Park at their table not only helped to raise funds, but lent them weight when dealing with diplomats and governments overseas.

'He was attending a meeting with the Home Secretary when Patrick Kingsman rang him. As you can imagine, Park wasn't happy about being interrupted. You're supposed to be finding missing people, not interrupting delicate surveillance operations.'

'Did he know I was in an alley with two thugs the size of tractors coming for me? That a third man stuck his Beretta behind my ear and threatened to blow my head off?' Her voice was starting to rise, along with her blood pressure. 'Jesus, Nick, they bloody kidnapped me in broad daylight!'

He stuck out his jaw. 'Roger told me you were okay. There was no reason to believe otherwise.'

'You didn't ring me. You didn't even send me a text!'

'There didn't seem any point since I knew you were okay.' Nick cracked his knuckles and fixed his gaze outside. His sudden inability to look her in the eye was as close as he'd get to giving her an apology.

Taking a deep breath, Jay held it while she counted to ten. It wasn't Nick's fault she'd taken it on herself to trot after Milot, then follow him down an alley. She couldn't blame him. Not really.

Exhaling, she picked up his bottle of capsules. She gave a loud sigh. 'It says two capsules with food. I think that could be a clue.'

'What, taken together? Or one at breakfast and one at dinner?'

'I don't think it matters.'

As she passed the bottle over, her e-mail pinged, telling her she'd received a message. It was from TRACE's office in Macedonia.

'Anything wrong?'

'Not really.' She tossed her head, flipping hair out of her eyes. 'I told Kiro I'd spotted Milot over here, and asked if he had any up to date info on him.'

'And?'

'Apparently the latest rumour is that Milot is looking for new smuggling routes into the UK. He's trying to corrupt top officials at both Heathrow and Gatwick, and infiltrate Customs with members of his gang.'

'Customs are hard nuts to crack.'

'Not everyone has your honour and integrity,' she told Nick. 'Besides, Milot may not try bribing them. Knowing him he'd be happy to threaten their families, kidnap their kids, whatever.'

Nick moved to read the e-mail over her shoulder. 'What do you want to do?'

She stretched her arms to the ceiling, gave a yawn, then began shutting down the machine. 'I guess I'll let Patrick Kingsman know. He's the one keeping tabs on him.'

He raised an eyebrow. 'And?'

'And what?'

'In his message, Kiro asked you a favour. To talk to your friends at Heathrow. And since half your old army buddies work airport security . . . '

'Stop exaggerating. I've got two friends there and you know it. My housemates. Angela and Denise.'

'The dykes.'

'I wish you wouldn't call them that. They're gay, okay? And yes, I was thinking of having a chat to them. They might have heard something.'

'Absolutely not,' he said emphatically.

'Come on, Nick. Kiro needs the information. It might help him plug a trafficking hole their end.'

'If MI6 hear you're sniffing around Milot they'll lock you up and throw away the key. You got a taster in Bristol. Wasn't it enough for you?'

'MI6 won't hear a dicky bird, I promise. I'll question Angela and Denise over a mug of tea in the bathroom with the shower on full blast.'

She was trying to make light of it, but to her dismay Nick's expression closed. 'You're a volunteer aid worker, Jay. Not a cop, not a private investigator. An aid worker. You'd best remember that,' he said, and walked out of the office.

The man pulled into the road behind her. He had to accelerate hard to keep up. She'd surprised him, taking off like that. It didn't help that the car he was using was a heap of crap. An ancient Land Rover Discovery with the performance of a butter bean. Its colour was entirely appropriate, given it was the same shade as a pile of freshly deposited cow dung: shit green.

She had the Golf nipping neatly around slow-moving buses and trucks, and he was absorbed in keeping up, when a transit van pulled out directly in front of him. No indicator. No warning. He was forced to brake, drop his speed to twenty m.p.h.

'Hell,' he cursed under his breath.

He inched out to overtake but was forced back by a rush of cars coming from the opposite direction. He cursed again. He didn't want to lose her.

A hundred yards on there was a gap in the traffic and he swung out and accelerated around the transit van. He pushed his car hard, one eye out for cops. He caught up with her as she approached Vauxhall Bridge. Once she had crossed the river, she cruised west along the Embankment before she turned north, and into Chelsea. He stayed two or three cars behind her as they threaded their way through the myriad of streets, over speed bumps and along one-way streets, until finally she was in a residential street of white stucco houses. She indicated left as she began to brake for a parking spot.

He cruised past her. She didn't look up. At the end of the street he paused, engine running, and watched her jog up the steps to a tall, white house and let herself in. He reversed back down the street but there were no more spaces and he parked illegally for twenty minutes until a space became free. Parking anywhere central in the city was always hell, but here – at the Chelsea end of Fulham – it was a nightmare. He wondered if it bothered her, and doubted it. She didn't look as though much would bother her. She had that air about her. He couldn't help but wonder what might shatter her seemingly unassailable confidence.

In spite of Nick's warning, or maybe because of it – Jay always had been insufferably stubborn – the second her housemates arrived home she told them about Kiro's email.

'Who's Milot?' asked Denise, pulling a Stella beer from the fridge and drinking straight from the neck. Despite the cold weather she was wearing nothing but tracksuit pants and a stretchy vest that hugged her upper body and showed off her muscles. Her toenails were short and painted bright red.

'Albanian Mafia,' Jay replied. 'A real bottom-feeder. Kiro's worried he's going to infiltrate Customs and Immigration over here, and in turn increase his human trafficking business.'

'Ooh, yes please,' said Angela. 'I could do with a juicy bribe or two. I rather fancy building a conservatory on the back of this place.'

'But what about the garden?' Denise looked through the kitchen window, her face a picture of dismay. 'Won't it disappear?'

'We'll still have one, it'll just be a bit smaller.'

Jay watched her friends with amused affection. Some days it was hard to believe that both women were tough ex-special reconnaissance soldiers supporting 1 PARA who had done Ops in Basra, Northern Ireland, Kosovo and Afghanistan. She'd first met them on the flight out to Sarejevo in a C130K, an ageing

Hercules, a lumbering great grey elephant that would have deafened her permanently if she hadn't been given ear defenders. She'd nodded off on the noisy journey but had come to with a jerk when the aircraft dropped out of the sky. One second they were on a glide path for landing, the next they were plunging straight down through the air. Seconds later the aircraft corkscrewed violently left then right, and continued twisting and turning wildly as it careered downwards.

'Jesus Christ!' Panic was in her voice. She was clutching her harness so hard her knuckles were white.

'It's okay!' yelled Denise, who was strapped in next to her. 'They have to chuck us around like this to avoid lock-on by missiles!'

The aircraft veered sideways, the fuselage groaning, and Jay felt the blood drain from her head. She was fighting the whimper in her throat when Denise took her ice-cold and clammy hand between her own two warm ones. Angela leaned across and gave her a sympathetic grin.

'Promise you this is completely normal!' she shouted.

'No it's bloody not!' Jay yelled back. 'It's fucking insane!'

Instantly, she felt better for yelling, and while the Hercules roared and shuddered around them, she and Denise and Angela yelled at one another until, with no apparent lessening of power, the pilot yanked up the nose and slammed the aircraft on to the ground with an almighty thump! Jay had been amazed that the machine was so rugged, and also amazed that she was still clutching Denise's hand. She hadn't held anyone's hand since she was four years old, and was grateful neither woman mentioned it again, not least in front of the guys. She would never have lived it down.

'But wicker chairs won't match the sofa.' It was Angela, colour-coordination obsessive. 'Not unless we spray-paint them cream.'

'Hey, guys,' Jay broke in. 'I'm sorry to break up your home re-modelling plans, but we were talking about Milot? Scum of the earth wanting to bribe our unimpeachable British Customs and Immigration?'

Denise took a final gulp of beer and chucked the empty bottle in the recycling box in the corner. 'Sorry, babe. I've heard zilch.' She turned her small, dark head to Angela. 'What about you, Ang'?'

'Not a squeak. Jay, do you want us to ask around? We'll do it on the quiet. Nobody'll know.'

Jay nodded. 'That would be great. Thanks.'

Angela made roasted vegetable lasagne that night, and they ate it off their laps while watching *Who Wants to be a Millionaire* and drinking too much red wine. Sitting with her empty plate at her feet, trying to guess the answers ahead of her housemates, Jay felt a peculiar sensation of watchful expectation seep through her. It wasn't a new feeling, she'd had it since she could remember, but she'd been so busy lately that it had fallen quiet. She looked over her shoulder and then at the windows, allowing the feeling to grow into an insistent sensation of waiting for something: something important. It was like waiting for the train to arrive when you're eager to start your journey. Or waiting for your lover's car to turn up outside your house.

Restless, she rose and went to the front door and opened it. The street was silent except for the rain pattering softly down.

She stood there for a while, listening to the sensation inside her and wondering what it meant.

Seven

Slightly headachy the next morning, Jay had to force herself to shop for groceries and household supplies. Standing on the pavement on Fulham Road, she was glancing left and right and waiting for the traffic to ease when she spotted an elderly man on the other side, peering at a restaurant window. There wasn't anything unusual about him. He wore brown trousers and shoes, and a bulky overcoat the colour of stale mustard. His wispy grey hair lifted in the winter wind but he didn't seem to notice. He appeared absorbed in studying the menu on display.

Goosebumps flashed across her skin, making the hairs on her body stand upright. It was the same guy she'd seen in Bristol when she'd been following Milot.

MI6 was tailing her.

Or, to be perfectly correct, MI5. Kingsman had said it was a joint op, and since her surveillance was being conducted on home territory, this guy had to be MI5.

Dumping her Sainsbury's bags in the kitchen, Jay picked up the walkabout phone next to the fridge to dial Nick, and then thought better of it. If they had stuck a tail on her, would they have tapped her phone? But why? It didn't make any sense. Just because she'd followed Milot to the back door of a restaurant in Bristol didn't mean she was worth all that time, effort and money, did it? Or was it because she'd asked her flatmates, two old army friends, to ask about Milot at Heathrow?

She recalled the way Nick's eyes had shuttered, the chill in his voice.

You're a volunteer aid worker, Jay. You'd best remember that.

Nick had to know more than he was letting on, and she'd bet it involved some old pals of his. Only last year Nick had utilised TRACE to find a missing retired Air Marshal friend, managing to embroil the agency in a diplomatic incident that still smarted. That was the thing about working with ex-service personnel; not only did they have a network that rivalled the old school tie, but they also had fingers in every pie imaginable.

Most people assumed if you worked for an NGO – a nongovernmental organisation – you were a do-gooder, someone who wore sandals and knitted your own vegetable soup, but nothing could be further from the truth. NGOs needed personnel who were tough and self-reliant, and who didn't fling their hands up in horror at people and places that could turn out to be dirty, rude, and sometimes downright vicious. A lot of applicants for the job believed all they needed was a keen desire to help, but there was no room for anyone who couldn't deal with rat-infested lavatories or getting spat on and worse by angry locals, which was why international aid agencies employed so many ex-military staff. TRACE was no exception. Out of the twenty-five people employed worldwide, only two were civilians, and even then those two had passed their advanced defensive-driving courses and were mountaineers in their spare time.

Jay considered Nick and his military cronies. If her boss knew she was being tailed she would, she decided, kill him very slowly when she saw him on Monday, but not before she'd wheedled the whole story out of him.

She went into the hall and sneaked a look outside, but the elderly man was nowhere to be seen. He'd switched with someone else, perhaps. Or they could be in one of the flats opposite, sitting comfortably behind a camera, waiting to take photographs of her and whoever came and visited.

What the hell was going on?

To stop her mind from spinning out of control, she busied herself unpacking the groceries. Porridge in the muesli jar, fresh

46

salads, milk and cheese in the fridge. Fruit in the bowl by the window. Her movements felt mechanical and unnatural and she wondered if she looked any different to her watchers now that she knew they were there. Her heartbeat was up, her breathing shallow. Hidden inside the bathroom she took several deep breaths, concentrating on letting her shoulders relax downwards as she breathed out. As usual it didn't take long to regain her equilibrium. She could hear her father's voice as if he spoke right next to her: *When you relax the body you relax the mind.*

He'd sounded like a self-help guru, a hypnotherapist, instead of the practical and tough ex-RAF officer he was. He constantly surprised her, her dad, which was probably why they got on so well. She desperately wanted to ring him but didn't want to involve him should MI5 – or MI6 – be listening. Best to keep quiet until she got to the bottom of what was going on, and besides, her father probably wouldn't answer the phone anyway. He was always flat out at this time of year, calving. Some retirement, working dawn till dusk, knee-deep in cow dung, but he seemed happy. In fact, she'd never seen him so contented; fly-fishing the burns for trout, caring for his herd of Highland cattle, and picnicking with his wife Nicola on the top of heather-drenched hills.

She started when the phone rang. Gingerly, she picked it up. 'Hello?'

'Oh, good. You're home.'

'Hello, Angus,' she greeted her brother.

'What are you doing tonight?'

'I'm busy.' She knew what was coming.

'Doing what?'

'None of your business, that's what.'

'No need to get snappy,' he said. 'I was just wondering, that's all. Can't I have a chat with my little sister?'

'Only if it gets around to whether I can baby-sit your two little horrors this evening, you mean.'

'They're not horrors.' He sounded hurt. 'They've been really good today . . .'

'Angus, I was joking. You know I adore them.' Particularly when they were fast asleep, she wanted to add.

'Sorry. Seriously, Jay, Sandra and I are in a bit of a tight spot tonight. You know I translate for the Albanian embassy?'

The embassy also called on Jay occasionally. Albanian was a relatively obscure language and trustworthy translators were in short supply. She and Angus had learned Albanian when their father – also a linguist – had been stationed in Tirana, along with Sandra's father. Both sets of parents had insisted that their children learn not just the usual French and German, but something that could be used locally too.

'They've invited us to a black-tie dinner,' Angus continued. 'Our sitter's let us down at the last minute and . . . '

'No, Angus.' She made her voice firm. 'I can't. Sorry.'

'But it's really important. I wouldn't ask otherwise.'

Like she hadn't heard that one before.

'Sorry.' No way did she want the kids in the house with watchers prowling about. 'Try Universal Aunts or something. Yellow Pages. I don't know.'

'Shit.'

'Send Sandra my love.'

'Yeah,' he gave a defeated sigh. 'Okay.'

Jay hung up and grabbed her newspaper. She'd gone for *The Times* today because of its headline, FAKE VISAS ACCEPTED AT JOB CENTRES. Taking the paper, she went and curled up on the sofa beneath the front window. It was a Saturday, after all. Her day off. Whoever had been assigned to watch her could get bored while she read the paper for the next hour. Then she had a better idea. She'd go for a run. Not only would it help her come to a decision about what to do next, but it would give her watchers some exercise.

He was halfway through his bacon sandwich when Jay McCaulay opened her front door, wearing sweat pants and sneakers, and her hair tied back. Why couldn't she stay at home drinking coffee and reading the weekend papers like most normal people?

Before she trotted down the steps, she glanced up and down

the street. Hell. She was checking to see if anybody showed any interest in her. What had tipped her off? It couldn't be him since he hadn't been on the street since eight p.m. last night. He was holed up in the house opposite, where he'd persuaded the owners – a married couple in their late sixties – to rent him their front room for the week.

He watched her jog down the street with a long, easy stride, sleek and powerful.

He decided to follow in his car; she'd spot him in two seconds if he jogged after her. Moving outside, he checked the area, more out of habit than in expectation of seeing anybody. He froze. There were two of them. A young woman at one end of the street, an elderly guy at the other.

He wasn't the only one watching McCaulay.

Sweat-soaked after three miles, Jay slowed her pace for the last section towards Redcliffe Road, cooling down. She hadn't seen anyone running behind her and assumed they'd followed by car or bike; far more sensible options. She felt soft-boned and loose, tension draining away as she concentrated on working her body. Running was her release, and if she didn't run regularly she felt cooped up and stale and became bad-tempered. Whenever she got snarly in the office Nick would fetch her trainers from the hall and offer them to her in silence.

Approaching her house, she couldn't see the elderly man, or anyone sitting in a parked car ostensibly reading a newspaper while keeping an eye out for her. The street was quiet and wafts of toast and frying bacon drifted past, making her mouth water and reminding her she'd missed breakfast. A blackbird gave a chattering alarm call from a cherry tree as she passed. Trotting up the steps to the front door, she felt a rush of gratitude to Angela and Denise. If it wasn't for them, she could never have afforded to live in such a beautiful house. Mind you, she should be thanking Angela's ex-husband. When he'd discovered his wife had fallen in love with another woman he'd settled the house on Angela in a desperate attempt to keep it hushed up. Apparently it didn't do high-profile barristers any good if they were married to lesbians.

Jay pulled her house keys from her pocket.

'Good run?' said a male voice behind her.

The tone was casual, but she jumped a mile.

'Christ,' she said. She put her hand over her heart.

'I'm sorry. I didn't mean to startle you.'

It was Max Blake, the field agent with cat's feet. He was on the bottom step, looking up at her, face open and alert. She glanced at his shoes, expecting to see desert boots or something with rubber soles, but he was wearing lace-up leather walking shoes. Brogues, for God's sake. How the hell did he manage to creep up on her like that?

'I'm the advance party.' He turned his head to indicate a shiny black car drawing up outside the house, a limo with smoked glass windows. Both rear doors opened and out stepped Patrick Kingsman and Roger Park, Cabinet minister and chief of TRACE's board. To her disbelief, the neat figure of Laura Sharpe joined them, followed by a morose-looking Nick.

'What the—' she started to say.

'If you wouldn't mind letting me in,' Blake said, gliding up the steps, 'I need to do a quick check inside.'

'Nobody's here. My friends are at work.'

'I'd still like to check.'

She stared at him, hoping for some sort of clue as to what was going on, but his dark brown eyes were unfathomable.

'It's not personal, you understand,' he added. 'It's my job.'

'I can't place your accent,' she said on impulse. 'What is it? Dutch? Or is it French? Algerian?'

'I've lived a while in each place, but didn't realise it was so obvious.'

'It's not.'

'Then you have a fine ear. Now, if you wouldn't mind letting me in . . .'

'Oh. Of course.'

Jay fumbled her Chubb key into the first lock, then unlocked the Yale and pushed open the door. Immediately came the beep-

beep of the alarm. While Blake slipped past her and down the hall, she disabled it.

'Mind if we come in?'

Nick stood on the doorstep, his expression guarded. She could see the tension in his hands, which were clenched together and held in front of him, as though he was in church and trying to strangle a rat without anyone noticing.

'You've met Roger, of course,' Nick said, and ushered the Cabinet minister forward. Greying and of medium build, he had a harassed air that was exacerbated by the fact that he needed a haircut. Wisps of hair drifted above his ears and forehead.

'Just the once,' she admitted. From the neutral look on his face, Roger Park didn't remember.

'Of course,' he said warmly, ever the politician.

They shook hands. Jay's was still hot after her run, Park's cold and clammy. She had to resist the urge to wipe away the stickiness against her tracksuit pants.

Nick turned to one side. 'And you know Laura and Patrick from your meeting with them yesterday.'

Jay nodded. She had a knot in her lower belly. 'What's going on?'

Nick said, 'We'll explain inside, okay?'

'An explanation would be nice.'

Kingsman shrugged out of his coat and stepped between them. 'Anywhere I can put this?'

She was tempted to tell him he could put his coat somewhere extremely rude but was distracted by Blake appearing at her elbow, leaning close. So close, that when he spoke she could feel his breath stir the hairs on her cheek.

'I'd like a quick word,' he murmured. 'In private, please.'

For no reason she could think of, her skin contracted all over her body.

'What is it?' Kingsman was looking at Blake.

'There's a basement alarm I need Ms McCaulay to help me with,' he said smoothly. 'We'll be back in a second.'

But there was no basement alarm ...

Blake said, 'I don't want to set it off by accident.' He cupped

51

Jay's elbow firmly in his right hand and steered her along the corridor and down the stairs. She remembered the sensation of his fingers on her carotid arteries when they stood in the alley. The army had trained her to fight and to shoot, and Nick had taught her some dirty tricks to use in close hand-to-hand combat, but every instinct told her not to chance them with Blake. She was out of his league, and anyway, he might have a legitimate reason for luring her down here, although she couldn't think what the hell it could be.

As soon as they were at the bottom of the stairs, he dropped her elbow and turned to face her.

'I found this on your walkabout kitchen phone.'

He opened his left hand to show her a small, round metal object.

Jay stared at it.

'It's a VHF listening device,' he told her. 'Which is legal.'

He then brought something from his trouser pocket and showed her another small metal object. Not the same as the first, but similar in construction, like a screw-fit light bulb is the same but different to a baton-fit light bulb.

'Another bug,' he said.

'Right.'

'Now, this bug' -- holding up the one from his pocket – 'is pretty much legitimate. It's VHF, and you've three in this house. I planted them yesterday for Kingsman.'

She felt her mouth fall open and closed it.

'But this one' – he showed her the device he'd found on the walkabout phone – 'is a problem. It's UHF, ultra-high frequency, which is illegal. I didn't install it, and I don't know who did.'

Shit. She was frightened now.

'I've only found the one so far, but I'd say it was a safe bet there are more. However, without specialist equipment, I'll be lucky to find them. I thought you should be aware.'

Jay looked at the bug then back at Blake.

'You're saying this house is bugged by the security forces, but also by someone else, and you don't know who?'

'Correct.'

She stared at him, not knowing what to think.

He turned his wrist and checked his watch. He said, 'You should go up now.'

Jay continued to stare.

'And be very careful what you say.'

She cleared her throat, tried to unscramble some of the tangled thoughts looping in her head. 'Are you going to tell Kingsman about this? Or Roger Park?'

His expression remained neutral as he scrutinised her.

'No.'

'So why tell me?'

'I have my reasons.' Then he turned and padded up the stairs.

Eight

'You won this?'

Roger Park was holding a mug of coffee and looking between Jay and the bronze medal propped on the mantelpiece.

'Yes.'

His eyebrows rose in startled admiration. She'd forgotten that Denise had put it there one drunken evening, telling her she should be proud of her achievement and that she ought to display it at every opportunity.

'Seven-point-five-kilometre sprint biathlon,' he murmured. 'Very impressive.'

'Like Jay herself,' interjected Nick with forced joviality. 'She's a valued member of my team and I'd like to keep it that way.'

'She'll be fine.' Roger Park waved a dismissive hand. She hoped he wasn't like that in Cabinet or he wouldn't be making many friends to help him get re-elected.

Nick said, 'She hasn't been in a combat zone for five years.'

'For heaven's sake, it's not a combat zone,' Park sounded irritated. 'It's got its post-conflict problems but nothing serious.'

'A bomb went off downtown only last month, killing two people and injuring five more.'

'She won't get blown up. If her army bio's accurate, that girl's got nine lives and she's only used up three.'

Jay didn't like being called a girl, and nor did she appreciate being talked about as if she wasn't there. She was about to say so when, across the room, Laura Sharpe sent her a warning look.

Kingsman cleared his throat. 'We've been doing some talking about you, Jay. Negotiating here and there with Nick. We've read your files and, well . . . we'd like to offer you a job.'

'I already have a job.' From across the room, she felt Nick's approval.

Kingsman frowned. 'You haven't asked what the job is yet.'

Jay turned her attention to Laura Sharpe, and as she looked into the woman's dark eyes, she felt a rush of foreboding.

'I'm happy with the one I've got, thank you.'

Although Laura Sharpe didn't move a muscle, didn't even blink, Jay immediately sensed that the agent approved of her negative response. She couldn't explain why she thought this, but since she made better snap judgements than cautious decisions, she trusted her instincts.

After a small silence, Park spoke up. 'You were offered a job in Whitehall four years ago, on the Balkan desk. Why didn't you take it?'

'I prefer command tours in the field.'

Which was only part of the reason why she'd left the army. She had buried the real reason so deeply it always came as a shock when she remembered it, like opening your fridge and seeing a dead rat inside and then remembering that yes, in a complete fit of madness you had put that rat there last week.

She swallowed as the scene unrolled in her mind. It had been raining when her platoon had come across a farmhouse in Kosovo, a low-slung building blurred by fog and with chickens pecking in the dirt outside. The war was over, but they were still needed to help with the ongoing Kosovo stabilisation under the mighty umbrella of NATO forces. Intel had heard a rumour that a bunch of well-known Serbian Orthodox Christians – all ex-soldiers – were in the area wanting to cause trouble with Muslim Kosovans, and had sent Jay's platoon to check it out.

They were a quarter of a mile away when they heard the screams. Immediately, they ran for the farmhouse. As they drew nearer, Jay could hear men shouting and jeering. The screaming stopped and the men's raucous voices filled the sudden silence.

Major Wayland gave orders. Her weapon ready, Jay had led the way inside. She couldn't remember precisely what happened over the next sixty seconds. It was as though her brain had shut down, only able to process single images, taking a picture every ten seconds or so and nothing more.

A snapshot of two soldiers, one drinking from the neck of a wine bottle, the other kicking an elderly man in the head. The elderly man was naked from the waist down. He had had his genitals ripped from his body.

The next snapshot was of two women; grandmother and mother. They were also naked and had their legs spread, their throats slit. The grandmother had had her left breast cut off and stuffed into the mother's mouth. The mother had a broken bottle rammed into her vagina.

Two little boys around three years old lay trussed on the floor, sobbing. Their arms and legs were bound tightly with barbed wire.

A stench of excrement and entrails and blood smeared the inside of her nose, choking her. Upstairs, a child began to scream.

The next image was of Major Wayland pointing up the stairs, ordering her to clear the upper floor, secure the child's safety.

Third snapshot. A soldier on his knees. He had his back to her. His neck was thick and pasty-looking. His trousers were around his ankles, his muscular buttocks pumping. He was raping a young girl. She couldn't have been more than ten.

After she had shot him, she knew it was over. She had reached her limit. Major Wayland had taken her weapon, his expression weary. 'Time to go home, Captain.'

She had to spend the next two months in psychiatric care, but despite the best efforts of her doctor she could never express any regret over shooting the girl's rapist.

'But during your army career, you did over six tours.' Park appeared puzzled. 'Didn't you think it was time to reap the benefits? You've a good working knowledge of Albanian and Serbo-Croat. You would have done very well.'

'I'd have been bored witless,' she said truthfully. Her psych report had stated that she had reacted emotionally to the scene without pausing to assess the situation before acting – they had no choice but to recommend that she take a desk job or leave the army. To Jay there was no option. She'd never been one for sitting still for long.

Park was now staring at her as though she was a sub-species of insect. 'Er ... Patrick. You're sure she's, ah ... suitable?'

'Jay is more than suitable,' Kingsman said. 'She's resourceful and adaptable, able to work independently, has a good sense of initiative, and above all, is a professional. As I've said repeatedly, I believe Jay is perfect for our purpose.'

'Which is' – this was Nick, who was obviously getting fed up with all the pussyfooting around – 'to send her to Macedonia to be your spy.'

For the first time since she'd made the coffee, Jay became aware of Max Blake. He'd been standing motionless by the French windows but now he raised his head like a hunting dog scenting its prey. He was gazing outside.

'You're perfectly placed working for an aid agency to insert into Macedonia and gather intelligence for us,' Kingsman told Jay. 'All we want you to do is go there and ask a few questions, take some old friends out for coffee, for drinks, and get them talking.'

'About what?'

'Milot Dumani.'

She raised both eyebrows.

'He's due to fly back to Skopje on Sunday and we'd like to keep a close eye on him. You see, we've heard rumours that he's bringing in the Georgian Mafia to operate with him in the Balkans. We need on-the-ground intelligence to confirm or deny this because, if it's true, we have to put measures in place to stop the partnership growing. The last thing we need is more weapons and drugs being smuggled into the UK.'

Jay drained the last of her coffee, trying to ignore the hop of excitement at the thought of returning to Eastern Europe. She'd like nothing more than to sabotage Milot's plans, throw a spanner in his works, but she wasn't sure if she'd be any good as a spy. She was too honest for all the subtleties required. What had her mother said?

You don't have to say what's on your mind and in your heart all the time, darling. Sometimes, it's kinder to others if you bite your tongue.

All she'd done was ask her mother's friend, Helen, how the heck she managed to look so young when she was as old as she was. She thought it was fantastic to look barely forty when you're pushing fifty, but Helen went bright puce and Mum kicked her shin under the table. If she became a spy, it wouldn't be for long. She'd only put her big foot in it and end up in a shallow grave with a dusting of snow on her corpse. Jay began to shake her head but Kingsman wasn't looking and ploughed on.

'You'll go out there as if you're on a normal TRACE mission. We'll match whatever TRACE is paying you, so you'll earn double until you come home. You'll be there for two, maybe three weeks. You might get a lead to those Moldovan girls,' he added ingenuously. 'Weren't they trafficked through Macedonia?'

She was about to reply when Blake moved from the window. He held a finger to his lips and flicked his eyes to the living room phone, then back to her. The bugs. She'd forgotten the wretched bugs.

'I'm not sure,' she said, earning a startled look from Nick. He knew as well as she did the girls had been shipped through Macedonia and on to Italy. 'Look, I appreciate what you're looking for here, but I really don't think I'm the right person for this.'

Blake gave her an approving look similar to the one Nick had given earlier and she wondered if they weren't in cahoots. It wouldn't surprise her. Nick knew so many people around the world, he could travel for the rest of his life without ever staying in a hotel.

Jay continued. 'Language is such a perishable skill that you'd

58

probably be better off with someone else. I haven't used my Albanian for ages, it's probably deteriorated—' She started when the doorbell shrilled. Laura jumped too, and Kingsman, but Blake didn't flinch.

'Excuse me,' she said. Partly relieved at the interruption, partly annoyed, Jay went to the front door and opened it.

'Hi.' Detective Inspector Tom Sutton was on her doorstep, smiling, and for a second her heart lurched. She forced herself to blink several times, but he didn't go away. He was wearing an old pair of Levis and a worn leather jacket. Jesus, he looked good. Six-two, brown hair, blue eyes, and as handsome as the first day they'd met.

'Hi,' she said. Her voice was hoarse.

She saw his gaze fix on something over her shoulder. She glanced around to see Blake propped casually against the wall, arms crossed, expression neutral.

'Okay?' asked Blake.

'Yes, thanks,' she said.

'You've been avoiding me,' said Tom. He was still looking at Blake.

'I've been busy.'

'So I heard.'

She blinked. How had he heard?

'Lily was hauled into the station yesterday. She told me you were looking for some Moldovan twins. Why didn't you ring me, let me know you were in town? We could have met up.'

'I didn't have time.'

A car drove past. She could hear next door's stereo playing, and the sound of a car alarm beeping several streets away. Her heart was jumping in her chest and she couldn't think what to say next.

'I'm in London for the weekend,' Tom went on. 'Do you fancy some lunch?'

Confusion flooded her. She desperately wanted to lunch with him, but if she did, it would be tantamount to giving in. Or would it? She tried not to look at his mouth, which last Saturday had explored her own thoroughly, and at great length, in the back of a taxi. He had a beautiful mouth, and kissing it was one of her favourite things.

'We could go to the Patara,' he added. 'My shout.'

The Patara only did the best Thai food this side of planet Jupiter and happened to be her favourite restaurant.

'But if you'd rather go to Longtemps, that's fine too. Except I might have to handcuff you to the table.' His eyes began to twinkle. She had bolted last time they were there.

She opened her mouth, unsure what she was going to say, when Blake said, 'Jay.'

It was a murmur, a tactful prompt, but she reacted as though she'd heard a warning siren. She had a Cabinet Minister in her house, plus an MI6 agent and a rep from the Foreign Office, and to top it all, her house was bugged. She had more important things to be getting on with than conducting a stilted conversation on her doorstep with a plainclothes cop.

Eyes on Blake, Tom said, 'Don't you want to introduce me?'

Jay became flustered. 'Look, Tom, I'm sorry, but I'm right in the middle of something. Can I ring you later?'

'Feel free.'

'I know. I should have called sooner, but—'

He held up both palms. 'Later, Jay.'

'Yes. Okay, then.'

Tom turned and went down the steps. He walked along the street without looking back.

Nine

It was raining hard when Jay hit the A11. Spray brought down visibility to a few yards, but it didn't deter the average motorway driver who had his foot pressed flat to the floor. She was relieved when she finally reached the turnoff north to Swaffham and Cromer.

The A1065 was a fast, busy road, and it was impossible to tell if she was being followed. Once she'd passed Fakenham the traffic eased, but she still couldn't identify the cars behind her through the spray. It was time to take the initiative. Instead of following her usual route along the B1388 to Langham, Jay turned north, winding her way along single-track rural roads through the tiny villages of Bale and Field Dalling. Two cars followed.

Just past Field Dalling, she turned right for Saxlingham. Now she only had one vehicle behind her, a four-wheel-drive. Did intelligence operatives use 4x4's? Surely not. She could almost hear the shrieks of objection from the civil service over the fuel bills. Or was this a sneaky way for them to blend into the countryside?

Only one way to find out.

When she came to the crossroads – Blakeney signposted left on the B1388, Holt to the right – she drove straight across and on to another narrow road that led to nothing but a picnic area which, considering the rain chucking down, wouldn't be at the top of anyone's places to visit. She held her breath to see what the vehicle behind her would do.

After pausing to check for traffic, it indicated left, and turned. It was a sludge-green Land Rover Discovery belching diesel fumes, indicating it had seen better days and probably needed a service. It wasn't following her at all. She was on her own.

Jay drove past the sodden picnic area and continued heading north, wondering if she was getting paranoid.

Her mother was peering out from the porch when she parked outside.

'You're late,' she said.

'Not by much!' Jay protested. 'You said twelve, and it's only half past!'

'I was worried you might have been in an accident.'

'No accident. Just slowed down by the weather.'

Her mother stared hard at Jay's car. 'Where's Tom?'

Grabbing her bag, Jay jogged through the rain and into the cottage. She didn't look at her mother when she spoke. 'He couldn't make it.'

Her mother lived in an old, low-slung flint house just off the main street in Blakeney. Once a thriving fishing port, Blakeney was now a sleepy village with an unspoilt coastline and a nature reserve that attracted hordes of bird-watchers, unless an easterly blew in straight from Siberia, which sent them scurrying home. She'd loved living here as a kid – walking the marshes, sailing, summer barbecues on the beach, cosy winter lunches in pubs – but as she grew up she found it stifling and dull, and the relief of arriving at Sandhurst and being plunged into a routine of non-stop training and parties had been fantastic.

Jay headed for the kitchen, where the air was warm and smelled of roast beef and scones. Some days, she found it hard to believe she was related to her mother. Not only was her mother short, barely five foot one, with mouse-brown hair and homely features, but she was the proverbial domestic goddess, joyfully washing and ironing, and baking for her guests. Jay, on the other hand, was a domestic philistine who hated housework, hated cooking, and when people came to stay, they always ate out.

She broke a piece off a scone and just as she was about to pop it in her mouth, a hairy salt-and-pepper missile launched itself at her knees.

'Hey, Tigger!'

She bent down to greet the miniature schnauzer and ended up giving him her titbit, earning herself a roll of the eyes from her mother. 'I wish you wouldn't do that. He'll be begging at the table for the next month.'

'He loves scones.'

Her mother sent her a narrowed look. 'Tom loves scones too. Which is why I baked double the amount.'

Jay shrugged and went and stood at the window, looking outside, her eyes flitting over her Golf and her mother's Astra to scan the mud-flats, studying the handful of walkers on the coastal path, looking for anyone that looked out of place.

'So what has Tom done wrong?'

'Nothing.'

'You used to say that when you were little. If I didn't believe you then, I certainly don't believe you now.'

'Okay.' Taking a deep breath she turned round to face her mother. 'Tom suggested we get married. Walk up the aisle and henceforth do everything that wearing wedding rings entails.'

'He proposed?'

'Yup.'

Her mother looked at Jay's wedding ring finger. 'So where's the ring?'

'He's still got it.'

'Still what?'

'I had a bit of a panic attack when he brought the box out so I went to the Ladies – we were at Longtemps, where it's in the basement – and while I was sitting on the loo I realised that if I returned to the table things would get heated. I mean, Tom would be expecting a response and I wasn't sure what I was going to say . . . '

Her mother was looking horrified. 'Tell me you didn't . . . '

'It wasn't intentional. It's just that I thought I'd get some fresh air, try and keep myself calm, and he was upstairs and couldn't see me walking outside . . . '

Part of her still couldn't believe she'd walked out, leaving Tom at the table. She knew it was appalling behaviour on her part. Perhaps if he'd given her some warning she might not have panicked, but with hindsight she should have guessed something was up because usually they grabbed a Thai meal or a takeaway. But Tom had suggested Longtemps, saying the reviews were amazing and he wanted to try it out.

She could remember frowning when he'd mentioned it, concerned about the cost. She'd heard that two courses with some bread and a bottle of wine took you into three figures.

'And don't worry,' he smiled. 'It's on me.'

'Will I have to get dressed up?'

'You can wear whatever you like.'

She'd turned up in a rush, straight from the office, out of breath, her hair awry. She was wearing an old rugby shirt of his tucked into a pair of jeans, and a pair of oversized hoop earrings.

'Sorry.' She kissed him on the lips. 'I didn't have time to go home and get changed. Something came up.'

Tom looked her up and down, a glint in his eye. 'Very sexy.'

'You think anything's sexy.'

'Only when you're wearing it.'

She had eaten the meal like a happy pig at a three-star trough. She had a large appetite, loved her food and wine, and the restaurant was like a slice of heaven.

Until, just after the *tarte au citron*, he'd brought out the black velvet box.

For a second, she couldn't believe it. Tom had been teasing her about taking her off the market, saying he wanted to make it illegal for her to have sex with other guys, but *marriage*?

The years poured away. She was eleven years old and sitting on the stairs listening to her mother and father row. They'd started fighting a couple of years before, vicious, bitter arguments that made her shiver and tiptoe back to bed, but this time something was different. Her father wasn't shouting at her mother, but speaking slowly and carefully as though he wanted to make sure her mother understood every word.

'It's not you,' he said. 'It's me. I can't help it, I'm sorry. But I just don't love you any more. I'm in love with someone else.'

There was a long silence, then he said quietly, 'I'll let myself out. Goodbye, Alice.'

Jay heard her father shut the front door behind him, start up his car and drive away. She crept downstairs to find her mother curled on the cold slate kitchen floor. Her eyes were wide open and expressionless and when Jay touched her hand, her skin was like ice. 'Mum?' she whispered.

Her mother blinked. She didn't look at Jay. 'Go to bed, darling,' she rasped. 'And stay there, would you?'

As Jay crept back up the stairs she heard what sounded like an animal roaring behind her. Terrified, Jay huddled on the stairs and listened to her mother's heart breaking.

'Jay?' Tom's voice had brought her back to the present. He was looking at her anxiously. 'Are you okay?'

'I need the loo.' Her voice was hoarse. 'Sorry.'

She fled downstairs.

Now her mother grabbed a chair and sat down heavily, as though her legs had just given out beneath her. 'I have a daughter who is a bolter. What did I do to deserve this? Most women would be doing handsprings in your position, but oh no, not you. Little Miss Independence.'

'But why do we have to get married? We were getting along fine before. Why mess things up?'

Her mother raised her eyes to the ceiling. 'You're not a teenager anymore, you're a grown woman! It's time you realised that.'

'God, Mum! You're as bad as Tom! It was like being at a lecture, him telling me that it was the right time in our lives for us to make a commitment, that there seemed no point continuing unless we take the relationship to its next stage, blah-blah-blah . . .'

'The man's right! You're nearly thirty years old! Just think of poor Gemma, would you? She's dreadfully unhappy. The last thing I want is that happening to you.'

Gemma was her mother's next-door neighbour. Married at university, Gemma was a career woman who had put off having children until her late thirties only to find she couldn't conceive. She was now forty-one, and almost suicidal because she hadn't tried to have children earlier.

'Mum, I'm not sure I even want kids. I just have to look at Angus and Sandra. They're always knackered, unable to stay awake beyond ten o'clock. It's all right for you, you'll be getting another brood of grandchildren, but what do I get? Nappies and screaming and sleepless nights. I think I'll probably turn Tom down.'

Jay saw her mother make a heroic effort not to scream with frustration. 'What does your father say?'

She stared at a heavy crystal vase sitting on top of the TV and remembered Angus, years ago, breaking it in the kitchen. Despite the fact that it had shattered into half a dozen pieces he had glued it back together. The glue was now turning yellow, but her mother didn't seem to notice.

'I haven't discussed it with him.'

'Why ever not?'

'He's busy. Spring's coming. He'll be calving.'

'And I suppose Nicola's taken herself off to the South of France or wherever she goes, until it's all over.' Her mother's tone was bitter, her normally generous mouth twisted. 'How Bob puts up with her vanishing like that, especially when he needs her support during the busiest time of year for him, is beyond me.'

'She's always been independent.'

'Selfish, you mean.'

Jay opted to remain silent. She liked Nicola.

'Will you be going up to help?' her mother asked. 'You usually spend Easter there, don't you?' She had pasted on her brightest expression to cover her distress, but Jay could see it was still there.

'Not this year.'

'Why not? Normally wild horses couldn't keep you away.'

'I'm going to Macedonia.'

Her mother blinked. 'On another mission?'

'Yes.' A smile began to rise inside her and she knew she'd made the right decision. She couldn't put her finger on precisely why she wanted to return to the Balkans, but she couldn't ignore the way her body had reacted as she'd spoken. Her heart had expanded, her spirit soared. The thought of travel always had that effect, which is why she'd probably been attracted to the army.

'Do you have to go?'

Jay spirits sank to see her mother's cheeks start to flush. Dammit, she thought. Why couldn't she keep her trap shut?

'It's not like I have to,' she said, always honest, 'but I want to.'

'You're running away,' her mother accused. 'You've only just got back from Afghanistan!'

'Hardly. I've been home for six weeks. Plenty of time to do my washing, answer the mail and sort my life out.'

'But you were away for two months!' her mother's voice began to rise. 'Two months in some godforsaken foreign country, getting shot at, shelled and bombed, and the second you're home you want to go back to a war zone! I blame your father for this. With your language skills you should have gone into the diplomatic service, not joined the army.'

'Jesus, Mum.' Jay's temper began to flare. 'I have the diplomatic skills of a buffalo, you know that. What is it with you? I left the goddamn army, remember? Just like you wanted.'

'So you've said countless times. I don't understand you, Jessica, I really don't.'

'My name is Jay.'

'You were christened Jessica and I shall use your given name as it was supposed to be used, not shortened to a single letter so you sound like some sort of bird . . . '

Jay got to her feet. She had to change the subject or things would only deteriorate. 'Shall I peel some spuds?'

'They're already in the oven,' her mother said stiffly.

'I'll lay the table, then. How about a glass of red to go with the beef?'

There was a small pause and then her mother nodded. 'What a good idea. I'll fetch a bottle from the pantry.'

Olive branch accepted, they settled down to lunch, but it wasn't until her mother was on her second glass of red wine that the tension eased.

'So, when do you fly out?'

'Tomorrow. I'm sorry, Mum. I didn't mean to upset you.'

'I just worry about you.'

'I know.'

Jay reached across and gripped her mother's hand. Her mother gave a sad smile. 'I don't suppose you can stay for tea?'

'I can't. I've loads to do before I pack.'

Although Jay could see her mother was hurt she couldn't stay longer, she hid it behind a bustle of filling Tupperware boxes with roast beef and scones.

'Angela and Denise will enjoy them,' she told Jay.

'Not half. They love your cooking.'

Expression determinedly bright, her mother stood with Tigger in the middle of the street and waved Jay goodbye.

Ten

Branko suffered his second night with Hana's parents with stoical good manners. He'd brought a whole haunch of prosciutto in the faint hope they might eat it, but no. They'd whisked away his expensive, delicious offering to be saved for God-alone-knew when, and given him a dish of *selsko meso*, village meat, instead. As if he wasn't heartily sick of meat and sausage stews served in earthenware pots. What he would have given for a plate of sushi, or even a plain platter of thinly sliced smoked salmon and wedges of lemon.

His host, Hana's father, raised his tumbler of rakija at Branko. 'To my daughter, Hana,' he said expansively. 'A good girl.'

'A good girl,' Branko agreed.

'You bring her home soon, yes?'

'Oh, yes,' he lied.

Hana's father downed his glass of oily brandy in one long swallow and Branko poured him another, praying the hairy old bugger would pass out soon. He didn't think he could bear another pathetic, macho-male drinking session. Please God, Zamira was on her way by now. He couldn't live through another day of this boorish shit, no matter how much Zamira might be worth. Sure, he'd seen the light of ambition at the back of her eyes, the set of determination in her chin, but walking down that stony, rocky trail at night wasn't for the faint-hearted.

She might get a hundred metres along and lose her nerve, run back to her fluffy sheep dog and her mummy.

Only time would tell.

He knocked back another glass of rakija, hoping it might numb his sensibilities. He wasn't looking forward to sleeping on a pallet of wood strewn with straw tonight, alongside a herd of sheep. Sheep stank. And although he showered and soaped and scrubbed himself twice, sometimes three times daily when he returned to Skopje, he never seemed to be able to wash the stink away. It was as though every time he returned to the mountains, the stench of poverty crawled into his pores, reminding him of where he came from and that he'd never be free.

Hana's father rose. 'Good of you, Branko. Looking after our little girl like you do.'

Branko didn't say anything. He didn't need to. Hana's father was well gone by now. Arms spread-eagled, he staggered across the room and lurched outside. Branko headed swiftly in the opposite direction, to his cold, stinking bedroom. Hana's father was probably going to throw up, and he didn't want to hang around for that.

Huddled beneath a pile of rough, prickly blankets, Branko lay staring up at the wooden beams supporting the roof.

If Zamira hadn't arrived by the time dawn broke, then bugger her. He'd find another beautiful girl to trade, a girl who wanted to escape the mountains as much as he had, and who'd help him forget.

Zamira dressed warmly. Thick socks, woollen trousers and shirt and jumper, and her big sheepskin coat that came down to her knees and kept her backside warm no matter what the weather. She packed a small bag with clean underwear and socks, toothbrush and hairbrush, and her smartest scarf. She'd need it if she was going to London.

Lastly, she put Hana's letter in her pocket and crept out of the front door. Outside, Bear's broad-shouldered doggy form rose to greet her. Pressing her face into his neck, she hugged him goodbye. As she breathed in his scent, heavily laden with the oily smell of lanolin from the sheep, she felt a trickle of apprehension. She hadn't thought what it would be like to leave Bear and her mother behind, she'd been so taken up with visions of Hana and her sunny apartment overlooking the park, the restaurant where she worked and the money she earned, but now she hesitated, wondering if she was being foolhardy to follow her.

But then she recalled Branko's voice.

She'll marry a local lad and have half a dozen children and live in the mountains until she's an old woman. Won't you, Zamira?

She didn't like any of the local boys. They were rough and boorish with thick accents and dirty fingernails. Some of them would follow in their father's footsteps and grow up to become smugglers, but Nana would never let her marry one of them no matter how profitable the cigarette or small arms trade. Nana believed in an honest day's work for an honest day's pay, even if some days she didn't even get paid. Her mother was too honest for her own good and it drove Zamira crazy.

Patting Bear's broad head, she firmed her resolve. She didn't want to live here for the rest of her life. She didn't want to wear her mother's stained and threadbare hand-me-downs any more, or look a hundred and three years old when she was only thirty-five. Nana's hair might be black but Zamira knew it had turned white a long time ago, and that her mother dyed it.

She thought of Hana's letter. She'd read it so often every word was ingrained in her mind.

I've got a new pair of boots, a Bench t-shirt, a leather jacket and cherry-flavoured lipstick. I'm making so much money! You must come, Zami, you can send your mother money for new clothes and some luxuries, perhaps some books and chocolates.

Zamira had already decided to send her mother a coffee-maker. Nana loved fresh coffee. She'd go to London and make her mother proud of her.

'Stay,' she whispered to the dog, holding up her hand to make sure he got the message. Bear sank to the ground. His tail stopped waving and his ears fell.

With her bag over one shoulder, Zamira stepped quietly down the rocky path. She didn't dare look back in case she cried.

*

71

It was just after dawn when she arrived at Hana's house. The sky was turning a soft purple velvet to the east but everything was still and silent. Chimneys were cold, empty of wood smoke, and the air smelled as clean and clear as spring water.

She tried to work out where Branko would be sleeping. Usually he bedded down on the couch in the living room, but now Hana was gone, would he be using her friend's old room?

Zamira tiptoed down the side of the house and tried to peer inside Hana's window, but it was pitch black and she couldn't see a thing. She tapped a fingernail against the glass. Again she pressed her face against the window and tried to see inside.

Nothing.

Her heart flipped. What if Branko had gone? What if she'd missed him? Urgently, she rapped the window with her knuckles. It sounded as loud as gunfire in the mountain silence.

Next door, a dog barked a couple of times.

She stopped breathing when she thought she heard a floorboard creak from inside the house. She rapped again and the dog started up, more loudly this time. It took a good ten seconds until it quietened.

Zamira started to shiver. She didn't dare knock again, not with that dog next door. It would wake up the entire village if she wasn't careful, and they'd take one look at her and send her straight back to her mother.

Her throat swelled into a balloon. She wanted to burst into tears. She hated the stultifying dullness that was her life in the mountains. She never wanted to milk another cow again. Tears began to spill down her cheeks. Where was Branko?

'Peaches, are you crying for me?' A man spoke softly nearby.

She jumped, afraid, until she realised who it was.

'Branko! You gave me such a fright!'

He chucked quietly. He was fully dressed and wore a thick overocat and woollen gloves.

'I've been waiting for you,' he said.

Her spirit soared. 'Really?'

'Are you ready to come to London with me?'

'Oh, yes. Yes, please.'

Eleven

'What made you change your mind?' Nick asked. 'I didn't think you wanted to go. Jay? Are you listening?'

Jay dragged her gaze from the sludge-green Discovery parked across from the café. Nobody was in the car, but having had a similar vehicle on her tail yesterday, it gave her the creeps. She memorised the number plate – K784 AWL – just in case. She was definitely getting paranoid.

'Lots of reasons,' she replied, manoeuvring a chair so she could sit next to Nick at the window. 'Like I haven't seen Kiro in ages, or eaten a Šopska salad, but the main one is that I'd love to mess things up for Milot. The thought of him teaming up with the Georgian Mafia is enough to give me hives.' She studied his gloomy expression. 'But I'm more interested in why you don't want me to go.'

'A good soldier doesn't necessarily make a good spy.'

'All I have to do is take some old friends out for coffee,' she protested. 'Have a chat. Surely it can't be that difficult.'

'You're a crap liar.'

'Let's hope I won't have to lie, then.'

Jay ordered his favourite coffee – a double-shot espresso – and a plate of assorted muffins, hoping the sugar hit would sweeten his mood. He admitted to having met Max Blake during a marine-assisted mission south of Tripoli a few years back, but denied any previous knowledge of Patrick Kingsman or Laura Sharpe.

'Blake's multi-talented,' Nick said. 'Specialises in ops whose provenance is, how shall I say it . . . unclear.'

'He's a mercenary?'

'Looks that way. He did private contract work in Russia apparently.'

'You know him well?'

'No.' He picked up a blueberry muffin and inspected it before putting it down again. 'So what do you think of our illustrious Cabinet Minister? And Kingsman?'

'Tricky. Both of them.'

'Political animals always are. And Laura Sharpe?'

'I quite like her.'

'I've been told she's a ruthless bitch.'

'Considering she swims with sharks, she has to be.'

'Point taken.'

'She's briefing me before I fly out.'

'So I was told.' His tone turned cold and disapproving. Jay waited until he'd eaten a muffin before she told him about the bugs in her house. Predictably, he was not impressed.

'You have to be out of your mind if you think I'm letting you go,' he said. 'Not until we know what's going on.'

'It might not be me they're interested in,' she pointed out. 'I don't live alone, remember?'

He considered Angela and Denise for about three seconds. 'I can't see they're after a couple of Customs officers. It's you. And the mission.'

'Shall I get someone in to remove the bugs?'

'No. Leave them. You can always use them for disinformation. And don't tell your housemates.'

As soon as he said the word 'disinformation' she knew Nick was hooked. He wanted to know what was going on almost as much as she did, but that didn't stop him from giving her a lecture on the three Ds of Diplomacy: deliberation, discretion and discernment. All of which they both knew she was hopeless at.

'Can I give you a lift anywhere?' he asked when they stepped outside.

She checked the street to see the sludge-green Discovery had gone. 'Only if you're going past Battersea Park.'

Nick raised his eyebrows. 'Shouldn't you be packing?'

'I've got to see Tom before I go.'

'Hop in then. I'll save you some time.'

When Nick dropped her off, he did what he always did when she left on a mission. 'Keep safe,' he said, and gave her a peck on the cheek.

Tom was standing with his back to the pagoda, looking out over the sluggish, mud-coloured Thames. There was a stiff, chill breeze and as she approached she could see his cheeks were red, his eyes bright. He was wearing a big leather coat with the collar turned up. His expression was neutral. It was his cop face.

She glanced at a barge cruising eastwards, still hoping he might forgive her. Part of her – a big part of her – longed for things to go back to the way they were before, but she knew it would be impossible now the M word had reared its ugly head.

They'd met two years ago, just after she'd started with TRACE. Tom had been a detective sergeant then, and Jay had been on her first mission, searching for a THB victim, a thirteen-year-old girl from Somalia who had allegedly been trafficked to Bristol. They'd worked the case together, and when they eventually found the girl and reunited her with her relatives, he'd asked her out for a drink. The drink turned into dinner, and within a fortnight they were in bed, unable to keep their hands off each other. Having Tom in Bristol was perfect for Jay. He wasn't on her doorstep, but he wasn't that far away either. She loved going to stay with him – it felt as though she was having a holiday – and when he came to see her they'd play tourists, visiting the Tower of London and taking boat trips up and down the Thames.

She loved the way he smelled whenever he dipped his head to nuzzle her neck – like sun-warmed spice, or freshly chopped wood. She loved the way his arm cupped her waist, her ribs.

They laughed a lot, and the sex was delicious. She couldn't bear the thought of losing him.

But marriage?

When it came to affairs of the heart, she had to confess to being skittish, to say the least. She liked her independence, and wasn't sure if she was cut out to be shackled to one person for the rest of her life, no matter how brilliantly they got on in bed and out of it.

'Hi,' she said.

'Hi.'

He didn't make any move to touch or kiss her.

'Thanks for meeting me.'

He looked around at the scattering of dog walkers wrapped in scarves, coats and gloves, and said, 'Interesting location you chose.'

When she'd rung him earlier, she'd thought it perfect. Tom was staying with a cop friend of his in Battersea, which meant they were both a ten-minute walk from the park, but now he mentioned it, she could have chosen better. It was as bleak as hell.

'I'm sorry,' she blurted. 'For walking out on you. I didn't mean to. I just . . . panicked.'

His expression softened. 'I rather gathered that. So where does that leave us?'

'I don't know.'

He raised a hand and brushed a lock of hair away from her face, tucking it behind her ear.

'What are you scared of?'

Startled, she said, 'What do you mean?'

'You're scared of marriage. Is it because of your father? He deserted your mother. You said he broke her heart.'

'He was still a great dad.' She felt defensive for her father. 'I saw him nearly every day until he moved to Scotland, and even then I spent half my holidays with him.'

Tom was studying her carefully. 'You told me about your first love, Chris, dumping you. You thought you'd never recover, remember?'

Jay rubbed her temples. 'Yes, I do. It was awful.'

'I won't abandon you, Jay. I promise.'

'Oh, Tom.' Her heart squeezed. 'I don't know how you put up with me.'

'I don't know either. You're impossible.' He was smiling.

He held out an arm and she stepped into his embrace. As she rested her head against his shoulder, she felt him kiss her hair.

'I'm sorry I panicked you,' he said. 'But I honestly thought you'd be happy to take our relationship to the next stage.'

'You caught me by surprise, that's all. How you can ever forgive me for running out like that . . .'

'Let's just say that you owe me one.'

They watched a man in a tweed coat walk past with two King Charles spaniels.

'Jay,' Tom said. 'Who was the man at your house yesterday, checking me out?'

'Max Blake. He's part of a mission I'm undertaking.' She cleared her throat. 'Which involves me going to Macedonia. I'm flying out this afternoon.'

'For how long?'

'A couple of weeks.' She twisted round to look into his face. 'Maybe this trip will give me some space. Help me discover why I reacted the way I did. Why I feel so confused.'

'I hope so.' He put his fingers under her chin and lifted her face to his. He kissed her on the lips before adding, 'Have you packed yet?'

'No.'

'I'll walk you home.'

On the tube ride to Heathrow, Jay watched a spotty teenager eat his way through a box of Pringles, one hand stuffing his face, the other texting on his mobile phone. Not for the first time she wished her mother had learned how to text, because then she could have sent her a goodbye message. If she rang, she knew she'd only end up feeling even more guilty that she hadn't stayed for tea. She'd send a postcard instead. Her mum loved postcards.

Before she checked in, Jay headed for the Terminal 2 short-stay car park where she'd agreed to meet Laura Sharpe. She was unsurprised to see the agent already waiting by the ticket machine. She bet that Laura was never late.

'Hi,' Jay greeted her.

Laura nodded and walked Jay to her car, a shiny black Vauxhall with alloy wheels. There was no twinkle in her eye, no warmth in her body language. She was one hundred percent business. The car's interior smelled of new leather but there was a hint of something sweet as well, like sugared vanilla. To her surprise, Jay realised it was Laura's perfume. She would have thought Laura would have gone for citrus and apple tones.

Reaching behind her, the agent pulled a beautifully made black leather briefcase off the rear seat and put it between them. She turned the twin brass combination locks until they clicked. Jay noted the number – 2581 – and the make of the case; Smythson of Bond Street. Stacked inside were files and notebooks, and a matching set of Mont Blanc pens. She wondered whether they had been a gift, and whether they showed the agent's pride in her job – or did she just like luxurious accessories? A Smythson briefcase cost more than anything Jay owned.

Laura picked up the top file and had a flick through. 'Right, let's get down to business,' she said. 'Milot Dumani. Highly intelligent and adaptable, he's a natural leader. He takes the initiative, makes things happen, but if he's confronted by someone with a difference of opinion, or if he feels undermined, he becomes vicious and uses threats and reprisals to get obedience from others. He is completely ruthless and dictatorial.'

'Your typical Mafia boss, then,' Jay remarked.

Laura went on to profile Milot's closest and most trusted gang members in the Balkans. The group consisted of two generals, five captains, and an unknown quantity of soldiers, though Laura reckoned there were around thirty.

'Quite a little army,' said Jay.

'Not so little if you take in his overseas troops. We put the total number of people working for Milot in the Balkans and Western Europe at around sixty, which makes it a sizeable but not overpowering corporation. But if he amalgamates with the Georgian Mafia . . .'

Laura turned to the next file. 'Tihomir Vadic. The boss.' She passed a photograph of a long-faced, cadaverous-looking man with thinning brown hair and a chin like a knife. He had an undershot jaw, and black eyes which seemed to have no pupils.

'He's also known as the Barracuda,' Laura said. 'I don't know what you know about the Georgian Mafia, but basically it's a loose assortment of organised crime groups headed by senior figures known as *vory u zakone* . . .'

'Thieves in law,' Jay murmured. Thanks to her job, she already knew quite a bit about criminal gangs, but she refrained from saying so. She wanted to hear what information Laura was going to offer.

'Yes. These criminal leaders first developed in the Soviet Union in the 1920s, aping the early Sicilian Mafia godfathers with their honour codes, but over time, the *vory u zakone* evolved their own rules and regulations, with Vadic as chieftain. His groups are mixed, including acting and former police and security officers as well as ordinary criminals. The structure is based on kinship and close friendship, which has made it almost impossible for us to penetrate. Vadic is devious and deceptive, and covetous of others' success, which makes him willing to do whatever it takes to preserve his superiority. He is relentless, obsessive, and destroys anyone who reminds him he isn't perfect.'

Laura was painting a profile of a man Jay wouldn't mind seeing wiped off the face of the earth. Laura passed her a wad of photographs.

'Vadic's chiefs of staff.' She passed over another wad. 'And Milot's.'

Most of the photographs were head-and-shoulder shots, taken when the subject was on the move, and although Jay studied them carefully, she knew she would be lucky to recognise any of them, aside from Vadic, if she saw them on the street.

'How long were you in the Balkans?' Jay asked.

'Oh, I've probably spent a year there in total. I drop in every few weeks or so. Trips to Prestina, Belgrade, Sarajevo.'

'You speak Albanian?'

'And Serbo-Croat, but not as well as you, Patrick tells me.'

A true spook, Jay thought, flitting from country to country, picking up morsels of information and reporting back. But something was niggling her.

'Laura.' She waited until the woman met her eyes. 'Forgive me for asking, but from what I know of you I have no doubt you do an excellent job gathering your own intel. So why do you need me?'

A flash of annoyance crossed Laura's face and went as fast.

'Because the more information we have,' she said smoothly, 'the better judgements we can make.'

'Aren't you pissed off that I'm treading on your toes?'

'Good heavens, no.' Laura looked genuinely surprised. 'You'll be talking to different people. I'll be meeting defence attaches, NATO chiefs and UNMIK cops. You'll be getting a contrasting view, one I'd be hard pushed to find.'

'You mean I'll be chatting to the bottom feeders.'

'Not quite.' Laura sent her a wry smile. 'But you've got the drift.'

They spent the next few minutes sorting out a rough plan for Jay – who she was going to see, where she might go. Then they swapped contact details.

'Now, I'm going to give you a number for emergencies. You ring this, and it'll hit the office as a code red. Someone will pick up immediately.'

Jay punched it into her mobile to speed-dial and returned it to her day pack.

'If I'm not there . . . ' Laura trailed off, biting her lip.

'What?'

'Nothing.' Laura gave herself a little shake. 'I'm sorry. I was miles away.' She put out her hand. 'Good luck, Jay. And if there's anything I can do this end, just call or text me, okay?'

Jay ignored Laura's hand. 'What were you going to say about the emergency number? If you're not there?'

'It's nothing.' She smiled. 'The number is fine.'

'Bullshit, Laura, something's wrong. What is it? You're not putting me in the field with a dodgy number, are you?'

There was a pause while Laura stared at Jay who stared back.

'The number is fine,' Laura repeated steadily. 'But if you could try and make sure you speak to me, it would be a help.'

Jay felt her eyes widen. 'Are you saying you don't trust everyone?'

'Of course not!' Laura protested. 'Honestly, Jay. You're like a cat on hot bricks, but I can't say I blame you. You're going to be spying on some extremely dangerous people, and they won't take it kindly if they find out what you're doing. Good luck, okay?'

Jay left Laura Sharpe in a state of high tension. She felt as though she was leaving the UK to commence battle, to approach the front line and face the enemy, but although her stomach was tense and her mouth dry, she acknowledged that she hadn't felt so alive or energised in months.

Twelve

For Jay, landing at Skopje airport felt like coming home. It wasn't anything like Heathrow or JFK or Frankfurt, or any of the international airports for that matter. A row of Russian Hind helicopters lined up next to the runway served as a grim reminder of the civil war, and you had to walk from the aircraft across the pockmarked concrete apron to the terminal building, which had an arrivals hall the size of Nick's office and a departure lounge only a little larger than her bathroom at home.

At the carousel she waited for her bag along with the other passengers, who were mostly dark-skinned and dark-haired, a mix of Albanian and Macedonian businessmen. Even though hostilities had ceased in 2001, few tourists came here, which was a shame since the newly independent Republic of Macedonia – about the size of Kent – boasted beautiful tectonic lakes and ancient ruins, outdoor nightclubs, and salsa bars. Most people who visited were part of the international community, and although many organisations had downsized a while ago they still had a tangible presence, trying to help lead the small country towards a successful future in the E.U.

Jay collected her backpack, slung it over her shoulder and headed outside. Although the sun was shining, it was cold. Beyond the small gravelled car park she saw the mountains still had snow on their peaks.

'Hey, Ice!'

She hadn't heard that nickname since she'd been in the army, but she reacted as fast as if someone had called her real name. Swinging round, she saw Kiro striding towards her, arms outstretched, a big grin on his broad Macedonian face.

Jay grinned back. 'Hey you!'

He swung her into a bear hug, smacking her cheeks with kisses. 'My beautiful Ice! Too long, my friend! What is it that you ignore me for so long then land on my doorstep like this? You finally realised you are in love with me?'

'Yup. I always have been, Kiro. You see right through me as always.'

'And Nick? Is the dismal old goat in love with me too?'

'Oh, yes. You know Nick, how he hides his emotions.' She let him take her backpack and lead her to his battered and dust-caked Lada Niva. 'He's ecstatic at my coming over here.'

'He was disgusting to me this morning,' grunted Kiro. 'Very rude.'

Which meant Nick had been his normal British self and Kiro had taken offence at the lack of warmth in his boss's demeanour.

'So!' he roared happily. 'You are here on a mission to find the twins!'

'If I can. Any news this end?'

'Not even a tickle.' He spat on the ground. 'I have heard nothing since they were last seen in Tetovo.'

Tetovo, the de facto capital of Macedonia's significantly sized Albanian minority, was the criminal hub of the country, filled with bars and brothels, restaurants and gambling dens – all run by the Mafia. Once a girl hit Tetovo, it was damned hard to get her out.

Kiro started his car with a roar, jammed the stick into gear and zipped his way out of the airport. The little 4x4 Lada Niva bounced across the potholed road like a cement-mixer on speed. Winding down the window – no electric extras for this ancient Russian-built car – Jay let the wind tug her hair as she thought about the twins. In all honesty, she didn't expect them still to be in the Balkans. They were too beautiful and too exotic. They would have been sold many times over by now, to rich Germans,

Belgians and French, possibly even shipped to the Far East for their atypical appeal. However, since the twins were her cover story, she may as well see what information she could garner.

'So, how is your love life?' Kiro asked with a grin.

'None of your business. How's yours?'

'I am in love!' he boomed delightedly.

'Oh, God,' she groaned. 'Not again. Who's the victim this time?'

'No, no.' He shook his head violently. 'Seriously, Ice, this is it. Rosanna is The One. She is like nobody I have ever met before. I swear it, we are getting married. I have never loved any woman like I love Rosanna.'

She studied his face, the stubble and strong chin, the nose that had been squashed out of shape from being punched over the years, and the soft, curly brown hair that he said made him look like a girl, but that he was secretly proud of.

'She's French.' Raising his hips, he pulled out a battered leather wallet and passed it over. 'Her picture. Have a look. Is she not beautiful?'

Jay's spirits sank as she looked at the stunning, sloe-eyed girl dressed in a miniature string bikini. Rosanna looked the same age as Kiro's daughter would be, if he had one. Barely seventeen.

'Very pretty,' she said quickly, and handed it back.

Depressed at men's inability to think with nothing but their cocks, Jay looked back through the windscreen. They were driving past a market where women were selling eggs and bundles of herbs from beneath red and green umbrellas.

'So, Ice. Are you single, or are you seeing someone?'

'I'm not sure.'

'In that case, you must have an affair immediately, so you can find out. You prefer an Albanian or Macedonian man?'

'Neither. They're too short.'

'What if I find you a nice tall one?'

'Maybe.'

Driving through town, Jay noted the changes since she'd last been here. A new shopping mall had appeared, with La Perla and Lacoste boutiques and a piano bar on the top floor, plus countless new coffee bars and restaurants, but what hit her hardest was the transformation of the people. Gone were the gaunt, hungry and fearful faces she remembered and in their place were crowds of well-fed, contented-looking folk who weren't afraid to raise their eyes from the ground and smile.

A rush of emotion closed her throat when she saw a young couple walking arm in arm, both chatting brightly on their mobile phones. To think Macedonia could have gone the same way as Kosovo – ripped apart from the inside, where everyone had blood on their hands and was still steeped in pain. She was so glad it hadn't. Macedonia had had its troubles, but unlike Kosovo it had managed to contain the violence, to bring the insurgents to the negotiating table rather than resorting to full-blown war.

'Did you find me a nice *pansion*?' she asked Kiro. She much preferred staying in a B & B than a blandly anonymous Western-style hotel, even if it did have a mini-bar, a gym and a spectacular view of the river.

Kiro pretended to look shocked. 'What, don't you want to stay with me and Rosanna?'

'It's very kind of you, Kiro, but I couldn't impose.'

'You think I will come to you in the night and seduce you? That Rosanna isn't enough woman for my passion?'

'Kiro, of course not.'

'Then it is settled. You will be best friends with my beloved, just you wait and see.'

Kiro's beloved had a dazzling smile, perfect skin, cheekbones to die for and shiny black hair cut into a smart bob.

'So this is the infamous Jay McCaulay,' she said warmly. 'I love your jeans. They fit really well. Levis?'

Jay was relieved when she saw the silver strands running through the woman's hair, and the fine lines around her eyes and mouth. Although Rosanna was beautiful, she was also closer to forty than twenty. Kiro's photo of her was deceptive.

'Gap,' Jay said.

'You must get me some the next time you're in the UK,'

Rosanna told Kiro, who was gazing at her adoringly. Rosanna could have told Kiro to jump off the balcony naked and he'd probably have done it. She offered an immaculately manicured hand for Jay to shake. Her grip was brisk and firm. She was wearing low-cut jeans, expensively distressed, and a tight V-necked blouse that showed off her figure.

'You look great,' said Jay.

Rosanna beamed. 'Armani. I just love Italian designers. Now, please, come inside.'

Kiro's home was tucked away behind one of the green markets, and was a two-bedroom apartment with coolly tiled floors that came with a cat called Marko. Marko was a big grey and white male who greeted Jay with a wide yawn that showed needle-point teeth and a bright pink tongue.

'Don't get up,' she told the cat.

Kiro dropped her bags into the spare room. In the hall behind them, Jay could hear Rosanna chattering in French on the phone, something about an embassy party coming up.

'So what do you think?' he asked Jay in a whisper.

Fortunately she had had time to formulate a response to the question she knew Kiro would ask. 'She's an amazing woman.'

'You really think so?'

'If she makes you happy, Kiro . . .'

'Oh, she does! So much!' He clapped his hands to his heart. 'Now, Ice, let me get you something to drink. Wine? Rakija?'

'Actually,' she admitted, 'you know what I'd really like? A big mug of tea. Really strong, with sugar and milk.'

His face twisted. 'I think a rakija would be better.'

Instantly, she knew something was wrong. 'Why?'

He didn't answer, just padded inside to return with a bottle of Bouin, forty percent locally brewed brandy, and two tumblers.

Oh shit, she thought.

Kiro poured a hefty shot for her and handed her the glass.

'Tell me, Kiro. You know I can't stand the softly-softly approach.'

'Zamira's gone missing.'

'What?'

'Nadire rang the office today. She was completely hysterical. She thinks Zamira's run away with a man called Branko Morillon.'

'Run away?'

'Apparently Branko turned up at their place in the mountains on Friday. He's a good-looking and personable son-of-a-bitch who everyone loves. He's related to half the village up there, brings them presents and stuff.'

'But Branko's a Slavic name,' she said. 'How can he be related?'

'Through marriage, rape, pillage. Christ knows.' Kiro ran a meaty hand back and forth over his head, making his curls dance. 'Whatever his background, Nadire says that in the New Year, he took Zamira's best friend, Hana, to London to live the supposed high-life. When he told Zamira, she was eaten alive by jealousy . . . she vanished Sunday night and hasn't been seen since. Nor has Branko.'

'Zamira's not fifteen yet,' Jay said. 'She won't have a passport.'

'You know that won't matter.'

A silence fell as they stared at each other. There was no need for words. Kiro knew the story as well as she did. Dozens of girls without legitimate documents were bought and sold every day and shipped across endless borders from Bosnia to Albania, Bulgaria to Turkey, Serbia to Macedonia, and beyond to Greece, Italy, and into Western Europe. They were raped and beaten and, most of the time, half-starved to make sure they were compliant.

Kiro said, 'What do you want to do?'

She'd been looking forward to a hot shower and a long, boozy dinner with Kiro, but after what she, Nadire and Zamira had been through together in the past, there was no way that she was going to turn her back on them now. They needed her, and by dint of coincidence or fate, she was here to fight for them once again.

Jay said, 'She could still be in this country?'

'Yes.'

'Then she'll be in Tetovo, where the money is.'

87

'I can't see they'd take her anywhere else,' Kiro agreed.

Jay went inside and grabbed her day pack. 'Let's go look for her. Can I use your car?'

'Of course.'

Jay held out her hand for the Lada's keys.

'No way,' said Kiro. 'I'm driving.'

Thirteen

Jay made calls while Kiro drove. He'd already rung the city cops and the border police, alerting them to Zamira's disappearance, but now Jay widened the net to include the Anti-Trafficking department at OSCE – Organisation for Security and Co-operation in Europe – and the head of the UN's THBS – Trafficking in Human Beings – investigation section. She also contacted a friend of Kiro's at Skopje's NATO Headquarters and another at IOM – International Organisation for Migration. The more people who were aware of Zamira's situation, the more chance they had of someone sighting her.

She was glad Rosanna hadn't kicked up a fuss when they left. To Jay's surprise, she'd been remarkably supportive, saying immediately, 'Of course you must go and help your friends. Ring me if there's anything I can do.'

Jay now called Sergeant Lucy Porter at UNMIK – United Nations Mission in Kosovo. 'Tell everyone I'm putting up a thousand-dollar reward payable in Denars, or Euros if they prefer. That should get the worms crawling out from under the logs.'

'Along with a lot of false information,' warned the police-woman.

'I can deal with the chaff,' Jay replied, 'but I can't risk missing something vital. Kiro tells me that she could be dressed in a sack and you couldn't miss her. She is seriously stunning. Someone, somewhere, will have seen her.'

'Have you got a photo?'

'Not a recent one, I'm afraid. Nadire only earns about fifty bucks a month so you can appreciate a camera isn't a priority. Just highlight the unusual colour of Zamira's eyes. Pretty much everyone out here has brown, but hers are bright green.'

'That'll be a help,' said the policewoman. 'Good luck, Jay.'

Finally, she called Nick. He was in the office, packing up to go home. He listened to her in silence, then said, 'I'll get on it now, put our usual protocol in place in case she's being brought here.'

'Thanks.'

'If I hear anything, I'll ring you immediately.'

It felt as though they'd only been in the car for ten minutes when Mount Tito came into view, rising proudly above the mist-coated plains and valleys and spearing a darkening sky with its snowy peaks. Skopje to Tetovo was forty minutes max along the highway, but with Kiro behind the wheel it took a lot less. They had a couple of narrow misses with vehicles pulling into their lane, but Jay was glad he didn't hang around. Every second counted when a girl went missing.

Nick's voice came to her. *She hasn't been in a war zone for five years.*

She'd almost forgotten what it was like to propel herself into a situation possibly filled with danger. Her body was alert, her nerves singing. She had to admit – she loved it.

Kiro barrelled through the town, the walls of its ugly and unimaginative blocks of Soviet-style buildings stained, and washing hanging from every window. The streets were busier than she remembered – and cleaner, more vibrant. Students crowded the coffee shops, and the pavements were bustling with shoppers.

'What do you want to do first?' Kiro asked. 'You want to see Nadire? She's staying with a friend in town.'

'Will she tell me anything new?'

'I doubt it.'

'Let's see her later,' said Jay. 'I'd rather check out a few clubs first. Which should we make a priority?'

'The Paris and Milano. They're in town, but the others' – he gestured south – 'are towards Gostivar. They're not really clubs, if you know what I mean.'

He was talking about the brothels that proliferated in the area, hidden in basements and at the back of people's homes. Prostitution formed a bedrock to the local economy. Not all the women were trafficked and held captive; many of them had turned to prostitution out of desperation in order to feed their families. Jay prayed Zamira was in Tetovo: the chances of finding her outside the city were virtually nil.

Kiro parked by a tailor's shop. As they climbed out of the car, Jay could hear the distant boom-boom of music and smell wood smoke, and when she looked up, she saw stars glittering in a cloudless sky.

'Okay.' He pointed in opposite directions. 'Which way shall we work? East to west or west to east?'

'How about I go west and you go east and we meet back here in three hours?'

Predictably, Kiro looked horrified. 'Holy Mother of God, you can't go alone.'

'It's much faster. We can cover most of the town this way. And I'll be careful, I promise.'

'Going into some of these places isn't a good idea even for me, let alone a single woman—'

'Shut up. I'll be fine.'

'*Ah, nanën.*' Ah, mother. He rolled his eyes as he cursed.

'You be good, now,' she told him, starting to walk away, 'I don't want you getting into trouble with any women just because Rosanna's not here.'

Jay walked from coffee shop to coffee shop, from restaurant to bar, asking questions. The temperature dropped further, the streets were becoming bitterly cold, and although she warmed up quickly in each establishment she never shed her scarf and coat; she didn't want to leave them behind if she had to make a rapid exit.

'Zamira's from Novo Selo. Her mother said she came to work in Tetovo, maybe as a waitress...'

There was a lot of head-shaking and shrugging of shoulders, but she didn't give up. After she'd covered the main drag she moved into the side streets, and that was when she stumbled across the Sugar Honey bar. Inside, the air was hot and thick with cigarette smoke, spilled wine and barbecued meat. Music blared from speakers set in the ceilings. About twenty people occupied the room, mainly Albanian men. Nobody looked at her as she entered; they were too busy talking and gesticulating and drinking. She caught sight of several weapons – a couple of AK47s as well as handguns – and swiftly checked out her nearest exits.

Jay let her eyes travel lightly over a girl sitting in the lap of a swarthy man with a moustache as thick as a dustpan brush. The girl looked about eighteen or nineteen. Big-breasted, her hips were full, her legs sturdy and strong, but from the way she was simpering and giggling against the guy's neck, Jay guessed she was actually no more than fifteen, sixteen at most. Whether or not she was trafficked was debatable, but that wasn't the issue. The girl shouldn't be here. She should be at home with her parents, maybe dating a boy from the next street, not in the grasp of some sweaty, greedy-eyed man three times her age.

Jay headed for the bar and asked for a beer. When the barmaid – a sinuous creature in a sequinned top and hipster hot-pants – served her, Jay asked her the question.

'I'm looking for a friend of mine, Zamira Kalisi. She's unusually pretty, with long black hair and green eyes.'

The woman surveyed her steadily, her expression flat.

'I'm not a cop,' Jay assured her. 'I'm just a friend, looking for a friend.' Surreptitiously she pulled out some already-prepared, folded notes from her pocket and slid them across the bar. The woman snuck the money into her hot-pants waistband.

Jay said, 'She's only fourteen. Have you seen her?'

'Green eyes, you say?'

'Yes.'

'I'm sorry. There's nobody here like that.'

'Are you sure?'

For a second the woman's stony mask softened. 'I'm sorry.'

'Thank you.'

She decided to finish her beer before she asked around some more, and she was chatting to a guy about Macedonia's economy when a rowdy group of men swaggered into the bar. They wore combats, with pistols in leather holsters slung on their hips like old-fashioned gunslingers. Almost immediately, a shoal of skimpily clad girls darted up to them, clinging to their arms and pouting. Jugs of wine and platefuls of food were pushed on to the bar.

Jay finished her beer and was about to move on to the next bar when one of the girls squealed. It was a yelp of real pain, and Jay's senses quickened when she saw a thuggish thickset man winding his fist around her hair, trapping her tight against his chest. He was pinching her right nipple between his fingers and grinning wetly. None of his companions reacted.

The girl was whimpering, trying to wriggle free, but he held her fast and twisted her nipple again. Jay said, 'Jesus', and at the same time the girl screamed.

'Shut the fuck up!' he yelled into the girl's face.

She was sobbing now. The other girls were looking uncomfortable, but they didn't look around, nor did they help. They didn't want the same treatment.

'Stop with the fucking crying!'

He was still pulling and twisting her nipple. Jay got off her bar stool, looking around as she did so, checking where the doors were, noting who was where.

'Please!' the girl begged. 'You're hurting me ...'

'Oh, for Christ's sakes, what is it with you fucking women?' Lazily he brought back his right fist and before Jay could move, let it loose, straight into the girl's face.

There was a soft, crunching sound, then the girl crumpled to the ground.

Everything went cold and silent in Jay's head. She couldn't hear the music, or see the bar staff. Her sight was filled with the thickset man, the disgust on his face.

The man's companions weren't taking any notice, nor was the barmaid. This happened every day. Nobody cared. Girls were two a penny out here.

He raised his mud-caked boot, preparing to kick the girl in the head. His expression was concentrated.

She had to distract him, take his attention away from the girl.

Jay crossed the room in five strides and grabbed the man's arm. He stumbled, and his boot missed the girl's face, slamming instead into the side of the bar with a dull thud.

'Haven't we met before?' she said, unable to think up anything else to say.

He glared at her.

'Who the fuck are you?'

'I'm from England. I thought I recognised you.'

'Fuck off.'

Behind him, the man's companions stared beadily at her. She noted there were eight of them and only one of her.

Come on, she told herself. Think of something!

The man looked down at the girl, who was trying to shuffle away, hands holding her shattered face. Blood poured between her fingers. Again he brought back his foot. Again Jay grabbed his arm, but this time he swung round, clearly angry, and shook her off.

'You touch me again, you get the same treatment,' he snarled.

Get up and run! she willed the girl, but she was hunched on the floor, dizzily weaving from side to side and moaning.

The man gave Jay a shove and turned back to the girl. Jay knew her options were running out when another man barged past her and, to her amazement, stuck a pistol against the brute's head.

'You make another move, you'll get this.' He spoke perfect Albanian. 'Did you hear me?'

The man nodded and swallowed. He'd turned as white as milk.

'You mess with my friend here' – he indicated Jay – 'you mess with me. Get it?'

Again, the man nodded, eyes glued to the floor.

'And you,' he spoke to the girl, who was on her knees, sobbing, 'go and get yourself cleaned up.'

With that, Max Blake put his hand under Jay's elbow and steered her outside.

Fourteen

Jay stared at Blake. If it hadn't been for his height she'd have taken him for a local with his unshaven jaw, faded jeans and trainers, and thick blue donkey jacket.

'What are you doing here?'

'Business. You okay?'

'Yes, thank you.'

Her legs had softened after the adrenalin rush and she felt weak. She put a hand against the wall.

'That was an interesting situation you got yourself in.' Blake cocked his head as he surveyed her. 'What would you have done if I hadn't arrived?'

He must think she was an idiot. You didn't interrupt a Mafia gang member when he was having time out and enjoying his sport.

'Head-butted him and busted his nose before running like hell before his pals could catch me.'

Blake looked at her. 'I take it you run fast.'

'Oh, yes. I'm an Olympian runner when I'm in a tight spot.' Her shivering increased as she recalled how tight a spot she'd been in.

'Wait here,' Blake said. He vanished briefly to return with a glass containing a hefty shot of rakija.

'Medicinal,' he told her.

Jay downed it in one swallow. The oily alcohol lit her throat and stomach like fire. Almost immediately, her legs steadied. She passed back the glass.

'Thanks.'

He gave a nod and placed the glass on the club's doorstep.

'What business are you here on?'

He raised his head to study the stars. 'This and that.'

A local thug stumbled past, reeking of wine and mumbling to himself. Blake watched him go before dropping his gaze to hers. His eyes looked like polished coal in the night light. 'If you're okay, I'll be off.'

'I'm fine. Thanks.'

'Try not to get into any more trouble.'

Goddammit, if the man wasn't smiling.

He raised a hand in a half-salute, leaving her to watch him lope off down the street and wonder what business Max Blake was conducting in the Balkans.

When she met with Kiro fifteen minutes later, his expression was dark and she wasn't surprised he had no news of Zamira. She told him about Blake turning up and Kiro frowned. 'He's with SOCA, you say?'

'That's what I've been told.'

'Remind me what they do?'

'Fight organised crime in the UK. They've got links all over the world with other police forces: Interpol, the FBI, the Chinese PSB.'

He mulled it over then shrugged. 'First time we've had one of those out here.' He didn't seem to make much of it, so Jay didn't say anything further. They began walking to his car.

'Let's go and see Nadire,' he said. 'I'm starved, and since she said she'd feed us any time . . .'

Nadire was staying with friends in what was known locally as The Valley, which comprised the multitude of villages spread along a narrow, dusty road that wound between Tetovo and Gostivar. Behind the snaking line of grocery stores and small houses were fields with olive groves and apple orchards, which were glowing silvery-blue in the starlight. The only sign that you had left one village and entered another, was when you passed the next mosque, always well-tended and brightly lit.

The apartment was small but neat, with tiled floors and wooden tables. Nadire's friend, Una, had a warm, generous smile, and was as short and round and homely as a cottage loaf. Despite Una's jet-black hair and olive skin, she reminded Jay of her mother. Una ushered Jay and Kiro into the living room where her twins lay sprawled face-down on the sofa, their pudgy two-year-old limbs spread wide. They looked as though they'd fallen asleep mid-leap across a cushion.

Nadire came into the room and ran for her.

'Ice,' she said on a half sob.

Jay tried not to look shocked at how much Nadire had aged. She was only thirty-four but her skin was rough and lined. Her hair was dyed black but you could see the white roots, and with her face red and swollen from weeping she looked closer to fifty.

They embraced tightly. Nadire was a good ten inches shorter than Jay; she laid her head against her breast while Jay rested her cheek against Nadire's head and briefly closed her eyes. Nadire smelled the same as she always had – of smoke and cinnamon – and Jay was instantly ambushed by the memory of their first meeting, the terror of smuggling Nadire out of Kosovo.

The only person who had known of her plan was Kiro. She'd been risking the life of a woman she'd never met to reunite her with her daughter, as well as risking her own career, and the fewer people who knew what she was up to, the better.

Leposavic was still under Serbian control, with armed checkpoints and Serbian soldiers on every corner. Jay knew that if a Serb caught so much as a glimpse of a Kosovo Muslim, he would kill them. Nadire, terrified of being gang-raped and brutalised before being murdered, had holed up in a basement.

Jay's plan had been simple. Jump into Kiro's car – which back then had been a white UN Toyota Land Cruiser – and drive from Macedonia to the north-east of Kosovo, sailing through any checkpoints along the way, before collecting Nadire and sailing back.

She made sure the car's tank was full and topped up the spare jerry cans. Then she added a shrink-wrapped tray of mineral water, a TRACE fleece and a baseball cap borrowed from Kiro, two hundred Marlboro cigarettes and a bottle of imported whisky. She took her standard issue SA80 rifle, and strapped a knife against her ankle. As she headed up Route Hawke for the border, she had to make a real effort not to think about what she was doing. She didn't want to bottle out. Having finally given Zamira her word, she couldn't bear the thought of letting the girl down.

As soon as she crossed the border Jay had focused on nothing but driving fast and not getting noticed. Shelled-out villages scarred the countryside and garbage blew across the fields like leaves. Soon she passed Pristina, and north of the capital the road became peppered with checkpoints manned by armed men in purple and blue uniforms, their faces as grey and hard as cement. She cruised through the first checkpoint, but to her dismay she was pulled over at the second. The last thing she needed was for that to happen on her return trip with Nadire.

'Open up,' a soldier demanded.

'Do I have to?' she pleaded. 'I'm in a real hurry today.' When the soldier shifted his rifle to point it at her groin, she hurriedly complied. He was built like an earth-mover, and his skin was smeared with dirt and dried sweat. He looked at the jerry cans and bottled water.

'Why are you going to Leposavic?'

'I'm meeting Colonel Campbell there,' she lied. There was no such colonel. 'He's with NATO. I'm needed as a translator.'

'NATO.' He spat on the ground before moving to inspect the rest of the car. It didn't take him long to find the Marlboros and the whisky tucked under the front seat. Immediately he confiscated them.

Jay rolled her eyes at him and then she gave a laugh and clapped him on the back. 'Happy Christmas,' she told him, keeping her expression light and amused. 'Or is it happy birthday, my friend?'

There was a second's pause, and then his face split into a

broad grin, showing he was missing two front teeth. 'You are very generous,' he told her.

'And you are a rogue and a thief,' she said, but she was laughing as she said it, and he laughed back.

Leposavic was a dump. Crumbling apartment blocks and office buildings were separated by rivers of mud and rubbish. On all sides, buildings were smouldering. The streets were filled with gaping holes from shelling and the trees had been hacked into lumpy stumps, every branch used for fuel. A few people wandered aimlessly, poking through the garbage for food.

Kiro had sketched a map for Jay, and it didn't take her long to find Nadire's apartment block. The door was pocked with bullet marks and inside it smelled of urine and boiled cabbage. Breathing shallowly, Jay descended the stairs to the basement.

Thanks to Kiro getting a message to Nadire the previous week, she'd already packed her suitcase. She had, apparently, been waiting for four days. She was neat, small and dark, with spiky hair, and when Jay showed her Zamira's little icon nestled at her throat and told her she was going to drive her out of the city to be with her daughter, she flung herself at Jay and wrapped her arms around her. She was sobbing.

'Quick,' Jay told her. 'We've no time to waste.'

She made Nadire put on the TRACE fleece and baseball cap, hoping she'd be taken for an aid worker, but she knew the skimpy disguise would be useless if Nadire was questioned.

They were waved through the first two checkpoints, but despite their smooth passage Nadire was getting increasingly panicky. As they approached the checkpoint that had stopped Jay earlier, she tried to keep Nadire calm.

'Just look straight ahead. Don't meet anyone's eyes. Try and keep your expression bland. Don't think about the soldiers. Picture Zamira waiting for you.'

Nadire started to shake. She was making little whimpering noises and her skin had turned the colour of putty.

'Keep breathing deeply. Keep calm. Think of Zamira . . . ' Jay could feel the hard stares of the soldiers as they approached. She pressed the accelerator lightly, and as the engine note lifted, a soldier stepped out, hand raised to indicate they must pull over.

Nadire gave a low moan.

'Don't look at them,' Jay told her. 'I'll show them my papers and they'll let us through, no problem.'

Mouth dry, Jay pulled in to the side of the road.

Two more soldiers appeared, grim faced. One was the man who'd taken the cigarettes and whisky. Jay beeped her horn at him and gave him a little wave. 'Remember me, you thieving bastard?' She forced a big smile on her face.

He looked at her, surprised, and then he smiled a gap-toothed smile and shouted something at the soldiers approaching the car. The soldiers paused and then they casually waved Jay through. They didn't even glance at Nadire.

By the time they got to camp Stenkovec it was dark and Jay was exhausted. She pulled up outside the camp gates and fell out of the car. Stumbling around the bonnet, she opened Nadire's door and pointed to TRACE's makeshift office.

'Zamira!' Jay called. 'Your mum's here!'

Like a miniature rocket, Zamira shot out.

Nadire and Zamira raced for each other, arms outstretched and faces lit with joy. Mumbling an excuse that she was tired, Jay went to the latrines, put her head in her hands and wept. It was a combination of relief and jubilation; reuniting Nadire and Zamira had given her an emotional kick like nothing else she'd ever experienced.

That night, over bowls of hot soup, Nadire told Kiro the story of her rescue. 'Jay was so calm at the checkpoints I couldn't believe it. No sweat, no nerves, no nothing,' she said, staring at Jay in awe. 'She was like ice.'

Which was how Jay got her nickname.

As Kiro had said, Nadire had few clues to offer them as to Zamira's whereabouts. Branko Morillon flitted into Novo Selo and out again every few months or so, talking of Rome, Istanbul and London as though they were suburbs in the city where he lived and making the young kids sick with envy. She did, however, have an envelope that Hana's parents had given her. Jay studied the postmark, red and circular, definitely British, but it was smudged and almost impossible to read.

'When did they get it?'

'Three weeks ago. Mid-February.'

'Can I keep it?'

'Of course.'

Jay tucked it inside her money belt. She'd take it back to England with her and get Tom to pass it to one of his experts and see if they could decipher the postmark. If successful, then it might help them track down Hana, who could lead them to Zamira.

The twins woke noisily and began squabbling over a woolly lion, and while Una cajoled them to bed, Jay asked Nadire to show her on Kiro's map where she lived.

'Here.' Nadire's cracked, dry finger tapped on a line of narrow contours about two kilometres south-east of Novo Selo. On the other side of the mountain, on the slopes of Mount Tito, was a symbol denoting several buildings. 'Ski resort,' she told Jay. 'I've never bothered to see it. It's over two days walk away.'

With her cows and sheep she was, Nadire told Jay proudly, self-sufficient, but Jay knew life would be hard, trying to live off the proceeds of nothing but milk and cheese sold in the local markets. 'We do better than a lot of people,' Nadire added, 'but Zamira doesn't see it like that. She hates her life with me. She wants nothing but tight jeans, boys and make-up.'

'It's her age,' Jay said. 'Girls are like that back home too.'

'I bet you weren't, Ice,' said Kiro. He had a glint in his eye. 'I bet you wore combat clothing on every date and that they had to arm-wrestle you for a kiss.'

For supper they shared a big Šopska salad – juicy tomatoes, cucumber and black olives, covered in grated white goat's cheese and drenched in thick, green olive oil – accompanied with crisp, salted strips of bread. The atmosphere was glum, and nobody ate much. Jay was relieved when Kiro eventually suggested they head back to Skopje. Her head was throbbing with fatigue, and they were barely five minutes into the journey home when she fell asleep.

Jay jerked awake in the middle of the night, damp with sweat. For a second she couldn't think where she was and she held her breath, listening and waiting for a spark of recognition.

Shit. Was she on duty?

No, she'd left the army. She worked with TRACE now. Seconds later, she registered the warm, furry weight lying across her thighs. Marko, Kiro's cat.

Exhaling, she pushed the cat aside and swung her feet on to the cool tiled floor. Her heart was beating fast and she was trembling. It was the same dream she always had, thinking she was trapped on the top floor of a house that she and her team were clearing. It always ended the same way: she was alone, without a weapon, and an enemy soldier – she never saw his face but she knew it was the girl's rapist with his fleshy neck – springing at her from behind a door and bringing up his gun to shoot her.

Once, she'd shouted in her sleep so loudly, she'd woken Tom. He'd taken her in his arms and held her close, stroking her hair and soothing her with gentle words until she'd fallen back to sleep, dreamless.

Tom's voice: *I honestly thought you'd be happy to take our relationship to the next stage.*

Marko crept on to her lap, purring. She stroked him until the small hours, thinking about Tom, and wondering what the hell she was going to do . . .

Her phone rang just after dawn and she had to force herself to crawl from beneath the covers to answer it.

'Hello?'

'Jay.'

Her stomach gave a swoop which she put down to being startled at hearing his voice. She'd been expecting Laura Sharpe.

'Blake?'

'Yup. I have a quick question for you. How old is Zamira?'

She was about to ask him how he knew her number, and then remembered him checking out her mobile phone when he'd jumped her in the alley in Bristol. Had he memorised it then?

She said, 'How do you know about Zamira?'

'You were asking questions all over town last night, remember? And since you're the only Jay McCaulay I know who's put out a thousand-dollar reward for information on a missing green-eyed girl, two and two on this occasion made four.'

'You've heard something about Zamira?'

'No, sorry.'

There was a brief pause, then he said, 'I asked around and discovered that Branko Morillon's tight with the Albanian Mafia. You know how good they've become at forging documents.'

Jay closed her eyes. 'She's only fourteen.'

'I take it she doesn't look her age?'

'How did you guess?'

'I've heard you can get almost perfect replica passports in forty-eight hours.'

'I thought it would take much longer.'

'It would have, last week, but they've got someone new on side.'

'What about visas? She'd need those if she was travelling out of the Balkans.'

'Same thing.'

'Oh, God.' Jay put a hand over her eyes. 'That is such bad news.'

'I'm sorry.'

'So she could have left the country.'

'Yes.'

Another pause.

'Jay, if I learn anything more, I'll ring you.'

With that, Blake hung up.

Fifteen

Zamira turned her passport round and round in her hands. Branko had given it to her yesterday, and she couldn't stop looking at it. Each time she checked her photograph she expected her face to have been replaced by someone else's, but there she was, gazing dead ahead, eyes as wide and round as a startled cat.

She wasn't sure how she felt. Excited to be sure, but there was a faintly sick feeling in her stomach too, which reminded her of the time when Bear had fallen ill – he'd eaten some poison put down for the wolves on a neighbouring farm – and they hadn't known if he'd live through the night.

She glanced across at Lina, who was glued to the TV. Lina drank coffee by the gallon and chain-smoked. She was a friend of Branko's, along with her boyfriend Jonuz, who rented the Tetovo apartment she was staying in. Lina had to be roughly the same age as her mother, but instead of cowshit-stained overalls and second-hand men's shirts, Lina wore tight hipster jeans and ankle boots with silver tassels. Her lips and fingernails were painted the colour of ripe tomatoes and when she laughed she honked like a goose. Zamira wasn't sure whether she liked her or not. Lina was polite enough, but she occasionally shot Zamira a sly glance, raking her body with an assessing eye that made her feel oddly exposed and vulnerable.

She'd thought it would take weeks to get permission to travel to England, but Branko had pulled some strings and here she was, with a passport and visa, and an air ticket. They were due to fly out with Macedonia Air at seven a.m. tomorrow, to Vienna, and then take the one p.m. British Airways flight from Vienna to Heathrow. Branko had wanted to fly out yesterday but apparently he had a succession of meetings he couldn't miss, so she had to wait here with Lina until he returned. Although the wait felt as long as a year she had to be patient, because soon she'd be flying across Europe – she'd never been on an airplane before, what would that be like! – and then she'd be with Hana, eating McDonald's hamburgers, going to the movies, shopping.

Getting up, she walked to the window and looked out. A light sleet was falling and she could barely make out Mount Tito's summit through the thickening clouds.

'Hey, you.'

Zamira turned to see Lina gesturing her away from the window.

'You know what Branko said.'

Zamira ducked back. Branko had warned her to keep a low profile or the next second her mother would be on the doorstep and dragging her back to their hovel in the mountains. 'And you wouldn't want that, would you, Peaches?'

Last night she'd said no, but right now she wasn't so sure. It wasn't the fact that the apartment was filthy as much as the way Lina's boyfriend, Jonuz, snuffled around her like a dog that smelled fresh liver. Thank God for Branko, or she might have been tempted to go home instead of waiting as he'd asked because, this morning just after she'd got up, she'd overheard Branko talking to Jonuz in the kitchen. He'd sounded angry.

'You lay a hand on her, I swear I will tear you limb from fucking limb. Do you hear me?'

'Come on, Branko,' Jonuz whined. 'Don't be a spoilsport.'

'Do you remember what happened to that captain of Milot's? The one who took a bribe from an UNMIK cop? They took him to the processing shed, remember?'

There was a long silence, then Jonuz cleared his throat.

'Yeah. I remember.'

106

'Does that mean you've got my message?'

'Yeah.'

Lina's mobile phone rang and she answered it without turning down the TV volume. 'I've gotta go, kiddo,' Lina said. She was plastering on more lipstick and fluffing out her hair with her fingers. 'See ya tomorrow.'

After Lina shut the door behind her, Zamira crossed the room to flick through the TV channels. Barely ten minutes had passed when she heard the front door open.

'Peaches, you there?'

Before she could reply he bounded into the shabby room with a bunch of tulips in one had and a family-sized bar of Milka in the other.

Without thinking she flung her arms around his neck. He smelled of coffee and brandy and was shaking with laughter.

'Now that's the sort of welcome a man likes when he gets home.'

He leaned back, smiling, his hands gentle on her waist as he looked down at her, but the his gaze moved from her eyes to her lips and his smile faded. 'Christ, Zamira,' he said. His voice was husky. 'You're beautiful.'

He began to move his hands away but she caught them and brought them to cup her waist once more.

'Peaches . . .' His tone was warning. 'You have no idea what you're doing. The effect you have . . .'

She reached up and touched the corner of his mouth with her finger. The grubby, shabby room faded away. Her whole being was centred on Branko, the breadth of his shoulders, the heat of his hands through her shirt, the way he was looking at her as though seeing her for the first time. He was so perfect.

'My sweet Peaches,' he murmured and, tilting his head, lowered his lips to hers.

It was the softest kiss, like being brushed with a chick's downy feather. He had closed his eyes but Zamira's were wide open. She saw his eyelashes were lush and thick, his lips smooth and full, and that he had a small, angry red spot just beneath one nostril.

She thought: I love you.

Sixteen

It was late morning when Jay returned to Tetovo. She found the perfect bar just around the corner from the Vero Supermarket, a small, neatly swept room with five tables and a TV blaring in one corner. Like a lot of bars here, the Mezzo Forte was off the main street and hidden between a parking lot and a scarred office block the colour of charcoal.

The place was crowded with people of all ages, old men in baggy trousers and shirts and young men in jeans and North Face fleeces. Settling herself opposite the door with her back to the wall, Jay ordered drinks and kept them coming for the endless flow of people drawn to her table. As the story of her reward of a thousand dollars for information on Zamira spread, so the crowd increased, much to the delight of the bar's owner.

Two guys in shiny suits at the next table appeared amused at her efforts to find Zamira. 'You'll be lucky,' one of them told her. 'If she's that pretty she'll be long gone by now.'

'Where to, do you think?' Jay kept her face open and innocent.

'Albania, Turkey, Greece, Germany.' He gave a careless shrug. 'Italy's the most popular destination at the moment.'

He made it sound as though they were talking about holidays, but she knew he was referring to THB hotspots. Jay wheedled for more information but he quickly got bored and turned back to talk to his friend.

Jay had been in the bar for three hours before she finally heard something that sparked her interest. An elderly man was moaning about the criminals in town, how they were the only guys who got to drive flash cars. 'Decent folk like us can't afford a BMW,' he told her. 'We have to make do with clapped out Ladas, and even then we're lucky. I'll never make enough money to own a car and even if I got my ugly face inside the big meeting coming up I never will.'

'Big meeting? What, like between drug dealers?' she asked, acting dumb. She didn't want him to think she was particularly interested in what he'd said.

'Not just drugs.' He shook his head. 'Anything and everything. Never done a day's honest work any of them.'

'They meet to barter goods? Weapons for women or something?'

'That happens.' He stubbed out his cigarette. 'But this meeting's nothing to do with that. This one's international. All the big men are flying in.'

'It sounds important.'

'Oh, yes.' He nodded. 'It's important all right, but for the wrong reasons.'

'What do you mean?'

He tapped the side of his nose with a tobacco-stained finger. 'You don't want to know. All I can say is that you won't find your young friend there.'

After lunch, the barman introduced her to Raman. About ten years old, he was a street urchin who earned money washing windscreens and sweeping floors, and today was helping to wash glasses at the bar.

'You want to find someone,' said the barman, 'you talk to Raman. There's nobody that kid doesn't know.'

Raman wore an impish expression and a pair of faded grey trousers rolled over at the waist. His hair was thick and scruffy, with a tuft that stood upright like a cockscomb. He put out his hand for her to shake.

'Hello, Miss.'

'Hello, Raman.'

'I hear you are looking for a friend?'

'Yes, she's . . . '

'I know everybody in town. Everybody.'

'That's great . . . '

'A thousand denar,' he said.

At that point the barman growled something at the boy, making him flinch.

'Two hundred,' he amended sheepishly.

Jay counted out four hundred denar, which was less than four pounds, and she'd barely begun to offer them to the boy when he snatched them as fast as a snake, beaming as though he'd just won the lottery.

'If we find your friend, will I get the thousand dollars?'

'Every last cent.'

He gave a little yelp and bounded down the pavement. 'I will find her, I promise! And then I can go to university and learn to be a doctor!'

At the end of the street, Jay paused. 'Raman, can you keep a secret?'

He looked affronted. 'Of course.'

Reaching into her pocket, she offered him another four hundred denar. 'There's something else I'd like you to do for me. Alone.'

He looked hungrily at the money, but he didn't take it. 'What is it?'

'I need to know if you hear anything about a meeting coming up. All the big men are flying in, apparently. I want to know who's attending, and where the meeting is, but I don't want them to know that I'm asking.'

A shadow passed over his eyes. He would have grown up with the recent hostilities, lived alongside bullets and bombs, seen NATO soldiers hunting for insurgents, learned all about spies and the value of secrecy – and the dangers of betrayal.

'Look,' she said. 'If you don't want to do this, I understand.'

He took the money and shrugged. 'It's okay.'

'You're sure?'

'Yeah.'

'Thanks.' Jay touched him on the shoulder. The boy was

110

nothing but skin and bone. 'How about if I see you at Mezzo Forte later? I'll buy you something to eat, if you like.'

His face cracked into a grin. 'They do great pizza!'

'Pizza it is.'

When Jay returned to the bar later that afternoon she couldn't see Raman. She was about to settle herself at a table by the window when the barman beckoned her over and pointed out a man slouched in the corner, nursing a cup of coffee. He wore dirty trousers streaked with what could have been tar, and a stained overshirt. His shirt was open at the neck, showing two gold chains tangled in thick chest hair, and his hair was lank and greasy.

'His name's Jonuz,' the barman told her. 'He works at the local meat-processing plant. He says he's got some information on your friend, Zamira.'

She eyed the man cautiously. 'How reliable is he?'

The barman shrugged. 'He comes in from time to time, drinks the odd beer or two, doesn't make a fuss. That's all I know.'

'Thanks.'

As she moved across the room, Jonuz raised his head to look at her. His beady eyes were quickly lowered to her breasts and stayed there.

'Hi. I'm Jay McCaulay.' She stood over him. She didn't offer her hand. 'I gather you've got some information for me.'

Jonuz shifted his gaze to her day pack. 'You got the thousand dollars?'

'Not with me, no.'

'Where is it?'

'In the bank.'

Getting to his feet, he threw a handful of notes on the table. 'Let's go and get it.'

'Not so fast.' Jay moved to stand in front of him. 'I need to know where Zamira is first.'

'And I need the money first.'

'How do I know it's the right girl?'

'Green-eyed little beauty with the innocence of a kitten, am I right?'

'Be serious,' she snorted. 'Just about everyone in the country knows I'm looking for a green-eyed girl. I'll need a bit more than that before parting with my cash.'

'She's staying at my place, I swear it. Just behind the meat-processing plant. Branko dropped her there Sunday.'

Despite her leap of optimism, Jay kept her expression neutral. 'And where can I find Branko?'

A cunning look crossed his face. 'Information on Branko's extra.'

Remember your priorities, she told herself. Zamira comes first.

'Give me a proper ID for the girl and your address and we'll go and get half the money. When I've seen Zamira in person, you get the rest.'

'Okay. She's got hair down to here' – he patted the side of his waist – 'and she's really pretty. Got a great figure too. Small and slim.'

'Come on, Jonuz, half the girls around here are like that.'

'Shit.' He ran a grubby hand over his head. 'She's wearing new jeans that Branko bought her ... and a pink top. Something tight and shiny. She's got a belt and boots ... Oh, and she wears a small blue thing around her neck.'

'What small blue thing?' Jay held her breath. Her St Christopher?

'A disc. On a silver chain.'

'Size?'

He pointed to his thumbnail. 'About that big. It's got a saint carrying some guy on his back.'

Jay's heart squeezed. It was her St Christopher! Zamira still wore it. Her rush of relief was rapidly followed by concern. 'How is she? Is she okay?'

'She's fine.' Jonuz didn't look as though he cared.

'Is she there under duress? Did Branko kidnap her? Has he hurt her?'

Jonuz looked astonished. 'What, Branko harm his precious Peaches? You must be joking.'

'Branko's her boyfriend?'

Jay wanted to know more about Zamira's relationship with Branko but Jonuz had obviously had enough small talk because he was gesturing impatiently at the door. 'Can we go and get my money now?'

'I want your address first.'

'So you can bugger off without paying me? Not bloody likely.'

They continued to haggle until finally, Jay agreed she'd hand over five hundred dollars when they were at the bank, when he would give her his address before driving her to Zamira. If everything went well, they would return to the bank for his final payment.

Jay waved to the barman as she left he but didn't see her. He was mopping a dark stain on the floor. It looked like blood.

Seventeen

Jay winced as Jonuz ground through his ancient Renault's gears. He'd stuffed the five hundred dollars in his back pocket and although she hadn't expected him to do hand-springs at receiving the money, she'd thought his expression might have cheered a little. As it was, he looked grim and tense, and she wondered what was going through his mind. Perhaps he was rehearsing how to tell his friend Branko that he'd stiffed him and sold his girlfriend to an Englishwoman.

They followed the road for about two miles to the northern fringes of the town before Jonuz pulled over and parked. Afternoon had bled into evening and when Jay climbed out of the car, the air smelled of snow. She looked around, her breath clouding. Jonuz's apartment block was another old Soviet building with the mandatory cracks and broken windows. The meat-processing plant stood opposite, a surprisingly modern square of concrete and steel with clean windows and a fleet of six trucks lined neatly in its forecourt. The street was empty of people, but two cats were balanced on top of an overflowing rubbish bin licking shreds of tin foil.

'Which apartment?' she asked Jonuz.

'Number eleven. And when you've seen her, I get the rest of the money, okay?'

'Okay.'

Jonuz led the way inside.

Maybe it was her anticipation at seeing Zamira again, or the fact that Jonuz had reiterated their deal that dulled her senses, but when she heard footsteps fall in behind her as she walked into the entrance hall, she was abnormally slow. She'd barely begun to turn to check on them when she was grabbed from behind, her arms pinned behind her back and hoisted into the air so that her feet swung six inches above the ground. She tried to jerk free but her captors were too strong. She could barely move but she continued to struggle until it dawned on her that it was futile.

For Chrissakes, she told herself, heart pounding, save your energy for later.

Immediately, she stopped fighting.

There were three of them, two holding her, the other covering her with a pistol. She recognised the guys with the guns as the men in shiny suits from the Mezzo Forte. Jonuz was standing back, his eyes fixed on the floor. He was sweating heavily.

The two men gripping her walked her back outside and across the road, towards the meat-processing plant. The third one followed. Jonuz stayed behind.

Fear stabbed beneath her breastbone. Didn't anyone live here? Where was everyone?

'What do you want?' she demanded.

One of the men slid a hand to her breast, and squeezed it hard. She bucked and twisted but he didn't relent. He began to laugh.

'Ah, fuck it. You're too old for me.' The man released his grip. 'I like them young and tender, not tough and scrawny like an old chicken.'

'You like screwing kids, is that it?' she said. 'Paedophilia's a crime where I come from.'

He slapped the side of her head, hard enough to shock her but not to do any lasting damage. Had he been told not to harm her?

'Shut it.'

Taking her to the side of the plant they walked her through a door and along a corridor where the brickwork was painted white and the concrete floor grey. Bare light bulbs hung from the ceiling and there was a strong smell of disinfectant. When they reached the door at the end, one of the men stepped forward and opened it. Inside was a cavernous room of steel and chrome. The floor was covered in shiny white tiles. There were four assembly lines, all empty, and along one wall rested waist-high stacks of plastic trays and tubs. In another corner stood what looked like a giant mincing machine. She could see two hoses, still leaking, and in the centre of the floor, a massive drain with a wide grille. The reek of fresh meat and blood hung in the air and small pools of water held pink streaks.

The door banged behind them and two more men walked in, towards the mincing machine in the corner. They wore plastic aprons and were hefting a carcass of a large, skinned lamb between them. Bewildered, Jay said, 'What's going on?' but nobody answered.

With a clunk, the mincing machine was turned on. The men raised the lamb to their shoulders and levered it head first into the mouth of the mincer. There was a brief splintering sound and then the machine settled to a steady grinding. The carcass shivered and juddered as it was steadily devoured. Coils of meat studded with splinters of bone snaked to the tiles. Gradually the rear legs vanished, jerking wildly. Last were the small, creamy hooves.

Why did they mince the carcass with its bones? They couldn't use it like that, could they . . . ? Jay's dread increased when the two men in aprons walked to a door at the far end of the room, opened it, and vanished. They had left the mincer on.

Jay looked at her captors. 'Will someone tell me what I'm doing here?'

One of the men in the shiny suits gestured behind her. She turned to see the men in aprons return. They were dragging something to the mincer. For a second she thought it was another dead lamb but then she saw it was a skinny bare-chested boy with a tuft of hair that stood upright like a cockscomb. His legs and feet were bound together with duct tape. More duct tape was plastered across his mouth.

Again, she said, 'What's going on?' Her breathing was tight.

Nobody replied. The men stopped next to the mincer. Raman was pinned in the men's arms but it didn't stop the boy from jerking and twisting like a fish on the end of a line. He was shouting behind his gag.

'Stop it,' she said. 'Let him go.'

The door banged again and she jerked her head round to see yet two more men entering the room. One was short and swarthy with bandy legs and virtually no neck. His black hair was flecked with grey and he'd run to fat, but that didn't stop him from wearing a shiny, tight red shirt that emphasised his saddlebags.

Milot Dumani.

Her eyes flicked to the second man, gaunt and white-faced with a chin like a blade. In his early fifties, he was dressed in a tan suit with a black polo-neck that made him look ill, as though he had cancer. His small black eyes held hers without emotion.

With a sick feeling in her heart, she recognised him from her briefing with Laura Sharpe.

The Barracuda, Tihomir Vadic. The Georgian Mafia boss.

Vadic said something to Milot and for a second the men by the mincing machine were distracted. Immediately Raman swung his bound legs around, lashing at the nearest man's groin. He missed but still caught the man's inner thigh.

'Please,' she said. 'Let the boy go.'

Vadic stepped forward.

'Raman's done nothing wrong,' she pleaded.

She was shivering inside and she hoped he couldn't see it. He gave a slow smile, and she knew he had. Still holding her eyes, he clicked his fingers and said, 'Hashim.' One of the henchmen moved to her side. He held a pistol in his right hand. He pressed the gun against her temple. She felt sweat beading on her forehead and trickling down the sides of her face.

'Hashim will shoot you if you so much as move a muscle. Do you understand?' Vadic's Albanian was perfect. If she hadn't known he was from Georgia, she'd have thought he was a local.

'Yes.'

Her neck felt as solid as wood and her heart was jumping as

though electrified. She tried to slow down her thinking, push Raman aside and concentrate on the opposition. Seven men in the room, mostly armed. No matter how hard she looked at her position, she couldn't see she had any chance of saving Raman. The barrel of Hashim's pistol was steady and unwavering, pushing against her skin. There was no way she could knock his arm aside in the time it would take for him to pull the trigger.

Without looking at the men holding Raman. Vadic said quietly. 'Do it.'

In one swift movement, they raised the boy to their shoulders and held him above the gaping maw of the mincing machine.

'No!' she yelled.

Immediately Hashim caught her around the neck with his left arm and pulled her tight against his chest. The gun was now rammed against her cheek and she could barely breathe.

'Watch,' Vadic commanded.

'No,' she begged, but she couldn't keep her gaze away as the men lifted Raman and began to lower him towards the gnashing, groaning metal mouth. The boy was thrashing about, trying to throw his body aside as his feet neared the blades, and Jay screamed at Vadic to stop. He didn't respond.

There was a tiny splintering sound. Raman's eyes grew wide, but behind the duct tape he couldn't scream.

Jay forgot about her stranglehold, the gun rammed against her skull. She lunged for the mincing machine, her voice cracking from the force of her shouts.

'STOP!' she yelled.

Vadic held up a hand. The men stilled. She was panting, sweat pouring through her hair, down her neck and back. Amazingly, she could feel Hashim's heart thudding against her shoulder blade.

Vadic turned to face her.

'You are a spy,' he said.

'I'm with TRACE,' she gasped. 'It's an aid agency and—'

'Do you know what we do with spies?'

'I'm not a spy. I'm trying to find a friend of mine. Zamira Kalisi. She's run away from home.'

'We kill them. That is, after they have experienced an intense and unpleasant physical sensation of some kind.'

He clicked his fingers at Hashim. She didn't think he could tighten his grip any more, but she was wrong. He forced her to lean backwards, raising her feet from the floor, the angle brutally unnatural and making it difficult to breathe.

'Please . . . ' she gasped. She felt any further pressure might snap her spine.

Vadic reached into his jacket pocket and withdrew a filleting knife with a sharp, pointed tip. He came and stood close and pulled up her fleece, then her undershirt, baring her belly. Desperately she tried to buck away, kick out at him, but with her spine bowed, her limbs flailed uselessly.

'In my country,' Vadic said, 'we're quite fond of making a small incision in a person's stomach, just here.'

He pressed the point of the knife just below her belly button. She felt it prick her skin. She went still but her heart was flipping frantically.

He brought out another steel implement, with a small hook at the end. 'And then we gently pull out the entrails, bit by bit.'

Jay couldn't help a moan escape her lips.

'As you can appreciate, it's very messy, and extremely painful. Milot, on the other hand, has his own methods. Since he owns this factory, he favours the mincer. It's a cleaner way of disposing of undesirables.'

'Raman's not a spy,' she begged. 'Nor am I, I'm here to find—'

'Your friend,' he sneered. 'Yes, so you said. Which is the perfect excuse to ask questions about things that do not concern you.'

Jay sent an anguished look at Raman to see he was still suspended in mid-air by the men. His eyes were on hers, beseeching.

'Don't kill him, I beg you. He's done nothing wrong.'

'But he told us he was a friend of yours!' Vadic turned to Raman, raising a pair of thin, dark eyebrows in mock-surprise. 'Befriending spies isn't to be recommended, but he didn't think about the consequences.' He swung back to Jay. 'Nor did you, obviously.'

Another click of the fingers and Hashim eased his grip, allowing her to stand upright again. Her legs shook.

Milot came over. He was holding an electronic organiser. Pressing some buttons, he raised it so Vadic could read the screen.

'Ah. Here we have your London address, three telephone numbers, your mobile, office and home, as well as ... '

Milot fiddled with the machine, and Vadic continued.

'Addresses for your parents. I see your father breeds some kind of special cows. I wonder what he'd say if they were all shot one night. Or perhaps we should shoot his rather attractive wife, Nicola? But then I'm curious what he'd do if his ex-wife – your mother – was knifed on her way back from the bridge club. I wonder if he'd mourn much?'

Jay held herself tight, trying not to let her fear and horror show.

'And you have a boyfriend too, I see. A policeman. He might find himself shot dead in the line of duty. Very noble of him. The funeral will be magnificent, I have no doubt.'

'What do you want?' she managed.

He came and stood so close to her she could smell his aftershave, bitter but sickly, like burned sugar.

'I want you to go back to Skopje and book your flight, leaving Macedonia on Sunday. That gives you enough time to file a convincing report to MI6 saying that you couldn't find anything. As far as you're concerned, Milot and I have never met, and you have no evidence whatsoever that we are ever likely to. We have great plans for the UK, and we have no intention of letting an annoying little insect like you mess them up.'

'I don't know what you're talking about.' Jay stuck to her cover story, as the army had taught her. 'I only came here to find my friend ... '

'And if MI6 are sceptical, you'll find a way to convince them,' Vadic went on, ignoring her. 'There is always a way, if you are motivated enough. Are you motivated, Jay McCaulay?'

Finally, she nodded. Once Raman was free and she was in England and safely away from this piece of shit, she would renege.

'I give you my word.'

'Your word,' Vadic sneered, 'is worthless.'

Jay tried to think how she could persuade him otherwise, but once again he'd turned his attention to the mincing machine. At his command, the men dragged Raman to one side. He was still bucking and groaning and although he'd lost a shoe, Jay couldn't see any blood.

'If you break your promise,' Vadic said, 'this demonstration will not be re-enacted on a worthless little boy.'

Vadic gestured at the two men in shiny suits who walked and opened the door. Huddled on the floor was a sobbing figure clutching two small children. Nadire and the twins.

Jay's heart went cold.

'No,' she said.

'Yes,' he replied. 'Because if I hear you telling anyone about our meeting, or reneging on our arrangement, I shall take your friends one by one and I will kill them. Starting with the snivelling little brats.'

Jay tried to lash out but Hashim held her fast. 'You bastard,' she hissed.

'I can do the same for anyone I choose,' he went on. 'Nick Morgan, your work colleagues, the lesbians you share a house with ... nobody is safe, you understand? I have friends throughout European law enforcement. I have powerful friends in Paris, Frankfurt and London. If you renege, I will hear of it.'

He came and stood in front of her. 'I despise women like you. Childless, without a husband. What good are you? You think you're equal to men, but you're pathetic. I could kill you so easily, Jay McCaulay. You could be dead right now, but there would be too many questions.'

He jerked his chin at the man holding her. Keeping the pistol against her temple, Hashim took a step backwards. She swayed violently. Her legs were trembling, but she managed to draw her shoulders back and push her chin high.

'Okay. I won't tell anyone of this,' she told Vadic, 'but I want something from you first.'

Vadic blinked. Obviously few people made demands at this point of the negotiations. She felt a flicker of satisfaction that she'd broken the mould.

'I want you to release my friends to me. Now.'

Eighteen

Jay staggered outside with Raman, Nadire and the twins. Night had drawn in and a bank of thick cloud loomed low in the sky. Puddles of pale, white light flickered from street lamps, struggling to illuminate the surroundings. She felt dizzy and close to vomiting and was glad the air was cold. It helped steady her.

Hashim threw her day pack at her feet before following Vadic and his henchmen to the line of Mercedes cars parked in the factory forecourt. Doors were slammed, engines started and headlights flicked on and, one by one, they pulled away.

'Are you all right?' Jay was urgently checking Raman. 'Your foot. I heard the machine make a noise.'

'It was my shoe,' he said. His voice was small. 'It fell off and got minced and I thought it was about to be me . . . '

His skin was waxy, his chin quivering, and he was doing his best not to cry but tears were trickling down his narrow face. Jay put her arms around him, and he returned her embrace with a ferocity that implied relief and terror.

'You're safe now. Jesus, I am so sorry.' She kissed the top of his head, holding him tightly and rubbing his back. 'I never meant for this to happen. Jesus.' Glancing across, she saw Nadire was on her knees, sobbing, the twins wailing and clinging to her like petrified monkeys. 'You okay?' she called.

'My head hurts,' choked Nadire. She spoke between sobs.

'They attacked us when we went shopping . . . I tried to stop them but they hit my head and I don't remember anything else . . .'

Jay shuffled across and tilted Nadire's head towards the street lights to check her pupils but as far as she could tell they weren't abnormally small. She hoped Nadire didn't have concussion. She had a large swelling where she'd been hit but the cut was minimal and wouldn't need stitches. Jay was shivering – the aftermath of shock – but she returned to continue hugging Raman until, finally, he made a little movement indicating he was readying himself to pull away.

She quickly checked the twins before ushering the little group to the street. An elderly woman shuffled past clutching two shopping bags, her shoulders hunched against the cold. Jay was amazed she didn't look at them. She felt as though they should stand out like fluorescent-yellow bollards after the horror they'd shared.

Pulling out her phone, Jay first called Kiro, and then Una. Both reacted fast, and within the hour Nadire and the twins were safely at home with Una, and Kiro and Jay were walking Raman to his front door.

Raman paused before he went inside. 'Will you be coming back to Tetovo?'

Jay ducked down to look the boy in the eye. 'No, I won't. But when I get back to the UK, I'll write to you, okay? You can be my pen friend.'

His expression turned puzzled. 'Don't you want me to find out where they're meeting?'

'Absolutely not! I don't want you ever to come in contact with any of those men again. The meeting isn't nearly as important as keeping us all safe, okay?'

'Okay.' He looked hurt.

'Will you write to me?'

'Sure.'

The last she saw of Raman was his silhouette as he stood in the doorway, watching them go. He was so small and skinny, his tuft of hair so pronounced, he could have been an ear of corn.

*

On the return journey to Skopje, Jay was glad Kiro didn't launch a barrage of questions but allowed her time to take stock, let the last of the adrenalin evaporate. Just because she'd served in the army didn't mean she was immune to horror and fear. In Basra she'd been near an explosion, a roadside bomb. Soldiers and civilians were down, bleeding, and she did her job, guarding her platoon and helping the injured. After holding a local boy in her arms while he died, she wanted to cry but she didn't. She had to be hard, tough in front of the men, and today had been no different.

'You did well,' Kiro said. He was cruising along the highway, fingers tapping on the steering wheel. 'Comforting Nadire and Raman, getting them out of there unharmed. You did a really good job.'

It was what she needed to hear. She immediately felt a trickle of calm seep into her.

'Thanks, Kiro.'

As her emotional strength gradually returned, Jay began to analyse the last few hours. She couldn't understand why Vadic had shown himself to her. Wouldn't it have been better to have Milot do his dirty work? Or did it have something to do with proving who was boss? What had Laura Sharpe said? That Vadic was vindictive and paranoid but, more importantly, was *willing to do whatever it takes to preserve his superiority.*

He'd certainly proved himself at the meat-processing plant. Milot had behaved like a lapdog, obsequious and compliant. Was that the point Vadic wanted to make? That he was the Big Boss in Tetovo and Milot just a foot soldier?

'It's time you filled me in.' Kiro turned his head to look at her. 'The real reason why you came to Macedonia. And no holding back.'

She glanced down at her hands, strong and square and criss-crossed with the tiny white scars she'd received from the bomb blast in Basra. God, another tour in Iraq seemed almost preferable to facing Vadic and his band of merry men again.

'Ice?'

She raised her head. She didn't want to involve Kiro, but he was right; the time had come to give him an explanation.

'MI6 asked me to scout around and see if the Georgian Mafia are going to team up with Milot's mob.'

Kiro didn't appear to turn a hair at her confession. 'And?'

'Milot was obviously told what I was up to. He picked me up to warn me off.'

'Jesus.' Kiro looked shaken. 'You're lucky to get out alive. He *hates* spies.'

Not as much, she thought with a shudder, as Vadic, who teased his victim's entrails from their bellies. Milot simply minced them to death, which was brutal but a lot quicker. Glancing ahead, she saw they were approaching the toll booths, lit orange and yellow. Only one was manned. Keeping the Lada rolling, Kiro chucked a handful of change into the automated machine and the barrier lifted.

The meeting was obviously important, Jay thought. Why take a sledgehammer to squash an ant? By threatening Nadire and the twins, as well as Raman, Vadic had exposed just how much it meant to him. She'd love to see who he was meeting and explode a stick of dynamite in his plans. Every soldier and police officer knew that organised crime groups funded terrorist activities, and where the Mafia hated spies, she loathed terrorists.

'You've got that look in your eye,' said Kiro, sounding weary. 'Please tell me you're not thinking what I think you're thinking, because it is a seriously bad idea.'

'I don't like being threatened,' she said.

'It's not just you they're threatening.'

'I don't need reminding, Kiro.'

They spent the remainder of the journey in silence.

They arrived outside Kiro's apartment just after nine o'clock, but it felt much later to Jay. Exhausted, she climbed out of the car, skirted an industrial-sized rubbish bin and nearly trod on a small dog curled among the tangled roots of a plane tree. Luckily it didn't bite her, just gave her a baleful look.

'Sorry,' she told it. The dog went back to sleep.

Jay was relieved Rosanna was away – in Milan, apparently, for the rest of the week – she felt she didn't have the strength to make small talk. And she was starving. She followed Kiro around to the front door at the side of the building, thinking of nothing but what might be in the fridge and possibly opening a bottle of red wine, when she saw a shadow materialise to the side of the front door.

Not again!

Immediately she went on the offensive. Three swift steps and she had the figure in a headlock, right arm rammed high between the shoulder blades. The body arched backwards, taut as a bow. Unconsciously, Jay had imitated Hashim's vice-like hold at the meat-processing plant.

'Jay, it's me. For God's sake, *Jay*.'

She took in the fact the figure was smaller than herself. Much smaller. And that it was female. She spun the woman around. 'Laura?'

'Jesus Christ, Jay.' The MI6 agent pushed back a lock of dark hair from her face. Her hand was trembling. 'You scared the crap out of me.'

'Yeah, well.' Jay didn't feel in the mood to apologise. Not after the day she'd had. 'You shouldn't be creeping around people's doorsteps at night and giving them a heart-attack either.'

'I dropped by to see how you were. I left a note.' Laura gestured lamely at the letterbox set in the door.

It was Kiro who opened the door and picked it up. He raised an eyebrow at Jay as he passed it across, asking her what she wanted to do. She glanced down at the note. She'd much rather have a hot bath and a meal than spend the evening dodging Laura's questions, but she was wary of palming the agent off. She didn't want any MI6 alarm bells to start ringing.

'Join us for a drink?' Jay offered.

'Oh, I wouldn't want to bother you . . .'

'Stop being so bloody British,' said Kiro, 'and say yes please, I'd love a drink.'

Laura looked askance at Kiro. Then she smiled. 'Yes, please,' she said. 'I'd love a drink.' She was an attractive woman, and from the solicitous way Kiro was now ushering her inside, he wasn't immune to the fact either.

With a bottle of red on the wooden coffee table in front of her, along with salted nuts, olives and pumpkin seeds, Jay nibbled and drank and prayed Laura wouldn't ask any awkward questions – she barely had the energy to blink let alone defend against a major verbal offensive.

Kiro fed Marko and switched on the oven before sticking his head in the fridge and having a look. 'Chicken, or chicken?' he asked them.

'I'd love chicken,' said Laura. She sent Jay a grin. She was learning fast.

'Lovely,' Jay agreed. She couldn't help the yawn that escaped. Tears collected in the corners of her eyes and she wiped them away. The wine had hit her system fast and was making her sleepy.

'Tough day?' asked Laura. Kicking off her shoes, she slipped on to the sofa next to Jay and tucked her legs neatly beneath her.

'Not particularly,' she lied.

'I heard you're looking for a girl who's run away. Zamira Kalisi.'

'Your intel's good.'

'Any luck finding her?'

'Not yet.'

Laura took a long sip of wine. 'I also heard a rumour you'd upset some people in Tetovo. What was all that about?'

Christ, news travelled fast! She busied herself pouring more wine, feverishly trying to work out a cover story but then just as quickly discarding it. Laura would see straight through her if she tried to lie.

Fixing her gaze on Marko, who was now washing his face next to his biscuit bowl, she said, 'They thought my asking questions about Zamira was an excuse to delve into their business. I managed to persuade them otherwise.'

'Did you?' Laura looked sceptical. 'I didn't think that lot were particularly persuadable once they got an idea in their Neanderthal little brains.'

In the kitchen, Kiro was putting a chicken in the oven, seemingly deaf to their conversation, but Jay could tell he was eavesdropping by the way his head was cocked their way.

'There was no reason for them to think I was spying on them,' Jay said. It was only now that she realised she still hadn't any news of Zamira, which made her feel even more exhausted and disheartened.

'Who did you speak to?' Laura asked. 'I know you'll give a full report to the office tomorrow, but it would help me in the meantime. I'm meeting with a bunch of defence attaches in the morning and they need to know.'

'Milot and a thug called Hashim.'

Laura blinked. 'You spoke to Milot himself?'

'Yup.' She wasn't going to mention Vadic's name if she could help it. She had to keep Nadire and the twins safe, as well as her parents, and Raman.

'Good grief.' Laura was still looking taken aback. 'You were lucky he didn't flay you alive if he thought you were poking your nose into his business.'

'He said it would cause him too much hassle.'

Another blink. 'He's right. We'd go mad if anything happened to you. He obviously knows that.'

Did Vadic know that? Was that why he'd released them unscathed? Or was he relying on the power of violent menaces and threats to keep them in line?

'Did you learn anything about Milot teaming up with the Georgian lot? If he and Vadic are in bed together?' Laura's demeanour remained the same but Jay saw something quicken at the back of her eyes.

'Nothing, I'm afraid.'

'Really? Are you sure?'

Please God, make the agent believe her. 'I'm sure,' she said.

Laura put down her glass and leaned forward. 'Look, those Mafia guys can be really scary. Did they try to intimidate you in any way? Because if they did, we've got to know so we can put preventative measures in place.'

'Of course they intimidated me! They bloody scared me half to death!'

Laura looked irritated. 'I meant did they threaten your family? Did they try to turn you against us?'

'They wouldn't be who they are if they didn't give me a good mental hiding.'

As Kiro moved into the kitchen, Laura dropped her voice to a whisper. 'In Pristina, I heard something about a big meeting coming up. Did you hear anything? I need it confirmed.'

Dread crawled over Jay's skin. Vadic's bitter, sugary aftershave was still clogging her senses, his threats echoing in her mind.

'I might have,' said Jay.

Laura stared. 'Do you know where it's happening?'

Jay shook her head.

'I heard it was in the mountains, near Tetovo.'

Jay felt a jolt of excitement. With Milot and Vadic already in Tetovo it made sense, and she'd bet if they were meeting in the mountains it wouldn't be in a hut, but somewhere flash and expensive, like one of the five-star ski resorts.

'It's just a thought,' offered Jay. 'But since it's out of season, a resort or private chalet could easily be commandeered, and being the Mafia capital of Macedonia—'

'It's also the perfect place for a clandestine meet,' Laura finished for her. Her eyes were bright.

'Have you covered the airports?' Jay asked, 'to see who's coming in? You could always follow them.'

'Yes,' Laura sighed, 'but no names have popped up, so there's no one to follow.'

'Which means everyone involved is either already here, or on their way overland.' Jay thought some more, and reckoned on the former. 'I think the meeting's imminent, like tomorrow or the next day.'

'I agree.'

'What will you do?'

'Keep my ears and eyes open. You do the same. The second we know where they're meeting, we move in, see what they're up to.'

They sat in silence for a moment. Kiro opened a packet of crisps and poured them into a bowl and brought them over.

'Chicken in half an hour, ladies.'

Scents of garlic were wafting across the room and making Jay's stomach groan. She could have picked up the chicken in both hands and eaten it whole she was so hungry.

Still keeping her voice low, Jay turned back to Laura. 'Who told you Milot had me pegged?'

'Sorry, I can't divulge that. But I'm glad the information he gave us has proved correct, because we were wondering if he was entirely trustworthy.'

It was Jay's turn to be surprised. 'You've someone on the inside?'

In response, Laura raised a finger to her lips, flicking her gaze to Kiro.

'I didn't think it was possible,' Jay said. Which one of the mob was reporting to MI6? Had she seen him today? Could it be Hashim? Or was it one of the men in shiny suits? God, this game gave her a headache. It was like trying to complete a jigsaw with only half the pieces. Out of nowhere, she recalled a tall, unshaven man dressed in faded jeans and a thick blue donkey jacket.

'It's Max Blake, isn't it?'

Laura's eyes widened. 'Blake? How the hell did Blake come into this?'

'He's, ah . . . ' Jay's mind began to scramble. 'I don't know.'

'You haven't seen him, have you?'

'Er, last week. At my house.' Which was true, but inside, her nerves were screaming. What the heck was going on? Why didn't Laura know Blake was out here?

'So why mention him?'

'He seems like an interesting guy,' Jay said lamely.

'Oh, God.' Laura rolled her eyes to the ceiling. 'Don't tell me you're smitten too. Half the bloody women in the office keep his picture on their desks.'

'Isn't he with SOCA?'

'SOCA, and anyone else who can pay his exorbitant fees.' Laura downed the remainder of her wine. 'Whoever pays the most wins that guy's loyalty. Which is why I wouldn't trust him as far as I could throw him.' Pushing back her hair, the agent resettled herself. 'But enough about Blake. I want to know where Milot took you, and what he said. Consider this an official debriefing.' She grinned cheerfully. 'But with wine.'

By the time Jay crawled into bed, she could barely keep her eyes open. Her last thought before sleep overcame her was: Christ, spying's hard work.

She slept heavily, dreamless, and only woke when she heard her mobile chirp just after dawn, alerting her that she had a text. Rolling over, she saw it was from Laura:

> Meet me outside the Museum Skopje 1000 hours.
> I know you are lying about Vadic.

Nineteen

'Keep your chin up,' Branko told Zamira. 'Don't slouch. You've got to look confident.'

He continued chivvying the girl to stop her from panicking. It was always a difficult balance to achieve as they approached the Immigration desks. The girls had to fear the authorities so that he retained control, but they also had to appear older than they were and not act like wide-eyed and terrified kids.

'Don't forget,' he reminded her, 'one slip and they'll be on you like a pack of dogs.'

Zamira was gazing at the passport officer, a handsome black woman with little gold-rimmed glasses and bright pink lipstick that matched her nails. The woman was smiling and chatting as she processed an Indian businessman's passport.

'She looks nice,' Zamira whispered.

'As nice as a snake in a suit,' he snapped. 'I've already told you it's all a sham. They're worse than the police at home. If you put a foot wrong they'll take you to a cell and rape you before beating you senseless. They don't want immigrants here. They hate us.'

He was relieved to see the fear return to Zamira's eyes. He didn't want her answering back or thinking for herself. He wanted absolute obedience, or he'd be thrown into jail faster than he could say the word lawyer.

Licking a forefinger he turned to the wall-sized mirror and

smoothed an eyebrow. He knew all about the officials that sat on the other side, scrutinising and evaluating everyone as they passed. They had the authority to interview whatever passenger they liked, whenever they liked, but they'd never stopped him. He knew he had the brains to go with the balls, which was why he was so successful at this game.

Across the hall, he caught a uniformed security guard staring at Zamira, who was staring back like a petrified rabbit.

He had to be careful when he broke the spell between them. He didn't want the guard remembering anything about Zamira later.

'Stop staring at the poor bloke,' Branko told her. 'He might think you fancy him and come over and ask you for a date.'

She jerked her head around, her cheeks flaming, and he chuckled. 'You shouldn't be so pretty,' he told her, and then he saw the Indian businessman was moving ahead and it was their turn to be processed.

This was the most dangerous moment, when he accompanied a girl to the desk. It didn't help that Zamira understood a handful of English words and phrases either, picked up from her spell in the refugee camp years ago. He would have to be doubly vigilant.

He greeted the black woman politely. 'Good morning.'

The woman ignored him and looked directly at Zamira, who smiled and said, 'Good morning,' just as he'd taught her.

The woman took their passports with a nod. 'Where did you travel from today?'

'From Vienna. Before that, Skopje.'

'And the purpose of your visit?' Again she was looking at Zamira who – unable to understand a word – was now looking desperately at Branko.

'Tourism,' he replied. He wished Zamira would stop looking like a stricken puppy but there was little he could do without giving the game away.

'How old are you?' the woman asked Zamira.

'Your age,' Branko prompted Zamira in Albanian.

'I am sixteen,' Zamira said in English.

The woman nodded, and looked at Zamira again. To his relief, Zamira came good by pasting a brilliant smile on her face. The woman stared, then dropped her gaze to her computer screen. After tapping on her keyboard, she double-checked their passports, then finally stamped them and waved them through.

Branko put his arm around Zamira. 'Good girl. I know you were scared, but you didn't panic. You didn't let me down.'

She gave a wobbly smile, near to tears, and he pressed a kiss on her forehead. 'My brave little Peaches. Now, I think you deserve a reward. Shall we get a London taxi?'

Instantly, her eyes lit up. 'A black cab?'

He laughed. 'Yes. We'll try and find one with a TV in the back, shall we?'

Zamira couldn't believe she was coming into London. The taxi was driving along a raised dual carriageway and she could see roads and buildings stretching in every direction, right to the horizon. Aircraft were lined up in the sky, coming in to land, and streams of traffic poured past; cars and buses and trucks. It felt as though every human in the world was in her sight, and for a second, she felt completely overwhelmed. It was so huge.

'Pretty amazing, huh?' said Branko.

She nodded, not trusting herself to speak. She felt very small, and not a little frightened.

'Now, Peaches. Where's your passport?'

She patted her breast pocket. She'd kept it close to her; she was terrified of losing it. Apparently if you got stopped on the street and didn't have your passport with you, you were thrown into jail.

'Can I have it? I think it would be wise if I looked after it for you. Is that okay?'

Zamira passed it over, relieved not to have the responsibility.

'Now, when we get to Hana's, I want you to be as good as you can, as good as gold. Hana's working at the restaurant this morning so she won't be there, but a friend of hers will be coming over later instead. He's called Quinton, and I want you to be nice to him. If you are, he'll look after you.'

Alarmed, she said, 'You're staying too, aren't you?'

'Of course I am, Peaches.' He reached across and tucked a stray hair behind her ear. His hand was as warm as bread and smelled of the lemony cologne he'd tried in Vienna's duty free.

'You don't have to worry about a thing. I'm just telling you about Quinton, so you don't panic when he turns up and not Hana.'

She nodded, her attention taken up by a pair of full-length emerald snake-skin boots that she spied in a shop window. What she wouldn't do for a pair of those! They were now in the heart of the West End, rattling past shops and red buses and mail boxes. She was still pinching herself, wondering if she was dreaming, when the taxi pulled up outside a handsome, tall red-brick building.

While Branko paid the driver, Zamira climbed outside. There was a faintly metallic smell in the air, overlaid by the odour of frying garlic and something weirdly abrasive, like washing powder. As she greedily inhaled the foreign smells she had a momentary flash of distaste. The clarity of the mountain air she'd known for most of her life seemed terribly far away and she swayed, feeling dizzy and displaced.

'Peaches? You okay?'

Branko was at her side, looking concerned.

She pushed the feeling aside. She wasn't a girl from the mountains any more. She was a city girl, a girl with a job, a career, and an incredible future ahead of her. And when she saw the apartment, for the first time since she'd left home she thought of her mother, who would have fainted with shock. It was ten times more beautiful than she had imagined. It had thick cream carpets and gold tables and mirrors, and as Branko had told her, it overlooked the park, and she could see a coffee shop and people walking their dogs, and pushing their children in pushchairs.

She felt as though her heart might burst. Her dream had come true. She was in London.

Twenty

'Can I borrow your car?'

'What for?'

'Because I want to vacuum your apartment with it,' Jay said. 'Why do you think, Kiro?'

He regarded her suspiciously. 'Where are you going?'

'Vladivostok?' She moved to the window and looked outside so he couldn't read her face. 'Seriously, Kiro, all I need it for is to get around for the day. I want to drop in to the OSCE and visit a couple of the lawyers who were involved in that THB trial last year, see if any of them can get me a lead on Branko or Zamira. Then I thought I might go up to Lake Matka and catch up with Art and Emine if they're around. I'd like to visit the monastery, maybe have lunch with them.'

'They'd love to see you.'

Art and Emine were friends of Kiro's that Jay had met when she'd last been in Skopje. 'You could join us, if you like,' she added. It was her best attempt at being devious, and she held her breath to see if it had worked.

'Okay,' Kiro agreed. 'Drop me off at the office and it's yours for the day. I can't do lunch, but if you could collect me around six tonight, that would be great. We can have supper at Intermezzo.'

Jay approached the Museum of Skopje in a state of high caution, aware that Laura's phone could have been commandeered, and that – God forbid – the agent could have been compromised, coerced or kidnapped. With the big Mafia boys only a stone's throw away in Tetovo, anything could have happened.

Leaving the Lada on the other side of the flower market, Jay walked along the Mito Hazi Vasile, traffic pouring past, and when she glanced right, to the broad pedestrianised street that led to Makedonija Square, she saw the cafés had already put their tables and chairs outside ready for the lunchtime rush.

Two uniformed policemen stood at the foot of the museum steps, smoking, but otherwise there was nobody about. The museum was shut for renovations. Crossing the street, Jay walked back on the opposite pavement. Still no Laura. She kept walking, unable to get the agent's text out of her head.

I know you are lying about Vadic.

Did Laura really know Milot and Vadic were working together, or was it a ruse to get her here? Jay continued to skirt the area but she didn't see Laura, or anybody who looked remotely suspicious, unless the ancient old woman selling herbs out of her baggy overall pockets was some sort of agent.

She walked her circuit twice more, and she had just decided to cap her time here, give Laura five more minutes, when her phone rang.

'Hello?'

'Hi, gorgeous.' It was Tom.

'Hi, handsome.'

'Everything okay?'

'Er . . . fine . . . ' Glancing north, she saw a small, lithe figure walking briskly past the cafes. She wore jeans, a high-waisted jacket and a pair of little pointy boots. Slung across her shoulder was a small, expensive-looking leather shoulder bag. It was Laura.

'Jay?'

'Yup.'

'How's Macedonia?'

Jay began to cross the road, dodging between rusting buses and trucks.

'Sorry, Tom, but you've got me at a bad time ... ' Jay's attention was caught by something behind Laura, a stocky, muscular man moving fast. Her breathing jammed in shock. It was Hashim, who'd held her while Vadic threatened to kill Raman and then pull her entrails from her belly. Hashim had something in his right hand. He seemed intent on Laura.

'Shit,' she breathed.

'What's wrong?'

'Tom, I've got to go. I'll call you back, okay?' She hung up. Hashim was quickly catching up with Laura, who appeared oblivious. Jay followed, accelerating her pace.

Hashim brushed past Laura, and if Jay hadn't been watching him at that second, she would have missed the movement, it was so quick. His hand brushed Laura's shoulder bag, and then he peeled away and began waving at a man in a café who, after a brief pause, began waving back.

What the heck was going on? Had the man dropped a live grenade in Laura's bag? Tried to steal something from her?

Laura's expression turned to alarm as Jay ran up to her. 'What's wrong?'

'One of Milot's men just tried to interfere with your bag,' she panted. 'Just now. He was right behind you.'

Laura immediately put her bag on the ground and opened it to check. Notebook, camera, purse, lipstick, dictaphone. Laura quickly sifted through the items. 'Nothing here that shouldn't be.'

Jay glanced at the café but Hashim had vanished. The guy he'd waved at was nowhere to be seen. Switching her attention back to Laura, she saw the agent was holding a book of matches. Her expression was one of astonishment. 'Fucksake,' she said.

'What is it?'

'It's a message.' Laura held the book of matches so Jay could see. On the front was a picture of a snow-covered Swiss-looking chalet, with skiers drinking cocktails on its balcony.

Sunny Hill.

Laura flipped the book open.

Written clearly on the underside of the lid in black pen were the numbers 1500 and the word *Denes.*

'Fifteen hundred hours,' Laura said, 'today.'

She closed the book and tapped the picture of the chalet with her finger.

'That's where the meeting's being held.'

The Lada's rear wheels slipped on an icy hairpin bend and Jay eased her foot from the throttle, bringing it back under control. Tetovo lay below them, a brown-and-white smear of low-slung buildings shrouded by wood smoke choked mist. She could only just make it out through the falling snow. The last of the winter freeze, and it had to be today.

An ancient VW Beetle trailed behind them, spewing exhaust. Two old people sat in the front, with what looked like a fully-grown sheep squeezed in the back. Jay guessed they were headed for Novo Selo, on the other side of the mountains near where Nadire lived – and where the road ran out.

Laura dug around in her shoulder bag and extracted the match book and, to Jay's surprise, a packet of cigarettes. Lighting up, she opened the window a crack and said, 'Who's Tom?'

Laura had been walking with her when Jay had rung Tom back. It hadn't been the best conversation, with her trying to reassure him she was fine when she had an MI6 agent breathing down her neck. Tom had picked up on her tension and nothing she said had dispelled his concern.

'Tom, I'm fine,' she said. 'I promise.'

'I've heard that one before.'

'I swear I'm okay.'

'Be careful, do you hear me? I happen to quite like you. Sometimes.'

She smiled. 'And I quite like you too. Sometimes.'

'Is Tom your boyfriend?' Laura prompted.

'I'll tell you if you give me a cigarette.'

Laura looked surprised. 'I didn't know you smoked.'

'Does that mean you don't know everything about me?'

'God, yes. I've learned over the years to trust the written report only so far.' She shook out a cigarette. 'Shall I light it for you?'

'Great.'

Laura passed it over before putting the pack and Hashim's match book in the plastic well between them.

The Marlboro was imported, not one of the locally produced counterfeits that were smuggled in vast quantities across Europe, and Jay's first pull made her head spin.

'Yes, Tom's my boyfriend. He wants to marry me.'

'Is that a problem?'

'Yes.'

'Do you love him?'

She shrugged. She didn't need a therapist to tell her she had commitment issues. Confrontation issues too. It was time she made a supreme effort to face them head on rather than bolting for the horizon like a panicked horse.

'Tell me about the guy who dropped off the book of matches,' Jay said. 'How long has Hashim been your snitch?'

'About six months or so.'

'I thought you said the Mafia was virtually impossible to penetrate.'

'Hashim's greedier than most. He also wants immunity should we ever take them down. It was Hashim who told me you'd lied about Milot and Vadic teaming up. You must have been really scared, Jay. I know I would have been terrified. Threatening a little boy like that ... '

What felt like a dozen ants scurried across the nape of her neck. 'Hashim told you about Raman?'

'And your friend Nadire being threatened, along with the twins. Hashim didn't give too many details, just ... Hey, slow down, will you? I think we're there.' Laura leaned forward, pointing at a narrow, snow-filled track leading almost vertically up the mountain. 'That's it. That's the road.'

'Road?' Jay repeated. 'That's not a road. That's a goat track.'

'This car will make it, though, won't it? I know it's a heap of shit, but it's still a four-wheel-drive.'

Jay slowed the car to a stop. Snow was the most deceptive off-road surface, because it didn't necessarily conform with the terrain it covered. The worst scenario would be if the track collapsed under the weight of the car and they got stuck. She hadn't realised it was going to snow, and if they had to walk back to Tetovo, they could be in trouble.

When she laid it on the line to Laura, the agent looked alarmed. 'I thought you said you could pretty much drive this car anywhere.'

'I didn't realise you were taking us up Mount Everest.'

'But it's the only way we'll be able to watch them and remain hidden. We've got snow-jackets and boots. We'll be fine.'

MI6 obviously hadn't sent Laura on any arctic-survival training exercises recently. Her grip on the reality of the situation was minimal. Dying of exposure was a real risk up here. The snow was coming in short bursts, followed by a brief pause, but what worried Jay was the top of the mountain, which had vanished behind a wall of grey cloud.

'Come on, Jay.' Laura was getting impatient. 'It's less than two miles before we reach the trees. They'll never know we're there.' She showed Jay the map, pointing out the green strip of conifers near the top of the mountain, overlooking the chalet. Jay had to admit it looked like the perfect vantage point. 'You don't want Milot getting the better of you, do you?'

It wasn't Milot as much as Vadic who Jay wanted to take a fall, but the agent sure knew how to drive in the nail. She'd love to get some information on Vadic that might help SOCA, Customs, Interpol – everyone involved in fighting the extending tentacles of organised crime – and the temptation to spy on him was incredibly tempting. She watched the VW Beetle crawl past and shudder around the next corner. It was definitely a sheep in the back.

'Two miles,' repeated Laura. 'We'll be out of here well before nightfall, I promise.'

'On your head be it,' Jay said.

'Put your foot down, then!'

Before she committed herself to the mountainside, Jay double-checked the map, then locked the centre differential. Keeping the car in the middle of the track, she drove with gentle adjustments to the steering wheel and speed, as though she was driving in slow-motion, and to her surprise the little car responded with a business-like, no-nonsense capability, and they reached the trees with a minimum of fuss.

'There,' said Laura. 'I told you we'd be okay.'

Jay parked the Lada between the trees, as well hidden as possible. She pulled on a down jacket she'd swiped from Kiro's apartment and zipped it up under her chin. Next came a scarf, woolly hat and sheepskin-lined gloves; she hated to be cold. Laura, on the other hand, hadn't bothered with hat or gloves and was already out of the car and crunching to the tree line. Jay followed at a distance, caution dogging her heels. She kept glancing around her, checking that no one else was about and that she could see the way clearly back to the car.

Finally, she took up position next to Laura on the edge of the trees where they were reasonably concealed, and looked down into the valley. A large Alpine ski lodge of yellow wood stood perched on the edge of some lateral moraines. Below the lodge were a variety of four-wheel-drives: Range Rovers, BMWs, Mercedes; and further west, on a raised apron, sat a helicopter, its rotors tied down. Laura was looking through a pair of high-powered binoculars and reciting number plates into a miniature dictaphone.

Jay studied the terrain and could see the wind scurrying across glimpses of jagged rocks, veiling them with spindrift. Thundering down the valley was a river, black and deep and swollen with snow melt. Ice-crusted boulders lined it on either side. She checked her watch. Fifteen minutes past two. The meeting was meant to start in forty-five minutes.

The faint buzz of an engine reached her.

She stilled her breath, listening.

The buzz grew louder, and with a lurch she recognised it as the continuous clatter of a helicopter's rotors.

'Last minute attendee,' remarked Laura.

Gradually, the shuddering clatter increased until they could see the machine heading up the valley. Soon it was banking sharply and circling over the lodge. Jay raised her binoculars to see it was a private helicopter with a civil aircraft marking. She couldn't see inside; the windows were tinted.

The helicopter banked a fraction, hovering directly above the lodge, then descended to around a hundred feet. It banked a little more and continued inching around the lodge, and she realised that whoever was inside was scrutinising the area, checking for tracks of people who shouldn't be there.

Although Laura had chosen her vantage point well – close enough to spy effectively with binoculars but far enough away not to pose an immediate threat if they were spotted – Jay was glad they'd hidden the car, and that their footprints were obscured in the forest.

Seemingly oblivious of their presence, the helicopter drifted to hover above the apron. Snow and spindrift circled the air, whipped by the downdraft.

The chopper was hovering fifty feet or so from the ground when it executed a full turn. A final three-sixty degree check.

Whoever was on board was either ultra-cautious or paranoid. Probably both.

The helicopter finally committed itself to land. The engines had barely been switched off when two men climbed out. One wore a suit and shiny, city shoes. Jay didn't recognise him, but she recognised the type. He wore success and power lazily, like a cape across his shoulders. His companion stood back, slightly obsequious, before they walked for the lodge. Jay took him to be a bodyguard.

'Jesus Christ,' Laura was gasping.

'Who is he?'

'Oh fuck, oh fuck.'

Laura was scrabbling at her jacket, cursing. She thrust the dictaphone in one pocket, brought out a camera from another and started snapping. Her breathing was shallow, her hands trembling.

A handful of men came out of the lodge to greet the arrivals. Once she'd identified Vadic, Milot, and Hashim, Jay turned her binoculars to the two newcomers and studied them carefully.

The first man, the one with the power, would be easy to identify again because he immediately reminded her of a bull, with his broad shoulders, short legs, and wide forehead, but his bodyguard was more difficult. He was smaller, and looked like most Albanians; short and even-featured with dark hair. Looking further, she studied the shape of his head to see it was narrower than most, and that his hair was cut with a little point at the nape of his neck. He also had a slightly receding chin. Although she looked hard, she couldn't see any further outstanding features. The impression she got was that although he appeared to carry himself well and with confidence, he was in fact wary. He was like an anxious Asian wolf dogging a bull's heels.

As Vadic's party began to usher their guests inside, Jay's binoculars moved to the back of the lodge, where a man stood guard over the rear door. He had his back towards her but something about him jarred. He wore jeans and what looked like a flack-jacket over a black roll-neck sweater. Nothing out of the ordinary, but then he turned his head and her heart gave a bump.

It was Max Blake.

Laura took some more shots of the disappearing group before putting down her camera. Her fingers were trembling.

'Who is he?' Jay asked.

'Just one of the most powerful organised crime bosses in the world, Luigi Protti. I can't believe he's meeting with Milot and Vadic. This is such bad news.'

Laura was right. It was bad enough having the Albanians and Georgians hooking up, but the Italians as well? Did this mean the three Mafia organisations were amalgamating into one giant clan, a collective business?

'We've got to get out of here and report at once.' Laura pushed her camera inside her jacket and began to head back towards the car. 'If the connections aren't immediately severed between the three clans ... Christ, I hope they haven't already taken root. They'll link not only to terrorist organisations worldwide, but every drug dealer, arms dealer, every smuggler ... It could become the biggest multinational business in the world.' Laura turned to look at Jay. 'It'll be just about indestructible.'

Jay said, 'What was Blake doing there?'

'That bastard.'

'He's not undercover?'

'As undercover as a scorpion in your shoe. That lying bastard, he's been a thorn in my side ... '

Crack!

Jay stumbled sideways as Laura collapsed into the snow. Her ears were ringing, her mind stunned as another crack slammed through the trees, echoing along the valley and rolling over and around her.

She took in Laura's sprawled form, the blood seeping at the neck of her jacket. Adrenalin gushed through Jay's veins.

Laura had been shot.

Twenty-one

Snow kicked from a tree trunk inches from Jay's face. She wanted to stop and help Laura, but she was too exposed. She turned tail and ran back the way she'd come, slipping and stumbling over the uneven frozen ground, her binoculars thumping against her neck and breastbone.

Voices shouted behind her, shots rang out. She heard a man yelling, 'Not her! You're after the wrong one!' and another screaming back, 'She's a fucking spy, you moron! Kill her!'

Another shot rang out. It sounded as though it came from an AK47 but it hadn't hit her. Thank God, it hadn't hit her . . .

Dumping her binoculars, she increased her speed, putting every effort into reaching the car before they did. Plan A. If she could do that, then she might have a chance. Belt down the mountain to the main road, and head for Tetovo, find help for Laura. Oh God, Laura. Jay wondered if the agent was dead, and if not, whether they would use her as a bargaining chip of some sort. She had no doubt the Mafia would attempt to use the MI6 agent to their advantage.

A few minutes later, she saw the outline of Kiro's car through the trees, but two guys stood next to it, rifles resting against their hips. The Lada's bonnet was raised, indicating the engine had probably been disabled.

Okay. Plan B.

Jay slipped away and headed back to the tree line, starting to scoop north, away from the lodge. They would find her tracks soon, she must hurry.

As soon as the lodge was out of sight, she plunged down the mountainside and into the valley, her eyes fixed on the roaring, tumbling river below. A flurry of snow obliterated the river and for a second, her world went white. Sweet Jesus no, she thought. The last thing she needed was a whiteout. All she could do in this situation was head downhill, head out of the mountains and get away from the storm.

Scrambling down the slope, she clutched a stunted shrub to keep her balance and glanced up to check on her pursuers. She couldn't see anyone behind her. The grey cloud that had blanketed the tops of the mountains earlier had descended, and was shrouding the trees. On the one hand this was good, because she'd be harder to spot, but on the other it meant she was alone in the wilderness with nothing but the contents of her money belt. Fat lot of good a Visa card was out here.

When she reached the river she checked her mobile phone for a signal and felt no surprise when the screen told her she had no connection. Pushing it back inside her pocket, she climbed on to a boulder and studied the other side of the river. She would have to make a series of big leaps from rock to rock to cross the freezing torrent, and pray her footsteps would be sure so that she didn't slip and fall mid-stream. If she got wet, her body temperature would plummet and she'd suffer from exposure within minutes.

Just do it, she told herself, and took a deep breath to prepare herself.

Then she jumped.

She didn't pause after the first leap, but kept up her momentum and her resolve by zig-zagging her way across the tumbling river. Sometimes she had to double back because the gaps were too great to clear, but all the same she was moving forward: Two rocks forward, one back; one rock left, the next three forward, another back.

She was three-quarters of the way across when a rock she'd just landed on wobbled violently and threatened to sink.

She willed it to stay where it was. She needed that rock because she couldn't go any further forward. She had to use it to lever herself back and then take the next rock to the right, which would bring her within springing distance of the far bank.

She had to trust the wobbling rock.

Never give up, never give in.

Jay leaped.

The rock shuddered, but held.

Immediately she sprang to her right, leaped again, and then – to her horror – she heard a shout above the rushing of the river.

A quick glance over her shoulder showed a man springing from rock to rock, following her fast.

Max Blake.

Laura's voice. *That lying bastard.*

Jay turned and vaulted for the bank, grabbing on to a lip of stone for balance, and then she was across. She looked back to see Blake was following pretty much the same route she had taken, but at twice the speed.

'Jay!' he called. 'Wait!'

And at the same time, the last rock from which he'd jumped toppled into the river, and sank.

The wobbly rock had finally capsized, effectively trapping him three-quarters of the way across. It was too far to the bank to jump, and now the rock had sunk, he couldn't return to try another course.

Blake teetered where he was.

'You'll have to swim,' she called.

'Okay,' he said. He didn't sound particularly fazed. He reached into his jacket and, before she could move, withdrew his pistol and ejected the shells.

'Ready?' he called.

Jay backed up the bank, eyes on the gun.

Blake lobbed his pistol across the torrent. It landed with a clatter on a scattering of stones near her feet. The shells followed. Jay grabbed the shells, and had the weapon locked and loaded and aimed at Blake before she took another breath.

'Ah,' he said. He put up his hands. 'I see Laura's had something to say about me.'

'She didn't have to, since you were with Luigi Protti's welcoming committee this afternoon.'

'I am not a traitor.' He said it clearly, holding her eyes, arms raised. He sounded sincere. But so would she, if she'd been in the same position. 'Why,' he went on, 'would I throw you my gun if I was?'

Good point.

'And why would I tell Vadic's men to look for you in the opposite direction?' He gestured behind him, where the cloud was sinking lower into the valley. 'You see anyone following you?'

She craned her neck but couldn't see anything. Just slopes of snow and cloud.

'Jay, I'm going to have to trust you with this.' Blake spread his palms. 'I can't go back, because I've blown my cover. I stopped them from shooting you. I saw Laura fall, and tried to confuse them, but they're not stupid. It won't take them long to realise I've sent them in the wrong direction, that I was trying to help you and Laura. I'm on the run, just like you.'

Jay replayed the initial pandemonium in her mind. A man yelling, 'Not her! You're after the wrong one!'

Had it been Blake?

'I've got a map,' he said, but when he began to reach into his ski jacket she yelled, 'STOP!'

He stuck his hands in the air. He flicked a glance over his shoulder before turning to face her. 'I just wanted to double-check it. Think where we might head next. We need a plan, right?'

'Right,' she said, 'but keep your hands where I can see them.'

'Okay.' He kept his palms spread. 'Look, I know this area pretty well from scouting it for Milot. I reckon we should head for Novo Selo. It's a small village—'

'I know where Novo Selo is.'

'Okay. So we go there, and get some help. The village is full of smugglers who'll help us across the border into Kosovo. From there, we can head north to Croatia.'

Jay stared at Blake across the rush of water. She had no idea if he was telling the truth. To hold his own with Milot and Vadic he'd have to be a consummate liar. He could be undercover, legitimate with SOCA, MI6, Russia's GRU and SVR for all she knew, or he could be lying through his teeth.

In a flash of recollection she remembered the Sugar Honey Bar: the thug yanking and twisting the girl's nipple, Blake pushing his gun against the thug's head and whisking Jay outside.

'I think you already know I'm telling the truth.' Blake lowered his hands, then bunched his body into a crouch. 'And I pray to God I'm right, because if I'm wrong . . .'

He uncoiled like a spring, arms reaching, unfurling his body like a big cat leaping, and for a moment she thought he'd make it, and then he dropped and plunged into the river, the water closing over his head.

For a second she remained fixed where she was, staring numbly at the space where he'd vanished, and then she said, 'Oh my God.'

Her words galvanised her, and she raced downstream where there were two large rounded boulders standing side by side. Pray God he'd get swept against them, and then she'd be able to reach down and pull him out. But Blake didn't appear near the boulders, nor was he in the next rushing pool. She saw no sign of waving arms and hands amidst the thundering water and foam. She began to run downstream. Where was he? She scanned the water, but it was only when she looked way down-river that she saw something shiny and humped lodged in the water near a rocky beach. Blake's jacket. He was lying face-down in an eddy, unmoving.

Jay raced for him.

She plunged up to her knees in the freezing water and grabbed his jacket, pulling him towards her. She hauled his head free of the water. With her elbows beneath his armpits, she dragged him on to the beach and laid him on his back. A thin trickle of blood seeped from his hairline.

She shook him hard. 'Blake!' she called. 'Can you hear me?'

He didn't respond. Quickly she rolled him on his side and tilted his head to check his airway was clear. Then she listened for his breathing. Nothing.

Hell.

She placed Blake on his back once again and knelt beside him. Tilting his head back she pinched his nostrils, took a deep breath and started mouth-to-mouth resuscitation.

She had barely pumped two lungfuls of air into him when he made a choking sound and rolled on to his side, gasping as the water drained from his lungs. Jay checked his pulse to find it was strong and steady. He flopped back and looked at her.

'Don't stop,' he said. The corners of his mouth turned up in a smile.

She couldn't believe it. The man had nearly died and he wanted to flirt with her?

'Wait here and I'll go fetch a bicycle pump,' she told him. 'Save me the effort of blowing up your lungs again.'

The smile increased. He raised himself up on an elbow and ran a hand over his head, his fingers exploring his hairline and the wound there, still seeping blood. He had begun shivering.

She felt a stab of anxiety. 'Are you okay?'

'Nothing an aspirin won't fix.'

Unsteadily, he got to his feet.

'Shouldn't we wait a bit?' she said. 'Until you're stronger?'

The smile returned. 'So you do care.'

Jay curled her lip. 'Blake, I hardly think this is the time . . . '

'Call me Max.' His shivers increased. 'I need to get somewhere warm, plus I'd rather not hang around with Vadic sniffing our trail.'

He began walking somewhat unsteadily across the beach. He was coughing, and had his arms wrapped around his body.

'Blake . . . '

He swung round and sent her a frown.

'Sorry, Max.' She took off her ski jacket and handed it to him. 'You need to wear something dry.'

Their four-hour hike over the mountain to Novo Selo was an

experience Jay wouldn't want to repeat. Occasional flurries of snow were whipped by a stinging wind that bit at her neck and shoulders. Blake had stripped out of his wet sweater and jacket and pulled on her down jacket, and since he'd been in danger of suffering from exposure, she'd also given him her hat and gloves. Her head and hands had turned completely numb.

They stumbled alongside one another, occasionally grabbing each other's arm or shoulder in order to remain upright when they hit a drift or a rock.

Low clouds had settled on the village when they arrived, and wood smoke drifted through a clump of trees that grew in front of a mosque. A woman, bent with age, carried an armload of firewood inside her house. The feeble, yellow light from an oil lamp shone from the door, and Jay caught a waft of something hot, something delicious, like lamb stew.

'I'm starving,' she mumbled.

'Ditto that.'

The street was peppered with sheep dung and the air smelled of lanolin. A quick peek through the shutters of the next house showed a small flock of sheep housed in the front room. Above the sound of the wind she heard someone call out. Looking up, she saw a group of men coming towards them. She glanced at Blake. He kept walking. The men stepped aside to let them pass, staring at them.

'*Si jeni?*' Blake greeted them. How are you?

'*Jam mirë.*' Okay. The youngest man was polite, but his eyes were sharp with mistrust.

'We're tourists,' Blake went on. 'We got lost in the storm. Is there anywhere we can stay for the night? We can pay our way.'

The man looked as though he didn't believe a word, but he gave a nod. 'Come with me.'

They followed him back down the hill to a ramshackle house near the mosque. He opened the door and motioned them to enter, then shouted for someone called Arta, who turned out to be his wife. Arta quickly ushered them beside a fire, taking their sodden clothes away to dry before producing steaming bowls of soup and hunks of bread. As Jay ate, she watched someone, who turned out to be Arta's sister, come inside with her baby and lay it on a bench opposite the table. Arta lit two more lamps and handed Blake a key for the byre and storage shed adjoining the house, along with a lamp and a pile of blankets. Taking Jay's hand Blake walked her outside, thanking the family with meticulous politeness. He spoke in a way that let them believe Jay was his wife, so nobody could be offended.

Wrapped in the blankets, she curled up on the large wooden storage shelf and gazed at the roof-high stacks of chopped wood. She could hear sheep rustling in the straw nearby, the wind whistling through cracks in the walls. The air was like ice. She could feel the lump of her mobile phone in her pocket but she didn't bother checking to see if she had a signal. Their hosts had already told them there was no mast around, not for miles. She would save the batteries for when she was guaranteed a signal. Next to her, she felt Blake roll on to his back. She didn't move. She hoped he thought she was asleep.

'You and Laura were compromised,' said Blake.

Her eyes snapped open. 'What do you mean?'

'They knew you were coming. Who do you think told them?'

'We could have been lured there.' She told him about Hashim and his box of matches.

Blake was quiet for so long that she thought he'd fallen asleep, but then he murmured. 'You're probably right. Hashim's not the type to snitch. I'm surprised Laura trusted him.'

It was almost as though he was talking to himself, and she didn't say any more. She was too busy wishing she was elsewhere, like at home watching TV with a glass of wine. She couldn't stop shivering. Oh, for central heating! she thought, realising she'd turned soft in the two years she'd been a civilian. She didn't think she'd be able to sleep, but she was also bone-numbingly exhausted and soon drifted off.

She awoke in the dark of the night. The wind had dropped and everything was quiet. Through a gap in the wall she could see stars, glinting hard and bright against a cold sky. Gradually she became aware of Blake's breathing, light and regular against the nape of her neck. His arm was around her waist, his body spooned against hers. Waves of heat rolled between them.

She waited for the insistent, nagging sensation she usually felt when she woke up in the small hours, but all was silent. She was, she thought, probably too tired to hear it. Closing her eyes, she fell back to sleep.

Twenty-two

'It's Quinton.' Branko opened the apartment door. 'Hana's friend.'

Quinton was pink and round and had red-rimmed watery eyes. He reminded Zamira of a pig, except that pigs didn't carry briefcases or bottles of whisky.

'Hi, Quinton,' Branko greeted him.

Quinton didn't respond. He was staring at Zamira.

She stared back. For some reason, she wanted to run, but she didn't know why. He looked innocuous enough with his neatly trimmed grey hair, his dark blue suit and red tie.

Branko was talking to Quinton in English and, although she couldn't understand what they were saying, she knew they were discussing her from the way their eyes would flick to her then away. She backed up slightly, crossing her arms, feeling uncomfortable.

Quinton made an exclamation, looked shocked, then Branko laughed and gestured at her. Quinton stared at her, and then he nodded. The men shook hands, both looking pleased.

'Come here, Peaches.' Branko beckoned Zamira over. 'Come and shake hands with Quinton.'

Reluctantly, Zamira obeyed. Quinton's hand was warm and damp.

'Pour him a whisky.'

Branko took the bottle from Quinton and passed it over,

gesturing to the drinks cabinet in the corner of the room. Zamira picked out a crystal tumbler, as heavy as a rock, poured in a shot and gave it to Quinton.

'Thank you,' Quinton said, and loosened his tie.

Zamira stared at Quinton. She felt off-balance and not a little frightened.

'Hell.' Branko looked at his watch. 'I didn't realise the time. I'm late for a meeting. Peaches, you'll be okay with Quinton until I get back?'

'I guess.' She tried not to let her voice tremble.

Branko walked across the thickly carpeted living room and into the hall. She scurried after him to see him open the front door and step outside. 'I'll see you in a tick, okay?' He sent her a grin, the kind that usually made her lower belly glow and heat as though it had been kissed by the sun, but now it made her feel oddly panicky.

'Branko . . . ' Her voice wavered.

'You be good now.'

He shut the door behind him, and then she heard a key turning in the lock, as though he were locking her in.

Instantly her chest went tight. She knew Hana was at work, but why did this feel all wrong? Her stomach lurched as she realised she hadn't seen any evidence of her friend in the apartment. No flowers or colourful touches. The knowledge that she was alone in an apartment with a strange man crashed over her like an avalanche.

She went to the door but she'd been right, it was locked.

'Branko?' she whispered.

Behind her, she heard Quinton speaking. She spun round. He was cradling his whisky against his chest. His eyes were glazed. He kept on talking. Didn't he know she couldn't speak English?

She tried the door again.

He came and put a hand on her arm. She shook him off, her panic building. He put his whisky down on the hall side table, then raised his hand and slapped her across the face.

Cheek stinging, ears ringing, Zamira stared at him in shocked disbelief. He started talking again, this time pointing down the corridor. He wanted her to return to the living room. She refused. She didn't know why. She just knew she didn't want to do as he said.

He flushed. His voice rose.

Still she wouldn't move.

When he brought back his hand to hit her again, Zamira launched herself at him. She didn't know what she was going to do. Thump him, maybe make a run for the bathroom, lock herself inside, she wasn't sure. She was running on pure undistilled fear. Her fist connected with his face.

Smack.

Quinton roared.

This time he didn't slap her, he let loose a punch that connected with her jaw and sent her spinning across the hallway into the wall. She collapsed on the floor. She saw little flashes of light and the floor swam, but she could see Quinton – his face puce with rage – towering above her. He was unbuckling his belt. Unzipping his flies.

Instinct took over. She kicked his knee. He howled. On all fours, she scurried down the hall but he grabbed her ankle and yanked her back. He was much stronger than her. Another blow landed, this time behind her ear. Dizzy, she tried to lash out but her movements were unco-ordinated, feeble, and she felt him tearing at her clothes, could hear his grunts as he tried to force his knee between hers. His breath was hot against her face, his lips inches away.

Zamira reared upwards and grabbed his lower lip between her teeth and bit down as hard as she could.

He screamed.

Twenty-three

It had been Jay's idea to run for the border and cross into Albania, but Blake had hesitated.

'The words fire and frying pan spring to mind,' he said. 'Albania's riddled with Milot's henchmen, we might get nabbed the second we step into the country.'

'It's the safest place to be,' she argued. 'Right in the heart of the lion's den.'

He thought it over. 'I'll say this for you, you're not faint-hearted.'

Jay pressed her advantage. 'It's also our best and fastest chance of getting to Western Europe. From the coast we can get a boat to Italy. From there, fly to Heathrow.'

He mulled this over for a minute or so. 'Okay. Let's do it. You got your passport?'

Jay patted her money belt. 'Yes. You?'

'No. But don't let's worry about that yet. Let's get ourselves a guide.'

Novo Selo was a hub of smuggling routes between Albania, Kosovo and Macedonia, and when the locals heard that the couple staying in their village wanted to travel quickly and quietly to the Adriatic Sea, several men turned up on their doorstep offering to escort them. Blake chose a bearded young man called Ali, who had eyes bright and greedy as a starling's and swore he'd not only provide them with the safest passage, but he'd also tell them the best jokes. When Ali let his jacket fall open on purpose, so they could see his gun, Jay didn't remark on it. He was only posturing, pretending to be macho. She doubted he knew how to fire it, let alone hit a target.

Jay said, 'Do you know Branko Morillon?'

Ali looked startled when she spoke, and when Blake indicated the young man answer, gave his reply to Blake.

Yes, he knew Branko.

'Do you know where he might be?'

London.

'Where, in London?'

He shrugged.

'What about Hana? She comes from this village. She went to London with Branko, do you know where he took her?'

More shrugs.

Jay questioned Ali for another couple of minutes without success. She wanted to ask questions around the village, but now wasn't the time. Her priority was to get out and away.

Ali proved to be a good choice as a guide. He was lean and fit and a fast walker, and appeared to know every trail and animal track they came across. To her relief, he barely said a word and didn't tell a single joke.

Blake wasn't much of a conversationalist either, leaving her mind free to roam. She thought of her mother, whom she hadn't spoken to since she'd left the UK, of Zamira and Branko – and of Tom. She wished she'd been able to reassure him yesterday. His concern reminded her of last Easter, when she'd been in Scotland with her father, helping with the calving. Three cows were in the barn, bedded in fresh straw and hours away from birthing, when disaster had struck.

Her father had been moving the bull from one field to another when it had swiped its horns at him. Her father had ducked away and slipped, and the bull – seeing the open gate – had charged for it, right over her father's prone body, treading on his elbow and crushing it.

The nearest A&E unit was an hour away in Elgin, and he refused to let her drive him there. Instead, he rang his neighbour

– another farmer who was in the thick of calving – and got the man's wife to drive him to hospital.

'Look after my girls,' he told Jay, white-faced and shivering from inside the muddy Land Rover. 'Vet's number's on the barn door, but you won't need it. You've birthed loads of calves.'

Not alone, she hadn't.

She had just returned to the barn and was getting together lubricant and some bailing twine, when Tom rang. After she'd filled him in, he said, 'Shall I come up? Give you a hand?'

She would have loved the company, but she couldn't see the point. Tom was a townie, and Jay reckoned he would be as much use as a cocktail umbrella. 'No,' she told him. 'I'll be fine. Besides, you're too busy keeping all those criminals under control.'

'There's nothing that can't be delegated.'

'Honestly, I'm okay.'

'If you're sure . . . '

'I promise.'

To her relief, nothing happened for four hours, until her father rang to say he had to stay in overnight. He sounded tired.

'We're all fine,' she assured him. 'Make sure you're well before you come back, okay?'

'Love you.'

'You too.'

After evening drew in, she watched two cows give smooth, uncomplicated births to two healthy heifers, and she was thinking everything was going to be okay when the third cow went into labour. To her dismay, instead of the calf's nose and one or two front feet showing, a single hind foot was coming out first. It was a breech. Shit. She didn't have much time. Working as fast as she could, she inserted a well-lubricated arm inside the birth canal. The calf's head was bent back. So was the other hind leg. She manipulated the head and limbs so both hind feet were pointing in the same direction. The cow – called Maisie – began to groan, distressed.

Jay tied the bailing twine twice around the calf's pasterns, and began pulling. Nothing happened. 'Come on, girl,' she told Maisie. 'Push, dammit.'

She was still pulling ten minutes later, sweating and cursing and wondering if she should call the vet when a voice said, 'Need a hand?'

Townie or not, she would have hugged Tom if she'd had an arm free.

Together they pulled a large bull calf free. While Jay tied the umbilical cord she told Tom how to clean out the calf's mouth and make sure it was breathing. Soon Maisie was on her feet, and although exhausted, was licking her calf hip to crown.

Tom had blood splattered up his jeans and slime and hay all over his hands, but he was grinning. 'Cigar?' she asked him.

'Come here, sexy,' he said.

Tom stayed for the rest of the week. He knew nothing about farming and Jay loved the fact that he took instructions from her and her father without batting an eye. He fell into bed with her at the end of each day with the smell of heather in his hair and whisky on his breath. When she asked him what made him fly up even though she'd said not to, he said, 'There was something in your voice.'

'But I swore I was okay.' She didn't get it.

'I just knew you wanted company.' He shrugged. 'I can't explain why.'

Tom was the only man who could read her like a book, and she was never sure whether she liked this or not.

Later that afternoon, they passed a ruined monastery clinging to the edge of a gorge, its whitewashed walls faded, the decorative ironwork broken. Jay paused to look at the view. The weather had cleared and snowy peaks stretched into the distance beneath a blue sky. In the valley below a scattering of tiny villages were tucked beside cascading streams and ancient terracotta roofs glowed warm-red in the sun, looking as picturesque as any postcard.

'Beautiful,' Blake murmured.

She turned, to see he was looking straight at her. To her

shame, a rush of sexual longing poured through her, from her throat to her belly and right to the tips of her toes.

The corners of his mouth curved into a smile.

'If I had a camera, I'd take a picture,' she said, and turned away. Her heart was bouncing. Please God, she prayed, he didn't see what I just felt. I know I haven't had sex for a while, but this is ridiculous. Had she reacted like that because she'd been thinking about Tom?

'You okay?' Blake called.

'Yup. Fine. Just want to get to where we're going. Keep the pace up.' She could feel his eyes beamed between her shoulder blades until she rounded the corner of the mountainside. She was grateful when he didn't catch her up but fell into pace twenty yards behind.

They spoke little until they came to a village that evening. There was nothing to indicate they had crossed the Albanian border earlier – there were no border posts or guards or razor wire up here, deep in the mountains – but Ali told them the village was ten miles inside the border and they were now officially in Albania.

Before they continued, Blake gave Jay his binoculars and insisted on hiding her in a tumble of rocks.

'Hey, hang on a minute,' she protested. 'I know how to fight, I can shoot—'

'I'm all for women's independence' – he was curt – 'but not today. If there's a trap I don't want both of us falling into it.'

At the look on his face, she decided not to argue and settled herself behind a slab of rock dotted with quartz. Ali was shaking his head, looking fed up, but Blake ignored the guide. He came and squatted close to Jay, and whispered, 'After we go, I want you to find another hiding place.'

'You don't trust Ali?'

'I don't trust anybody. Wait until I give you the signal before you show yourself. If I don't give it, make your way to Tirana. I'll be at the British war cemetery near the park in the centre eight a.m. and six p.m. every day until you turn up.'

The signal was a clenched left fist against his heart.

She watched him approach the untidy collection of stone and mud-plaster houses, Ali at his side, with a feeling of dread rising in her belly. Had Ali or one of the Novo Selo villagers tipped off Milot and his men? Were they hidden in one of those buildings, waiting for them? Would they shoot Blake on sight, or grab him, and torture him until he died?

Hurriedly she found another hiding place, higher up the hillside and behind a screen of low bushes. Her hands became slippery on the binoculars as she watched the two men vanish inside the village. She checked her watch. Six-ten p.m. She scanned the village, but the only person she saw was an old man wearing a white fez, sitting on a tree stump smoking a pipe. Chickens scratched in the dirt and in the distance, a donkey brayed.

Six-fifteen. Six-twenty. Six-thirty.

Her heart jumped when she saw a figure appear, but it was only a woman in a peasant headdress, coming to bring the old man inside.

At six-forty she saw Blake striding to the edge of the village, his left fist over his heart. The rush of relief was so strong it made her fingers tremble.

Once again, Blake and Jay shared a bed on the upper floor of a barn. She was exhausted, her leg muscles throbbing from the unaccustomed gradients, but she was unable to relax. She couldn't stop thinking about Tom, the way he kissed her, and then wondering how Blake's mouth would feel. She couldn't believe she was obsessing about sex when she was on the run from a mob of terrifying gangsters. It had to be her biorhythms or something, PMS or hormones, or perhaps she was just missing Tom. Or maybe deep-down she was looking for an affair so she had a proper excuse to end their relationship. But if she was honest, she knew she didn't want to break up with Tom.

She kept waiting for Blake to move over and spoon her as he'd done the night before, keep them both warm, but he didn't move. He slept quietly on his back, making her wonder if she'd imagined his look earlier. Yes, that had to be it. She was in such a state over Tom she was fantasising about other men. This thought settled her for a while, and she finally fell into a doze. She began to dream.

She was with her platoon, clearing a house. She was on the top floor and weaponless when an enemy soldier sprang from behind the door and raised his gun to shoot her. It was the girl's rapist.

'All clear!' someone yelled, and the man vanished. Poof, just like that, he evaporated. She must have imagined him.

'All clear!' she yelled back.

'Good job, soldier.'

She awoke to find herself in a man's arms. For a split second she thought it was Tom, but then she took in the cold night air and the faint rustling of sheep below.

'You okay?' Blake murmured against her hair.

She gave a small nod.

He said, 'You were having a bad dream.'

'I get them sometimes.'

'Me too.'

Jay fell back to sleep with her head against his chest, listening to his heartbeat.

At noon the next day Ali led them into another tiny village lurking in the hillside. While their guide vanished to visit his cousin, Jay and Blake tucked themselves inside a dusty little café and ordered lunch. She was glad of the break; her legs were tired and beginning to weaken. Perched on a rickety stool, she watched Blake try his mobile phone and then he immediately started punching numbers. At last, they had a signal.

'Who are you ringing?'

'Kingsman.'

A chill brushed her skin. 'What are you going to tell him?'

Blake paused. 'You're worried about Vadic?'

She had already told him about the horrifying scene at the meat-processing plant, Vadic's threats.

'Yes. If he hears MI6 is aware of his involvement with Milot, and that he's hooking up with the Italians, he'll go mad. Until we know what's happening with Laura, can we sit tight for a bit? He's the sort of guy to use someone like me to send a message to the troops. "Disobey the boss and look what happens to your loved ones."'

A man entered the café and gave them a suspicious look. Like most Albanians he was short and narrow-faced, with stumpy legs. Blake waited until the man was out of earshot.

'Good point,' he murmured. He kept his eyes on the man, who went and sat with some buddies in the corner.

'Vadic despises women like me.'

'So I heard. It's become personal between you. Makes things tricky.'

Jay shuffled her stool closer to Blake. 'We have to tell MI6 about Laura, I appreciate that, but can we keep the information about the clans amalgamating quiet for a little while?'

He thought it over. 'Okay,' he agreed. 'I'll say you and Laura surprised Milot in the mountains. I won't mention Vadic or the others. Not straight away.' His expression became distant. 'We need leverage to get Vadic off our backs. It's the only thing he'll understand.' Blake started re-dialling. 'Meantime, let's keep your folks safe.'

While Blake made the call to Patrick Kingsman, Jay called Nick.

'Something wrong with your mobile?' he said.

'I've been out of range.'

'Like where? Kiro's been going nuts. Says you nicked his car.'

'I'll tell you everything when I get home.'

'When's that likely to be?'

She did some swift calculations. It was Friday today, which meant they'd be travelling for most of the weekend.

'Monday, all going well.'

'Are you okay?'

'As okay as I can be under the circumstances.'

Small silence.

'Can I help?'

She only had to say the word and she knew he would jump on an airplane and parachute to her rescue if necessary. 'Not today,

Nick, but thanks. I'm with an old friend of yours, who you met on a mission near Tripoli.'

'That's good.' He sounded relieved. 'He's a capable guy.'

'Are you saying I'm not?'

'Put it this way, you're ex-army, he's ex-special services.'

'You never told me that.'

'Well, now you know.'

Jay looked over at Blake with new respect. She said, 'Any news of Zamira your end?'

'No, sorry. I'm still looking.'

After a small pause, she said, 'I'd better go.'

Hanging up, she watched Blake redial. 'I'm trying Laura,' he told her, and a few seconds later added, 'Nope. It's been disconnected.'

Jay tried not to think of Raman dangling above the mincer in the meat-processing plant, and prayed that Laura was all right, that she'd managed to escape, but the worry gnawing at her belly told her she wasn't being realistic. To distract herself she rang Kiro, who wasn't going nuts as much as – in his own words – demented as a man who has had his earlobes nailed to the floor.

'You cow!' he roared, 'you kidnap my car and expect me to forgive you?'

'Sorry.'

'So where is it?'

After she gave him instructions, he said, 'Now, tell me where you are. I shall come and get you. You are obviously in need of my help.'

'No need, Kiro. I'm already on the road, headed for—'

She bit back a yelp as a warm hand covered hers and pulled the phone away from her mouth. Blake was shaking his head at her.

'It's Kiro,' she told him.

He glanced sharply around the café, the handful of men drinking coffee and watching them out of the corners of their eyes. Despite the fact she'd been talking in an undertone, and didn't think any of the men could speak English, Blake was right, she had to be ultra-cautious.

She took back the phone. 'We're headed home,' she murmured to Kiro.

'Where are you?' Kiro repeated.

Not liking his insistence, she was brisk. 'Safe and sound,' she told him. 'I'll ring you when I get to London.'

'But, Ice' – his voice was worried – 'something is wrong, I must be able to help, please, all you have to do is ask.'

'Promise me you won't stop looking for Zamira?'

'Of course not, but are you sure—'

'Bye.'

After she hung up, she had an almost overwhelming urge to ring her mother, but wasn't sure if it was such a good idea. She turned the phone over and over in her hands, undecided.

'Problem?' Blake asked.

'I'm not sure whether to call home or not.'

'Your decision.' He was looking past her shoulder at a girl with peroxide hair who was heading their way with a tray of fatty grilled lamb, sheep's cheese and tomatoes. The fat was crisp and brown, the cheese white and crumbly. Jay put her phone back in her money belt. She'd call her mother when she hit London. If her mother sensed that the slightest thing was wrong she'd worry herself sick.

The rest of the day was a blur of walking and grindingly slow bus journeys up and down steep gradients and around hairpin bends that made Jay shrink inside and pray the brakes worked. In the late evening Ali dropped them at a harbour overlooking a moonlit Adriatic Sea, and shook their hands.

'You will be safe now.' He sounded sincere.

'Thanks.' Jay was reserved. She wouldn't believe she was safe from the Mafia's clutches until she was breathing freshly belched fumes from a number fourteen bus on Fulham Road, and even then her safety wasn't guaranteed since the Albanian Mafia had their claws as deeply entrenched in London as they did in Tetovo.

It didn't take long to find a fishing boat willing to take them across, and although the fee used up nearly all their cash, Jay didn't quibble but climbed aboard before the skipper had second

168

thoughts. After they had set sail, Jay left Blake on deck with a pair of binoculars, watching for patrol boats, and went below to sleep – on a pile of old rope with her thermal hat and gloves for a pillow.

It was dawn when they docked at a small harbour south of Bari. Italy had never looked more beautiful or a strong espresso tasted so good. Even the laconic Blake made appreciative noises as he glugged his down. Jay ate two croissants in quick succession, while Blake moved to a shot of Punt e Mes which, translated, meant a point and a half he told her, and was a vermouth-type alcohol that Milanese stockbrokers would knock back before they went to work. It sounded like a good story.

After they'd recharged their batteries and had a quick wash in a service station bathroom, they caught a bus to Bari airport. Jay bought her ticket with her Visa card.

'I'll see you in London.' Blake was standing at the departure gate with her. They'd agreed to travel separately to help avoid detection.

'How will you get back?'

'I have a couple of options. I should be there Wednesday. I'll ring you. Make a plan.'

She felt awkward and self-conscious at saying goodbye. What did you say to a man who had saved you from being hunted down by a bunch of sadistic villains? Who held you in his arms when you were chased by nightmares?

'Safe flight,' he said, and reaching up, touched her face with his fingers.

If he'd taken her in his arms and kissed her it couldn't have had a more powerful effect. She felt the full force of his chemistry in that fleeting gesture.

And then he was walking away, through the crowds. He didn't wave. He didn't look back.

Jay stood on Fulham Road, breathing deeply. She couldn't believe that a lungful of diesel fumes could taste so good. It was seven in the evening and everywhere was blanketed in freezing fog. The streetlights wore orange halos and she could barely make out the lemon blur of the lamps which lit the shop windows. She was cold and damp and exhausted, but she couldn't stop grinning. The sheer relief of not being on the run, constantly looking over her shoulder, was immense. She'd made it, escaped from the clutches of one of the scariest criminals around, and she felt like a hare who had outrun the hounds. Ducking into Mr Patel's, her local corner shop, she bought two bottles of champagne. Angela and Denise could help her celebrate.

As she walked home, she quickly rang Nick. 'I'm back, safe and sound.'

'Thank God.'

'Any news on Zamira?'

'Not yet. I'll ring you the second I hear anything, you know that.'

'I know. Sorry. I'm tired.'

'Then go and rest. Come in when you're ready. Not before.'

Aside from a stack of messages by the phone, the house looked pretty much as she'd left it. She put the champagne in the fridge and went upstairs, stripping off her clothes as she went. She hadn't bathed properly in five days and couldn't wait to get clean.

Standing in the shower, she let the hot water play over her shoulders and neck as she considered the past week. She wondered where Laura was and whether she was okay . . . what Hashim the double-crossing snitch was up to . . . what the three Mafia chiefs were plotting – to take over the world, probably . . . She tried not to think about Max Blake, how his heartbeat sounded as she rested her head against his chest, but it was impossible since he was part of everything that had happened.

After towelling herself dry, Jay pulled on her bathrobe and took her dirty washing downstairs, loaded the machine and switched it on. She opened the champagne, poured a glass, and toasted herself before flicking through her mail which, aside from a postcard from her stepmother Nicola, was mostly bills. Turning to her messages she found six from her mother, two from Nick, one from Sandra her sister-in-law, asking her to baby sit all weekend – no, thank you – and two from friends asking her to supper. She shuffled through them again. She knew he was probably fed up with her after her last phone call, but her heart hollowed to find nothing from Tom.

Bracing herself, Jay rang her mother. She hadn't forgotten the bugs in the house and was tempted to make the call outside from her mobile, but since she wanted whoever was listening in to believe she was unaware she was being bugged, she had to act as normally as possible, and that included day-to-day phone calls.

'Hi, Mum. It's me.'

'Jessica.'

With just the one word, Jay's instincts came on full alert.

'What's wrong?' she asked.

'Aside from your vanishing into the Balkans without saying goodbye, there's the small matter of a nasty little man knocking on my door and threatening to do all sorts of horrible things to me if you don't keep your mouth shut.'

'*What?*'

'It's all right. I took down his number plate and the police are looking for him.'

Feeling faint, Jay had to put a hand on the wall to steady herself. 'You didn't take him seriously?'

'Certainly not! I don't know what you've been up to, but I won't have my family threatened, least of all by a midget with the breath of a troll.'

'Mum ... ' She didn't know whether to laugh or cry. 'Please don't upset him or his friends.'

'He's got friends? I don't think so.'

Long pause while Jay reassessed her mother. She'd never heard her like this before – pugnacious and belligerent – but then she didn't suppose her mother had ever been threatened by a midget. 'I'd better come up and see you. Talk the situation over.'

'When were you thinking?'

'How about if I arrive around lunchtime tomorrow?'

'Would you prefer roast chicken or a moussaka?'

'Are you doing bread sauce?'

'Of course.'

'Roast chicken, then. Mum, you're okay, aren't you? He didn't hurt you or anything?'

'You've obviously forgotten about Tigger. He didn't like the troll much either. He bit him in the pants.'

Twenty-four

Unfortunately, before she could drive up to see her mother the next morning, Jay had a call from the Foreign Office requesting an immediate debriefing. Her spirits sank. She knew Kingsman and his troops would have put an alert out for her re-entry into the UK, but in her relief at being home she'd rather hoped they'd give her a little more time before calling her in.

She tried to put the meeting off until the next day, but the acid-voiced woman on the other end of the line wasn't having any of it. 'If there's a problem, we'll send a car to fetch you,' she said, which Jay easily translated as 'we'll strong arm you if we have to.'

She'd just hung up when her father rang. She'd called him from her mobile the night before to tell him about the troll threatening her mother and to warn him to be watchful of strangers, and she'd been grateful when he asked very few questions and simply suggested he should join Nicola, saying he would move his cattle to the bottom fields to be looked after by the neighbouring farmer. She could have kissed him for his no-nonsense, sensible attitude. He never panicked, and would always find a workable solution to a problem. This time, it was to leave the country with a minimum of fuss. Nicola, Jay knew from her postcard, was currently in Toulouse. If her father joined her, then Jay wouldn't have to worry about them.

Now, she said, 'Hi, Dad. Where are you?'

'Not in the British Isles,' he said.

'Great. How's the weather?'

'Surprisingly cold, since you ask.'

'And Nicola?'

He chuckled. 'Hot.'

'Dad,' she groaned. 'I didn't need to know that.'

'Sorry. Things okay with you?'

'Yup.'

'Let me know when the coast is clear. If I can do anything . . . '

'I'll let you know.'

Jay was locking the front door when she heard her name being called. To her surprise, it was Sandra, her sister-in-law, with both kids in tow.

'I was picking up some wine for Angus,' she said. 'Thought I'd check and see if you were up for a coffee. Haven't seen you in ages.'

Sandra had thick auburn hair and skin like cream, and although she could be as bossy as a drill sergeant she also had a heart as big as a barn. Jay liked her enormously.

'I'd love to stop,' she said, 'but I can't. I've got a meeting to attend, and then I'm going to Mum's.'

'I wish I had a meeting to go to.' Sandra gave a twisted smile. 'Some days I wonder if I ever had a real job or if I was a full-time mother since time began.'

'You want to go back to work?' It was the first Jay had heard of it. She'd thought Sandra was content with things as they stood.

'I'd love to, but who'd look after Mark and Katie? You know my job. It's not always nine-to-five.'

Sandra was a psychoanalyst and her patients could be incredibly demanding.

Jay said, 'You need a live-in nanny.'

'If only. Look, we won't keep you.' Sandra gave Jay a hug. 'I'll ring you later. Maybe we can meet up over the weekend.'

'That would be great.' Jay kissed Sandra on her cheek and waved at the kids. '*Lamtumirë*.'

They both waved cheerfully back. '*Lamtumirë*, Auntie Jay.'

*

The debriefing took place in the same grey and chrome office at Heathrow, and this time it was just Kingsman and his younger side-kick with the sandy hair, Alistair Ingram. They had covered the preliminaries – Jay and Laura spying on Milot's ski-chalet, Laura being shot and Jay and Blake's escape – and it took every ounce of concentration not to make a slip and mention Vadic or Protti by name. Would her mother and father be safe from Vadic's vengeful claws? She thought of the troll, the man who had visited her mother, wondering whether MI6 knew about him, but unless they had been in touch with the Norwich police she doubted it.

'Where is Blake now?' Ingram asked. He had stationed himself directly opposite Jay and their knees were almost touching. Each time he leaned forward he invaded her personal space and she assumed it was a psychological tactic to make her feel pressured. Sitting behind the table, Kingsman studied a pile of papers. He didn't appear to be listening to their conversation, but when Blake's name was mentioned, a strange stillness descended over him.

Jay said, 'He left me at the airport.'

'Bari.'

'Yes.'

'What would you say if I told you he was now in Calabria, making contact with the Mafia down there? Historically, the Italians have strong links with the Albanian Mafia, and since you've just come from Albania ... ' He trailed off suggestively.

'I'm sure he has his reasons.'

'We'd like to know what they are,' said Ingram.

'I honestly have no idea.'

'Not even having spent five days in the man's company?' Ingram looked disbelieving.

'We didn't talk about the Mafia much,' she said. 'Except how to avoid them.'

'You said you walked for three days across the mountains. Surely you didn't do it in silence.'

Jay arched her eyebrows. 'You've met him, what do you

think?' She thought she saw a flash of humour cross Kingsman's face but it was gone so fast she must have imagined it.

'Oh, come on, Jay.' Ingram leaned back and crossed his arms. 'I'm not stupid.'

'What on earth is that supposed to mean?'

'You're an attractive woman, and I'm told he's not an unattractive man. I bet you found lots of things to talk about.'

'Hardly.' Her skin began to tighten. 'We were just trying to survive.'

'He didn't try and come on to you?'

'What?'

'The number of women I've debriefed who have fallen for him and just about crucified themselves trying to protect him—'

'I'm not trying to protect him! He said he'd see me in London, probably sometime this week, and then he left. He didn't give me his itinerary of what he was going to do for the next forty-eight hours.'

'Has he rung you?'

'No.'

'Do you have his number?'

'No.' And boy, did it smart. When she'd arrived home she rang him to let him know she'd got back safely, but his number had been disconnected. She'd thought they were a team, but obviously she'd read him wrong.

'Well, if you hear from him, would you let us know? We need to speak to him urgently.'

'Don't you have his number?' She was looking at Kingsman as she spoke, but he gave nothing away.

'He seems to have changed it.'

She switched her gaze to Ingram. She couldn't think how to couch her question subtly. 'Don't you trust Blake?'

'Of course we do.'

'Then what's the problem?'

'We're concerned for him.'

'Why?'

'Let's just leave it at that, shall we?' He gave her a thin smile, which she didn't return. 'And run over what you saw at the ski chalet again.'

She repeated the same abbreviated version of her and Laura driving the Lada into the forest, seeing the helicopter landing, and the two men climbing out, the way the power sat on the broader man's shoulders.

'Two men?' Ingram's voice was sharp.

'A big guy and his bodyguard.'

'You didn't mention a bodyguard before.'

Jay pushed back a hank of hair. 'Sorry.'

'Describe him.'

Jay started with her overall impression of the man, that he looked Albanian with his swarthy skin and dark hair, before moving on to describe the narrowness of his head and his receding chin.

'Good observation.' Ingram looked pleased. 'Perhaps we could run some photos past you. How about if I bring them to your office tomorrow?'

'You think he might be important?'

'Once we've identified him and his boss, we'll know, won't we?'

Jay turned her head when someone tapped on the door. A small, lithe figure with short-bobbed dark hair stepped inside.

Jay's pulse immediately began to rev at twice its normal speed. 'Laura?' She jumped to her feet, her mind whirling, backtracking over the interview. What had Laura told them? Did they know she was withholding information?

'Jay.' Laura was smiling, but it was guarded.

She wanted to give the agent a hug, to touch her in some way to show her relief at seeing her safe and well, but Laura's body language was stiffly reserved, and Jay kept her distance.

'Laura will continue the debriefing.' Kingsman was watching them closely. 'Ingram, I'll see you later.'

Ingram was indignant. 'But sir, I wanted to—'

'Later, Ingram.'

The young man flushed and pushed back his chair. The look

he shot Laura as he walked past her was pure poison, and he shut the door with more force than was necessary.

Kingsman readjusted his glasses and returned to his papers, seemingly oblivious. 'Carry on,' he told them.

'Yes, sir.' Laura pushed back the chair Ingram had vacated, giving Jay lots of space. She said formally, 'Welcome back.'

'It's good to see you.'

Laura nodded. Her expression was perfectly neutral, giving nothing away. 'I managed to escape the day after they captured me. Hashim helped. I flew out of Skopje Thursday evening.'

Which meant the agent had been with Vadic and his men for twenty-four hours. Plenty of time for them to get their hooks into her, but aside from the fact that her left arm was in a sling, she looked in pretty good shape. However, when Jay looked further, she saw how drawn Laura looked. She had dark rings around her eyes, and their depths were shadowed, reminding Jay of Nick and his ghosts. She wondered if anyone else had noticed the pain Laura was carrying.

Laura said, 'Tell me what happened from when we met in town, when Hashim dropped that book of matches in my bag.'

'I've already told Ingram.'

'I'd like to hear it.'

Jay felt prickles of fear. What had Laura told MI6 about the ski-lodge meeting? Did they know about the three clans amalgamating, or not?

She carefully re-told the same story she'd given Ingram, without mentioning Vadic or Protti by name. When she finished, Laura nodded. 'Thank you.'

To Jay's surprise, the agent got up, and without another word, left the room.

Completely at a loss, Jay stared at Kingsman. He had put down his glasses and was watching her.

'There are a few discrepancies, but I'll sort them out with Laura later,' he said. 'Thank you for undertaking the mission. If you remember anything you forgot to tell us that you think might be important, please ring me.'

She continued staring at him.

'Thank you, Jay.'

She had been dismissed.

Sitting in her car in the car park, Jay scrolled through her mobile phone contacts list, searching for Denise's number. She wanted to touch base with her housemate, tell her she would be staying in Norfolk for the night – drinking quantities of red wine in an attempt to get her head around everything, including Tigger the mini-schnauzer biting the arse of one of Vadic's men – but she paused when she saw a name that hadn't been there before.

Blake, Max.

He must have swiped her phone at some point to put his number in her contacts list. Jay dialled the number. 0777 5665 565. A nice easy one to remember, making her wonder if he'd chosen it for that purpose. It rang twice, then he said, 'What's up?'

Her heart gave a little hop. 'I've just had the joy of being debriefed by Ingram, then Laura.'

'How did she get away?'

'Hashim helped her escape.'

There was a small silence.

'Maybe Hashim's playing both sides of the game,' he said. 'Is Laura okay?'

'Physically, yes.'

'You?'

'Pretty good. Where are you? Oh, don't answer that or I'll have to report it in. They told me you're in Calabria hobnobbing with a bunch of hoods.'

'Nice one,' he said. 'Anything else?'

'The Mafia approached my mother.'

His voice sharpened. 'Tell me.'

'They sent one guy. Her dog bit him on the bum.'

She thought she heard a snort of laughter, but when he spoke, his voice was serious. 'And?'

'She took down his number plate and reported him to the local police. She described him as a midget with the breath of a troll.'

'Your mother sounds like my kind of girl.' Now he was definitely laughing. 'Tell her well done from me.'

No way was she going to tell her mother about Blake. She'd rather staple her hand to the table first.

She was about to start the car when her mobile phone rang. 'Hello?'

'Jay, I need to see you,' Laura said. 'Wait for me.'

The rain was blurring her view of the office entrance, so she put the wipers on intermittent. Five minutes later Laura came jogging across the car park. Jay leaned across and opened the passenger door.

'Drive,' Laura said.

Jay immediately started the car and accelerated out of the car park. 'Where to?'

'It doesn't matter.' Laura wiped her face of rain.

Jay turned on to the A4 and headed east, towards London. 'Do they know you're with me?'

'Probably.'

'You want to tell me what's going on?'

Laura rested her head against the headrest and closed her eyes. 'I don't know where to start.'

'With Hashim. You said he helped you escape, but Blake thinks it was Hashim who lured us into the mountains.'

'Where is Blake?' Laura asked.

'No idea.'

'Do you trust him?'

'With my life.'

There was a pause, then Laura said, 'Fuck it. Everything's such a mess I'm tempted to emigrate.'

The agent's head was turned away so Jay couldn't read her face. Switching on her indicator she took the next exit off the A4 into a residential street lined with two-storey brick homes. Fifty yards on she pulled the car to the kerb and parked. Switched off the engine.

'Tell me,' she said.

Laura took a deep breath, then exhaled. 'I'm reporting to

Vadic. I'm reporting to Kingsman. I'm walking a tight-rope held by them both and it's driving me crazy.'

'Does Kingsman know about the three clans meeting at the sky chalet?'

'Not yet.'

'Vadic got to you.'

'Yes.' The agent turned and looked Jay in the eyes. 'Just like he did you.'

Jay let this sink in. 'Our stories matched.'

'Pretty much.'

'But Kingsman doesn't believe us.'

'No.'

Jay drummed her fingers against the steering wheel. A young woman was walking down the pavement with two bags of Sainsbury's shopping in one hand. A little boy held the other. Her shoulders were hunched, her head ducked against the rain, but the little boy didn't seem to notice the weather. He wore blue and red striped wellies and was splashing and jumping into each puddle he came across. He was squealing with laughter.

Jay said, 'What shall we do?'

'Nothing at the moment. Vadic thinks he's got control of me but I'm going to get evidence to put him behind bars. Permanently.'

'How?'

'I'm going to lure him over here and set him up.'

'He'll expect it.'

'Not the way I do it, he won't.'

Jay watched a grey Ford cruise past them and turn left at the end of the street. 'You're telling me to do nothing.'

'Correct.'

'For how long?'

'Until I tell you.'

There was a small pause, and then Laura said, 'You need my new mobile number.'

After Jay had punched it into her phone, she studied the agent's gaunt expression, the shadows lurking in her eyes. 'Laura, is anyone helping you with this?'

'I've got to do it alone or Vadic will hear.'

With a start, Jay remembered her alarm bells ringing when she'd met Laura in Heathrow's car park, before she'd flown to Macedonia. Laura had hesitated over the emergency number she'd given Jay, which had made Jay question whether she trusted everyone there.

Jay's skin began to crawl. 'Someone in MI6 is working for Vadic?'

'Yes.'

'But you don't know who.'

'I've got a pretty good idea.'

'Which you're not going to share.'

'No.'

There was a long pause while they looked at each other. Laura turned away first. She said, 'Take me back to the office.'

Jay nearly told Laura about her house being bugged by a party aside from MI6, but at the last minute decided against it. The agent had enough on her plate without having to worry about her as well.

Back at the house, Jay called Denise. 'I'm off to visit Mum. I'll be back tomorrow.'

'How was Macedonia?'

'I'll tell you about it when I see you.'

Driving north, Jay tried to make sense of the morning's events. If Kingsman knew she was lying, why had he let her go? Why was he letting Laura continue her work as usual if he thought Vadic had got to her? Perhaps he had his own plan. Perhaps he was Vadic's mole in MI6. Perhaps Ingram was the traitor. Jay's mind then turned to Zamira, and she wondered where the girl was, and whether she was in the UK with the snake Branko, or if she was still in Macedonia or – God forbid – in Albania, prostitution capital of the world. She still had Hana's envelope with its blurred postmark. It could turn out to be a good lead and she'd follow it up once she'd seen her mother.

There was another vehicle parked outside her mother's house

when she arrived. It was a dark blue Audi, and when she saw the number plate, her heart did a double tap.

It was Tom's car.

Twenty-five

Zamira lay curled in the corner of the hall. She ached all over; her arms from trying to fend off Quinton, her breasts, which he'd punched, her thighs, which he'd gripped and bruised with his fingers, her legs, which he'd knelt on, but the worst pain was the one deep inside her, which was bleeding and throbbing as though she'd been impaled on a stake wrapped in barbed wire. She knew nothing would be the same again.

She didn't cry. Dry-eyed, she watched Quinton straighten his clothes and leave. The door closed behind him, and then she heard the click-click of the door as it locked.

Feeling as old and bent as one of the ancient peasants working the fields back home, Zamira pulled up her panties and jeans. Then she rolled on to all fours and willed herself to her feet, recoiling from the blood on the hall carpet. Unsteadily, holding her lower belly, she made it into the living room and stumbled to the windows. They all had locks on them. She looked around for a key, but couldn't see one.

She had to get out of here.

She checked each window in the apartment, and although one was cracked – a tiny feather was stuck in the glass making it look as though a bird had flown into it – they were all locked. Besides, she'd need a ladder or a rope to descend the four storeys to the street. Trying to move faster, she continued through the apartment, checking every drawer and every cupboard. There was no phone, and none of the interior doors had locks on them.

When she heard a key in the door, her heartbeat went into overdrive. Was it Hana? Or was it Quinton again? Zamira hurried for the bathroom and closed the door.

'Peaches? You there?'

It was Branko. She stood in the bathroom shaking, unsure what to do. She heard him calling but she didn't move. She felt as though she was frozen, paralysed.

The next instant the door was flung open.

'Sweetheart.' His face was a picture of dismay. 'Oh, Peaches, whatever did he do to you?'

The sympathy in his voice was too much and she burst into tears. Branko came and wrapped her in his arms. 'You poor little thing. Did he hurt you? I told him to treat you like a princess, but he's obviously a brute.' She was sobbing and clutching his shirt in her fists, her tears coming hot and fast. 'I'm so sorry, my darling. I really thought he'd be gentle, I really did, but look . . . '

He pulled back and reached into his pocket. He withdrew a fat roll of bills. British pounds. She had never seen so much money.

'It's yours. Quinton's way of saying sorry.'

For a moment she didn't understand, and then it hit her. She was being paid for being raped.

She forced herself to speak through her tears. 'I don't want it.'

'Don't be silly. Of course you want it. You can send some of it home, to Nadire. She needs the money.'

Somehow Zamira found the strength to shoulder her way past Branko. She didn't want to touch him, but she wanted to be held by him. She hated him, but she loved him too. She didn't know what to think. She hurt so much.

'Sweetheart, let me help you get cleaned up.'

She felt his hand on her shoulder and said, 'Don't.'

He dropped his hand. 'Okay.' He sounded wary. 'How about if you speak to Hana? Would that help?'

Zamira spun round. 'Oh, Branko . . . Yes, please.'

Stepping past her and into the living room, Branko spoke into his mobile phone. He was talking in English and she could only understand a handful of words, like 'yes' and 'money'. He seemed to speak to more than one person, and then finally he passed her the phone.

'Hana?'

'Oh, Zami . . . '

'When are you coming to see me?' Her voice began to break. 'I really need you.'

'I can't. I'm miles away. I got sent out of London. I didn't do as I was told. Zamira, if there's one thing you've got to do it's be obedient. Don't misbehave. You don't want to come here, believe me, it's awful. Just be *good*.'

'He raped me,' she wailed. 'A fat man, he was like a pig and really old and he hit me then he *raped me*.'

'Listen.' Hana's voice turned low and urgent. 'Get used to it. I know it's tough to start, really hard, but the sooner you begin to be nice to them, the better. You'll make heaps of money, and you'll be living somewhere nice . . . I'd do anything to still be in the apartment. It's hell where I am now. It's dirty and the men are disgusting. Do what Branko tells you, okay?'

Her world was toppling around her. Her ears were roaring with the sound of it.

'You're telling me to stay here?'

'Yes, Zami. Stay there and do what he says and you'll be fine. You're beautiful, you'll be in high demand . . . you'll be rich. Promise me you'll do that? Don't fight them or you'll end up here . . . '

'Where are you?'

Branko came and took the phone from her. 'Thanks, Hana. She needed a little sense talked into her. She doesn't realise how lucky she is yet.'

Lucky? Zamira stared at Branko. The word reminded her of her row with her mother and she stared around the room at the beautiful pieces of furniture, the gilt-edged mirrors and heavy bronze lamps. What would Nana say if she knew what was happening?

Tears trickled down her face but she made no effort to brush them away. 'I'll be good,' she whispered. 'I promise.'

'That's more like it.' Branko smiled. 'Why don't you go and have a wash? You'll feel much better afterwards. Okay?'

'Okay.' She looked up at him. 'Can I have my money?'

He put back his head and laughed. 'You're all the same, you women. Of course you can.'

He gave her five pounds.

Dismayed, she looked at the single note. 'I thought you said I could have it all?'

'I'll put the rest in the bank for you. When you need more, just ask and I'll give it to you. Now, will you be okay if I got out for a bit? There's food in the fridge. You can watch some TV. I'll be back later.'

She nodded. She pocketed the five pounds.

'Good girl.'

She didn't move as he patted her on the shoulder and left. She heard the front door open and shut, then the sound of him locking it. She didn't know how long she stood there. It could have been minutes or hours, she had no idea. She supposed she was in a state of shock. She'd heard you needed sugar in this sort of situation, or a shot of rakija, and so she went to the drinks cabinet and poured herself some whisky. It was disgusting and made her choke, but the trail of fire it left through her stomach felt good.

Gazing outside she watched people crossing the park, struggling with their umbrellas against the wind. A newspaper blew across the road. Red buses and black cabs cruised left and right. She saw a man climb into a taxi which then executed a U-turn and vanished up the road.

She wished she could jump into a cab and disappear.

She felt a sensation of doom tinged with terror descend over her. She was in a beautiful apartment in central London and she couldn't get out. She was a prisoner.

After a while, she went to the bathroom. She pulled off her clothes and stepped under the shower. Her skin was covered in bruises. She began to shiver as she washed between her legs. She washed and soaped and washed herself again, but she still didn't feel clean. She didn't think she ever would.

Dressed in jeans and with her hair slicked back, she went into the living room and studied the bookshelf. On the bottom shelf, within easy reach, was a miniature A-Z. She pulled it out and had a look. She wasn't sure where she was, which park she overlooked, so she turned the pages to study the area north of Camden Town. After a while, she pushed the book into her back pocket and went to wait for Branko in the hallway. She ignored the smudges of blood, now dry and dark, almost rust-coloured, on the carpet.

The minutes inched by. She sat down and rested her head in her arms. The clock tick-tocked soothingly, and eventually she slept.

She awoke with a start when she heard a key in the lock. Instantly, she was on her feet and pressing her back against the wall as the door opened. Branko stepped inside, and as he turned to close the door behind him Zamira sprang forward and pushed him into the hall with all her might.

He gave a startled shout, stumbling sideways. It was all she needed. She dived through the door.

'Zamira!' Branko yelled.

She pelted for the stairs. No time to wait for the lift. She could hear shouting behind her and then Branko appeared, tearing after her. If she could reach the street, someone would help her. She could hear Branko's thundering steps, gaining on her. She mustn't let him catch her.

Suddenly an apartment door opened in front of her and she nearly collided with it, startling the man emerging, who cursed.

She yelled, 'Help me!' and, pointing at Branko, continued her headlong charge. She piled down the next set of stairs. Just two floors to go.

Branko gave a yell. 'You fucking shit! I'll fucking kill you!'

A quick glance behind her showed the man had tripped Branko, who was scrambling upright from the floor, enraged. His attention wasn't on Zamira. It was on his new-found foe.

Only one floor to go. Then she was at ground level and running for the front door.

'ZAMIRA!'

188

His roar filled the building.

She yanked the big brass handle, pulled open the door and belted outside, swinging right, looking for a taxi with its yellow light shining. He'd never outrun a taxi.

She didn't look over her shoulder. She didn't want to slow her sprint. She'd spotted a taxi at the traffic lights ahead and she waved at it as she'd watched people do, and it put on its indicator, telling her it had seen her and was pulling over.

Branko was shouting her name. She catapulted into the back of the cab and slammed the door shut. The cab driver said something. She assumed he had asked where she wanted to go. Branko was ten metres away and closing fast.

She said, 'Forty-two Brecknock Road, N7.' The words felt peculiar in her mouth. She hadn't spoken them since she'd memorised them with Jay all those years ago.

The driver asked a question, gesturing at Branko. 'Friend?'

'No,' she panted in English. 'Please, go.'

The taxi driver stamped on the accelerator.

When she looked through the rear window, Branko was standing in the road with his hands on his hips. He was still shouting.

Twenty-six

'Hi,' said Tom.

'Hi.'

'How was Macedonia?'

'Interesting.'

He looked her up and down. 'You've lost weight.'

'I did a lot of walking.'

He said, 'Must have been a mighty long walk.'

'It was.'

She went and hugged him, and kissed him on the lips. He kissed her back. 'Hmm,' he said. 'You've been eating treacle dabs.'

He led her to stand in front of the fire. They were in the snug at the far end of the house, where her mother had put them along with a pot of tea and a plate of freshly baked double-chocolate brownies. Her mother had looked like the cat that had eaten the canary when she'd left them, ostensibly to start preparing supper.

A log tumbled in the grate, sending a flurry of sparks up the chimney. 'I had a walk too, earlier,' Tom told her. 'Your mum rang me and invited me to lunch, and when you didn't turn up, I thought I'd get some fresh air. I didn't lose much weight, though, thanks to the flapjack she gave me. It was as big as a brick.'

Belatedly she took in the marsh mud spatters up his jeans and the fact he was wearing socks. His shoes must have got soaked. 'Tom, in case you didn't know, there's a type of rubber footwear called wellies that you—'

'God, you drive me crazy,' he interrupted. He was shaking his head. 'You are the most hot-headed, foolhardy, most stubborn and impetuous woman I have ever known, and . . . '

Jay held her breath.

'I've missed you.'

'I missed you too,' she said.

'That's good to hear.' He smiled. 'Tell me, what exactly does Max Blake – the man I saw at your house last week – do?'

'Oh, he's with SOCA. He's been working undercover in the Balkans.'

'Is he the reason why you went to Macedonia?'

'No, that was MI6. They sent me to Skopje to ask around about a guy called Milot Dumani, and I bumped into Blake out there. We got into a bit of trouble with the Mafia and did a runner through Albania and on to Italy. But I'm here now, safe and sound. Blake's still overseas.'

'MI6?' Tom's eyebrows had shot up. 'Mafia? Please God, tell me you're making this up.'

'Unfortunately not,' she said. 'Which is why I came to see Mum. The Mafia are threatening my family to try and stop me going to MI6 with some vital information I discovered in Macedonia.'

There was a long pause and then Tom lifted his head to stare at the ceiling. 'Why can't I get engaged to a normal woman? Someone who works in a bank or a department store instead of tangling with mobsters and spooks?'

'We're engaged?'

'I'm not sure, from the look on your face.' His voice turned gentle. 'But do we have time to go into that right now?'

'No,' she admitted.

'Later, okay?'

'Okay.'

'Right. Let's start at the beginning.' His demeanour turned

crisp and professional. 'I want to know everything. Take your time, Jay, and don't leave anything out.'

By the time Tom left, Jay had as much energy as a wrung-out dish towel. She had told him everything – except that she'd shared a sleeping shelf or two with Blake, she didn't think he needed to know that – and the relief at sharing the whole grim and terrifying story had been huge, like extracting a painful thorn from her foot after walking on it all week. He had listened quietly, interrupting with the odd question to clarify a point, and by the time she had finished with her chat to Laura in the car, she had eaten several brownies and felt faintly sick.

Tom had taken Hana's envelope, said he'd give it to forensics, and then told her he'd investigate the restaurant where Jay had followed Milot.

'I'll also liaise with the Norwich cops, see how they're doing tracking down the guy who threatened your mother.' He leaned forward. 'I appreciate why you're withholding stuff from MI6, but don't you think we should meet with SOCA? They're specialists in organised crime, they'll know these guys. They should be able to help get Vadic off your back.'

'We can't, Tom. That's the point. Vadic said he has contacts everywhere, including the British police. If he hears of me stepping out of line, he comes after us.'

'I can't believe Vadic thinks he can keep such big news quiet. Someone will talk at some point, somewhere. A foot soldier of Protti's or Milot's. I bet it'll be out within the month.'

'I'd rather it wasn't me who blabbed.'

'McCaulay, listen to me. We have to go to SOCA. It's the only way.'

'Not when my loved ones are at risk.' Jay looked away. 'He knows about you. He said you could get shot in the line of duty . . . '

Tom's expression tightened. 'Okay. So let's give it twenty-four hours. See what I can come up with.'

He left looking grim and determined, and when she followed him to his car, he turned and kissed her goodbye. He tasted of coffee and chocolate and she wished he didn't have to leave.

Now Jay took another slug of wine. Her mother was demanding to know the full story, and although she deserved to know why she'd been targeted by a Mafia henchman, Jay decided to keep the story to its bare minimum, but her mother thought otherwise. It was like being interrogated by the KGB.

'You shared a bed with this Max Blake?' Her mother's expression was intent.

'There wasn't anywhere else to sleep. Besides, we kind of had to pretend we were married, to avoid causing offence. You needn't worry. He was the perfect gentleman.'

'Where is he now?'

'God knows.' She yawned. 'Look, Mum. I'm exhausted. Can we finish this tomorrow?'

'Of course, darling. I'm sorry. You go to bed and I'll bring you a mug of hot cocoa.'

Jay let her mother fuss over her and tuck her into bed as though she was four years old. She slept deeply, no dreams, and when she left for London in the morning it was with two ham and mustard sandwiches and a freshly baked carrot cake.

Twenty-seven

Branko watched Zamira's taxi accelerate down Kensington Gore. The little bitch, giving him the slip like that! When he got his hands on her, he'd give her a hiding she wouldn't forget. He had honestly thought she'd been cowed by her experience with Quinton, but she'd fooled him.

Picking up his mobile phone, he called Reda. Reda owned the brothel where Hana worked. 'I need to talk to Hana. Put her on.'

'She's with a customer, Branko.'

'I don't care, I want to talk to her *now*.'

'Ring back in ten minutes.'

To his fury, Reda hung up.

Branko prowled the apartment, trying to think where Zamira would run. He'd made sure she was frightened of the authorities, so she wouldn't go to the police. Then he remembered her talking about some friend she had in London, an army captain. A woman. He couldn't remember the captain's name but instinct told him she was his best lead. He just had to hope Hana could give him an address before it got out that he'd lost a girl. Milot would laugh himself sick. He shuddered. He didn't want to work with Milot and his gang any more. They were thugs. Primitive brutes with the sophistication of a herd of swine. They wore chicken-shit imitation leather jackets and although their suits were labelled Armani and Versace, they were nothing but cheap copies. Their cologne was ripped off, and so were their cigarettes. Nothing the Mafia used was authentic. Everything was counterfeit.

You could dress them in Savile Row suits and give them Cristal champagne to drink and they'd still be nothing but thugs. It was imprinted in their blood.

One day, he'd have made enough money to turn his back on them. He'd buy a mansion in Hampstead and an apartment in Paris and spend his evenings with beautiful women at the opera.

But first, he had to find Zamira.

Five pounds didn't take Zamira far, but at least the taxi driver was kind enough to show her where she was on her A-Z, and where she had to go to.

'Long way?' she asked. 'I walk.'

'Two hours.'

A two-hour walk was nothing. She'd been brought up walking the hills all day and she should be there before night fell.

The cab driver squinted at her face. 'You okay?'

'Yes. Thank you.'

Her face and body ached unrelentingly as she walked. A few people stared – they obviously hadn't seen a battered woman before – and she stared back until they looked away, her soul shrivelling as she trailed painfully north. She couldn't understand why Hana hadn't told her what awaited her in London. On the phone she'd said she hadn't been good and that she was in a bad place, why hadn't she warned her in her letter? And where was she?

Eventually, Zamira came to a huge park, and as she gazed at the cream and white houses overlooking the broad green space she momentarily forgot her pain. They were enormous and beautifully cared for with immaculate paintwork and trimmed hedges. The amount of money you would need to own one of those places made her feel faint.

After she'd rested, she walked through Camden Town, distracted from the aches in her body by the restaurants and pubs, bookshops and grocery stores. She followed Camden Road, her lungs tight from the stench of pollution – she hadn't realised how dirty London would be – and then finally she arrived.

Brecknock Road was busy with traffic, but the house Jay lived in looked nice. It was freshly painted white and had a large tree that would shade the ground floor apartment in summer. Zamira peered through the big front window to see the stripped floors that Jay had told her about, and the fireplace set between two bookshelves. Going to the door, she pressed G, for ground. Nothing happened. She pressed it again. Tears threatened to rise. Please God, Jay wasn't away.

She jumped when the door was flung open. A tall black man in a pair of pink running shorts barked, 'Yeah?'

'Jay McCaulay,' she said. 'I'm her friend.'

'Well, bully for you.'

'Jay here?'

'Nope. Nobody here by that name. Sorry.' He shut the door in her face.

Fighting back tears, Zamira tried another bell with no luck. Then another. Finally, she tried the basement.

'You want Jay?' a woman said on the intercom. 'Hang on, I'll come up.'

The woman was huge and wore a tent-shaped dress printed with gigantic daffodils. Zamira had never seen anyone so overweight and had to make an effort not to stare.

The woman said, 'Crikey, love, what happened to you?'

'Jay is here?'

'Not any more. She moved a couple of years ago.'

'Where is she?'

'I have no idea, but you could try her work . . . '

The woman looked over Zamira's shoulder, her expression brightening. 'Why, hello handsome. What can I do for you?'

Zamira didn't look around. She didn't want to be interrupted. She said, 'Where she work?' She was intent on the fat woman, not caring who was behind her, and as she repeated the question, getting impatient, her arms were grabbed from behind. She gave a startled yelp but then a hand went over her mouth, an arm around her waist.

'Zamira,' said Branko. He was hauling her towards the street. 'If you shout or scream or run from me again, I shall whip you so hard you will bleed.'

She jerked her head, trying to bite his hand but his grip was relentless. At the end of the path, she saw a white van come to a stop. A thickset man jumped out and opened the rear doors. She screamed behind Branko's hand but it was muffled. She glanced back to the house, looking for the fat woman, but she had gone.

Zamira doubled her efforts to free herself, fighting with all her strength, but it wasn't enough. He flung her roughly in the back of the van. She landed on her side, skinning her knee and her elbow, and then the doors were slammed shut. She lunged at them, banging with all her might, shouting. Then the van gave a lurch and drove away.

She was thrown to one side when they rounded a corner, and she had to wedge herself behind the wheel arch to brace herself against the movement of the car. She couldn't stop sobbing. How had Branko known where she'd go? She'd never told him where Jay lived ... her mind leaped. She'd told Hana, though. Hana must have told Branko. Her friend's treachery was the worst, and tears poured down her face and ran into the corners of her mouth. Eventually the van stopped veering left and right, and settled to a steady cruise. They were on a highway. Her face was hot and sore from weeping, her body aching all over. She couldn't think where Branko was taking her, but it was well out of the city.

She thought of Hana, their early childhood – long summers when the sun was hot and the sky as blue as glass, when they ran barefoot across hillsides speckled with wildflowers. They'd strip off their clothes and leap into the shallows of a nearby river, shrieking, before sprawling on a small sandy beach and telling one another stories.

Why had her best friend betrayed her?

The van drove for a long time, maybe two hours or more, before it lurched off the highway and began twisting and turning. She heard engines alongside, and a siren. She was in a town, or a city. At last, the van slowed to a stop. She listened to footsteps come round to the back of the van and tried not to cower when the doors opened and cold night air rushed inside.

'Out,' said Branko.

On her backside, she shuffled to the doors and was immediately grabbed and lifted outside. She was in a street lined with small houses. Streetlights glowed orange, and dustbins stood on the pavement, one for each house. It was raining and the air smelled metallic.

Gripping her upper arm, Branko marched her to the front door of one of the houses. It didn't have a number, and the garden looked overgrown. He didn't knock or ring a bell, just opened the door and pushed her inside. Ahead was a staircase and to the left a living room that led into a kitchen. The living room had threadbare brown carpet with orange swirls, a dark blue sofa and a beige armchair. It reeked of stale cigarettes and old food.

'Reda!' he yelled.

'Yeah, yeah, Branko.' A skinny woman in a purple smock came down the stairs.

'Here she is.'

Reda looked Zamira up and down. 'Very pretty.'

Gripping Zamira's hand, Branko hauled her through the living room and into the kitchen. 'Put the kettle on or something,' he told her. 'I'll be back in a minute.'

She was quaking inside as she looked at the window. It was barred with thick black metal posts and on the other side, just three feet away, was a brick wall. No plants or view of a garden. It was like being in jail.

She peered into the living room. She watched Branko click his fingers at the woman. 'Come on, Reda. I don't have all day.'

'Three thousand,' said Reda.

'You must be kidding. I saw the way you looked at her. She's a filly in her prime, sleek and full of stamina. You know they'll go mad for her.'

'She'll be bloody difficult.' Reda stuck her lower lip out like a bull dog. 'You can tell by the fire in her eyes. She'll give me hell.'

'Six thousand.' Branko turned businesslike.

'Four.'

'No fucking way. That's the price for tired old cows who are past their sell-by date. You insult my intelligence, Reda.'

'Okay.' The woman licked her lips. 'Five.'

Zamira was numb with horror. She couldn't look away, couldn't speak.

Branko rolled his eyes and sighed. 'Five and a half and we've a deal.'

Reda reached into her smock pocket and withdrew a roll of money. She flicked through it and Zamira's eyes widened. It made the roll of money Branko had shown her earlier look pathetic.

'Deal,' said Reda, and handed the wad of notes to Branko.

Branko counted the money. 'I'm fifty short,' he said.

'Sorry.' Reda returned her hand to her pocket and extracted a smaller roll of notes and peeled off five, handed them over.

Branko pocketed the money and Zamira ducked back and leaned against the kitchen wall, heart pounding. She felt nauseous and wondered where the bathroom was.

'Hey, Peaches.' Branko was smiling down at her. 'You okay?'

Her mouth opened but no sound came out.

'I'm going to show you your bedroom. It's upstairs. You'll be sharing with Hana, okay?'

Zamira began to edge away, for the living room, the front door.

Immediately Branko's face darkened and he lunged for her, grabbing her wrist. He dragged her forcibly up the stairs and pushed her into a room and slammed the door behind him. She heard the lock turn.

She raced to the window, flinging back the flimsy orange curtains, but it was boarded up. She couldn't even see outside. Panic flooded her. She whirled around. There was a double bed in the middle of the room, and nothing else. The room was bare. She sank on to the bed and stared at the wall. She was shivering, too scared to weep.

After a while, she heard the door unlock. In a flash, she fled to the furthest corner of the room. She couldn't hide behind the door because it opened outwards, and into the hall.

The door opened to reveal Reda. Behind her stood four men.

'Now, Zamira,' said Reda. She tossed a short skirt inside the room, along with a flimsy halter-neck top. 'You'll need these for work.'

Zamira stared at the clothes.

'You are in debt to me for seven thousand pounds. This covers what I bought you for, along with your air fare, your travel costs, and your accommodation. When you have worked off your debt, you can go.'

Reda gestured one of the men forward. 'This is Shaban.'

Shaban looked just like the men back home. Short and squat, dishevelled and bearded with no neck.

'If you try and escape, Shaban will kill you. But not before he makes you hurt. He knows more about causing pain than I've had cups of tea. He's good at it, because he enjoys it.'

Zamira tried not to whimper, but the sound escaped. Shaban's eyes gleamed.

'Branko says you're a troublemaker,' Reda said. 'That you bite and scratch and fight. From the sound of it, you need breaking in.' She gave a narrow smile showing a row of uneven, discoloured teeth. 'She's all yours, Shaban.'

Shaban stepped into the room. He was already unbuckling his belt. To her horror, the other men came inside too.

'You're going to love us, sweetheart,' said Shaban. He was grinning.

Twenty-eight

Jay, bleary-eyed, yawned as she stirred her porridge on the stove. She'd had a restless night, unable to stop thinking of Zamira and where she might be, and when she'd finally dropped off, she had fallen straight into her familiar, terrifying dream. She was in combat kit, clearing a house. She was on the top floor and waiting for the girl's rapist to spring from behind the door when a British soldier charged past and kicked it shut. To her amazement, nobody was hiding behind it.

He yelled, 'All clear!'

'All clear!' she yelled back.

'Good job, soldier.'

She awoke and lay staring at the ceiling, stunned. The British soldier who'd burst into her dream, altering it for ever, had been Max Blake. And she realised it had been Blake who had yelled, 'All clear!' when she'd last had the dream, and vapourised the rapist.

Jay replayed the dream in her mind. She wondered if you could be in love with two men at the same time. This question kept her awake for a long time.

'You look tired.' Denise was in an old pair of tracksuit pants, making tea to take up to Angela. 'You should take the day off.'

Jay yawned again. It was a tempting thought, especially since it was chucking down rain outside. 'Too much to do,' she said. She was about to ask Denise a favour, and then considered the bugs.

She dithered until Denise made to go back upstairs. Grabbing a pen and Post-it note from next to the phone, she scooted across the kitchen. 'Can you flag someone coming into the country for me?' Her voice was a murmur.

Her flatmate paused, her eyes narrowing. 'Like who?'

'You remember I was talking about a guy last week?' She scribbled the name Milot Dumani on the Post-it note.

Denise looked at it with a frown. 'Sure, we'll flag him.'

'Could you extend it to include another scumbag?'

Another scribble. Tihomir Vadic. 'He's from Georgia.'

Denise studied Jay. 'You're not in over your head, are you?'

'No, everything's fine.'

'I've heard that one before,' Denise sighed as she pocketed the post-it-note. 'You need backup, just call.'

'Thanks.'

Adding a spoonful of brown sugar to her porridge, Jay ate it, looking through the window and thinking of Blake, where he might be, and whether he was also having breakfast. She was washing up her bowl when her mobile rang. It was Nick, calling from TRACE's office.

'I've just had a call from the Camden police. Apparently a man kidnapped a girl outside your old home in Brecknock Road. It sounds like it could be Zamira. A woman called Pat Vellum dialled nine-nine-nine but by the time the cops turned up, the girl was gone. Pat says she knows you. Do you want her number?'

Jay grabbed a pen. 'Fire away.'

'Pat said the girl was asking for you, but before she could give the girl your Fulham address she was grabbed and thrown into the back of a white van. The number plates were bogus, the van stolen. Pat Vellum said the girl's face was bruised, and that she looked as though she'd been beaten up.'

Oh God. Poor Zamira.

'Description of the kidnappers?'

'She only got a good look at one. A very attractive guy according to the witness. Around five-ten or so, dark hair and eyes, Mediterranean looking, nicely dressed ... '

It had to be Branko. Zamira had run away from him but he'd managed to track her down and reclaim her. 'I'll go and see Pat,' Jay told Nick. 'See what else I can get.'

'Good luck.'

Despite questioning Pat closely for over an hour, Jay learned nothing new aside from the fact that Pat had joined Weight-watchers and managed to lose five pounds in her first week. Before Jay left, she gave Pat her new address and all her phone numbers, including her mother's. 'If you see or hear anything from the man or the girl, ring me, day or night.'

She got into her car wanting to weep over the fact Zamira had run to her for help only to find she'd moved.

Jay spent the remainder of the day in the office, dealing with her in-tray and a stack of e-mails longer than her arm. Kiro had rung with the depressing news of six more girls going missing; apparently traffickers were sourcing more girls from Macedonia than before.

'And you're okay?' Kiro asked for the third time.

'Never better,' she told him. 'I'm sorry about your car.'

'I can only forgive you if you tell me the whole story.'

'I will, Kiro,' she promised. 'But it's not over yet.'

Ingram had rung from the MI6 office twice, wanting to bring round his photographs to see if she could identify the two men from the helicopter, but she put him off. Instinct told her to keep buying time for as long as she could.

She was speaking to the duty officer in the Norwich police, getting an update on the troll who'd threatened her mother – no news of his whereabouts yet – when her e-mail pinged. It was from Tom.

Re: Hana's letter. Postmark is dated 25 January this year, Bristol. You want to come and question your usual suspects?

She wound up her call and e-mailed back: *You bet. I'll drive over in the morning.*

Tom's reply was instantaneous. *Chocolate brownies at my office, 11.00 a.m.*

*

True to his word, Tom had a plate of brownies waiting when she turned up. They were roughly sliced and crumbling at the edges, obviously homemade, and when she peeked at the bin she spotted a familiar wrapper from a Clifton deli.

She took a brownie and looked around. He'd moved offices since she'd last been here, and this one was bigger, with a view of the car park rather than the road. It reminded her of MI6's office; blue painted walls, grey synthetic carpet, fluorescent strip lighting. No personal photographs or pictures on the walls. A space for work, not for day dreaming.

'What have you got?' she asked.

Tom was wearing jeans and a soft blue shirt over a white t-shirt and she wished he didn't look so damned good.

'Milot owns a chain of restaurants in town, along with two clubs and a chunk of real estate on Canon's Marsh worth over ten mill.'

'Legit?'

'It seems so.'

'What else?'

'I got the weekend teams on duty to ask around about Zamira. One of the constables heard of a brothel specialising in newly recruited Eastern European girls but when they pressed for an address, the witness clammed up.'

'Who was the witness?'

Tom bit into a brownie while he shuffled through some papers. 'A Welsh girl called Hilary. Short, dark, in her twenties. She was questioned just off Old Market Street.'

Lily's pitch, Jay thought. She'd talk to her when she'd finished with Tom.

'I got in touch with SOCA about Zamira. I didn't mention Milot or Vadic,' he assured her. 'Just the girl. They sent me this.' He pushed across a photograph. It was of a dark-haired man with chiselled looks that wouldn't have looked out of place on an advertising billboard for Chanel or Dior. 'Branko Morillon.'

For a moment, she was dumbfounded, but then she pounced on it. 'Tom, that's fantastic. Can I keep it?'

'All yours. I've made copies for the teams on duty to show around.'

Jay tucked it into her day pack, her spirits soaring. If they found Branko, then they'd find Zamira. She was about to grab another brownie when Tom pushed forward a second photograph saying, 'About this guy . . . '

She forgot all about the brownie as she stared at a picture of Max Blake. He was looking into the camera, expression narrowed and hard, as though the photographer was someone he hated.

'He's not with SOCA. I checked with them. He's a mercenary. A gun for hire. They consider him a loose cannon and wouldn't touch him with a barge pole.'

Jay touched Blake's face with her forefinger. She ran over her first meeting with MI6, replaying everyone's instructions. Blake had told her he worked with SOCA and nobody in the room had corrected him. Did this mean Blake was working for MI6? Or did he have his own agenda?

'Jay.' Tom looked at her sombrely. 'Whatever this guy's told you, take it with a pinch of salt, okay? I know he helped you out of Macedonia, that you probably feel a kind of loyalty towards him . . . '

'Not probably,' she interjected. 'I do feel loyal to Blake.'

'I can understand that, but he's not to be trusted.'

'Who says?'

Tom blinked. 'SOCA, of course.'

'They've worked with him? Done an op with him?'

'Not that they've said, but I gather they know him pretty well.'

Her blood pressure began to rise. 'How can they know him pretty well if they haven't undertaken any kind of mission with him?'

Tom ran a hand across the nape of his neck. 'Just listen, would you? They warned me against the guy, said that he's a chameleon who changes sides as fast as he can change his socks, that he—'

'Stop,' she said. She held up her hands. 'I don't want to hear any more. The man helped save my life.'

'From what you said, it sounded more like you saved his.' His voice was cold.

'That too, but we were a team out there, Tom.' She leaned forward. 'He proved himself a hundred percent and I won't have that undermined by anyone, least of all you.'

Tom stared. 'Jesus Christ. You slept with him, didn't you?'

For a second she wasn't sure if she'd heard correctly and then it sank in. She rose to her feet. Her breathing was tight.

'Well, aren't you the detective,' she said. 'Yes, we shared a bed. Yes, we fell asleep together each night with farm animals farting and shitting next to us. Yes, we hugged to keep warm. Yes, I slept with him. So sue me.'

Back ramrod straight, she stalked out of the office before he could see the tell-tale flare of guilt on her cheeks. She may not have had sex with Blake, but sometimes she wished she had.

Twenty-nine

During her first three days in the brothel Zamira was continuously beaten and gang-raped by four men. She was given no food, just water, and was only allowed out of the room to use the loo – in full view of whichever man was guarding her.

She stopped fighting on the first day, but it made no difference. They'd slap her, wanting her to respond, and if she moved, they'd slap her again to keep still. By the end of the second day she became a rag doll, limp and compliant, with her mind splintered into compartments.

There was a compartment for Branko, where she took a knife to his belly and slit him wide open. One for the four men and Reda, whom she would douse with petrol and set alight. Another for Hana, where she'd hit and punch her friend for lying to her. But the place she went to when the men were pumping and thrusting inside her was clean and pure and smelled of snow. She'd imagine Nadire chopping logs, the great sprawling doggy form of Bear nearby, ears cocked as he watched over the sheep. She could taste the scent of fresh resin from the wood, hear the streams bubbling and the birds trilling; the taste of freedom.

On the fourth day, Reda came into the room. 'I've a friend of yours wanting to see you.'

The next second, Hana shot inside. She was wearing a miniskirt that barely covered her sex and a bikini top covered in little silver mirrors. She'd lost a lot of weight and looked gaunt.

'Zami,' she said. She was crying.

Zamira looked away. She couldn't bear to meet her friend's eyes.

'Clean her up,' barked Reda. 'Have her ready for work tomorrow.' Then the woman left, shutting the door behind her.

'Zami, I'm so sorry.' Hana crept on to the bed. Zamira scurried to the other side. 'I tried to warn you ... I told you to be good. You should have listened to me. You could still be in the apartment, making tons of money ... '

'You betrayed me.' Zamira's voice felt rusty from not having spoken for days. 'You told Branko where Jay lived.'

'Shaban said he'd break my arm,' Hana whimpered. 'He really meant it.'

Zamira stared at her friend as though she was a stranger. 'Why did you write that letter to me?'

'Branko made me. I tried to code a warning but he spotted it. He threatened to sell me to Shaban if I did it again.' She began crying once more. 'I didn't want you to come, I promise.'

Zamira was too crushed to hate Hana. She wanted to, but at least now she could understand the betrayal. She might have written the letter too, rather than be owned by the brutal, evil-smelling Shaban.

'Let me help you to the bathroom,' Hana said. 'I've got painkillers and some arnica. Arnica's great for bruises.'

Zamira let Hana bathe her and put her to bed. When she felt Hana climb in beside her, she closed her eyes. Hana cuddled up to her like she used to when they shared a bed as children and, at last, her mind went numb.

'No,' Hana said. She was shaking her head furiously. 'I won't do it.'

'Please,' Zamira begged. 'She trusts you. She lets you go out shopping. Just leave the door open for me. Two seconds will do it. I won't tell her it was you.'

'I can't.' Hana's face was screwed up. 'She said my family would be harmed if I didn't behave. She just has to call Branko and he'll call someone in the gang. My little brother, he's only six . . . '

While Hana continued to bleat, Zamira shovelled another spoonful of cornflakes into her mouth. She'd been eating like a horse over the past two days, trying to build up her strength. If she stayed here, she knew she would crack. She wasn't like Hana, able to manage this horrific lifestyle and keep her sanity. Within weeks she knew she would become a zombie, permanently unfeeling, unthinking and numb. She would rather be dead.

'Hana, once I'm out of here, I will find Jay and we'll come back and free you.'

'But you don't even know where Jay is!'

'I can find her.' She wasn't going to tell Hana her plan, in case she told Reda, who would then tell Branko.

'I can't do it.' Hana got up and started to walk out of the kitchen.

'You mean won't!' Zamira yelled. 'You selfish bitch! It's your fault I'm here and now you won't even help me!'

The next second, Reda was there. 'What's this all about?'

'Nothing,' said Zamira.

'Hana?'

Hana ducked her head and remained silent.

'Hana, if you don't tell me what was just said, I shall send Shaban to you tonight.'

'Please . . . ' Hana shrank into the corner. 'It's just that . . . Zami wanted me to leave open the front door. So she could escape.'

For a moment, Reda looked stunned, as though she didn't believe what she'd heard. Then she came over to Zamira.

'I should never have bought you,' she said. Her eyes were like flint. 'You're unbreakable.'

'Let me go. I'll pay you.'

'With what?' Reda laughed.

'My English friend is rich.'

'I don't think so.' Moving into the living room, Reda pulled out her mobile phone. 'Shaban? You know anyone who might want to buy our beautiful little princess? Have her all to themselves? What? You'd like her? Really? How much?'

Terror speared Zamira. She shot into the living room and fell to her knees. 'No!' she cried. 'Please! I'm sorry, I'll be good! I promise I'll never try and escape, I swear it!'

Reda looked at her. Her eyes were empty. 'It's too late,' she said. 'Shaban is on his way to collect you.'

Thirty

'Sweetie!' Lily greeted Jay effusively.

'Wow,' said Jay. 'You look amazing.'

Lily had teased her peroxide hair into a wild beehive above a gold tank top and a pair of spandex leggings the colour of mustard. Her shoes had heels the height of the Empire State Building and were patent leather red.

'And you look dull and dowdy. You should wear more colour, honey, bring some light into your life. Cigarette? Or have you still given up?'

'What the hell.' Jay took one and lit up. Smoke scalded her lungs as she watched a blue van slow on their side of the street. The driver, a guy in a boiler suit, waved cheerfully at Lily.

'That's Dave,' Lily said, waving back. 'Self-employed builder with a Catholic prude of a wife at home. He nearly went through the roof when I gave him his first blow job.'

'Lucky Dave.' Jay began to bring out the photograph of Branko but paused when her mobile phone rang. It was Denise, her housemate.

'About those guys you wanted flagged. There's no sign of Milot, he's still overseas, but Vadic's already in the UK. I got Angela to check with Immigration. He flew in on Saturday.'

A high-pitched ringing started in Jay's ears. 'You got an address for him?'

'Number twelve, Kensington Gore. Since he is who he is, I wouldn't hold your breath that it's legit.'

Kensington Gore was one of the most expensive streets in London, a stone's throw from the Albert Hall and almost opposite Kensington Palace.

'I'll try it anyway. Look, thanks a lot. I really appreciate it.'

'You're going to approach him?' Alarm tinged Denise's voice.

Shit. Jay realised her slip. Please God, Vadic wouldn't find out about this conversation. 'Probably not.'

'What's going on?'

'I'll tell you later.'

There was a short pause before Denise said, 'Remember we're here for you, okay?'

'Okay.'

Apologising to Lily for the delay, Jay finally showed her Branko's photograph. 'Do you know this guy?'

'No.' Lily studied it. 'I'd remember him if we'd met. Bet he's a bastard. That type usually are.'

Jay tucked it back in her pocket. 'What about Hilary? Do you know her? She's a Welsh girl who works around here. She says she knows him.'

'Sure, I know Hilary. Wait here, I'll get her for you.'

It didn't take Lily long to find Hilary, and when Hilary balked at Branko's photograph, it was Lily who did the strong-arming. Jay didn't hear what Lily said, but from the way she took hold of the young Welsh girl, hissing into her ear and making her pale, Jay gathered she wasn't talking about how to best prune your roses. Not meeting Jay's eye, Hilary gave an address in the suburbs towards Fishponds before scuttling off.

'Thanks, Lily.' Jay ground her cigarette beneath her boot before giving her a twenty pound note.

'I'd be careful if I was you,' Lily warned. 'That brothel's got a particularly nasty reputation.'

Jay parked her Golf at the end of the street and walked to the address Hilary had given her. Standing outside, she studied the house before she decided her next move. Identical to its neighbours, the only thing that set it apart was the fact that it had bars on every window and that one of the upstairs rooms appeared to be boarded up. Its garden was messier than most, with rubbish spilling from black refuse bags – empty lager cans and takeaway pizza cartons smeared with tomato and congealed cheese – but there was nothing about it that indicated it was a brothel.

She considered knocking on the door and asking if Branko was there, but instinct told her she'd be better off doing it with Tom and a couple of constables backing her up. Pulling out her phone she turned away and trudged back to her car. She checked the time. Six p.m. Tom was probably still in the office. She wondered if she should apologise for storming out earlier, or if it was for him to apologise for assuming she'd slept with Blake, but then she heard her father's voice in her mind, and realised it didn't matter. *Never let the sun go down on an argument.*

She punched in Tom's number. He answered on the first ring.

'Tom, I'm sorry,' she said. 'I shouldn't have stormed out like that.'

'And I shouldn't have acted the way I did,' he replied. 'I'm sorry too, okay?'

'Very okay.' She smiled.

'You fancy supper this evening?'

She was about to say yes, when he cursed. 'Hell, Jay. Sorry, the chief's waving at me, reminding me I've got a meeting tonight. How about the weekend?'

'Great.'

'Got to go, gorgeous.'

She was nearing her car when she registered a sudden movement alongside her. A man was leaping for her, his hand outstretched. Immediately she brought up her arms to defend herself and then a stream of spray hit her full in the face. The pain was instantaneous. Her eyes felt as though they were being eaten by acid. She gave a hoarse shout and then she was stumbling desperately for her car, trying to get to the door, scramble for safety, but already her responses were uncoordinated, her motor skills breaking down.

Unable to see, unable to breathe, she managed to kick out once, but then her senses ceased to co-operate. Her hearing had gone. She couldn't smell. She felt herself tipping sideways as her legs buckled and she was falling, and she wanted to brace herself before she hit the gutter but someone had filleted her and she had no muscles, no bones.

Her last coherent thought before she passed out was: hell, I hope I don't break my head open on the pavement.

Thirty-one

Jay swallowed salt water.

Choking, she flailed her arms and legs. The cold was immense. Water slapped against her face. Her throat was burning, her eyes stinging as though they'd been rubbed in chilli peppers. Everything was pitch black.

She was drowning in a bath. No, she was in a swimming pool.

Briny, salty water.

Oh, Christ! She must be in the sea.

She kicked and thrashed in the water, trying to keep afloat while she searched desperately through the darkness for a point of reference.

There was no sky. No stars or moon. No light anywhere.

There was nothing except black, freezing cold salt water. An impenetrable darkness that stretched into a seemingly endless void. Terror streaked through her, and she was sinking and lashing out, confused and panicky, and then her brain kicked into life: Get rid of your boots. They're dragging you down.

She had to move her limbs freely or she'd drown. She managed to grab a lungful of air before searching for the zips. Her fingers felt swollen and stiff and she struggled to force them to do what she wanted. She had unzipped one boot when a wave slapped against her face and she began to sink again.

She stopped fighting the water and let herself drift downwards, putting all her effort into releasing the boot. Her fingers pulled and tugged and twisted and her chest was aching but she refused to give in and at last the leather loosened and she yanked her foot free.

Kicking to the surface, gasping and choking, she tugged off the second boot but she was still being dragged down so she struggled out of her fleece and shirt. She wanted to strip off her jeans but it would be impossible.

Treading water in jeans and bra was much easier, and she steadied herself, looking around into nothing. Her adrenaline spiked and she forced herself to keep her breathing steady and not to lose control. She must stay calm, but already she could feel the fear building inside. The wind blew salt spray into her eyes. Waves slapped against her mouth.

'Help!' Her voice sounded tiny, like a beetle crushed in the corner of an amphitheatre.

'HELP!'

Fear and horror gave her voice strength but the wind snatched her words away.

She was taking another breath to yell when she heard an outboard motor start up. Her heart leaped. Someone had heard her! It wasn't that close, but it wasn't that far away either. She swung her head to where the sound came from, but she still couldn't see anything. There were no lights.

'Help!' she shouted. 'HELP!'

The engine engaged gear.

No! What if they left her behind? Jay floundered then kicked out. She had to get to the boat.

'HELP!'

The throttle began to ease open, and then the lights were snapped on. It was a small cabin-cruiser. Red and green lights burned on the bow. A figure stood at the helm but it wasn't looking her way. The boat was facing in the opposite direction.

'HELP!' she yelled again and lunged after it but the throttle opened wide, swallowing her shouts as the propellers churned the sea into a lather and powered the boat forward. Panic speared her when she realised it was motoring away from her.

Jay put her head down and charged after it. She didn't think, didn't wonder who was at the helm of the boat, or weigh up any options about conserving her energy. Her instincts were screaming not to be left behind and she put every ounce of effort into swimming as hard and fast as she could for the rapidly disappearing blur of lights bounding across the waves.

It was only when a large wave crested over her and came down like a pile-driver, burying her underwater, that good sense prevailed. She came up, spluttering and gulping to see the boat was now at least a quarter of a mile away. The throttle was wide open and the bows were up on the plane, leaving a foamy wake as it raced into the distance.

Still staring after the boat, she prayed it would turn around. It didn't. She could feel wavelets slapping against the back of her neck and hoped the wind driving them was a westerly, and that it was blowing from the Atlantic and across the Bristol Channel for Avonmouth. If it wasn't, and she'd been dumped off the Welsh coast, or somewhere off southern England, she'd be dead before the sun came up.

Mustn't think of that. She had to believe she was in the Severn Estuary or she'd give up, and she didn't want that. She was a survivor. Survivors didn't fold at the first fence.

Scrunching her eyelids to ease the saltwater burn, she began to swim after the tiny yellow dot in the distance that was the cabin cruiser.

Thirty-two

Jay swam in long, unhurried strokes, trying to pace herself and prolong her store of energy. She was relatively fit and strong and although the water was cold, it wasn't Arctic cold. She should be able to swim for at least a couple of hours, making a headway of two miles or so. She just had to hope that she hit a shoreline before her energy gave out.

It took a while before she relaxed into a rhythm. Swimming blind, not knowing if she was about to collide into a cliff face or a pile of rocks was disconcerting and frightening, but she pushed the fear aside.

Those with courage will prevail.

Cold dug deep into her muscles. She'd thought she'd been cold when she'd been in the mountains of Afghanistan in January, but it was nothing compared to this. Her feet and hands were numb, her limbs as heavy as if they were filled with rocks. For the first time in her life she wished she was fat, as fat as Pat Vellum, and that she had a nice, insulating subcutaneous layer between her and the water.

She wondered when Tom would notice she'd vanished. And what about Denise? Would she worry if she didn't turn up tonight? The first person she could count on reporting her missing would be Nick, when she didn't turn up for his weekly prayers at five o'clock on Friday.

It was Wednesday today. Could she survive until Nick hit the panic button? Mustn't think about it. Of course she could. She was not going to bloody well drown. She had loads of stuff still to do, like rescue Zamira, ride the London Eye with her niece and nephew, and kiss Max Blake.

She thought about Blake and Tom as she swam. Whether there was something wrong with her that she couldn't commit to Tom. Whether she ought to be locked up and psychoanalysed about the strength of her attraction to Blake.

The waves seemed to get larger and the wind stronger. She saw a yellow dot in front of her, larger and steadier than the one on the disappearing boat. Was it a boat at anchor?

Jay kept plugging away.

She was travelling too damned slowly. The light didn't seem to be getting any nearer and she tried to think whether the Bristol Channel had any currents or rip-tides.

I will not drown, she chanted to herself. I will not drown, I will not drown.

She rolled over and finned on her back for a while. Looking up, she saw the shape of a cloud. Either her eyes had adjusted to the pitch black, or it wasn't as dark any more. She flipped on to her front and forced her feet to paddle harder and propel her through the waves.

It took several seconds for her sluggish brain to accept what her eyes were telling her.

The yellow dot wasn't alone. It had been joined by a string of dots. Pinpricks of light. White and yellow. She looked around and saw some more further away, to her right.

She wasn't looking at boats, she realised, but a coastline.

Her spirits soared and energy flooded her veins.

Don't blow it, she told herself. Don't rush. Just keep up a nice, steady pace until you get there.

Concentrating on the brightest light, Jay swam. She swam on autopilot, not thinking about the cold gripping her muscles or the salt swelling her eyelids and tongue. Her world was cold and water and salt and steady, repetitive strokes.

Time floated by.

She rolled on to her back once more. Her legs drifted down,

pulling her towards the endless ocean bottom. It took an effort to raise them up, keep them kicking. She was nearing the end of her strength.

She checked the string of lights. Too far, she thought. It was too damn far. Lights and life and people having supper, watching TV, but they could have been in Australia as far as she was concerned.

She wondered whether her mother would have her buried or cremated when her body washed up on shore. She'd never made a will, never told anyone what music she wanted played. What would Tom think if Blake came to her funeral?

Stop being so pathetic!

She turned on to her side, and swam. The alternative was impossible. She would die mid-stroke, or she wouldn't die at all.

When a brighter light entered her consciousness, it took her a while to get her exhausted body to respond. She raised her head to see a house. Set high up a hillside, or a cliff, its wall appeared to be made of glass. For the sea view. Her vision travelled to another house above it, and then more alongside. A street's worth of houses.

She would have swum faster if she'd had any reserves. She was barely moving but the houses were getting closer. The tide was helping her, perhaps. Maybe God had intervened, because she could hear the sound of waves softly breaking, the shushing noise as they receded, and then her belly and thighs were sticking against something, making it almost impossible to move. Mud. She was swimming in mud. She was in an estuary.

She heard some birds nearby scuttle away from her with cries of alarm. She flopped and squelched feebly on her belly until she lay at the edge of the silt-thickened water. She was gasping and coughing. If she had had the energy, she would have wept.

Jay had no idea how much time passed before she managed to get herself clear of the water and collapse on to stiff, bristly grasses. Shuddering in the cold night air, she stared at the nearest house. It wasn't far. Maybe a hundred yards along the muddy beach and then another hundred up a slope.

It looked impossible, but even if it took all night, she would make it. Dragging herself on her hands and knees she made it across the beach. Then she tackled the slope. She was half-panting, half-sobbing when she reached the top. She could hear music and someone laughing. Happy sounds, sounds of life.

A final effort took her crawling to the side of the house, past a plastic tricycle and part of a kite that stood beneath an outside light. On the front doorstep, she tried to stand, but she was too weak. Raising her hand, she made a fist and let it fall against the door. Thud. It wasn't her usual smart rap and she hoped they'd hear.

Thud. Thud.

The door swung open. A woman standing in her dressing gown made a startled exclamation and then the door closed with a bang.

Jay slumped and closed her eyes. Obviously having mud-caked, half-naked women lying on your doorstep wasn't the done thing around here. She came to the realisation she couldn't move any more. She would sleep on the porch, and in the morning, if she wasn't dead from cold, she might have recuperated enough to crawl and get help. She closed her eyes.

'Now wait a minute,' a man said. 'You can't sleep here ... '

She struggled to raise her head. 'Help,' she managed. 'Me.'

He ducked down and peered at her. 'Jesus,' he said. 'What the hell ... '

'Ship,' she said. 'Wreck.'

'Christ. Hang on ... I'll be back in a tick ... '

He vanished briefly and returned with the woman. They slid their hands under her armpits, and between them they lifted her into a hallway with a pink and white floral carpet. Warmth wrapped around her like a hot towel and she gave a groan of appreciation.

'Love,' she said. 'Lee.'

'Lovely,' the man translated to the woman, who Jay took to be his wife. Their sitting room had a fake gas fire and a wall of glass that looked over a black empty view of the sea. Shuddering, she turned her gaze away. She wouldn't be swimming in the ocean any time soon.

They were about to deposit her on their sofa when she said, 'No, no.'

They paused, anxious.

'I'm filthy,' she said. 'Covered in mud.'

The man glanced at his wife who said, 'Wait a second.' When she dropped Jay's elbow she swayed but the man had her around the waist and she didn't fall.

They wrapped blankets around her, and she collapsed on to the sofa. Bliss. It felt as though it had been stuffed with goose-down and warmed with a dozen hot water bottles.

'Shall I call the Coast Guard?' he asked. 'Were you alone? Are there any other survivors?'

'Alone,' she said.

'I'll call an ambulance. Then who shall I contact? Your family?'

She wanted him to ring Tom but she paused, trying to get her exhausted brain into gear. Someone had just tried to kill her. If she popped up all hale and hearty, who was to say they wouldn't try again? She needed some time to think before she did anything.

'Nobody,' she said.

He looked shocked. 'There must be someone. You can't be like this on your own.'

He was right. Common sense dictated she didn't have the strength to go solo. She couldn't call Tom, she realised. He would take one look at her before punching every panic button within reach, bagging her jeans and undies for forensics, getting the team on duty activated, alerting the Coast Guard and a variety of marina security guards to look out for the cabin cruiser. Whoever had tried to kill her tonight would simply come back and finish the job. She couldn't risk it.

She thought of Denise and Angela, highly trained soldiers, and then her mind switched to someone even more capable. She gave him Max Blake's number. He had said he'd be in the UK by Wednesday.

Thirty-three

It was after midnight when Shaban drove Zamira to his house and took her inside. He'd handcuffed and blindfolded her. She told him she was tired, and wanted to sleep, and he laughed.

'You can have this first,' he said, unbuckling his belt.

When he had finished, he tied her to the radiator in the hall. She heard him moving around the house, and then the sound of a loo being flushed. Not long after she heard a rhythmic rattle that she guessed was his snoring.

She didn't sleep much that night. She could feel Shaban's sperm leaking from her, smell him on her skin. She couldn't get comfortable, and had to keep moving to stop her limbs from going numb. In the middle of the night, her bladder began to ache. She tried to hang on, but eventually gave up and urinated where she lay.

The next day Shaban untied her and dragged her upstairs. 'Get clean,' he told her. Unmoving, he watched her shower, and then tied her back to the radiator. She was naked.

He returned a few hours later with a couple of friends who were drinking heavily. Shaban released her from the radiator to be raped. They continued drinking and took turns to rape her until finally they were all passed out. Zamira could barely move, but she saw a chance and had to take it. She pulled on her shirt and jeans and crept for the front door.

She had just put her hands on the door handle, praying the door wasn't locked, when she heard a roar behind her. Shaban.

She didn't cry as he dragged her down the corridor by her hair. She felt hollow, as her spirit had been sucked from her. She'd never get away now.

Shaban gave her the most brutal beating yet. Before, he'd always hit her body, her thighs and breasts and buttocks, but this time, he went for her face. Before she could raise her hands he smashed his fist into her nose.

She heard the crunch and felt the pain but she didn't make a sound. She knew she was going to die. He punched her in the mouth and against her cheekbones, and then he began hitting her nose again.

She was on the floor. She rolled over and threw up.

He began kicking her.

Gradually everything dimmed.

She thought she heard a dog bark, and she realised it had all been a terrible dream. She'd never left Macedonia, she'd never turned her back on her mother or the mountains. The great shaggy form of Bear was bounding towards her, his tail waving a greeting. Nana was in the doorway of their house, wiping her hands on a cloth. She was smiling.

Arms outstretched, Zamira ran for her mother.

Thirty-four

Jay awoke for the umpteenth time feeling as though she could sleep for another decade. Her lower back was aching and she felt as weak and vulnerable as a baby blackbird. She kept her eyes shut, listening to trolleys rattle past her cubicle. In the distance she could hear the distinctive jingle of Radio 2, people chatting brightly as they wished each other good morning.

The ambulance had dropped her off at A & E sometime the previous night. She had been checked over by a nervous looking doctor who looked about twelve. He told her she didn't need to have her lungs pumped – thank God – but she would need to be kept warm and nourished until she was ready to go home.

'What, stay here?' She raised herself up on one elbow and he pushed her back down with surprising firmness.

'Yes. It's important you receive preventative care.'

Preventative care involved lots of hot soup, and a nurse prodding her every hour or so during the night and peering into her eyes. It was intrusive and annoying, but felt wonderfully safe.

Now she lay in bed wondering what time it was. After a couple of minutes she opened her eyes. A pair of steady brown eyes stared back.

Jay scrambled upright, clutching the sheet to her chest.

'Hi,' said Blake.

'Hi.'

He got up and walked out of the cubicle. Thirty seconds later he was back with a doctor in tow. This one wasn't much older than the first, with a pair of wire-rimmed spectacles and acne on his chin.

'Did she take in much water?' Blake hovered while the doctor ran his checks.

'About half the ocean,' Jay replied.

'Has she got hypoxia?'

'What's hypoxia?' She felt alarmed.

'Nothing for you to worry about,' the doctor said, shooting Blake an irritated look.

'No respiratory stress?' Blake continued. 'No risk of pulmonary oedema?'

The doctor paused, looking over his shoulder at Blake. He raised his stethoscope. 'You'd like to check?'

Jay drew her flimsy hospital robe tightly around her. 'No he would not,' she said.

The doctor quickly ran Blake through Jay's results and when he was looking happier, pronounced her fit enough to go home.

Blake said, 'How long does she need to rest for?'

'I would suggest taking things slowly for the rest of the week. Her lungs are sore and the last thing she needs is any strenuous exercise. If she has any trouble however, bring her in immediately, but I doubt she will need further care.' The doctor gave her a smile. 'You're in very good shape, considering.'

When Blake opened his mouth to ask him another question, the doctor hurriedly excused himself, and vanished.

Blake reached for a plastic carrier bag resting beneath the chair. 'Here,' he said, dropping it on the bed. 'I thought you might need something for the ride home.'

She emptied the bag to find underwear, socks and shoes, a pair of jeans, some stretchy t-shirts and a fleece. Each item still had its shop tag attached.

He said, 'I'll wait outside.'

'You told anyone about this?' Blake asked.

He was driving fast along the M4 towards London in her Golf, which they'd collected earlier. Amazingly her car keys were still in her jeans pocket, and although the remote alarm didn't work, at least they could get the vehicle started. He hadn't told her how he'd got to Bristol, or where he'd got the clothes she was wearing, and she didn't ask. Especially since the underwear he'd provided was a selection of sheer silk, cherry coloured G-strings and low-cut matching bras in different sizes. One set fitted her perfectly, as did the jeans. Most guys couldn't buy you a pair of socks without getting the size completely wrong, and the fact he'd got most of it right just from picturing her – which she assumed was how he'd done it – was rather alarming.

'Jay?' he prompted.

She dragged herself into the real world. 'I haven't told anyone. I thought it best to play dead. To stop them coming for a second try.'

'Good. That means we have the advantage.'

'You've got a plan?'

'I'm cooking one up.'

He accelerated hard past a Mercedes SLK. Jay glanced over to see he was doing over 100 mph.

'Do you have a get out of jail free card?' she asked.

'Yup.'

She rolled her head to study his face, the straight, narrow nose, his stubble. She recognised that he hadn't shaved for over twenty-four hours. She should know, having seen his beard grow every day when they'd been on the run through Albania.

'Talk me through everything's that happened,' Blake said. 'From when you first got back.'

There was a long silence while Jay tried to arrange her thoughts. Her head was woolly and it didn't get any better when she started telling the story, which came out in disconnected bursts. When she had eventually finished, they drove in silence. It had started raining and Blake flicked on the wipers.

Jay leaned back and closed her eyes, trying to work out why there had been an attempt on her life. She hadn't told anyone about Milot and Vadic teaming up, nor, as far as she knew, had Laura, which meant she must have touched another highly sensitive nerve. Was it the MI6 mole who wanted her out of the way? Or could Branko have spotted her outside the brothel and seen her as a threat? And what about her asking Denise to flag Milot and Vadic at Heathrow? Had that been picked up via a bugging device and seen as breaking her promise to Vadic?

'I don't get it,' Blake said. He was shaking his head. 'Why you? Why now?'

'He despises women like me.'

'That's not it.'

'Maybe it's the MI6 mole.'

'Could be. Run over it again.'

She groaned. 'Do I have to?'

'Sorry.'

Jay relayed the story for a second time. 'Any help?' she asked.

'No.' His fingers were tapping on the steering wheel. 'Let's take it back further. To your trip to the ski lodge.'

Jay spoke with her eyes closed. She started with the drive up the mountain road with Laura, the old couple following them up the mountain with a sheep in the back of their VW, the helicopter arriving, Protti and his bodyguard getting out.

'Describe the bodyguard.'

She opened her eyes. 'Didn't you see him?'

'No. I was at the back of the lodge.'

Jay gave as detailed a description as she could, but this time she included the way the man's hair was cut, with a little point at the nape of his neck.

'So you'd ID him easily if you saw him.'

'Yes.'

'How about if I showed you some photographs, see if you can pick him?'

'Sure. Ingram wants me to do the same, but I've managed to put him off so far. I'm dreading making a mistake that Vadic will get to hear about.'

Blake's head snapped round. 'Ah,' he said.

'What do you mean, "Ah"?'

'Not sure. I'm thinking.'

After a couple of miles, he gave a nod, as though he'd reached a satisfactory conclusion, but he didn't say anything.

'Max?' she prompted.

'Sorry.' He gave his head a brief shake. 'I know why Vadic wants you out of the way.'

She stared at him in surprise. 'Why?'

'Because the guy you thought of as Protti's bodyguard is important. Really important. And Vadic doesn't want you identifying him.'

It felt as though a tricky jigsaw piece had fallen into place. Her instincts told her his theory made perfect sense because, like Tom, she'd always doubted Vadic's paranoia over the secrecy of the three clans' amalgamation.

'If MI6 knows you can ID the guy, then so does the mole. And since you're the only witness to see this guy meet with Vadic . . .'

'Aside from Laura.'

'She recognised him?'

'She hardly looked at him she was so excited about Protti.' Jay thought further. 'But why aren't they after you?' she asked.

'I didn't see the guy. I didn't even know he was there. My reports say the same, which means the mole knows I don't have a clue, which in turn keeps me safe.' He glanced in the wing mirror, then back at the road ahead.

'I'm surprised the Mafia aren't after you for being a spy,' she remarked.

'They tried last week.'

'What?'

'They failed. I don't think they'll bother trying again.'

What did that mean? That he'd killed whoever had come after him?

He said, 'Don't ask, okay?'

'Okay.'

Ten more miles passed in a blur of spray and trucks and rain before Blake spoke again. 'You say Laura's reporting to Vadic?'

'And MI6.' Jay stretched, curving her spine against the soft leather of her seat. 'She's walking a tight-rope between Kingsman and the Mafia. She wants to trap Vadic somehow, bring him down.'

'And she says she's working alone?'

'Yes.'

Blake mulled this over for a while. 'Maybe we should team up.'

Jay didn't dare mention what Laura thought of him, that she had called him 'that bastard'. Which reminded her. 'Max, do you work for SOCA? Or do you work for MI6?'

'It depends who you talk to.'

Instead of being frustrated at such an enigmatic response, she didn't ask any more. It was typical of him to give away as little as possible, and there was no point in pushing him. She tried to make some more sense of what had happened but her brain was having trouble doing anything but float around in a fog of exhaustion. She yawned, tears collecting in the corners of her eyes.

'You need to rest up for a couple of days,' he told her.

She nodded.

'I'll take you home. We can pick up some DVDs on the way. You can watch movies and read some books. Relax.'

'I'm not sure if taking me home is such a good idea.'

'I meant my home. It's not far.'

She blinked. 'You live in Berkshire?'

'Where did you think I lived? Siberia?'

Blake's home was tucked in the folds of a hillside and away from prying eyes. It had a perimeter alarm and, he told her, two interior intruder security systems that operated independently and involved infra-red beams as well as heat sensors. When he pulled up next to a sludge-green Land Rover Discovery, she was so knackered it took her a few seconds to take in its number plate.

K784 AWL.

It was the same Discovery that she'd spotted outside the café when she'd been talking with Nick.

'That car,' she said.

'Yeah. I used it to keep an eye out for you. I thought you might get approached by the mole, maybe offered a bribe.'

'I thought I was going paranoid.'

'Having a tail can do that to you.'

Eyes still on the Discovery, she said, 'There was also an elderly guy, and a young woman.'

'Kingsman put them on you, for the same reasons.'

'Didn't he know you were already watching me?'

'No. I thought I'd keep it quiet, leave the field open.' Hopping out of the Golf, Blake led her inside.

Like the man himself, the house was a contradiction. Outside showed one facet of living – rustic, countrified – but inside it was a bright, modern space with oak floors and chrome fittings.

There was a jacuzzi and steam room, a kitchen equipped with every appliance known to man, and a living room with wide-screen TV and wall-to-wall views. There were few personal touches but she couldn't miss the framed photograph hanging next to the fireplace, of an angular woman with wild, curly black hair and a laughing mouth.

'She's beautiful,' Jay said.

Blake didn't appear to hear. He pointed through an alcove behind them, saying, 'Bedroom's through there. Okay if I leave you for a bit? I've some business to attend to.'

She nodded.

Before he left, he showed her how the alarms worked, and which were the quickest exits. He even had a semi-camouflaged door set in some bookshelves in his state-of-the-art office that opened just twenty yards from the woods. 'Useful way out,' he said, 'if you need it.'

He ushered her back to the sitting room saying, 'a friend is dropping my vehicle off in an hour or so, okay if I use yours?'

'What about the Discovery?'

'It's out of action. Needs a new alternator.'

'Sure.'

He gave her a nod. 'Make yourself at home.'

After he'd gone, Jay turned on the stereo to find it was tuned to Radio 3. Very civilised. She trailed into the bedroom, another broad space with oak floors and lots of masculine tones; chocolate, caramel and coffee. There was an old steamship trunk at the foot of the bed, covered with tattered stickers that told of luxury travel in another era: QE2, P&O, Paris, Venice, Cairo.

Then she took in the book on the bedside table, the radio alarm clock, and realised it was Blake's room, but when she searched the house further she discovered any bedrooms that had been there before had been converted into a mini-gym, a games room complete with pool table, and the state-of-the-art office.

Too tired to worry about where he was going to sleep, Jay stripped down to her cherry undies and slid between the sheets. Her last thought as she slipped into unconsciousness was that it was rather like having a sleepover with Batman.

Thirty-five

'Christ, Shaban,' said Branko, 'you think you could have messed her up any more?'

Zamira pushed the image of Branko away. She didn't want to see him. She wanted to be back in her mother's arms with the smell of lamb stew cooking on the fire and the sound of cows lowing.

'She's an absolute mess,' Branko went on. 'Completely worthless.'

Pain seeped into her senses and despite her best efforts to burrow into unconsciousness, her mind began to crawl awake. It couldn't be Branko. He'd sold her to Reda and abandoned her. It had to be another dream, a nightmare.

'I'll take her off your hands for five hundred.'

'You sold her to Reda for five and a half grand!' Shaban protested.

'Look at her, Shaban. Nobody's going to want her now. You've ruined her.'

'A thousand.'

'Nope. Five hundred, take it or leave it.'

'Come on, Branko. Make it seven hundred and we're quits.'

'I'm not negotiating.'

Zamira heard Branko walking away. She tried to get up but her limbs wouldn't move. She tried to shout, but her throat wasn't working and nor were her eyes; they were swollen shut.

233

'Fuck it,' Shaban said. 'You win.'

'Put her in the back of the van.'

Shaban picked her up like he would a sack of potatoes and carried her outside. She waited to be flung on to a hard metal floor, but she fell on to what felt like a mattress.

'Peaches.' She felt Branko's hand on her shoulder. 'I want you to take some medicine. It'll stop you hurting. Make the journey manageable.'

Past all caring, she obediently swallowed the pills he gave her with some water from a plastic bottle.

'Good girl.'

When she heard the rear doors closing, she sank back. She was pathetically grateful to Branko for saving her from Shaban. She would be good now, really good. She would sleep with anyone Branko chose. She would suck their cocks and let them fuck her in every hole, ejaculate all over her face if they wanted. She'd be the best prostitute he'd ever known.

Zamira was aware of the van starting up and driving away, and then a softness stole into her brain, like a giant fluffy cloud, and she drifted into sleep.

She came to briefly to hear a woman protesting. 'We can't use her like this, Branko. She's a mess, and far too vulnerable. Yes, she's a match, but we don't want to lose her.'

'Are you sure? She's very strong.'

'We can't risk it.'

'Shit.'

'Look, I'll clean her up now, but you'll have to take her home until she's better. Okay?'

When Zamira's consciousness finally dragged her awake she didn't know what day it was, or whether it was morning or afternoon. She was lying in one of the softest beds she'd ever slept in, against the coolest, crispest sheets. Her eyes felt gummed shut and she could barely crack them open.

She blinked twice, unable to believe it.

She was back in the London apartment, lying in the king-size bed overlooking the park. She could smell fresh coffee and warm pastry.

A young girl popped her head around the door. She looked about the same age as Zamira, and was slender and blonde. Zamira felt a hundred years old. She used to look like this girl. Innocent and wide-eyed and waiting for her life to start.

'Would you like coffee?' the girl asked. 'Or some water? My name's Jasmin. Branko told me to look after you.'

Zamira licked her lips with a tongue dry as blotting paper. 'Water,' she managed.

Jasmin vanished, to return with a tray which she popped on the bed. She had included a plate of sweet pastries and a bowl of sugar lumps. After drinking all the water, Zamira sucked on some sugar. After a while, she felt a little strength ease into her veins, and she picked up a raisin-spotted pastry. She wanted to eat all the pastries but couldn't manage more than three bites. Having not eaten properly for so long, her stomach had shrunk to the size of a peanut.

When Jasmin came back, she croaked, 'Thank you.'

'Branko left some painkillers, would you like one?'

'Yes, please. I really hurt.'

Jasmin trotted off and came back with a bottle of pills. Zamira swallowed three.

Jasmin grimaced. 'It must have been awful.'

'What?'

'The car accident. Branko said it was a motorway crash.'

'He lied.'

Jasmin looked away. 'He told me you'd say that.'

'Have any men been here yet? Quinton or anyone?'

'No, it's just Branko and me.' She looked puzzled. 'And now you.'

'If men come here and want to fuck you,' Zamira said, 'don't fight them. Do what they want and you'll be okay. If you fight them, you'll end up looking like me.'

Jasmin stared. 'I don't understand.'

Zamira wanted to explain, but then she heard someone unlocking the front door.

'Peaches!' he called.

Jasmin's face lit up. 'Here!' she called back, and ran to greet him.

Thirty-six

Jay didn't leave Blake's bed for twenty-four hours, drifting in and out of sleep. When she woke up properly, she felt better. Not that she was up for competing in a biathlon yet, but at least she didn't feel as though her legs were going to collapse beneath her.

After a shower, she got dressed and trailed into the kitchen. She opened the fridge to find a stack of steaks, fresh vegetables and a bottle of Polish vodka. Hunting further she found a half-litre of milk and a pack of Colombian roast. She stood gazing at the view as the scent of brewing coffee permeated the house.

'Smells good.'

He spoke right behind her, making her spin round in shock. 'Jesus, Max. You just about gave me a heart attack. When did you get back?'

'Just now. You're looking better,' he said, and as he studied her, his eyes darkened.

'Yes. I slept well. Very comfortable. Thank you.' Her words sounded stilted. Her heart was hammering. If he made to kiss her, she didn't know what she'd do. Moving to the other side of the kitchen, she busied herself pouring coffee. A quick glance showed he was watching her, looking amused.

'Do I scare you?' he said.

'Sometimes.'

He beckoned her with a forefinger. 'Come here.'

'No.'

'I won't bite.'

'That's what I'm afraid of. Look, Max. I'm with someone. I'm supposed to be engaged ... I shouldn't really even be here. If he knew I was with you ... well, he'd go ballistic.'

He didn't move, or say anything, just looked at her steadily.

'Coffee?' she offered. Her cheeks were now aflame.

'Great.' He gave a nod before moving to the space she'd been standing in earlier, and stood looking out over the view. His expression was unreadable.

She already knew he took his coffee black, no sugar. She brought it over. 'Thanks.' He didn't look round, just took the mug. After pouring milk into hers, Jay began hunting for some sugar. She found a cupboard filled with Villeroy & Bosch china, another with Le Creuset cookware, and a shelf of Venetian crystal glasses, all hand blown. Boy, this man had expensive tastes. He'd make more than a match for Kiro's new lady love, Rosanna.

'What are you looking for?'

'Sugar.'

'Sorry.'

'You don't have sugar?' She stared at him. 'But everyone has sugar.'

'I'm not everyone.'

Isn't that the truth? she thought.

'I've got honey,' he offered.

'I guess it's better than nothing.' She was appalled to hear she sounded like a sulky child.

Blake went to a cupboard to the right of the cooker and opened it. 'Take your pick.'

To her amazement, a whole shelf was crammed with honey jars of every size and description. There were miniature jars you'd find on a hotel breakfast table alongside great litre-sized bottles, and tucked to one side she spotted a tub of eucalyptus honey-comb from the Barossa Valley, South Australia. Jay picked up a jar filled with honey as dark and thick as molasses. It had no label.

'Lebanon,' he said. 'I was there before the conflict in May, two thousand and six.'

She pointed at another pot of honey the colour of straw, also unlabelled.

'Sumatra, July ninety-nine.'

'You collect honey?'

'It's more useful than collecting stamps.'

Jay felt antsy all morning, unable to stop thinking about her killer. She wanted to ring Laura Sharpe, but if she was going to play dead, she'd better do it as thoroughly as possible. She didn't want the mole to find out she was alive and send Vadic after her again. Besides which, if Kingsman hadn't trusted their de-briefs, the agent's phone was probably bugged.

She was still pondering Vadic when Blake came and joined her on the sofa. He put a heavy-looking box file on the table in front of them before returning her car keys saying, 'Tank's full.'

'Thanks.'

He opened the box file. It was filled to the brim with photographs, colour, black and white, some taken with a tele-photo lens, others close-ups, mugshots.

'Homework,' he told her.

'You think our mystery man is in here?'

'It's worth a try.'

She picked one up. It showed a dark-haired man in dungarees glaring at the camera. He looked like an Albanian peasant farmer. 'Where did you get these from?'

'If I told you, I'd have to kill you.'

She was glad his eyes were twinkling as he said it.

He left the house ten minutes later. He didn't say where he was going or when he'd be back, just gave her a brand new mobile phone and said, 'I've already put my number in.'

Jay used her new phone to call Tom.

'Sutton,' he barked.

'Hi handsome.'

'Hello you,' Tom said. 'Your number didn't display. There must be something wrong with my phone.'

'There's nothing wrong with it. I'm ringing from a new mobile, that's all.'

'Why? What happened to yours?'

Since he invariably saw straight through her, Jay decided on the truth. 'It joined me for a rather long swim and didn't come back.'

'Swim?' he repeated in a strangled tone. 'I hope you mean in a nice hot bath, or a heated swimming pool.'

'Actually, it was in the Bristol Channel.'

There was a brief silence during which she could hear people talking in the background, meaning he was either in the squad room or reception.

'You want to fill in any details?' he finally said. 'Like how you got to be swimming in the Channel in the middle of winter? Come on, Jay. Spill it.'

She sank on to Blake's leather sofa and curled her legs beneath her. 'Someone tried to kill me.'

More silence, then Jay spoke.

'I followed the lead you gave me, about the brothel specialising in newly recruited Eastern European girls, but when I turned up to have a look someone jumped me and sprayed me with some kind of gas, probably CS, and when I came round I was in the Channel. I swam until I found land, and a very nice couple called an ambulance which took me to Frenchay for a check-up. They said I was fine, which I am. I've had a good sleep and I'm ready for action.' Which wasn't true, but Tom wouldn't accept anything less without hitting the roof.

'You're okay?' His voice was hoarse.

'Couldn't be better.'

'You reported this to the cops?'

'If I reported anything it would be to you, you know that. But I don't want this reported.'

'Why not?'

'I don't want anyone to know I'm alive. If they think I'm dead they can't come and try to kill me again.'

'That's probably a good idea.' Tom's voice sounded faint. 'Stay dead to keep yourself safe.'

'Tom, I need you to raid the brothel and see if Hana is there.' She rattled off the address. 'She might know where Branko and Zamira are. I'd go myself but I want to keep a low profile.'

Silence.

'Tom? You'll raid the brothel? Talk to Hana?'

'Yes. Later today.' Short pause, then he said, 'I'll ring you when we're going in, okay?'

'That's brilliant, Tom. Fantastic. You're a star.' Jay hung up fast and before he could ask any more questions, like where she was.

After Jay had unsuccessfully looked through Blake's photographs, she spent the rest of the day reading through the stack of newspapers he'd brought earlier, and eating toast spread with varieties of honey. Come four-fifteen she was snoozing in front of the TV, volume turned low, when her mobile rang.

'We've done it,' Tom said. 'Busted the brothel. Seven arrests including a witch of a woman called Reda. We're back at the station. Hana's here, but she's not talking. I mentioned Zamira's name, and yours, and she recognised both but won't say a word. I can hold her for a couple of hours if you think you might have more luck. You can interview her pretty discreetly. Nobody should find out you've been here, so long as you can keep Hana quiet.'

'Can I stay with you tonight?'

'You can stay all week if you want.'

'I'm on my way.'

Before she left, she wrote a note to Blake telling him where she'd gone, and why, and stuck it on his fridge door.

Hana was huddled on the floor in the corner of the interview room, cowering. Her eyes were swollen and bloodshot from weeping, her mascara smeared like charcoal down her cheeks. She had purple bruises on her arms and neck, and a fresh scab the size of a bottle top stood on her forehead. She couldn't stop touching it. Her fingernails were bitten to the quick.

This was Zamira's best friend, the girl she'd played with, gone to school with and dreamed impossible dreams with, until now.

Swallowing her emotions, holding them tight inside, Jay joined Hana on the floor. She didn't sit too close, she didn't want to alarm the girl, but she didn't sit too far away either. She didn't want to appear aloof or distant.

'Hana,' she said softly. 'My name is Jay. Captain Jay McCaulay. I saved Zamira's life a few years back.'

Hana's gaze flew to Jay.

'I'm here to help you in any way I can.'

Despite the mess the girl was in, Jay could see she was pretty. Once she'd bathed, washed her hair and put on some weight – God, she was thin! – she'd be even prettier.

'I want to give you something.' Jay unclipped the silver chain around her neck. 'Zamira gave this to me when she was little, to give me luck when I went to bring her mother out of Kosovo. I want you to have it.' She held it out to the girl and waited. Hana gazed at the icon blankly before she eventually stretched out a hand. Jay dropped the icon into Hana's palm. The girl stared at the miniature picture of mother and child for a long time and then she crumpled, as though her bones had dissolved.

Hana gave a shout, and her face contorted as she shouted again and again, 'I'm sorry! I'm sorry!' The shouts tore at Jay's heart. Tears were pouring down Hana's face and she was shouting and sobbing so hard her voice was becoming hoarse.

'Hana . . .' Jay tentatively touched her on the arm and the girl immediately turned towards her and then she had her arms around Jay's neck and was sobbing into her shoulder.

'I'm so sorry!'

'It's okay, Hana. You're safe now.'

Hana didn't notice when the door opened and Tom peered inside, eyebrows raised. 'Okay?' he mouthed. Jay nodded, and he left.

'It's okay,' Jay soothed the hysterical girl, stroking her hair. 'It's okay now.'

Jay held Hana for a long time before she stopped crying. Eventually she leaned back and looked into the girl's ravaged face. 'I've got loads of questions for you, but they can wait until you feel better. Would you like to come and stay with me? At my boyfriend's place?'

Hana gave a choked sob. 'Yes, please.'

Thirty-seven

'How much?' Zamira was staring at Branko.

'Three thousand pounds. And when it's over, I'll return your passport and get you a nannying job.'

'What, with this face? I don't think so.' She walked to the gilt-edged mirror over the fireplace. Gone was the pretty girl she used to know and in her place was an ugly creature with livid scabs raised all over her face like feeding leeches. Her nose was flattened, her nostrils distorted, and her lips swollen and scabbed like the rest of her face. Every time she looked at her reflection, she felt sick, but this was quickly replaced by a rush of rage so strong her whole body trembled.

'You want to go home?' he asked.

Alarm flooded her. 'I don't want my mother to see me like this.'

'Okay, so you start a new life here,' he told her. 'Three thousand pounds will go a long way.'

'You sold me for five and a half.'

'I have overheads. Like buying your passport and visa, paying for your air fare, taxis, renting this place ... '

'I am not selling my kidney for less than five thousand pounds,' she told him.

'Peaches, three thousand is all—'

'Don't you dare call me that,' she snarled. 'I'm not your pet any more.'

'Sorry.' He held up his hands. 'But the current value for a kidney is barely ten thousand pounds, and out of that I have to pay the hospital staff. The nurses, the surgeon, the anaesthetist. They're private specialists. They're not cheap.'

'Who's going to get it?'

'Get what?' For a moment he looked bewildered.

'My kidney.'

'Oh. Er, some guy. I think he's from one of the Arab countries, I'm not sure. I don't get to meet the recipients. I'm just the middle man.'

She thought it over. 'Arabs are rich. I'm sure he can afford to pay me five thousand.'

'That's not how it works,' he said with a sigh. 'Remember, the overheads are massive. Everyone takes their cut.'

'Including you.' Her voice was hard. 'You owe me, Branko.'

'Zamira.' He was patient. 'If you don't do this, what are you going to do?'

'Beg on the streets.'

'What if the police catch you? They'll throw you in jail.'

She noticed he'd stopped the old threats of the police beating and raping her. She said, 'Maybe jail is preferable to losing a kidney.'

'I don't think so. You like your freedom more than most, even I know that.'

She felt a wave of dizziness and had to put a hand on the mantelpiece to steady herself. It was frustrating, but she kept getting waves of weakness like this. She wouldn't last two seconds begging on the streets. 'Make it four thousand, and I'll do it. Tomorrow.'

'Three and a half and you can recover here. For as long as you like.'

She felt a moment's horror. She hadn't thought where she might recover after the operation.

'Deal,' she said quickly.

Branko grinned. 'Good girl,' he said.

Thirty-eight

It felt strange being at Tom's again, as though she'd seen his apartment in a movie, with everything looking familiar but feeling alien. There was the same granite worktop in the kitchen, the same spider plants begging for water, photographs of his family and their trips abroad; Tom and his brother diving, Tom and his father skiing, Tom looking fit and tanned in each.

When she'd asked if she could take Hana there – she still had Tom's key on her key ring – he had looked at her and the weeping, broken girl, and said, 'I'll tell social services where she is.'

Hana hadn't seemed to mind that she was staying with a policeman. Since breaking down at the station she appeared to have put her total trust in Jay. She was like a lost child who'd found a beloved aunt she'd been told about but never met. Jay showed her the spare room before handing her a towel and a new bar of soap. She then sat numbly staring at the TV while Hana took one of the longest showers on record. After an op she wasn't any slouch when it came to washing away the stench of adrenalin and fear, but Hana was washing away more than that, or trying to. When she finally joined Jay in the living room she was wearing a pair of Jay's tracksuit pants and top, clothes she'd left in Tom's wardrobe for slobbing about at weekends. The girl's damp hair was tied back in a pony tail and her skin was clear. She stood shyly in the doorway, looking every inch the child she was.

'Are you hungry?' Jay asked.

Hana nodded.

Jay peered inside Tom's fridge. Beer, pizza, a hunk of cheddar, some salami, and a packet of watercress salad that had green goo at the bottom. She decided against pizza when she remembered the old cartons outside the brothel and raided the freezer for a steak and mushroom casserole she remembered buying last month, along with a packet of frozen peas and another of chips. She microwaved the food and put it on the kitchen table. Light jazz was playing on the radio and as they ate, she watched Hana unwind.

'Zami always said you'd help,' Hana said. It was almost a whisper. 'I didn't believe her.'

Jay couldn't think of anything to say to that.

'Branko said we'd go to jail if we were found without the proper documents. That the police would beat us until we bled from our eyes and mouths, that they'd take a blow torch to our faces ... ' Her mouth wobbled. 'But the police were really nice.'

'That's their job.' This wasn't the moment to say not all of them were nice. Hana needed as much reassurance as she could offer. 'They arrest the bad guys and put them in jail, and help the good guys, like you and me.'

'Branko lied,' Hana said.

'Yes.'

Hana looked up and in that instant Jay saw her bewilderment. 'But I liked Branko. I loved him.'

Jay remained silent.

Hana put her head in her hands. She didn't cry. She just sat there as though numbed.

'Hana,' Jay said. 'Where's Zamira?'

'I don't know.' She raised her head and Jay saw the anguish on her face. 'It's my fault she left. She wanted to run away but I told on her and Reda sold her to Shaban ... ' The tears began to fall again. 'It's all my fault ... '

Jay moved her chair next to Hana's and put her arm around

her. 'It's okay, sweetheart.' She waited until Hana had regained control before she asked where they could find Shaban.

'I don't know. I wish I did, I swear it.' She took a shuddering breath. 'I'd like to see Shaban dead.'

'What about Branko? Do you know where we could find him?'

'You could try the apartment in London. He goes there a lot.'

'Where in London?'

'Kensington. I don't know the address, but if you took me there, I could show you. It's a beautiful place.' She sounded wistful. 'It's not far from the shops and looks over the park.'

When Jay tucked Hana into bed that night, the girl didn't want to let her go. 'Stay with me until I fall asleep?' she begged. 'Like Zami used to?'

Jay shook off her shoes, climbed on the bed and curled herself around Hana's slight form. Almost immediately, Hana fell asleep, and before Jay knew it, she was drifting off too.

When she awoke it was past midnight, and although she still lay on top of the bed with Hana curled against her, she was as warm as toast beneath a duvet Tom had pulled over her. What a nice guy, she thought, not waking me up and making demands. I'll get up in a minute and go and see him, ask if he can put pressure on Reda to tell us where Branko is. She was still thinking about Branko, that death was too good for him, when she fell back to sleep.

'Okay,' said Tom. 'Tell me again. You want to take Hana where?'

'To Kensington.'

'Why?'

'To identify Branko's apartment.'

They were standing in his kitchen, and rain was pelting against the windows. Hana was next door watching cartoons on the TV and the table was covered with breakfast items; marmalade, Weetabix, milk and butter – but no honey. Tom didn't have a single jar of honey but he made up for the lack with a large bowl of caster sugar and three packets of treacle dabs.

'There is a reason why we have a police force,' Tom said. 'We

248

can get the address off Reda or one of her cronies and have an officer round there by the end of the day.'

'You must be joking. You think Reda's going to give up her main man just like that? Tell me, how much has Reda given you since her arrest? Branko's address maybe? His telephone number?'

Tom stared at her, immovable, but his fists were clenched.

'I don't want to wait until Branko hears the brothel's been raided.' Her voice was fierce. 'I don't want him to slip through our fingers. I want you to put the Met on the alert so when I have the address we can go in and grab him. You've got Hana's statement about the place, what goes on there. They won't hesitate to bust the door down.'

He reached out and picked up the milk and butter and put them in the fridge. He spoke over his shoulder. 'You are like a pit bull when you're on a case.'

'Is that a yes?'

The Weetabix went into the cupboard next to the fridge, along with the marmalade. Finally he turned and looked at her. He ran a hand over his face and looked at her again. He said, 'Shit.'

'Thanks, Tom.'

Jay went and kissed the corner of his mouth before digging out a pair of old combat boots she'd dumped in his wardrobe after Christmas. She and Hana left ten minutes later wearing borrowed fleeces and showerproof jackets several sizes too big, plus baseball caps. Despite the pouring rain, Jay refused to take an umbrella. She'd only lose it.

To Jay's frustration, two miles past Reading they hit a traffic jam. All three lanes were blocked and in the distance, through the rain and spray, she could see blue twirling lights. An accident. Great.

Switching on the radio, she searched until she found a local station and waited for the news. Nothing about the accident was mentioned, but then a traffic report came in. A lorry had turned over on the M4, spilling its load. Long delays. Find an alternative route. Jay rested her head on the steering wheel. She had no alternative route. She and Hana were stuck.

For the first two hours, they talked. Jay told Hana she'd stayed in Novo Selo recently, and described the few people she had met, what she'd eaten and where she'd slept. Hana knew just almost every wooden board that Jay and Blake had trodden, the names of the sheep they'd shared a byre with, and was desolate at the fact Jay hadn't dared find her parents. But when Jay asked Hana if she'd like to return to her village, the girl shook her head. 'I hate being poor,' she said. 'Besides, nobody would want to marry me now, except the brutes.'

A burly trucker knocked on their window, offering them biscuits from his tin of assorted creams. Jay and Hana took two each. For the next hour they listened to the radio, and then they made themselves comfortable, and napped.

It was past three when the road finally cleared, and it took them another hour to reach the park. Jay cruised along Bayswater Road, and when Hana didn't recognise anything she made her way south. They were heading west on Kensington Gore, past the Albert Memorial, when Hana sat bolt upright. 'We're here. I recognise the deer above the gates.'

Jay felt a frisson of excitement. The address Denise had given her for Vadic was on Kensington Gore. Jay would bet her last penny it was the same apartment that Branko used but she didn't say anything to Hana; she didn't want to influence her.

Parking at a meter near the top of Queen's Gate, they continued on foot. The sky was darkening into evening and the rain had eased into a light drizzle. As they walked, Jay noted the calibre of vehicles pulling in or out from the kerb, the Bentley Continental with tinted windows, the silver Porsche, the black Rover and several taxis.

'The window,' gasped Hana. 'It's got a crack, like a bird flew into it or something. That's the one!'

Jay phoned Tom. 'We've got it. Number twelve Kensington Gore, it's on the fourth floor, overlooking Kensington Gardens.'

'You sure?'

Jay glanced at Hana who was staring at the windows as though mesmerised.

'We're sure. And check who owns it. Vadic gave this address to Immigration when he arrived.'

'I'll call the Met. You promise to stay well out of range when they arrive? Not get in their way?'

'We're going to the park,' Jay told him, and hung up before he could elicit a promise from her. She didn't want to break it.

Jay sat in her car with Hana for over two hours, getting more and more frustrated. She felt as though she'd spent the entire day in the car and now it was dark she was getting stiff and bad tempered. Surely it couldn't take this long for the duty inspector to authorise a magistrate's search warrant? What the hell was going on? She was seriously considering ringing Tom for the fourth time when – finally – a patrol car arrived. As the officers climbed out, putting on their caps, readying themselves, another patrol car turned up. The Armed Response team. Tom had warned them Branko was part of the Albanian Mafia and they weren't taking any chances. While the two officers from the first car went through the building's front door, the others stood by their car, listening to their radios.

Jay shifted on her seat, her heartbeat picking up.

'What will they do if he's there?' Hana asked in a small voice.

'Arrest him.'

Hana looked worried. 'They won't hurt him, will they?'

'No, they won't.' Even though they'd love to, she wanted to add, but kept her lip firmly buttoned. It was understandable that Hana felt confused over Branko. He was a long-time friend of the family who she'd trusted. It would take some time before Hana saw him for the cold-hearted reptile he was.

Jay's finger hovered over the receive button on her mobile, waiting for Tom to ring her. She counted the seconds, which turned into minutes, until finally her mobile chirped.

'They've found a girl,' he said. 'She's hysterical, thinks the police are going to kill her. I don't know if it's Zamira or not but see if you can calm her down.'

Jay sprinted for the building, Hana hot on her heels. She didn't have the patience to wait for the lift and she took the stairs two at a time. There was an officer guarding the door. He looked her up and down. 'You're the translator? Assigned from Trinity Road?'

'Yup. And this is Hana, she's Albanian. It could be her friend inside.'

He checked Jay's identity and motioned them through the door. Jay's spirits plummeted when she saw the girl huddled in the living room, sobbing. She was silver-blonde and as slender and wan as if she'd been clipped from the moon.

Jay ignored the cop standing by the windows. 'Zamira? Where is she?' she demanded.

The girl stopped sobbing and stared. 'Who are you?'

'Zamira's friend. Where is she?'

'What are the police doing here?' The girl scrambled to her feet. 'They broke down the door, what do they want?'

'They won't harm you, I promise. I'll let you know what's going on, but first you have to tell me where Zamira is.'

'Why should I tell you?'

'Because . . . ' Jay took a breath and stifled the urge to scream. 'I'm worried about her.'

'Oh.' The girl sniffed and wiped her nose with the back of her hand. 'Branko took her to hospital. She needs an operation.'

Alarm shot through Jay. 'What for?'

'She was in a car accident. She's a real mess.'

Hana looked at Jay. Her lips were trembling. 'Shaban,' she whispered. 'He does that to girls. He smashes their faces into pulp.'

Jay pushed aside her horror and concentrated on the girl. 'Which hospital?'

'I don't know.'

'Come on, *think*.'

The girl started to cry again. Hana went over and put her arms around her. 'It's okay,' she said. 'I won't let anyone harm you.' Although the girl didn't know Hana, it appeared she trusted her instinctively despite her bruises and the ugly scab on her forehead. Hana said, 'What's your name?'

'Jasmin.'

'I'm Hana.'

Jasmin gave Hana a wobbly smile while Jay felt like cracking their heads together. They were wasting valuable time.

'Jasmin,' said Hana. 'Can you remember anything about Zamira's operation? It's really important.'

'She's coming back here to recover tomorrow,' the girl said.

'Will Branko be with her?' Jay asked.

'I don't know. Maybe.'

To Jay's annoyance the fingerprint team arrived at that moment. Jay met DI Wilkinson, a brisk florid-faced man who immediately arranged for a social worker and WPC to come and look after Hana and Jasmin. Standing in the hall and out of his team's way, Jay translated his questions to Jasmin, unfolding a story almost identical to Hana and Zamira's, except she'd been promised bar work and not a waitressing job. After a while the fingerprint team left and the evidence guys moved in, bagging everything from bathroom towels to toothbrushes. Jay spent the time with the Yellow Pages on her lap, ringing around the hospitals, but none of them had a Zamira Kalisi registered.

By the time the fingerprint team were finishing, the rain had returned to strike noisily against the windowpanes. They were seated back in the living room, Jay still ringing hospitals, Hana and Jasmin looking exhausted, when one of the cops stepped inside.

'Sir? You should see this.'

Jay followed DI Wilkinson into the hallway – the girls trailing behind her – where the cop was pointing to a stain on the carpet behind the door. 'It looks like blood,' he said. 'Someone didn't make a very good job of cleaning it up.'

The DI didn't hesitate. 'I'll call forensics. Get Sally Norbutt here.'

He was still talking but Jay didn't listen. She was riveted to Jasmin who had jumped as though she'd been stuck with an electric cattle prod.

'What's wrong?' Jay asked her.

'He said, Norbert?'

It was close enough. 'That's right.'

'It's the name of the hospital Branko was taking Zamira. St Norbert.'

Thirty-nine

When Jay rang the St Norbert Hospital, the male receptionist was brisk and efficient, telling Jay they didn't have a Zamira Kalisi or Branko Morillon listed, nor had they admitted anyone today who had suffered a recent car accident or registered anyone of Eastern European extraction that happened to be female and fourteen.

She headed east towards the hospital, determined to trawl the wards until she found Zamira. Jasmin had been adamant that Norbert was the right name and Jay wasn't about to leave this particular stone unturned.

She parked outside the front entrance just after nine p.m. She would have been there earlier but she'd waited until Hana and Jasmin had met their social worker and the WPC assigned to them, introducing them and assuring them they'd be well cared for. She gave both girls her home and mobile numbers and told them to ring her any time, day or night. This seemed to reassure them, but when they were asked to accompany their new keepers, it was Jasmin who went without a peep. Hana didn't want to go.

'I want to help you find Zami.' Tears began to well.

'I know you do.' Jay put her arms around the girl. 'But I also don't want to have to worry about you while I try and find her. Do you understand? I want to know you're safe and sound.'

Hana's grip turned fierce as she buried her face in Jay's shoulder. 'You're wonderful,' she said.

'Not everyone would agree with that.' She smiled. 'But thanks anyway.'

The St Norbert was a private hospital with massive flower arrangements displayed in Chinese vases and a smart little shop – currently shut – selling sweets, magazines and trinkets. There were comfortable chairs in muted colours, and water coolers, and it felt a million miles from your usual NHS offering. A few people who looked like patient visitors came and went, but otherwise it was quiet. The night receptionist, a tall black man with a Yorkshire accent, confirmed there was no Zamira Kalisi registered. She began to ask about Branko when her mobile phone rang. The receptionist frowned. Phones weren't allowed in the hospital.

'Sorry ... ' Jay went outside to answer it.

'I got your note,' said Blake. 'What's up?'

'We've busted the brothel and Branko's love nest in Kensington. Hana and another THB victim are with social services.'

'Good work.'

'How about you?'

'Oh, this and that. My paper trail of Vadic's bank accounts is proving interesting. Where are you?'

'At the St Norbert Hospital looking for Zamira.'

'What?' His voice was clipped. 'Why?'

Pacing along the cobbled mews at the back of the hospital, she quickly told him about Zamira being sold to Shaban, and then supposedly being in a car accident. 'Her face is a real mess, apparently. Hana reckons Shaban is responsible. Zamira's not the first girl he's hospitalised.'

'Jay.' His tone sent a flurry of apprehension up her spine. 'I've been tracking Vadic's funds. I found another business he has expanded into.'

'So?'

'It involves trafficking human organs.'

Jay felt as though she'd been thrown in front of an express

256

train. She knew about the organ trafficking industry, but hadn't thought of Zamira being involved.

'He's set up a whole structure of organ trafficking in the Balkans, but what concerns us is that he's broadened his business into London.'

'No,' she moaned. 'Please, God. No.'

'The fees vary, but a new kidney, for example, would cost the recipient around sixty thousand dollars. It's big bucks.' His voice dropped. 'Jay, if Zamira is no use to Branko as a sex slave, what else could he use her for?'

'I've got to find her.'

'They've got tight security. You wait until I get there. I can get us in.'

'I can't wait.'

'I'll be there in an hour. Maybe less. Sit tight, okay?'

He hung up without waiting for an answer.

Jay strode back inside the hospital, her adrenalin pumping wildly. She wanted to charge up and down corridors yelling Zamira's name, but that was impossible. She had to be as cautious as a cat and not alert them that she was coming, and then she might stand a chance of rescuing Zamira. She couldn't wait for Blake. For all she knew they were prepping Zamira right now, the surgeon and nurses scrubbing their hands, the anaesthetist talking her down into oblivion.

Picking up a clipboard from the waiting area – thoughtfully provided for patients to lean on while they filled in their admission forms – Jay held it against her chest and walked to the lifts. When one opened, she waited while an elderly man got out before stepping inside. None of the buttons were labelled. She pressed three.

The third floor hall had a bank of windows overlooking the mews. Opposite was a glass door set in a glass wall, and operated by a keypad security system.

Jay was biting her lip, wondering what to do next when she saw someone appear on the other side of the glass wall. Immediately she started walking for the door. An Asian nurse pushed open the door and Jay put out her hand and caught it.

'Evening,' she said, and kept going.

The Asian nurse didn't turn a hair. If you had a clipboard, you could obviously go anywhere. Brilliant.

Straight ahead was a nurse's station, which was empty. Jay leaned over the counter to have a look. She picked up a hospital directory and had a quick flick through. She was, apparently, on one of the general wards for patient recovery. Operations were held in the basement.

'Can I help you?'

A starched, brisk-looking woman, thin as a broom, was regarding her suspiciously. Her dark blue uniform and sensible flat shoes told Jay this was the Ward Sister. The ward guard dog.

'I'm visiting a friend of mine.' Jay gave her a warm smile. 'I didn't know which room to go to.'

The Sister glanced at her watch pinned to her chest. 'I know we don't keep strict visiting times, but it's very late. Who are you visiting?'

'Mrs Hemsworth.' Jay plucked a name from the list of patients she'd spotted behind the counter. 'Amy Hemsworth.'

'She's fast asleep. She had a long operation, but she's doing well. Why don't you come back in the morning?'

'Can I just peep in and see her? Leave her a present on her table?'

The Sister softened. 'Of course you can. She's in room three-oh-eight.'

Dutifully Jay headed for 308 but stopped as soon as she saw the Sister turn around and head down the opposite corridor. Quietly as she could she jogged back and let herself out, and caught the next lift. Her spirits dropped to the bottom of her boots when she saw you needed a key to access the basement. How the heck was she going to get down there?

Then she remembered the Ward Sister. She had worn a belt with a set of keys attached.

Never give up, never give in, she chanted to herself as she returned to the third floor. A quick glance at her watch showed her it was nine-twenty. Blake would be here in forty minutes or so. Not soon enough. A lot could happen on an operating table in that time.

Again, Jay waited to tail-gate someone in or out of the door, but nobody appeared. It was nine-forty-five when the Sister appeared at the nurse's station. Jay knocked on the glass door and gestured frantically.

Startled, the Sister came and opened the door. 'What's wrong?'

'Mrs Hemsworth,' gasped Jay, waving her arms. 'Amy Hemsworth. It's not her in room three-oh-eight. I've never seen that woman in my life! Where have you put Amy? Where is she? Is she still in the operating theatre? The surgeon said it would be a late op but this is crazy, and why is that woman calling herself Mrs Hemsworth?'

All the time she was speaking Jay was scanning the woman's belt, and the keys dangling there. They didn't appear to be chained on or anything, just attached with a metal clip like you'd find on a dog lead.

'She's not Amy Hemsworth?' The Sister frowned, but she wasn't panicking yet. She was too experienced for that.

'No she's not! I should know my aunt! Where the hell is she?' Jay let her voice grow into a shout and she blundered past the Sister, purposely clumsy, and the Sister said, 'Now, just you wait a minute . . . ' Jay tripped and grabbed at the woman and at the same time her hand snicked the dog lead clip and freed the keys. They jingled, loud in her hand, and she fell to the ground, giving a shout to try to cover the sound. 'Oh, for goodness sake!' she cried, scrambling to her feet. 'Get out of my way, you silly cow! I'm going downstairs to sort this mess out and if you still have a job tomorrow I'll be very surprised!'

Jay turned and pushed open the door and legged it for the lift. Behind her the Sister was at the nurse's station watching her. She looked more confused than concerned. She didn't appear to realise Jay had her keys. Maybe if Jay was quick enough she'd get to the basement and find Zamira before the woman put two and two together and alerted security.

Heart pounding, Jay jumped into the lift and pressed G. While the lift descended she ran through the keys. Tried the first without luck, but the second fitted perfectly. The lift paused at Ground where she turned the key and pressed B. The lift doors closed, and she descended.

There was no *ping* when she arrived. The doors opened smoothly and silently into a blue space that was overly cold from air-conditioning. Everything was quiet and still and smelled faintly of citrus, as though someone had just peeled an orange. Peering up and down the corridor, she was surprised to see it was deserted. She'd expected locked doors, maybe even a guard, but there was nothing. Was this why Branko had chosen the St Norbert? Because of its lax security? Or had he bribed security to turn a blind eye on certain nights?

Not knowing which way to go, right or left, Jay tossed a mental coin and went left. She passed a variety of operating theatres, all dark, their machines switched off. Her footsteps on the blue linoleum sounded unnaturally loud no matter how quietly she trod.

She crept to the end of the first corridor and peered around the corner. At the far end, lights were on and she could hear voices. Jay tiptoed down the corridor. She came to an open area with monitors and prints of tropical islands on the walls. Ahead was an operating theatre. She peeked through the window to see three people garbed in green. They wore gloves, the face masks hung below their chins. They were chatting and wheeling instrument trays and equipment across the room.

There were no patients that Jay could see.

She hurried past the theatre and to the next room. The lights were low but she spotted a small figure lying on a bed beneath a pale blue blanket. She crept inside to see the figure was a sleeping girl hooked up to a blood pressure monitor. She had a hideously broken nose, lying off kilter against her cheek. Her lips and eyebrows were broken and bruised and thick scabs bulged all over her face, but her hair was thick and long. She wore a blue-enamel St Christopher at her throat.

Jay almost fell to her knees.

She had found Zamira.

Forty

Jay was backing away from the bed when Zamira opened her eyes and looked straight at her. Her gaze was remarkably clear, her expression bright.

She said, 'Jay! I'm dreaming.'

'Shhh.' Jay put her forefinger against her lips. 'No you're not. It's me, but we've got to keep quiet ... '

Jay fell silent when she heard footsteps in the corridor outside.

She was already in motion, scooting to hide behind the door when a man's form appeared in the doorway. She stopped dead. For a split-second, their eyes met. It was the sleek, dark-haired man with sharp good looks from Tom's photograph.

He said, 'Who the fuck—'

'It's Jay,' blurted Zamira. 'Branko, she's my friend, don't hurt her, please don't—'

But he was already moving, reaching down for something at his ankle. She couldn't let him arm himself, but she had no weapon.

She launched herself at him, and as she sensed his muscles tensing to retaliate, she turned sideways and lashed out with her big combat boot. Her leg was as rigid as a block of wood when she rammed it straight into his right kneecap.

There was a soft, wet crunch as it broke, and then he crumpled to the floor, screaming.

You must keep him down!

Bringing back her boot she kicked him between the legs, hard as she could. The breath whooshed from his lungs. His eyes turned upwards into his head. She brought back her boot for the second time, and repeated the blow.

Her instincts were telling her to put the final boot in. Smash his nose, disable him completely, and it took a huge effort to bring herself under control and pause – gasping – to assess the situation.

Branko was groaning on the floor, spittle oozing from his mouth. Jay bent and unstrapped his ankle holster, which held a hunting knife with a serrated edge and blood gutter.

Outside, voices filled the corridor.

'What the hell was that?' a man said, and a woman's voice asked, 'What's going on?'

Branko rolled on to his side and threw up. He began to groan.

'Shouldn't we go and see?' the woman said. 'It came from the donor's room.'

At the top of her voice, Jay yelled, 'Police! FREEZE!'

There was a brief pause followed by footsteps clattering wildly on linoleum, some curses. She prayed they were running away.

Branko gasped, 'Please don't kill me, please don't.' His eyes were fixed on the knife. Tears leaked down his face.

Jay went to the door and glanced up and down the corridor to see there were no green-garbed surgeons or nurses rushing towards her, nor any security guards. The basement theatre block they were in lay beneath the mews and not beneath the hospital, but even so, hadn't anyone heard Branko's screams, or were the floors and walls so thick they had absorbed the sound? And what about the Sister? Was she still oblivious of her missing keys?

In a rush she checked the operating theatre. Empty. She put Branko's knife aside, yanked a flex free from one of the machines, and returned to bind Branko's wrists behind his back. She ran a length of flex from his wrists to his good leg, pulling it tight. With one leg flopping uselessly, the other trussed to the small of his back, he wouldn't be going anywhere.

A quick glance showed Zamira sitting on the edge of the bed, staring at Branko. Her face was bleached white.

'I need to check the area,' Jay panted. 'Don't move. I'll be back in a tick.'

She ran past the theatre and into the next room along the corridor to find a young Arab-looking man sitting up in bed looking bewildered. An older man in an armchair at his bedside stood up. He said, 'What is going on? I thought I heard someone scream.'

'Nothing,' she replied. 'A male nurse got a fright. A large spider dropped on his hand. He's terrified of spiders.'

'Are they ready for my son yet? We have been waiting for a very long time.'

'You're here for ... ?'

'A kidney transplant,' he said irritably. 'We have been here for half the day, I had no idea how inefficient you English could be. I wish we had gone elsewhere.'

'Sit tight,' she said. 'They won't be long. Thirty minutes max.'

He sat back down looking disgruntled. His son began to yawn. After she left the room, she found a chair and wedged it beneath the door handle. If she could have locked it she would – the pair would make valuable witnesses – but she didn't have a key so the chair would have to do.

Jay hurried back to find Zamira was still staring at Branko. She looked as though she was in shock. Jay sat next to her and took one of her hands.

'Zamira,' she said. 'Tell me what you're doing here.'

Zamira turned to look at her. Her eyes were wide. 'Is this real? You're really here?'

'Yes, it's me.' She pressed a kiss on Zamira's knuckles. 'Please, Zamira, can you tell me what's going on?'

'I'm selling one of my kidneys to an Arab guy for three and a half thousand pounds. Then I'll be free.'

'How, free?'

'Well, that amount of money should keep me going for at least eighteen months, during which time I can learn new skills and get a really good job. Secure my future.'

'Is that what Branko told you?'

'Yes.'

'He lied.'

Zamira looked at the unconscious Branko.

Jay said, 'Three and half thousand pounds will pay your rent for that long, but only if you live in a rat-infested hole under the railway lines with no running water, sewerage or electricity. You certainly won't have any money for food or clothing, or heating. Three and a half thousand pounds is nothing in England.'

Zamira kept gazing at Branko. Her expression was blank.

'Do you know the current value for a kidney on the black market?'

'Ten thousand pounds.'

'Sixty.'

Zamira turned her head and looked Jay in the eye. 'The Arab man's paying sixty thousand pounds for my kidney?'

'I don't know for sure, but it would be in that region. Maybe even more.'

Zamira looked steadily at Branko. Then she stood and walked over to him. Leaning over his slumped form, she spat in his face. Her sputum glistened like a slug's trail at the corner of his mouth.

He gave a moan. 'Peaches? That you?'

'You snake,' hissed Zamira.

'Help me.' He opened his eyes. 'Christ, my knee ... '

Jay crossed the room to squat in front of him. 'Look at me, Branko.'

He cracked open his eyelids and squinted at her.

'I want to know who you work for. Who's behind this organ trafficking business. I want names of nurses, surgeons, how you organise the operations, how you find the recipients and the donors. I want to know everything.'

He remained silent. Despite the icy air-conditioning, sweat was beading on his forehead and running down his face, which was no longer a healthy biscuit-brown but dirty yellow.

'Also, there's the little matter of a traitor on our side. A mole in MI6. Who is it?'

'A what?' he said.

His eyes gave a genuine flick of surprise when she asked the question, so she moved right on. She doubted Branko would be privy to such information, being a mere captain in the Mafia's army, but it had been worth a shot.

'Who gets the money for this little scam, Branko? Is it Milot?'

'I wouldn't know. I'm just the middle man.'

'So who do you pay? Who gets the profit? You don't have the brains to set all this up. Someone smart is at the top and if you don't tell me who it is, I'm calling the police. You'll get thrown into jail. You'll be there for a long time, at least twenty years, charged with trafficking under-age girls, sexual exploitation, false imprisonment, and rape.'

'I never raped them!'

'And that makes it okay to let others do it?'

'I looked after them! I never harmed a hair on your head, did I Zamira?' He looked at the girl desperately, but she didn't respond. Her expression was frigid but her eyes blazed with hate.

'You'll soon find out what it's like to be raped,' Jay went on. 'You're quite a pretty boy, aren't you? The guys will love you inside.'

'Go fuck yourself.'

His words were brave but the quiver at the corners of his mouth gave him away.

'The apartment in Kensington Gore,' Jay prompted. 'It's owned by Tihomir Vadic.'

'Who says?'

'Vadic gave the address to Immigration officials at Heathrow.'

He gave a little jerk of surprise.

'Vadic's your boss, isn't he?'

'Fuck off.'

Moving fast she grabbed his bound wrists and imprisoned his right thumb. 'You want a broken thumb as well as a smashed kneecap?'

He squeezed his eyes shut. 'If that's what it takes.'

Jay knew if she didn't get answers from Branko, she wouldn't get any at all. He was her only door to Vadic, and the only source of information that could lead to releasing her friends, her loved ones, from the Mafia's hook. The instant she rang the cops and they turned up she had no doubt he'd turn mum, get the best lawyer in town, and she'd never be free. She pictured her father's cattle lying dead in the heather, her mother knifed, Tom shot down some back street in Bristol, and firmed her resolve.

She glanced up at Zamira, who gave a nod.

'I'm not kidding, Branko.'

He had started to pant, sweat pouring down his face. 'I know you're not,' he gasped.

'You're going to scream yourself hoarse,' she told him. 'And nobody's going to run to your rescue, are they? Because you've bribed them to stay away from this area tonight.'

'How the hell . . . ?'

'Just a guess.' And as long as the Sister didn't come running, Jay reckoned they'd remain undisturbed.

'Last chance, Branko.'

'Fuck . . . '

Gritting her teeth, steeling herself, Jay grabbed his right thumb and twisted it, yanking it violently backwards. The gristly crunch was shocking in the silence. Nausea flooded Jay's stomach as he flung back his head and screamed but she didn't release the pressure. She leaned forward, getting close to him, speaking into his face.

'How do you pay Vadic? Money transfer? Through a bar or a club? I want to know *every single detail.*'

'Fuck . . . yourself.'

'How many fingers do you want broken? All ten?'

'F-fine.'

He wasn't frightened enough for Jay. He knew broken bones could be healed. He was, Jay realised, more scared of what Vadic would do to him if he squealed than anything she might do.

Branko flicked sweat out of his eyes and glanced up at Zamira. 'Come on, Peaches,' he gasped. 'Help me out here. Can't you see I'm in agony?'

'Not enough,' Zamira said bleakly, and before Jay could move the girl brought back her foot and kicked him in the side of the head. It was a hard, vicious blow, made with all her strength, and if she'd been wearing shoes it could have done some serious damage.

'Jesus Christ.' Branko stared at Zamira.

Zamira looked at Jay. Her eyes were remote, as though she was looking at a horizon in her mind's eye. She said quietly, 'I want to take him into a forest and kill him.'

Jay felt a rush of euphoria as a plan fell neatly into her head. 'Zamira, I've got a far better idea.'

Forty-one

Branko watched as Zamira looked over the gleaming instruments on the aluminium tray. There were scalpels and pliers and needles, probes, scissors and bone cutters, and wicked looking things he didn't have names for, and didn't want to know what they were either.

His knee was pounding with pain. He wanted to shout and beg for mercy, but there was no point. Zamira appeared deaf to his pleas. He was in deep shit. He could yell all he liked and nobody would hear. The walls were ancient and absorbed sound like blotting paper. He should know, since he'd tested them last year. He'd also told George, the fat security guard on duty tonight, to avoid the basement, which meant the only person who might help was the receptionist, but they'd never hear him. They were too far away.

He squinted at his captor. He didn't like the way Zamira was studying a scalpel that looked sharp enough to slice open his shirt if she brought it within a hairsbreadth of the cloth. To his horror she picked it up and began turning it from side to side, as though admiring the way it gleamed beneath the bright lights of the operating theatre.

'Christ, Zamira, put that thing down, will you?'

To his relief, she returned the scalpel to the tray, but then she picked up a long, slender aluminium instrument topped with a delicate hook that was sharper, finer, than any fishing hook.

'You wouldn't hurt me, Peaches, would you?' He hated the quaver in his voice. 'I know I told a few fibs, but I got you to England, didn't I? Helped you realise your dream?'

She ignored him. He tried to think how to get through to her, and make her realise that *he* was her friend and not that army thug next door. It had been McCaulay who had dragged him into the operating theatre and tied him to a ducting pipe in the corner. Despite his pleading, she had also bound his head to the pipe. He was trussed and immobile aside from his mouth and eyes. When McCaulay came and squatted in front of him, he'd had to grip hard on his sphincter muscles. Her weird yellow-brown eyes were flat and held as much emotion as a corpse.

She said, 'I will only come in and stop Zamira if you give the answers I need. But not before then.'

Caught between the devil and the fucking blue sea, he'd remained silent as the bitch left, locking the door behind her.

'Zamira,' he pleaded. 'Don't hurt me. I'm your friend.'

'You were going to sell my kidney for sixty thousand pounds,' she said. 'And only give me three and a half.'

'She told you that?' He tried to inject his tone with outrage. 'The cow! She lied! I only get ten grand a kidney, I swear it!'

Zamira stepped so close to him he could smell her sweat, mixed with the lemony soap she'd used in the flat. She lifted the little hook to his right eye.

'Fucksake, Zamira. What the hell ... '

He tried to jerk free but the army bitch had tied him well and he barely shifted.

'Keep still, Branko,' she whispered.

'Fuck, no!'

He scrunched his eyelid shut. He could see the operating theatre lights behind his eyelid. He squeezed it tighter. Then he felt a tiny prick just inside his lower lid.

He moaned. 'Please, Zamira ... '

'Shut up.'

He felt her pull a little and the hook dug deeper. He needed all his self-control not to scream. He didn't want to move in case the hook slipped and took out his eyeball or ripped open his lower lid.

'Who do you work for?' she asked.

'Zamira, I can't tell you, you know I—'

She yanked on the hook, pulling out his lower lid and forcing the hook into the pink, fleshy part below.

He felt the warm trickle of blood seep down his cheek. 'Please.' It was a sob.

Suddenly the pressure eased and she removed the hook. His eye watered. He blinked several times, trying to clear his vision.

His stomach clenched when he saw she was now holding the scalpel.

'Branko, if you don't tell me, I shall remove your lower lid with a single stroke.' She put her head on one side. 'I wonder if your eye will fall out?'

He felt a sudden urge to urinate.

'Please,' he said, but she didn't seem to hear.

Raising her hand, she steadied her wrist against his cheekbone. The scalpel approached. It was so close he couldn't focus on it.

He strained against his bonds. 'Peaches, please,' he gasped, and he scrunched his eyelid shut and a second later the scalpel sliced, burning through his skin. For a second he couldn't believe it. Then he screamed.

'Okay, okay! I'll tell you, I swear I will! Take the fucking thing away from me!'

Zamira moved the scalpel to his other eye. 'No.'

'Okay,' Branko choked. Blood streamed from the wound, down his cheek and into the corner of his mouth. He tasted it, warm and salty. 'Don't cut me again, please ... '

'Who heads the business that uses girls like me and Hana?'

'Milot Dumani. He brings in women from Russia as well as Eastern Europe. He's recently teamed up with Tihomir Vadic to go into the organ transplant business. Milot provides the donors, Vadic the recipients. Vadic has a huge operation running between the Balkans and Turkey – he takes people from Moldova, Kosovo and the like to Istanbul – where the operations are done late at night using hospital facilities he doesn't have to pay for.' He was panting like a stricken dog in his haste to speak. 'It's a brilliant scheme, rumours have it that he's made over fifteen million dollars so far, but he's not stopping at that. He wants to crack the European market. We're going to make zillions.'

There was a brief silence.

And then he had a brilliant idea.

'You could join us, Zamira.' He turned his voice soft, persuasive. 'You're tough, smart, they could do with someone like you, and they'll pay you so much money that ... '

'Shut up!'

He fell silent.

'I don't want to hear any more of your lies.'

'Okay.' His voice was thin and trembled.

'How do you get the money to Vadic?'

Alarm shot through his veins. 'Oh, no. I couldn't tell you that. Sweet Jesus, Zamira, if Vadic finds out I've given him that sort of detail he'll kill me and my family, my wife ... '

'You have a wife?'

'No, no.' Christ he was losing it, he must concentrate. 'That was a slip of the tongue. I meant it metaphorically ... '

But it was too late and he felt the scalpel fall smoothly on to his lower lid and the pain was as though someone had poured acid into his eye.

Branko shouted so hard his voice cracked. Blood ran into his eye, blinding him, and he was sobbing, but Zamira didn't move.

'Talk to me, Branko, or you'll lose your eye.'

'Don't, please ... I'll tell you which banks, which countries ... I'll tell you everything ... '

He began talking fast, details of deposits and accounts, where the majority of the money was laundered and what bonuses he and his fellow officers in Milot and Vadic's expanding army received.

Vadic scared him, but Vadic wasn't here. Zamira was.

Forty-two

When Blake arrived at the hospital, it was only ten-fifteen but it felt much later, like four o'clock in the morning. He resembled a cat burglar in black jeans and polo neck shirt, black soft-soled shoes and matt black leather jacket. He looked neat, fresh and alert, whereas Jay was rumpled and sweaty and felt a mess.

'How did you get in?' she asked.

'One day I'll show you. Advance B and E. How about you?'

'Gift of the gab and theft.'

'Good work.'

'Did you see any security guards?' she asked him.

'Yup. A couple were running around with one of the ward sisters but I sent them in the opposite direction.'

'How?'

'I showed them my ID. Gets me out of jail every time.'

When he stepped into the operating theatre, he looked at the unconscious form that was Branko, trussed, still bleeding, and shook his head saying, 'Jeez, will you look what happens when you don't wait for me? Untie the man, will you?'

Jay and Zamira stared at him.

Ignoring them, Blake opened a leather case clipped onto his belt and withdrew a handy-looking device that, when pressed, produced a wicked-looking knife. He sliced the flex between Branko's wrists and leg. Branko stretched out his leg, moaning.

'What are you doing?' Jay asked.

Blake paused and looked at her. 'You want to be up for GBH when the cops get here? Let's tidy the man up, and get our story straight. And what's with the guys in the room with the chair against the door?'

As Jay filled Blake in, he disposed of the flex in a bin labelled 'medical waste only' and replaced it with a pair of handcuffs. Jay fetched Branko's holster and passed it to Blake, who strapped it on his ankle. 'Handy,' he said, then, 'You called nine-nine-nine yet?'

'No.'

'Let's do it.'

Since her mobile couldn't get a signal in the basement, Jay went and found a phone down the corridor. While she dialled, Blake talked to the Arab man and his father. What he said to them she never knew, but within five minutes they were standing meekly with her and Zamira, eyes down, shoulders slumped like condemned men.

'They've agreed to give a statement.' He turned and looked at Branko. 'You're going away for a very long time, my friend.'

To Jay's relief the same DI was on duty – DI Wilkinson with the florid face – so she only had to explain the latter part of the day's events. He even managed to rustle up the same woman from social services who had taken Hana and Jasmin under her wing, and who promised faithfully that Zamira would be sharing a room with her two THB charges, and that tomorrow they would go and see a doctor about her face. When Zamira clung to Jay, not wanting to let her go, Jay explained why she couldn't stay with her.

'The Mafia may well try and come after me,' she said. 'They tried to kill me once, and when they know I'm still around, they might try again. I'm going into hiding until Vadic's been put away.'

'Where?'

She glanced at Blake, who gave her a minute nod that she took to say, yes, you're welcome to stay in my mini-fortress for as long as it takes.

'It's a secret.'

'Can't I come too?'

'I'm sorry, sweetheart. It's better if you don't. Just in case.'

She gave Zamira her mobile phone and all her cash. 'I'll buy myself another phone tomorrow, okay? I can borrow Max's until then.' Jay showed her Angus and Sandra's numbers, as well as Denise and Angela's and Nick's. 'They'll all help you if you need them.' The inconvenience of not having her mobile phone was outweighed by the sense of security she knew it would give Zamira.

The last Jay saw of Branko was as two uniformed constables helped him into a wheelchair and headed to the lifts. His blueberry coloured jacket was creased and stained with blood, his normally immaculate hair dishevelled. He was crying.

The police held them for five hours. By the time they were let go, Jay was exhausted. She was barely able to keep her eyes open during the journey to Blake's house. When they arrived, they tripped what seemed to be a hundred floodlights.

'Wow,' she said. 'It's like *Close Encounters*.'

'The foxes hate it. Scares the crap out of them.'

'I'm not surprised.'

He let her in and gave her a set of house keys which controlled three sets of alarms, the garage, his office, the barn – she hadn't realised he owned a barn as well – and the cellar.

'I'll be back in time for breakfast.'

Jay blinked. It was two o'clock in the morning. 'Where are you going?'

'To get the jump on Vadic before he knows what's happened tonight. If we don't get him while he's on British soil, we'll never get him. It'll be like trying to catch an eel between two pieces of soap once he's on home territory.'

'Shall I come too?'

'No. You'll only hold me up.'

Thanks a bunch for the vote of confidence, she thought, but then a wave of exhaustion washed over her. She'd be more use after she'd had some sleep. 'Bring me back a newspaper?'

'Sure thing.'

After he'd gone, Jay drank two glasses of water and put some bread on to toast. She hadn't eaten since breakfast and was starving. Tonight, she sampled some honey from Bulgaria. Thick and dark, it had hints of lavender and rosemary and was so delicious she ate three spoonfuls on their own and had to force herself to put the jar back inside the cupboard and out of sight.

She went through Blake's bedroom and into his spacious en-suite to run herself a bath. It was too late to ring Tom, besides which she doubted he'd be overly worried since the last time they'd spoken she had been in the Kensington apartment, surrounded by police. He hadn't texted or phoned her since, which meant he was either flat-out busy on some case, or fast asleep.

She peered inside Blake's bathroom cabinet and found a bottle of Jo Malone bath oil. French Lime Blossom, delicious and very feminine. Not something she could see Blake bathing in and not for the first time she wondered about his love life and who the gorgeous dark-haired woman was in the photograph, whether she was an old girlfriend or current, or even an ex-wife. She slipped out of her clothes and climbed into the bath, leaned back and closed her eyes. She tried to imagine Blake married, but it was like trying to imagine a tiger with a pink bow around its neck sitting at a tea table.

Before she realised it, she'd nodded off and when she came to, the bath water had cooled. Shivering a little, she towelled herself dry before wrapping herself in Blake's bathrobe and climbing into his bed.

She slept deeply, no dreams.

When she awoke, for the first few seconds she had no idea where she was. Immediately her heartbeat picked up. Was she on duty? On a front line? She sat bolt upright and recognised the outline of the steam trunk at the foot of Blake's bed. Unmoving, she sat there for another few seconds, listening to the silence. A quick glance at the digital clock on his bedside table showed her it was four a.m. She didn't know what had woken her, but then she recognised the harsh glare of the floodlights through a crack in the curtains.

A fox, or an intruder?

Jay pulled on her shirt and jeans, hardened with old sweat, and padded barefoot to the hallway. She peeked at the video-intercom that showed the front forecourt to see a dark-coloured sedan standing on the gravel. Someone was walking briskly up the path, a florid-faced man in dark trousers and a fleece zipped to his chin. Jay did a double-take.

It was DI Wilkinson.

On the screen, she watched the detective reach out and press the doorbell. Inside, it emitted a polite buzz.

The intercom crackled. 'Miss McCaulay, are you there?'

For several moments, all Jay could hear was the thudding of her heart.

'We've got to talk. It's urgent. Vadic is on your tail and we want to offer you protection until he's in custody. Take you to a safe house. Let me in, will you?'

Jay stared at the image of the detective scuffling on the steps. How did the policeman know she was here? Why was he here at four in the morning, and why was his right hand in his pocket? Fear shot through her.

'Miss McCaulay?' His voice rose. 'This can't wait. I tried your mobile but got Zamira instead. Believe me, I'm here to help protect you! You're in terrible danger!'

No shit, Jay thought. She pressed the intercom button. 'How did you find me?'

'You were seen leaving the scene at the hospital with Max Blake, and since Blake was seconded from MI5 to MI6 . . . Well, all agent details are on our files. I just looked them up and drove over.'

She stared at the intercom monitor. Her heart was tripping at twice its normal speed. Was it true that cops were able to access intelligence details? She didn't think so. Had Vadic got to the policeman? Or was this the mole's work?

Jay was about to back away from the door, her mind already planning ahead – phone Blake, then the cops, head to the kitchen and find the biggest knife she could find – when she saw a shadow dart between the trees at the edge of the drive, and then another. Two men, keeping low. Both with dark objects in their hands. Pistols.

'Miss McCaulay – Jay – please would you let me in?'

She counted two more shadows. They were closing in. Who was the target? Was it her, or DI Wilkinson?

Using the cover of the DI's car, one of the shadows crept on to the forecourt. He was twenty yards from the front door.

The gunman aimed his weapon at the policeman.

'Please, Jay. Trust me and open the door!'

Forty-three

Jay put her hands on the door locks, readying herself.

The seconds ticked away. DI Wilkinson kept ringing the doorbell. The gunman didn't shoot.

A full minute passed before the gunman lowered his weapon. DI Wilkinson turned and raised his hands at the gunman. He appeared to be saying, 'It didn't work. What next?'

The gunman glanced over his shoulder. He looked as though he was talking to someone hidden in the trees.

They had tried to trick her into opening the door, and letting the policeman in.

Jay spun and pelted for the kitchen. She needed weapons, and fast. She flung open drawers and grabbed what she needed; a small paring knife, a large carving knife with a wickedly sharp blade, and a length of cord to use to strangle and garrotte. She had just flicked on the kettle – to give her boiling water to throw at an assailant – when she heard the sound of an engine. A powerful engine, revving hard.

She turned to see a pair of headlights approaching across the forecourt. The vehicle was accelerating, headed for the large picture window. They were going to ram it.

She dived to the ground as the window shattered. A four-wheel-drive BMW bounded into the kitchen spraying glass and metal everywhere, and slammed into the central oak console, crushing it into jagged sticks and splinters. Dark figures holding pistols emerged from behind the car but Jay was already in the corridor and moving fast for Blake's secret door at the far end of the house.

There was a muffled 'pop' from a silencer behind her and a bullet whizzed past, walloping into the wall alongside and kicking out a chunk of plaster. She didn't feel it slice into her cheek. Every ounce of effort was concentrated on getting out of the house.

'Stop!' a man's voice yelled.

She sprinted through the sitting room, carpet soft beneath her feet, and then she was on oak floors and skidding, careering into Blake's office and the bookcase and the secret door.

Another 'pop' and Jay grabbed the door handle and twisted it, shoved open the door and fell through.

Pop. Pop.

She slammed the door behind her, ramming home the bolts a second before the door handle twisted and the man pounded his fist against it.

There was no point in going for her car, the men would have it covered. She raced for the trees. The ground was harsh beneath her soles, used to the protection of boots, but she didn't slow. Breaking an ankle or getting a few cuts was preferable to being caught by Vadic.

Jay plunged into the woods, dodging between the trees, branches snatching at her clothes. She glanced behind her to see flashlights bobbing. Angry shouts. Curses.

She aimed downhill towards the stream. She would follow it to the road, and from there, hitchhike to a phone box.

She continued moving between the trees at a light jog, keeping her knees soft in case she hit a rabbit hole or an ant hill. Her feet were grazed and torn, but she shut the pain out of her mind. The moon was behind a cloud, and Jay willed it to stay there. She didn't want the men to have any advantage in tracking her.

The slope steepened and she skidded, sliding the last few yards through cold mud, churned up by livestock. She grabbed at exposed tree roots to help keep her balance until she reached the stream. She was tempted to walk in the water to soothe her feet, but the stones were sharp and she daren't risk damaging them further in case she couldn't walk.

Through the ringing of her ears she could hear the odd shout, distant, angry, but otherwise the night was still and silent. Jay pushed on as fast as she dared, following the stream. Soon she passed under a wooden bridge, and not long afterwards she came to the road. She broke into a run. The bitumen felt smooth and solid and she was glad there were few stones to puncture her soles.

She soon settled into a steady rhythm. Ignoring the pain in her feet, she felt her breathing relax, her body working efficiently and smoothly. She heard a car behind her. She leapt on to the grassy verge and made to hide behind the hedge but it was thorny and impenetrable, so she slid into the ditch running alongside. Water seeped through her clothes, but when headlights speared the darkness, she held herself as low as she could. A single glimpse of her skin or shirt would flare as brightly as a firework to her pursuers.

The car swept past, and then she heard them.

Sirens. Lots of sirens, and they were coming her way.

Against the darkness she could see blue lights twirling. Cop cars approaching fast. Blake's house must have been hooked up to the police. Or he had a personal alarm on him that alerted him to intruders.

For a moment she paused. Part of her wanted to surrender herself to the safety of the police, who could give protection to her and her family until Vadic was in custody. But the other part was terrified she'd be murdered in that same safe haven. DI Wilkinson was in Vadic's pocket. Even if the police believed her story that he wasn't to be trusted, another cop might tell Vadic where she was, and she'd be dead. If Tom had been in one of the cop cars, she wouldn't have hesitated, but he was in Bristol. He couldn't protect her from there. She had to make some time to think, to make a plan.

Jay climbed out of the ditch and ran down the road, looking for a gate through the thick hedge.

She must get off the road.

Her breath hot in her throat, Jay spotted a gap in the hedge which revealed a gate. Leaning her torso over the top bar, she vaulted it and kept running. Half a minute later three cop cars drove past. Jay watched them go.

It was eight a.m. when the taxi dropped Jay at home, and her housemates had already left for work. Hobbling inside, she raided the kitty jar to pay the driver. 'You sure you're okay?' he asked. He looked at her feet and then tapped his cheek at her.

She touched her face to find it caked in dried blood. 'I'll be fine once I'm cleaned up.'

Which wasn't true – her feet were agony, the skin ripped and still bleeding – but the cab driver looked happier as he drove off. It was thanks to a spotty teenager manning the tills of a twenty-four hour garage that she'd managed to ring him. If she hadn't, she'd probably still be walking. In the kitchen, she plucked a yellow Post-it note free from where it was stuck to the kettle.

Your mum's rung three times. Apparently she has got the troll. She repeated this ten times to make sure I got it right. Whatever she's on, can I have some? Love, Deni.

Limping up the stairs, Jay wanted nothing more than to have a hot bath and go to bed, but she had to keep moving. She was only here to plant some bait. After a hurried shower, she slathered her feet with antiseptic cream before binding them with some crepe bandage she found in the bathroom cupboard. She quickly packed some supplies; binoculars, water, chocolate bars, sleeping bag, warm clothing, waterproofs, walking boots, a flask of whisky, a camera.

She jumped when the phone rang. She picked it up, but didn't say anything.

'There's a BMW in my kitchen and bullet holes in my walls,' he said. 'You care to explain?'

'It was a bit of a wild party. Sorry.'

'I leave you alone for two seconds ... ' He sighed, and she pictured him staring at the ceiling in mild despair.

'Sorry,' she said again.

Brief pause.

'You okay?' he asked.

'Sore feet.'

'You ran barefoot?'

'Yes.'

'Ouch.' He cleared his throat. 'Sounds like it might be a good idea if I brought your car round.'

'God, Max, that would be brilliant. Oh, before I forget ... ' She paused, wondering how to request what she wanted without her listeners catching on.

'What is it?'

'Er, it's a bit embarrassing. I've a huge spider in the bath. Would you mind removing it for me? I can't stand spiders.'

It was an oblique reference but Blake seemed to understand what she meant. 'On my way,' he said.

Jay brewed a pot of fresh coffee and gave a mug to Blake. He drank it while de-bugging her house of the VHF devices. He had brought a small metal box with him, a specialist-type gadget, to help him track down the illegal UHF bugs. At her request, he left them where they were. One was hidden inside the plug of her bedside light, one in the kitchen walkabout phone, the third in the smoke alarm between the living room and hallway. She was hoping to use the one in the phone to plant a trap for the mole. In Jay's mind, the mole was the key to saving her from Vadic, because then she could use the mole to set up another – more deadly – trap for the gangster.

It didn't take long before Blake came and joined her in the kitchen, washing his hands and rinsing out his mug in silence. They hadn't spoken much since they'd covered what had gone down at his house. Jay was too tired and she suspected he might be too, even though he didn't look it.

She'd been right about Vadic getting to DI Wilkinson. Apparently Vadic's thugs had been with Wilkinson's ten-year-old granddaughter when they'd called him and told him if he didn't do as they wanted, they would rape her, then cut her throat. The information confirmed that she'd been right not to run to the police last night. Some people would say she was being stupid, but she felt safer on her own.

'Did the cops catch anyone?' she asked Blake.

'Nope.'

'How's his granddaughter?'

'Traumatised, but yeah, she's okay.'

'And what about Vadic? Where is he?'

'If I knew, I wouldn't be here. I'd be tearing his head from his shoulders and sticking it on a pole. I liked that console in my kitchen. It was hand-made.'

He ran a hand over his stubble. She felt a sudden urge to touch his cheek, and had to look away before she acted.

'I've got some more photos for you to look at,' he said. 'I'll send someone over with them later.'

'I might not be here.'

He gave her a long look. 'Any chance it's because you're going away for a few days? Somewhere safe?'

The surface of her skin shivered as though someone had walked over her grave. Did he know what she was planning? Could he read her mind?

'How did you know?'

'The bag sitting in the hall gave me a hint.'

He didn't ask any more so she didn't volunteer any information. The less everyone knew, including Blake, the better.

They stood silently as a woman and her pet pug walked past the window. The woman wore a pair of purple Wellington boots and a trilby with a red plastic flower stapled to the front, the pug a faux diamond collar. Some days Jay couldn't believe the eccentrics in her neighbourhood.

'Max, can I ask you something?'

'Sure.'

'Do you work for MI5?'

'Not all the time, but today I do.'

He was as enigmatic as ever and she didn't have the energy to pursue the line of questioning. She watched him check his phone before putting it back in his pocket. He moved close to her and plucked a piece of fluff from her sweater. 'It should all be over by the weekend,' he said.

'Really?'

'Yes.'

She noticed she wasn't the only one keeping her cards close to her chest. Blake obviously had his own plan and she just had to hope it didn't conflict with hers or it might get messy.

'How about we do something Saturday?' he said. 'I could pick you up around six or so and we could be in Venice in time for dinner. I know this really cool place, Locanda Cipriani. Have you been there?'

She felt her head go light. Was he serious?

'It's on an island. Torcello . . . ' His phone began to ring. He flipped it open, saying, 'Yeah, I'm done in town.' He glanced at his watch. 'I'll see you in forty, okay?'

Putting his phone back in his pocket Blake lowered his head and for a second she thought he was going to kiss her, but instead he brushed a lock of hair behind her ear and whispered, 'There's a present for you in your glove box.'

As she felt his fingers brush her skin all the hairs on her body rose. A rush of blood poured into her stomach and heated her lower belly, making her feel faint.

'See you Saturday,' he said.

Before she left, Jay rang Angus and explained about Zamira and Hana.

'They might ring you,' she said. 'I hope that's okay.'

'God, the poor kids. Of course it's all right.'

'I'm going away for a couple of days. Would you check on them for me?' She gave him the social worker's mobile number.

'No problem. I'll call later today. Will they need somewhere to stay? We've got loads of room, you know.'

'You are wonderful,' she told him sincerely.

'But not when I ask you to baby-sit.' He sounded amused.

It took Jay nine hours to drive to the Scottish Highlands and when she arrived at her father's house the light was softening, and dusk was drawing in. She drove past the farm buildings and up the rough track to the house, which was perched further up the mountainside. As she climbed out of her car to open the gate, exhaustion hit her.

She'd forgotten how quiet it was here. There were no roads nearby, no villages, no neighbours. She was on the edge of the moors in the company of nothing but rabbits, grouse, and the odd brown trout in the depths of the peat-browned burns.

As usual, she felt as though she'd landed on a different planet, and her spirit lightened and stretched in the great expanse of sky and winter-brown heather. Despite the abnormal and dangerous situation she was putting herself in, it felt good to be here.

Tucking the car out of sight from the farm buildings, she unpacked her supplies. The house was chill inside and she switched on the central heating before downing a couple of painkillers. Thanks to her father having left the Rayburn ticking over, the kitchen was reasonably cosy, and she heated some tinned game soup and ate it with her back against the range. After she'd washed up, she switched out all the lights and went to bed.

Nobody knew where she was, and her subconscious seemed to recognise that, because she slept like the dead until dawn. She awoke to see pale grey light trickling through the curtains. Her breath made little puffs in the still, cold air and in a rush she felt her energy return. Quickly, she bathed, and put on olive-green moleskin trousers, a khaki polo neck jumper and matching outer fleece, the colours muted so she'd blend in with the countryside. She felt refreshed and invigorated. Ready for battle. It was six a.m. and time to set the bait.

Blake's gift had been another mobile phone and charger – did he have a supply at home he raided? – but Jay used her father's phone instead, so her call would appear genuine to anyone who checked the phone records.

First, she rang Kingsman.

'Jay,' he said. 'How are you?'

'I have something for you,' she replied. 'Or rather, someone.'

'Does this have to do with the St Norbert Hospital debacle?'

'Yes. You see, Branko knew more than I imagined. He knew the name of your mole.'

Huge silence.

'I'd be very careful what you say next, Jay.'

'In that case, I shall say goodbye.'

She hung up.

Next, she dialled her home number. 'Denise, it's me. Sorry if I woke you.'

'I was already up, no worries,' her friend said on a yawn. 'Long time no see.'

'Yeah, I know. I've been busy. Look, this is a quick one to let you know I'm staying at Dad's place for the next week or so. Taking an impromptu holiday.'

'Lucky you.'

'It's bloody cold. There's still snow on the tops.'

'Get stuck into the whisky, that'll warm you up. Oh, send our love to your Dad, will you?'

'He's overseas, lucky bugger – but when he comes back, I'll tell him. Do me a favour, Denise?'

'Sure.'

'Don't tell anyone where I am.'

A small pause, then Denise said, 'Problem?'

'Put it this way, a low profile is a good thing for me right now. I've discovered the identity of someone who's meant to be secret.'

'Like who?'

'Think of a small animal that lives underground, with a black velvet coat.'

'God, Jay, you're up to your neck again, aren't you?'

'I'm okay, promise.'

'Ring us if you need us.'

Fetching some milk from the fridge, and oats from the earthenware jar by the window, Jay made herself some porridge. She could hear her father's voice. *Never fight on an empty stomach.*

She spent the next couple of hours preparing the house; she

didn't expect any trouble but there seemed little point in not taking precautions. She hid knives and skewers at strategic points throughout the house, plus lengths of twine to use as impromptu garrottes. She drilled a tiny hole through the sitting room floorboards, down into the cellar, where she rigged up a handful of tin cans with some of her father's invisible fishing line.

Next, she switched off the electricity at the mains. Using a syringe from her father's veterinary medical kit, she injected petrol through the base of four light bulbs. She put the first and second in the lights by the front and back entrance, the third in the main hall and the last in the cellar.

Then she stripped the ends of three electric cables – one in the kitchen, one in the master bedroom, the last in the sitting room – and made sure each was tucked well out of reach to avoid someone treading on them by accident and electrocuting themselves. Lastly, she turned the mains back on.

Come twelve o'clock she was hungry again. Frying some bacon, she made herself a thick butty with ketchup and ate it while she phoned her mother.

'Jessica, where in the world have you been? I've left—'

'Five messages. Yes, I know. Something about the troll?'

'The police caught him! Can you believe it? The silly little man got picked up for running a red light and when the traffic police rang back to base to check his number plates they were told to apprehend him immediately. Which they did! So he's in custody!'

'That's great, Mum.' Jay swallowed a lump of bacon. 'Has he said who told him to threaten you?'

'Oh, yes. Some foreign man called . . . ' There was the sound of rustling paper. 'Vadic. That's V A D I C.' She spelled it out. 'Apparently he's from Georgia. They've put out a warrant for his arrest, but haven't caught him yet.'

There was a brief pause, then her mother said, 'Jessica, do you know this Vadic man?'

'I met him once. We didn't exactly get on. He sees me as a threat.'

There was a long pause.

'Where are you?'

'Somewhere safe.'

Her mother said tightly, 'Don't you dare do anything stupid.'

Jay looked at the cellar door, then at the can of petrol, the bailer twine, the electric cables and her father's twelve-bore shotgun, and said, 'I won't, I promise.'

Forty-four

With her father's house brightly lit, the sitting room fire stoked and sending smoke spiralling into the chill air, Jay hefted her backpack on her shoulders and set off up the hill. Having spent most of her holidays here during her teenage years, she was used to moving alone in the mountains, but it was the first time she'd gone walking with her feet mashed to pulp. She'd taken more painkillers before leaving the house, but every step still hurt.

Damn him, she thought. Damn Vadic for her pain, her trepidation and fear. Please God, let my plan work.

She hadn't dared tell anyone what she was doing. She couldn't risk it getting back to the mole. She could have had Blake or Tom alongside, and a SWAT platoon armed to the teeth, but the mole would no doubt check on all her friends and her family before they took her bait, and if they found anything amiss, they wouldn't come.

She had to do this alone. It was the only way.

Usually it only took Jay half an hour to get to the deserted, shepherd's hut – known locally as a bothy – which was set in a deep fold near the top of the mountainside, but today it took over forty minutes, with the pain in her feet getting sharper.

Damn Vadic.

She kept walking, passing an ancient, crumbled wall she used to hide behind when she was a kid, and a multitude of burns full of brown trout she used to fish, and it was with enormous relief that she finally made it to the tumbledown building and pulled open the wooden door. Inside was a single room with a dirt floor. The air was icy, but the roof was in good repair and it was dry. Her father and Nicola used the bothy in the summer as a picnic hut – the views were spectacular – where they could shelter if the weather changed, and she was glad to see the gas cylinder was nearly new and that the battered old armchair was still there. She went and filled up her water bottle from the narrow burn cutting through the heather nearby, and with her binoculars around her neck, settled herself to wait.

The bothy was in a good position to keep an eye on her father's house. Glenfiddich Forest was behind her, a rounded, wooded mountain, but the land before her was bare of trees and stretched unimpeded across heather-clad slopes to the scattering of farm buildings and fields at the bottom of the valley. Opposite her, on the other side of the road below, rose the majestic Ben Rinnes.

Through her binoculars she spotted her father's herd of Highland cattle tucked in a meadow at the bottom of the valley, with access to shelter and hay inside a barn. Several cows had calves, and not for the first time she sent her father a blessing for entrusting them to his neighbour. She couldn't have done this if he'd been here. She would have been too scared of him being hurt.

At the bottom of the glen she could see the hamlet of Kirkhill and the B9009, the Dufftown road. There was no traffic, just a tractor trundling along with stacks of pine logs on its trailer. Jay's shoulders relaxed a little as she studied the bleak, frosty wilderness. She loved coming up here, even in winter. The air was clear and cold and held the smoky scent of peat. People here had more space than folk down south, and more time to chat and gossip in the shops. She could understand why her father had retired up here. There was something elemental about it, walking on earth instead of pavements, breathing pure air rather than city fumes. It fed a fundamental need in her father, and some days she wondered if she didn't need the same diet too.

Lunchtime came and went. She ate a sandwich and drank

coffee from her thermos. She didn't know when the mole would come. Flights from Gatwick to Inverness left at regular intervals between nine in the morning and nine in the evening. It didn't matter if they drove up here or if they flew and hired a car at the airport. She was as ready as she would ever be.

She napped from time to time, waking to check the Dufftown road and the track leading past the farm buildings to her father's house, and there was nothing to alert her until two-thirty, when a pale blue sedan turned off at Kirkhill and crossed the first cattle grid to the farm buildings.

She trained the binoculars down the valley. All she needed was one look, a single glimpse of the mole, to see who they were, that was all. She wasn't going to confront them, not yet, not until she had backup. She just wanted to know who they were, and then – hopefully – they could be turned against Vadic.

To her surprise there appeared to be only one person in the car and she quickly scanned the B9009 to see another vehicle, a dark blue 4x4 Toyota, also turn off into the hamlet. While the pale blue sedan bounced and jolted its way to her father's house, the Toyota paused at the cattle grid and a man got out, but he was too far away for Jay to make out his features. He had a pair of binoculars and appeared to be watching the pale blue sedan's ascent. He only got back inside his car and started driving when the sedan had parked next to her own Golf. He was, Jay realised, following the sedan.

She swung her binoculars back to see someone hurrying for her father's front door. A small, lithe figure in pencil trousers and a thick padded jacket that did little to hide her femininity.

It was Laura Sharpe.

Through the lenses, she watched the agent reach out and press the doorbell.

For several moments, all Jay could hear was the rustle of the wind through the heather.

Jay stared at the MI6 agent rubbing her hands together on the steps.

She couldn't believe how stupid she had been. She remembered Kingsman listening to Laura debrief her, his neutral expression as he said, *There are a few discrepancies, but I'll sort those out with Laura later.* She'd bet Kingsman had known all along that Laura was the mole and had used Jay to try and trip his agent into showing her duplicity.

All along the agent had been playing her for a fool. Jay remembered Hashim supposedly dropping the book of matches in Laura's shoulder bag, and Blake musing, *I didn't think Hashim was the type to snitch.*

She remembered her instinct not to tell Laura about the second lot of bugs in her house. Her subconscious had obviously kicked in, suspecting Laura as the illegal listener. Laura had made sure Jay rang her first with any new information, so that she could filter and use it accordingly. When she had seen that Jay wasn't going to fold under Vadic's threats made in the meat-processing plant, Laura had lured Jay to the ski chalet to get her killed. But Jay had survived. Laura must have been spitting chips when she realised Jay wasn't keeping her end of the bargain they'd made after Kingsman's debriefing – to lie low and do nothing until Laura told her – and had decided Jay had to go. Laura must have arranged for Jay to be drowned in the Bristol Channel. And now she was here, to make sure she finished the job.

Jay checked on the Toyota to see it had parked behind the cow byre and that three men were approaching the house on foot. Something was wrong here.

She swung the binoculars to stare down at Laura walking around the house to the back door, which Jay had left open. She didn't reappear, which Jay took to mean she'd gone inside.

After three minutes, no more, Laura appeared at the side of the house. She was looking up the mountain and around, presumably searching for Jay's figure walking the heather.

Jay studied the men as they neared the house. With a lurch, she recognised Hashim, but not his companions. She watched them walk to the rear of the house and vanish, while the third man continued along the front drive. Even from this distance she could see the man was tall and cadaverous with dead-flesh skin.

Vadic, the Barracuda, was here.

Gripping the binoculars Jay watched Laura go to her VW Golf and peer inside. The two men appeared from behind the house and began to creep up on her. They both held pistols. Laura appeared oblivious of their approach.

No! Jay thought. This was all wrong. What was going on? Was Laura the mole or not? She had to be, because the only way she could know of Jay's whereabouts was by listening in to her phone call to Denise this morning, on the illegal UHF listening device. But why were Vadic's men stalking her?

Jay watched the men raise their guns and aim them at the agent.

Jay was on her feet. She wanted to shout to Laura, warn her of an imminent attack, but she was too far away.

One second Laura was beside Jay's car, the next she was bolting for her pale blue sedan. She must have spotted the men in the Golf's wing mirror. She was small but she moved as fast as a whippet. One of the men aimed his pistol at her fleeing form.

He fired.

Laura seemed to stumble. She fell to her knees.

Only then did Jay hear the crack reverberate down the valley. *Crack, crack, crack.*

She was surprised they weren't using silencers. She wondered who else had heard the gunshot, and if they would recognise it as a pistol and not a rifle. She didn't have time to ponder the point because Vadic's thugs had Laura by her arms and were hauling her to her feet. Laura's head was hanging, but it was impossible to see where she was wounded thanks to her padded jacket. Vadic gestured at the men. While one held Laura the other sped into the house. He returned shaking his head.

Vadic then walked to the agent. With one arm, he encircled Laura's throat. Her features spasmed, and Jay could see she was choking, gasping for air, but then Vadic grabbed one of his men's pistols and thrust it behind Laura's ear. He raised his head, and scanned the mountainside. The message was unmistakeable: Come down, or we'll shoot her.

Laura struggled against Vadic's grip. Her mouth was open in a silent scream and Jay fought a wave of nausea. She didn't wait to see any more. As fast as she could, she texted Blake and Kingsman, her fingers trembling in her haste. When she pressed *send* the messages bounced straight back.

No signal.

Shit, shit, shit. She left the messages in the outbox, to be sent when the signal kicked in. Please God, make it soon.

Grabbing the knife and shotgun, she sped out of the bothy. She didn't feel the pain in her feet as she raced down the mountainside. She was running on adrenalin. Flying over heather and grass tussocks, she only slowed when she reached the ancient, rotting wall.

She steadied herself against its old stones and studied the house. It took a couple of minutes, but eventually she saw a movement – a figure at the kitchen window – but then they stepped away. Because they hadn't found her on a brief search of the house, they assumed she was up the mountain, but they didn't have any evidence. She ran her mind through several options, and decided to see if she could lure them apart and pick them off, one by one.

She crept along an old game trail concealed by clumps of thick heather at the back of the house. She would be unseen from all the windows apart from the gun room, and soon she was squirming on hands and knees through bushes and tall grasses as she approached the house. Her trousers and fleece were soaked by the time she reached the stand of pines, a stone's throw from the back door.

She wanted to burst inside the house, shotgun blazing, but her training couldn't allow her to give in to the impulse. *Check, and double check.* She could endanger Laura's life if she acted prematurely. Vadic wasn't going anywhere for a while. He would wait for her for as long as it took. She just had to be patient.

Her caution saved her life.

She heard a footstep and then another. Someone was creeping towards her. She smelled a waft of stale nicotine. He was so close! But he hadn't seen her – not yet.

In slow motion, a millimetre at a time, she turned her head. She couldn't move any faster in case the movement alerted the man to the fact she was nearby. A crunching sound as he took another step. He was checking the perimeter of the house. Pulse pounding, she finally spotted him, moving between the trees. He was around eight feet away, looking at the house. He held a pistol in his right hand and had his back to her.

Those who hesitate, die.

Silently, Jay put down her shotgun. She withdrew a length of cord from her pocket and wound it around both hands.

Hands high, she launched herself at him.

He didn't have time to move before she had the garrotte around his neck, her knee in the small of his back. She jerked him violently backward. The movement was swift and vicious, as she'd been taught.

Both his hands went to his throat. He collapsed on to his knees, gurgling. Brutally, she increased the pressure.

It's either me or you, mate, and it's not going to be me.

The man's legs began to kick and thrash but she didn't lessen her grip. *Go down!* her mind yelled. *Go down!* Almost as if he'd heard her, the man stiffened and then shuddered, his feet drumming on the ground. His body abruptly slumped. Keeping up the pressure, Jay waited a few seconds more, but he was a dead weight. He wasn't breathing. Jay eased the body to the ground.

She was shaking, and part of her couldn't believe she'd killed him, but the rest of her brain was cold and hard and calculating. One down, two to go.

Forty-five

Breathing hard, Jay swiftly checked the corpse to find a mobile phone – which she switched off – and a Sig Sauer nine-millimetre pistol, its magazine fully loaded, a round already in the chamber. Gun in hand, she crouched in the bushes, trying to detect whether Hashim was outside guarding the house or not. Everything was silent but she didn't move. Despite the cold air, sweat poured from her hairline. She didn't brush it away but let it trickle unheeded down her face and neck. She concentrated on the house and surrounding area. Nothing moved. Not even a bird.

After fifteen minutes, she slunk to the back door and turned the handle. It opened smoothly. She slipped inside, closing it behind her. Immediately she heard voices coming from the kitchen. Vadic's and Laura's. Where was Hashim?

Holding the pistol in both hands she tiptoed down the corridor. The voices continued talking, unaware.

'Why would she know who he is?' Laura asked, sounding bewildered.

'She was in the army.'

'The British army, not Italian!'

'Everyone in NATO knows everyone.'

'Tihomir, I swear to you, Jay doesn't have a clue who your general is. She thought he was Protti's bodyguard!'

'Nicomedo doesn't look like a bodyguard,' he snorted. 'She's trying to trick you, Sharpe. I want her dead.'

With her back against the wall, gun held high, Jay steeled herself to look inside, but they had stopped talking. The silence only aggravated her tension. Holding her breath, she counted, one, two three.

Not wanting to alert them with a sudden movement, she inched her head around the door jamb.

Vadic was sitting at the kitchen table, a pistol in one hand, a cigarette in the other. Hashim stood with his back to her, looking outside. He also held a pistol. Laura was tied to a chair opposite. Her narrow face was bloodless and tight with fear. She seemed to sense Jay's presence, because she glanced at the doorway. Her eyes widened, her expression changing immediately from terror to hope. Thank God, she seemed to say. You can save me.

Jay ducked back before Laura could give her away. She didn't dare risk shooting at Hashim and Vadic with Laura in the room. The agent might get killed by accident. She had to cause a distraction, split the men up. Pistol ready, she aimed it down the corridor. She didn't trust them not to have more men around. *Better safe than dead.*

She felt cold even though she was sweating – a symptom of high stress. Peeking into the sitting room, she saw it was empty. She went to the corner of the room and crouched behind the drapes. She picked up the loop of almost-invisible fishing wire she'd left earlier, attached to a handful of tin cans in the cellar. Before she could lose her nerve, she gave it a good pull.

Immediately the cans toppled over, clattering and banging on the floor below.

She heard Vadic's exclamation. 'What the fuck's that?'

Footsteps pounded on the flagstones.

'She's in the fucking cellar!'

'I didn't see a cellar,' Hashim replied. 'Or a basement, but—'

'I don't give a shit what you did or didn't see, get the fuck down there and get the fucking bitch!'

Hashim immediately headed off. She listened to doors opening and closing, tracking him out of the kitchen, past the larder and into the laundry. As he headed for the gun room – where the cellar door was obscured in the wood grain beneath the stairs – she pulled up her courage from her boots and followed him. With her finger light on the trigger, she let the gun lead her into the gun room where Hashim had just found the cellar door. Opening it, he peered down the stairwell. It was pitch black inside and he did what anyone would in his circumstances. He switched on the light.

The light bulb was on Hashim's right, almost at eye-level and when it exploded, it hit him full on the side of his face. An eye-searing flash and an explosion of petrol and tiny shards of glass erupted in the small space, and slashed his bare skin. Hashim screamed as he dropped to his knees, his hands to his face, and at the same time Jay stepped in close and shoved him down the stairs.

Slamming the door shut she locked it and pushed the key beneath the dog bed. She rushed through the laundry and aimed the Sig into the corridor. When she saw it was clear, she belted for the kitchen. A quick glance showed Vadic standing behind Laura, pistol raised, and then a bullet whizzed past, whacking into the wall and missing her by a whisker. Jay hastily scrambled back out of sight, and flattened herself against the wall.

'McCaulay!' Vadic shouted. 'Throw down your gun! Come out now or I will shoot your friend!'

'She's not a friend,' she called back. 'She's a traitor. Go ahead and shoot her, see if I care!'

'No! It's not true!' Laura yelled.

'You led them here, Laura!'

'I came to warn you! I didn't know they'd followed me!' 'Bullshit!'

'I didn't have anything to do with your getting dumped in the Channel, okay? I'd never hurt you, Jay, I swear it!'

'You have three seconds!' Vadic yelled. 'One! Two!'

Jay's mind flew over the past few weeks, scenes of her and Laura drinking wine in Kiro's apartment, Laura laughing, Laura lighting her a cigarette in the Lada, Laura's blood on the mountain snow, the haunted shadows in her eyes on her return to England.

She asked herself a vital question: if Vadic killed Laura, could she live with herself?

'Okay!' she shouted. 'I'm coming out!'

'Push your weapon into the kitchen!'

Jay ducked down and pushed the Sig along the flagstones with a clatter.

'Put your hands behind your head and come out!'

Legs trembling, Jay inched around the corner into the kitchen, dreading the thump of a bullet in her chest, the searing pain of her flesh being torn apart.

Vadic had moved in front of Laura. The barrel of his pistol was levelled at Jay's face as she appeared. Her arms were high and although her hands weren't behind her head as he'd asked, he didn't seem to notice.

'Keep coming,' Vadic growled.

Jay obeyed, walking closer, concentrating on the Sig out of the corner of her eyes, and she was almost level with the gun when Laura screamed, a blood-curdling scream that had Vadic spinning around and Jay's adrenalin surging.

Even though she knew she'd be shot, Jay dived for the Sig, desperate to get to it before Vadic could shoot her first. Her fingers closed around the butt of the gun at the same time that Vadic pulled his trigger.

She felt something punch her hard at the top of her breast and, to her horror, her fingers slid from the Sig.

She heard Laura shouting but she focused on trying to grab the pistol. An aching numbness began to spread from her breast into her shoulder and down into her heart. She could feel something warm soaking her shirt, pouring down her chest. Everything started to slow down.

She felt incredibly tired, as though she could sleep, but then she heard her father's voice in her head.

Never give up, never give in.

With fierce concentration Jay forced her senses awake. She

heard footsteps approaching. This was when Vadic would shoot her. Execute her with two shots to the head.

'Good,' he said in satisfaction. 'You're still alive.'

Vadic paused beside her and dug a shoe into her ribs.

'You have caused me so much trouble,' he went on, 'that shooting is too good for you.'

She glanced past his ankle at the dresser, and spotted the length of cable she'd left tucked beneath it. With an immense effort, she began to crawl across the kitchen. Vadic laughed. 'Still trying to get away? I have you to give you this, you don't give up easily, do you?'

With every movement, she groaned. She felt cold. She felt sick. But she didn't stop crawling.

'Rather than a bullet to the back of the head, I have something much better in mind,' Vadic spoke to her. 'I wish to make an example of you, Jay McCaulay, to prevent anyone else from thinking they're clever enough to bring me down. Nobody wants to die a slow death with a small incision in their belly and watching their own entrails being hooked out, bit by bit. I haven't heard you scream yet. I'm sure you will make your father's rafters tremble.'

The dresser was only a yard away but a dull, deep ache spread through her breast and into her ribs, slowing her even further. She had to get there before she got any weaker.

'I'll cut you first. Laura can listen. It'll help sharpen her mind when I ask her about her masters and what she's been up to lately. Why she changed her coat so often.'

There. The length of cable was tucked behind one of the dresser's feet, well hidden, along with a skewer. She shuffled close. Sheltering her right hand from Vadic's view with her body, she unwound the cable, avoiding the stripped ends. Another agonising shuffle allowed her to check it was still plugged into the mains. With the electric cable in one hand, she gripped the skewer in the other.

'Let's roll you over, shall we?' Vadic said softly. 'And begin.'

In slow-motion, Jay did as he said and rolled over and buried the end of the live cable into Vadic's thigh.

He stiffened and then shuddered. He fell to the floor.

She scrambled on to his chest and with the last of her strength, rammed the skewer up his nose and straight into his brain.

Forty-six

Jay was curled up on the sofa at home, watching a re-run of *CSI* and drinking tea. She had just finished talking to Kiro. As she'd promised, she had told him the whole story, and for once he hadn't interrupted.

'Are you sure you're okay?' he said when she'd finished. He sounded anxious.

'I'm fine, Kiro. I swear.'

It had been four days since she'd been shot, and she wasn't going to tell him she was still on double-strength painkillers and felt appallingly weak.

She had had a succession of visitors since she'd arrived home. After killing Vadic, Jay had crawled to Laura and freed her. It had been Laura who called the police, for despite her injury – she'd been shot just above her shoulder blade – she'd lost less blood than Jay and had more strength. The police had arrived to find two corpses and a guy in the cellar with a bloodied, sliced-up face and a broken arm from falling down the stone steps.

'The paramedics will be here soon,' a policeman told Jay. He was pressing a sterile pad on her wound. Her skin felt clammy, her head light. 'What happened? Did they break in?'

'Yes.'

'Who attacked them?'

'I did.'

'Christ,' the policeman said.

Jay and Laura were airlifted to hospital in Inverness, where they were given blood and stitched up. When Jay came round, it was to see Max Blake sitting by her bed.

'Welcome back,' he said.

'Thanks.' Her voice was hoarse, her mouth dry.

He got to his feet and poured her a glass of water from a jug on the bedside table. She drank it straight down. He poured her another.

'I heard what you did,' he said. 'Good job.'

'I nearly didn't make it.' She shuddered at how close Vadic had come to killing her.

'Next time,' Blake said, coming to stand close, 'I want you to promise me something.'

'Like what?'

'Ask me along.'

'Max, I couldn't risk it. Laura would have known.'

'I know.' He raised both hands. 'But just promise me, okay?'

'Okay,' she said. 'I promise.' Her voice faded as a wave of weakness flooded through her. Grey shallows lapped at the edges of her mind. She closed her eyes.

'I'll leave you to rest,' he murmured. She felt him pick up her hand and press a kiss against her palm. His lips were warm and soft. She wanted to touch his head, stroke his hair, but the grey shallows were deepening into black. She heard him say, 'Don't forget our date Saturday,' and then she knew no more.

When she resurfaced again she felt much stronger, which was fortunate since her next visitors were Kingsman and Laura. Laura's arm was in a sling and there was a large mound of bandages over her left shoulder. Her skin was drawn and pale but the anguished shadows had gone and her eyes were clear.

Apparently Kingsman had been tracking Laura since she'd returned from the Balkans last January. He hadn't known for sure that it was Laura who was reporting to Vadic, but he'd had his suspicions, and when Jay fell into his lap after following Milot, he'd decided to use her to stir things up.

Which satisfied Jay to a certain extent, but what interested her more was *why* Laura had changed sides, and when Kingsman was drawn outside by Alistair Ingram to answer an urgent phone call, Jay asked the question.

'I was stupid,' Laura admitted. She moved to stand at the window and stare at the car park 'I thought I could control it . . . I met Vadic in Macedonia two years ago. He asked for a couple of small favours that were easy to grant, and in return he gave me some vital information about a particularly nasty gun-running mob in Holland . . . we managed to stop them in their tracks. My colleagues thought I was brilliant. So did Kingsman.'

She leaned her head against the glass, as though to cool her forehead. 'So I asked Vadic if he had any more, similar, information, and he gave it to me. Some really good stuff. I didn't see it at the time, but I was getting hooked by being one step ahead of everyone at work, knowing things they didn't . . . I was soon feeding the Mafia more and more titbits from the office, tipping them off, keeping them away from any raids, keeping their noses clean. Vadic gave me some fantastic leads to terrorist cells in the UK – we stopped one mob from blowing up the Albert Hall. I got promoted . . . '

Jay lay in bed remembering the agent when she'd first seen her, the ambition oozing from every pore. But it wasn't just a drive to succeed, Laura had been greedy for praise, for recognition, and she'd found it in bucket loads, but only through doing a deal with the devil.

'When you arrived in Macedonia,' Laura went on, 'things started to get out of hand. Vadic didn't like you meddling, being able to speak the language and insinuate yourself into the general population, make friends. He considered you an extreme risk. He wanted to kill you but I persuaded him it would be worse for him if he did because MI6 would come down on him like a ton of bricks. Needless to say, he didn't listen to me, but I didn't know that then.'

Laura pinched the bridge of her nose. Her eyes were closed. 'Hashim and I set up that scene in town to lure you to the mountains. I swear I didn't know they planned to kill you. I was told to get you there so they could give you a good going over. I didn't know they'd already done that. You made your meeting with Vadic at the meat processing plant sound like you'd had a walk in the park rather than a terrifying experience with a giant mincer.'

Laura took a shuddering breath. 'But then I discovered where my true loyalties lay. The second I saw Protti and General Nicomedo get off that helicopter, I knew I had to report it back to the office. I couldn't let the four of them get together – three criminal gangs with the power of a NATO General behind them – it would create an unstoppable tide of filth across Europe with criminal gangs and terrorists working together to destroy everything I love.'

Jay remembered the agent's excitement, the way her fingers trembled as she photographed Protti as he walked to the chalet.

'I turned over a new leaf at that moment.' Laura's voice softened. 'I began using their information against them.'

Jay struggled up on her pillow. 'Why did they shoot you on the mountain?'

'That was Hashim winging me, taking me out of action. He never trusted me and thought – correctly – that I was going to run with you and report what we'd seen. God, how I wish we'd never gone up there.' Her expression turned earnest. 'I like you, Jay. I'd never hurt you, I swear it ... '

Jay said, half-exasperated, half-affectionate, 'You are a crap spy.'

'So are you.'

'At least I knew it before I took the job.'

At that point Kingsman had appeared with two men to take Laura away, where to Jay was never told, but no doubt to an ignominious end as an agent, possibly charged, definitely fired. Kingsman stood at her bedside as she watched Laura being escorted outside.

Jay said, 'What will happen to her?'

'You don't have to worry.' He gave a thin smile, his half-moon glasses winking. 'We won't hang her for treason.'

'I like her.'

'I know.'

She shuffled up in bed. 'Does Max Blake work for you?'

'From time to time.'

'Where is he?'

'He didn't say, and I didn't ask.'

She wasn't surprised at the evasive answers and didn't bother asking further. She wouldn't learn anything.

Kingsman cleared his throat. 'I was wondering if, when you're better, we could meet about a little situation we have in Brussels. You speak German, I take it?'

'Well, yes. But I'm not sure if I'm the right person—'

'How about if I drop around at the weekend to discuss it? We really could do with your help. The doctors tell me you should be okay to travel home on Thursday. I'm due in Belgrade on Saturday evening but I have a brief window before my flight.'

'Mr Kingsman ... '

'Patrick, please.' He beamed. 'I'll call round on Saturday, say six-ish. I won't hold you up for long, I promise—' He paused when Alistair Ingram stuck his head inside the room, looking expectant. 'I am sorry, Jay,' Kingsman said regretfully, 'but I must go.'

Forty-seven

Zamira was drinking a cappuccino in a smart brasserie on Sloane Square. She had a window table and was watching the cars drive past; Rolls Royce, Mercedes, a Lamborghini. Two months ago she would have been agog, unable to believe her eyes, but today little could permeate the feeling that there was nothing that would captivate her again. She had lost her zest, her enchantment with life, and wondered if she'd ever get it back.

Even talking to Nana hadn't helped. If anything, it had made everything worse. Jay's friend, Kiro, had arranged for them to speak on the phone first thing yesterday. To her immense relief, neither Jay nor Kiro had told Nana about the brothel or Reda or Shaban, and what they'd forced her to do. Jay had said it was up to Zamira to tell Nadire whatever she felt comfortable with. So Zamira lied.

'I'm a waitress,' she told her mother.

'You sound funny. Are you all right?'

Her bruises and cuts were healing, but her nose was still mashed out of shape and her breathing was loud and distorted. She sounded like a pig. 'I've got a cold, that's all.'

'Are you sure you don't want to come home?'

The thought of Nana seeing her like this made Zamira shudder. 'No. I want to stay here.'

'I wish you hadn't run away.' Her mother sounded close to tears. 'But if Jay's looking after you, and you're happy ... '

'Yes, I'm happy.'

'Come home when you can. I miss you. Bear does too.'

'Maybe in the summer.'

'I love you, Zamira. So much . . . '

'I love you too, Nana.'

'Zamira?'

An unfamiliar voice broke into her thoughts. She looked up to see a woman about Jay's age looking at her. She wore jeans and a checked jacket and was smiling. She looked nice.

'I'm Sandra,' she said. 'Jay's sister-in-law. May I join you?'

Relieved Sandra spoke in Albanian, Zamira pulled out a chair for her and watched her order a coffee. Her movements were firm, her voice temperate but confident. She had creamy skin and shoulder-length chestnut hair that reminded Zamira of a horse's mane. She was an attractive woman, strong and secure in herself.

Zamira felt small and shy and terrifyingly embarrassed about the way she looked, but unlike other people, Sandra didn't flinch from Zamira's gaze. It was as though she didn't see the scars, but looked past them and straight at her soul. She said, 'Jay told me you and Hana need somewhere to stay.'

Zamira nodded.

'Jay's brother – my husband, Angus – and I have a big house in Putney. We have two young children, two and four. Do you like children?'

Feeling shy, Zamira said, 'I wanted to be a nanny.'

'I think you might change your mind once you've met my two,' Sandra said with a smile. 'They can be monsters.'

She went on to say that if they all got on okay, then Zamira and Hana could move into the top-floor flat of the house while their asylum applications were being processed. Because they were victims of trafficking, it was highly likely that if they went home they might be trafficked again, and nobody doubted they'd be granted permission to stay.

'We'll help you learn English,' Sandra went on, 'and in return you can help us with the children. I want to go back to work, and it would be fantastic if you and Hana could look after Mark and Katie while I'm with my patients. I've been missing my job terribly.'

While Sandra chatted on, telling Zamira about Angus, about her parents who lived nearby and who couldn't wait to meet the two Macedonian girls, Zamira felt something inside loosen, as though a piece of string balled into a tight knot had just been unwound.

'And maybe one day you'll feel strong enough to see a plastic surgeon,' Sandra said. 'The NHS might be able to help, certainly with your poor nose, which affects your breathing. I have a friend who has a practice on Harley Street. He's already said he'd be happy to see you to give you an opinion. Angus and I will pay, of course. We'll do anything to help ... ' She cleared her throat. 'And if your mother would like to come and visit, we'd love to have her stay too.'

Zamira stared at Jay's sister-in-law, the woman who was offering to have her and Hana live with her family, almost unable to believe her ears. Tears filled her eyes.

She'd forgotten the kindness of strangers.

Sometimes, it was almost overwhelming.

Forty-eight

'How are you feeling?'

Tom stood on Jay's doorstep with two Styrofoam cups of cappuccino and a big brown paper bag emitting wafts of warmed yeast and sugar.

'Is that for me?' She pointed at the takeaway bag.

'Of course it's for you.'

'In that case I'm feeling much better, thank you. I'm starving.'

'You always are,' he said, stepping inside. 'I've never known a woman eat as much as you do.'

He put the bag on the kitchen counter. Jay opened it with her left hand to find an assortment of croissants and pastries, still warm. Biting into a *pain au chocolat*, the chocolate soft and melting in its middle, she made a small groaning sound. 'This is delicious. Thank you.'

'It's the least you deserve,' he said, touching his cup against hers. 'For busting what appears to be the largest THB ring in Europe almost single-handed. The Met have done a deal with Branko and he's squealing as loud as a stuck pig. He's petrified of going to jail and is doing everything to try and keep himself safe.'

'I hope he rots in hell.'

Tom came over and gathered her in his arms, careful of her bandages. 'I know,' he said. He pressed a kiss against her forehead. She found herself relaxing, dissolving into his embrace.

Resting her head against his shoulder, she closed her eyes. He felt *so good*.

'I'm glad you got him.' He cleared his throat. 'And I'm glad you got Vadic too.'

They hadn't yet talked about her killing two men and maiming a third. She wasn't sure how she felt about it and she sure as hell didn't know how Tom felt about it either.

'Thanks to you,' he went on, 'we've got Reda in custody. She's considered a serious flight risk and hasn't been granted bail. We've also got Shaban and the bunch of guys that raped and beat Zamira. Branko just about fainted when we told him we'd found Zamira's blood in his apartment, he couldn't wait to tell us it wasn't him who beat her up but a guy called Quinton. Quinton is currently answering a lot of questions at the Kensington police station. He's got a nasty scar on his lower lip. Zamira says she bit it.'

'Good girl.'

Tom leaned back to look down at her. 'We've raided over ten brothels so far, in London, Manchester and Bristol. The network's falling like a pack of cards. Every time we hit one we offer to do a deal and they fold. They can't wait to dob in their pals if it means they get off more lightly.'

Taking their coffee and pastries into the sitting room, they settled on the sofa. Jay had lit a fire earlier and it emitted a low glow.

'Nice,' said Tom.

'Yum,' said Jay, tucking into an almond croissant, thick and gooey with nut paste. 'So what about Vadic's troops?'

'They've all turned tail and fled.'

'Back to the Balkans?'

'Maybe. We don't know for sure, but we've alerted UNMIK and NATO, everyone who needs to know over there, including the Americans.'

'What about Milot?'

'We heard he flew to Frankfurt, probably on a false passport or we'd have picked him up at the airport. Interpol are keeping an eye out for him. We'll catch up with him at some point, don't you worry.'

She didn't think Milot would come after her with Interpol on his tail, but she had to admit it was a shame that he wasn't behind bars.

'And General Nicomedo?' she asked. 'Any news on how NATO are dealing with him?'

'He's been sent to the Hague for crimes against humanity.'

Tom paused and looked over at her. 'How are your parents?'

Her father had been a bit surprised at the mess in his cellar. Apparently Hashim had bled profusely as he stumbled around in the dark, trying to get out. He'd broken two garden chairs, a vase and a hideous statue Nicola had bought in Prague. Her father had been delighted about the statue, Nicola pragmatic. Her mother, on the other hand, was now a local celebrity and unsure how to take the headlines.

'It's all very well being a Housewife Heroine,' she'd said to Jay that morning, 'but how does that stack up in real life? Does it get me a discount at the local Spar? I think not.'

'They're fine.' Jay asked Tom about the case he was working on – two Somalis murdered in the centre of town – and they chatted some more until Jay felt her eyelids droop. She was always feeling so damned tired, it was frustrating.

'Jay.' Tom cleared his throat. 'I've been thinking a lot about us since you've been in hospital.'

She tensed.

'I'm aware now that I rushed you. I'm sorry.'

A car alarm started up outside but was quickly shut off.

'I'm sorry too,' she managed.

'Look, I know this isn't the time . . . you need to be a hundred percent fit and well before you make a decision, but could you do me a favour?'

She nodded.

'Just say you'll think about it.'

Jay swallowed. 'Okay. I'll think about it.'

He tucked her head into his shoulder and pressed a kiss on her hair. 'Thank you.'

Jay was curled on Tom's lap, listening to him talking about where they might holiday when she was better – he fancied diving in Egypt – when the door banged and Angela and Denise appeared, clutching boxes of chocolates, bottles of wine and a stack of DVDs.

'Hi, Tom,' Denise said cheerfully. 'Not disturbing anything, are we?'

'Not at all,' Tom said with a roll of the eyes.

'We've got *Black Hawk Down*,' said Angela. 'It's brilliant. Shows how useless the bloody Americans are.'

'No way!' protested Jay. 'That movie gave me nightmares for weeks! Far too realistic. Haven't you got *Pretty Woman* or something?'

'I'm definitely not staying for *that*,' Tom said. He twisted and kissed Jay on the lips. 'See you later, sweetheart. You up for supper out tonight? I've booked Rossopomodoro around the corner, but if you're still feeling shaky, I'll get a takeaway.'

Jay looked at her friends who were settling themselves on the floor with piles of cushions, already unwrapping the Cadbury's boxes, and said, 'Maybe out would be good.'

Tom got to his feet and stretched. 'I'll bring a taxi about six, okay?'

She smiled. 'Very okay, thank you.'

Jay watched two movies back-to-back and it was dark outside when she headed for a shower. Trying to wash single handed as well as keep her bandages dry was torment, but she managed to shampoo and rinse her hair, and even give it a bit of a blow-dry. She put on her favourite pair of jeans and a stretchy shirt, a big belt and boots, some eyeliner and mascara, and fluffed out her hair.

She was halfway down the stairs when it happened, and she was so unnerved, so surprised, she stopped dead.

She stood on the stairs, the hairs at the nape of her neck rising as she listened to the sensation inside her. She realised she had been so distracted recently, so terrified, that it hadn't been able to make itself heard.

Hell, she thought. What day was it?

Saturday. She'd forgotten about Kingsman. Hadn't he said he'd drop in about six-ish? And what about Blake?

She stared at the front door, every nerve in her body awake, and when the bell rang she didn't flinch.

She simply went and opened the door.